# A Fair Prospect

## A Tale of Elizabeth and Darcy: Volume I

## Disappointed Hopes

# A Fair Prospect:
## A Tale of Elizabeth and Darcy
In Three Volumes

~~~

Volume I: Disappointed Hopes
Volume II: Darcy's Dilemma
Volume III: Desperate Measures

Published by Createspace.com

**ISBN:** 978-1482098358

**ISBN-10:** 1482098350

*This book is dedicated to*

Gwen and David Grafton

with deepest affection and heartfelt gratitude for indulging

my passion for reading throughout my childhood and for

unconditional love and support in my adult years

# Author's Note

*A Fair Prospect* is a story inspired by Jane Austen's *Pride & Prejudice*. It begins at the point in that story where Mr Darcy makes his first, ill-fated proposal of marriage to Miss Elizabeth Bennet.

For the purpose of this particular story, the Gardiners have no children of their own and the Militia left Meryton before Elizabeth travelled to Hunsford to visit her friend, Charlotte Collins.

# Acknowledgements

A heart-felt thank you to those who supported me in the writing of this tale, tolerated the lengthy breaks between chapters and the two-year break between Volumes I and II! Your patience, support, and your kind and generous feedback were what kept me going to the end, and I thank you for making the journey with me.

A special thank you goes to the following:

Adrea, Barbara, Helen, Marita, Mary, Rita, Sandy, Sylvie, Tara and Tess – words alone cannot express what my Pinker sisters mean to me!

The Readers at *Pen & Ink* and *The Derbyshire Writer's Guild*, with a particular shout out to Mel and Jan for their encouragement and support, to Renée for promoting my story on the wonderful *Mrs Darcy's Story Site*, to Abigail and Sybil for the feedback, suggestions and priceless editing advice, and to everyone who ever took the time out to comment throughout the four years that this story took to be posted online!

Adrea and Diane, for the beautiful artwork they produced for all three volumes of this story, and to Rebecca for the lovely cover design – you are all awesome!

Last, but never least, to Julian – for everything.

## Thank you!

# Prelude

## One inclement Sunday in April...

FITZWILLIAM DARCY STRODE RAPIDLY down the path, a man in torment, his mind and heart in conflict with one another.

Fetching up beside his tethered conveyance, he released a frustrated breath. Almost against his volition, and certainly against his reason, he had engaged upon a pursuit that he prayed would satisfy – oh how he hoped it would do so – his fascination with one Miss Elizabeth Bennet by securing her hand in marriage. Having been raised in a family where wealth and status meant little was denied, Darcy suffered no doubt of his reception; his struggle remained all with himself, for what he desired so strongly vied with what he knew to be his duty to his family and went against the conventions of his upbringing.

He cast a wary glance heavenwards at an ominous rumble from the thickly quartered clouds above. Then he regained his seat on the bench and flicked the reins, urging the pair forward as the curricle he had hastily acquired from the mews at Rosings, a concession to the threat of a storm, made its way along the lane.

Darcy's call at Hunsford Parsonage had failed to deliver the end to his quest, hence his now scouring the landscape for sight of Elizabeth. The lady, who had cried off from drinking tea at Rosings that afternoon with a plea of indisposition, had taken herself off on a solitary ramble. He could only assume she had thought the cool spring air a balm to whatever ailed her, unless she hoped he would act, that he would grasp this opportunity to speak, for she must surely discern his interest and knew of his impending departure for Town.

Throwing another glance at the heavily laden sky, Darcy resumed his search, soon rewarded by a glimpse of colour amongst the trees, and before long he drew the conveyance to a halt, dismounted from the bench and wrapped the reins about a convenient branch. Patting each steed on its silken neck, he straightened and drew in a calming breath. The moment had come, and he must silence once and for all the dissenting voices in his head.

With determination, he turned and made his way along a dirt track, his feet soon finding a flagged path under an over-hanging of branches, guiding his steps towards a circle of birch trees.

Memories of childhood days flooded his mind, rendering him insensible to the sporadic droplets that foretold the rain's proximity. He had forgotten this place! Nature had formed a natural canopy, providing shade from the sun's heat and shelter on more inclement days. Oft, when seeking a place of solitude to escape his overbearing aunt or his boisterous Cousin Richard, he had taken refuge under its protection, a favourite book to hand or even his writing case, a letter to his mother being foremost in his mind.

The distraction of such thoughts stood Darcy in good stead, so much so that, as he emerged from the pathway into the circle of trees to find Elizabeth seated on the stone bench there, he silenced any remaining doubts with little effort and focused upon his carefully rehearsed speech.

Elizabeth gave a visible start on discerning his presence before getting slowly to her feet, the letter she had been perusing still held in one hand as it fell to her side. Her cheeks appeared pale, but she seemed otherwise well, and he felt his heart swell within his breast as he gazed at her. Then, he recalled himself.

"Miss Bennet." Taking a step forward, he bowed formally, and as his eyes met hers, he swallowed against the tightness that gripped his throat.

He knew he must speak, yet before he could utter a word the heavens opened fully. Though the overhanging branches afforded them some relief, the spring leaf was not yet at its fullest and raindrops would persist in finding their way through, and conscious that time was of the essence, Darcy hurriedly began:

"In vain have I struggled. It will not do. My feelings will not be repressed. You must allow me to tell you how ardently I admire and love you."

# Chapter One

RAINDROPS STUNG DARCY'S FACE as he emerged from the stone pathway and black clouds rolled menacingly overhead, a fitting backdrop to his inner turmoil.

How could it have gone so wrong? His encounter with the lady, far from realising his dreams, had unfolded into a nightmare of wretched proportions, and his mind reeled with the relentless sound of her voice and its cutting accusations.

"... *your arrogance, your conceit and your selfish disdain of the feelings of others...*"

Oblivious to the expletive that escaped him, so intent was he on gaining distance from her, he remained insensible to the rain and unheeding of the thunderous noise in the heavens.

"...*the last man in the world whom I could ever be prevailed on to marry.*"

Darcy willed her voice into silence, but failed to displace her image from moments earlier; the expression of mingled fury and shock upon her face smote him to his core, and he winced, his pace slowing as he neared the curricle and pair. How he hated the prospect of returning to the soulless house of his aunt, yet what choice had he? He was soaked to the skin and could remain exposed to the elements no longer.

With little option, he walked on, attempting to unclench the fists he had made earlier.

*The fists he had made...*

That had been the only physical thing he had been able to manifest to prevent himself from doing the unthinkable – grabbing Elizabeth by her damnable, stubborn, misdirected shoulders and kissing her soundly.

Darcy bit back another oath. What madness possessed him? How dare he permit it to cross his mind? And worse, how was he to endure the truth of the matter: that he repented the thought far less than not acting upon it.

"...*had you behaved in a more gentlemanlike manner*"

The import of such words was not lost upon him; with so ill an opinion of him, would satisfying his momentary desire to silence her tirade with his mouth have made it any worse?

Angry with the direction of his thoughts, Darcy came to an abrupt halt as he reached the curricle. Though the raised hood of the conveyance had protected the seating, no such benefit had been afforded to the horses, one of whom greeted him with a baleful eye.

In the meantime, a disgruntled Elizabeth Bennet paced back and forth in what little shelter was afforded by the copse, outraged and distressed at Mr Darcy's nerve in so addressing her.

Questions raced through her head: how dare he even approach her? Was it not blatantly obvious to him how much she despised him? What conceit could have him believe she would welcome such an application? Elizabeth sighed and brushed a hand across her damp forehead. Was she ever destined to be offered marriage by men she could not respect?

Coming to a halt, she dropped down onto the stone bench once more, insensible to the chill stealing through her clothes. Had her manners been so at fault throughout their laboured acquaintance? Or was her family's position in society so very dreadful that he would expect her to welcome his offer, despite her marked aversion to his company? And to be proposed to in such a way – Elizabeth's cheeks burned at the memory, and she quickly got to her feet and resumed her pacing.

Over and over she dwelt upon his words: his arrogant assertion that he willingly parted Jane and his friend; his disdain for Mr Wickham's reduced circumstances; the mortification of his appraisal of her situation. How dare he tell her that he loved her despite her family's shortcomings?

Her anger and disgust carried her along on a wave of temper that heeded not the rain as it further permeated her shelter. That he could admit to ruining her sister's chance of happiness, and with no sign of remorse – how dare he?

Preoccupied as she was, it was a moment before Elizabeth realised she was no longer alone and, with a gasp, she found herself face to face once more with the source of her displeasure.

"Mr Darcy!"

Forcing himself to execute a bow, Darcy ignored her outraged tone and launched into speech.

"Be not alarmed, Madam. I have no desire to continue our discourse. I am come merely to escort you back to the parsonage; you cannot walk in conditions such as these."

"Really, Sir? Is that so?"

He was unsurprised at the indignation in her tone. Yet despite her lack of regard for his conduct, when presented with the curricle and thus the means to remove her safely home and dry, he had been unable to do anything but rein in his own humiliation and anger and return to do just that.

As the older brother and guardian of a young teenage woman, Darcy knew full well how to stand his ground, and he met the challenging look in her eye with one of his own. Yet before he could respond, she spoke again.

"And how do you propose to *escort* me, that I might have no need of the power of walking?"

"I have a curricle waiting at the end of the path, Madam. I must insist upon your accompanying me. This storm shows no sign of abating."

"And pray who are you, to determine what I may and may not do?"

Darcy was cold and wet, almost to the point of numbness. It went without saying that she must be experiencing something similar, if not worse, for her garments were hardly proof against the rain that was even now making its presence duly felt. If he was not so very angry, he was certain he would feel something – frustration, despair even – but this was no time for such indulgence.

"Your response, Madam, whilst not unexpected, does you no favour."

"How so, Sir?"

"What do you gain from refusing to return to the warmth and security of the parsonage in such a swift and easy manner?"

"I retain the freedom to choose the manner and timing of my return, without recourse to one such as yourself!"

Part of him wished he could leave her there but Darcy knew he would regret it later, and he said in a biting voice: "If you will not accompany me willingly, then you leave me no choice. I shall remove you to the curricle myself!"

He was in no fit state to acknowledge his triumph as, for the first time in their acquaintance, he appeared to have robbed Elizabeth Bennet of the power of speech. She glared fiercely at him, a blush staining her damp cheeks, her mouth slightly open.

Then, she bit out, "You would not dare, Sir!"

Darcy let out a bitter laugh. "Do not tempt me, Madam. I am in no humour for games."

Pursing her lips, she threw him one more glance full of fire, then stormed past him down the path at a rapid pace.

Within moments, they were both installed under the raised hood of the curricle, and Darcy guided the horses up a bank in the direction of Hunsford parsonage. The journey progressed in a powerful silence; the only sounds were the soft thud of hooves against the sodden earth and the staccato raps of the rain on the leather hood.

He focused his gaze on the horses, his fierce desire to look at Elizabeth countered by the disparagement he might perceive on her countenance. Impatiently, he flicked the reins. Despite his endeavour, it was impossible not to be conscious of her beside him. The sodden fabric of her coat was so close to his own equally saturated leg that every lurch of the conveyance threatened a touch he was ill-equipped to contend with. Thus it was with no little relief that he determined the low wall that formed the boundary to the parsonage's garden, and soon he halted the curricle and vaulted from his seat with almost indecent haste.

Hardly pausing to draw breath, he made his way round to the other side. Despite her ill opinion of him, he could not allow her to descend from such a height without assistance, yet it was no surprise when he fetched up in front of her to see that she was poised upon the edge of her seat, clearly intending to dismount unaided.

She met his look with a glare, raising her chin as their eyes locked. Resolutely, Darcy held out his hand, his intention apparent, struggling to contain the flash of anger that flared when he detected the look of disbelief that briefly crossed her features.

The fury Elizabeth had felt during her earlier confrontation with Mr Darcy vied with her annoyance at being obliged to accept a place in his conveyance. There had, for a fleeting moment, been a look in his eye back there that had persuaded her she had pushed him as far as it was wise to go and that his proclaimed intent to pick her up and bodily throw her into the curricle was no idle threat.

Yet here she was, safely returned to the sanctuary of the parsonage, blissfully empty of its sycophantic incumbent for a few hours, and certainly drier than the gentleman in front of her, who was currently being drenched anew by the treacherous onslaught of a fresh downpour, whilst she remained protected by the large hood of the curricle.

Elizabeth refused to acknowledge his outstretched hand. Agitated as she was by their angry confrontation and by his insistence on seeing her safely home, she remained in no mood to give him credit for his gesture and in no humour to accept it.

Refusing to break eye contact, she fixed him with a glacial look as she stood up and took the prideful step that must preface a fall. Her foot slipped on the wet footboard, and she fell forward with nothing to grasp onto but the shoulders of the one man she least wished to encounter.

As the full weight of Elizabeth's body struck him, Darcy took a step backwards. His arms had reflexively caught her, but as the speed of her fall propelled her forward into his unintentional embrace, he found himself clasping her to his body, her hands tightly gripping his shoulders and her eyes wide with surprise mere inches from his own.

For a long, portentous moment silence reigned. Unable to tear his eyes away from her, achingly conscious of her weight against him, he swallowed hard on the sudden constriction that gripped his throat. How he had dreamed of holding Elizabeth in his arms, yet he knew that this would be his only taste of such painful pleasure. Though his mind screamed at him to release her before she regained her senses and lashed him once more with her tongue or, more likely, her palm, his heart begged for one more moment, one further second of stolen comfort.

Unable to help himself, his eyes dipped to her mouth. Her lips were slightly parted from surprise, and he swallowed hard. He was too close to her – much too close. If he had been tempted by the raw emotion pulsing between them earlier, it was nothing to the desire he now felt as she rested unresisting in his arms. Yet he feared perceiving the expression in her eyes – at present lacking in censure and almost accepting of their situation – change to one of loathing and disapproval. He had suffered sufficient for one day and wished for no more.

Resolutely, he released his grip, his arms falling to his sides as he awaited the backlash of abuse that was certain to rain down upon him.

The mist that had clouded Elizabeth's mind slowly lifted. Suddenly, acutely aware of her situation, she caught her breath. Taking a stumbling step backwards, she righted herself and released her grip on the gentleman's shoulders as though the fabric burned her hands.

Mortified and chagrined, both by her fall and its aftermath, she felt the warmth flood her cheeks and cast her eyes to the ground. The man opposite her spoke no words, yet she could sense his consternation, for with her eyes lowered she could perceive the agitation of his hands as they hung at his sides.

There were no words she could summon in such circumstances, and only the consciousness of the rain beginning to trickle down her neck, exposed as it now was to the elements, roused her from her silent contemplation of the muddy ground. With a hurried glance in Mr Darcy's direction, she nodded briefly before turning to flee up the path to the parsonage.

Darcy stood motionless where Elizabeth had left him. There had been no chance to respond to her parting gesture – indeed, he was too deep in thought to even be conscious of the loss of her company. For some moments, he remained where he was, staring at the place where she had been, until an impatient stamping of hooves and a disgruntled snort alerted him to the presence of the horses, and he finally turned to take his leave.

# Chapter Two

ELIZABETH CLOSED HER bedroom door and sank onto the chair nearest to the fireplace, though little heat emanated from its residual embers, the bitter exchange between herself and Mr Darcy resounding in her head and beating a rhythm that slowly elicited a dull ache.

She gave an involuntary shudder, becoming acutely aware of the state of her clothing. She was damp and cold, her dress and coat wet through and the hemlines soiled with mud. Her bonnet had fallen to the floor by her feet and lay, limp and unnoticed, as she got wearily to her feet and pulled the bell for a servant.

The maid was soon on her way back downstairs, having stoked up the fire and, dressed in dry clothes once more, Elizabeth sat on the edge of her bed and began to brush her now towel-dried hair. The sudden storm had ceased as abruptly as it had arisen, the clouds being hurried on their way by a blustering wind, and even now a tentative ray of sunlight seeped through the window. The fire crackled brightly in the grate, yet she felt no warmth from either source.

A coldness had settled on her limbs, and somewhere deep inside she ached, though she knew not why. Her initial anger was all but spent, but though her indignation remained, it continued to be overshadowed by the memory of that moment when she had found herself clasped within Mr Darcy's embrace.

Elizabeth stirred restlessly. Never in her entire life had she experienced such proximity to one of the opposite sex. She had looked into the depths of his eyes, studied the length of his fine lashes, every nuance of his face. With a sigh, she owned what she had long denied – he was a well-featured man; an extremely handsome man, who had professed not moments before to being deeply in love with her. Yet she despised him heartily, did she not?

Getting to her feet, Elizabeth began to walk about the room, arms folded around her middle. Mr Darcy was a proud man who perceived her as decidedly below himself – how had he come to offer for her? Whence had come this depth of affection that he claimed and – if his proposal stemmed from such ardent love – how acute must his disappointment be?

Darcy remained on a damask-covered chair near the window of his room, elbows resting upon his knees, his head in his hands. The change in the weather made no impact upon him; he remarked neither the cessation of the earlier downpour, nor the sun breaking through to disperse the remnants of grey cloud.

His valet, Thornton, had taken away his soaking garments and mud-spattered boots with a barely concealed grunt of displeasure and, dressed once more in dry clothes, Darcy had dismissed him for the remainder of the day with the strict instruction that he was not to be disturbed. Thus, he had been sitting like so for an hour or more, the only disturbance to his contemplation being his cousin, Fitzwilliam, rapping on his door, but he had ignored him.

He had to put this debacle behind him, but how to make a beginning? His head pounded; he felt chilled to the bone and deep inside he was conscious of a dull heaviness that had settled close to the region of his heart. Further, despite his efforts to the contrary, his mind would persist in replaying over and over the recent encounter.

*"Your character was unfolded by Mr Wickham"*

Darcy stirred in his chair. Elizabeth's defence of Wickham had cut him badly. His anger towards her was all but gone, so much so he could hardly bear dwell upon it, yet his mind persisted in tormenting him with questions for which there were no answers.

How intimate were they? Was her outrage on Wickham's behalf born of tender feelings for the scoundrel? If he had imposed himself upon her... the ache within his breast intensified, and he caught his breath. He knew not how he would bear it if it were so. Darcy rose quickly from his chair and began to pace to and fro across the room.

Wickham was evil; he was degenerate and unworthy. That he had maligned Darcy's character to her surprised him not, for it was hardly the first time, but to what extent had he imposed upon her open and generous nature? How was it that, in their brief acquaintance, Elizabeth had such a picture of him from Wickham? With a groan of frustration, Darcy threw himself down on a chair adjacent to an ornate writing desk. Such thoughts were counter-productive; none of it signified, for even had Wickham not vilified his name, he had to accede that, in Elizabeth's eyes, his faults lay in more than one quarter.

Head in his hands once more, he finally began to admit the portent of her words. Her refusal had been a profound shock, but to learn of her dislike of him, her poor opinion of his character... the pain occasioned by such knowledge, accompanied by the devastation of all his hopes for the future, was almost more than Darcy could bear, and for a time he became lost in the depths of his own despair.

With a frustrated sigh, Elizabeth stopped pacing and stared down into the fire. That Mr Darcy had been shocked by her refusal was clear, and the depth of hurt and disappointment on his countenance she knew she would likely never forget; yet she wished she could be rid of it. Mr Darcy was a man she could not respect; his actions against Jane, Mr Bingley and Wickham spoke for themselves.

Elizabeth frowned. The subject of Wickham clearly disturbed him; could it be that he felt remorse for his treatment of him?

*"You take an eager interest in that gentleman's concerns!"*

Or perhaps it was the depth of her interest that riled him so? Her mind all confusion, Elizabeth walked slowly over to the mirror and stared at her reflection.

She could not help but dwell upon Mr Darcy's words – his seeming pleasure in his success in parting Jane and Mr Bingley; his failure to accept either responsibility or affect contrition for Wickham's present circumstances – all this far outweighed her embarrassment over his appraisal of her family, a situation she had lived with for so long that she could hardly fail to acknowledge its truth, no matter that is was galling to have it spoken of in such terms.

Yet her confusion over Mr Darcy and his character reigned. That he had acted the true gentleman in seeing her safely home could not be ignored. Nor could she deny that he had saved her from the mortification of a fall brought about by her own stubbornness.

And overriding all these things was the man himself: his air and countenance, the breadth of his shoulders and the pain and confusion in his eyes. She had clearly failed to read his feelings throughout their laboured acquaintance, yet she was certain – with complete conviction – that he had been tempted to do the unthinkable and place his lips upon her own...

A sharp rap on the chamber door caused Elizabeth to start, and welcoming the interruption, she hurried to open it.

Slowly, Darcy became conscious of his whereabouts, and he leaned back in his chair, his gaze falling upon the desk in front of him. Elizabeth's accusations haunted him, the discovery of her ill opinion consumed his every thought, and he could perceive no respite from it. He needed resolution, to defend himself and his character – but how?

Her opinion of him was a matter of no little import. If there was aught he could do so that she despised him less then do it he must. Attempting a private interview for the length of time it would take to explain his dealings with Wickham and his reasoning for his actions towards Bingley and her sister was impossible. Besides, in the face of her displeasure and the knowledge of her rejection, he would struggle to retain the power of coherent thought or speech.

His troubled gaze fell upon the letter-writing materials on the desk, and he studied them thoughtfully. A letter went quite against the form; moreover, in all likelihood she would refuse to accept it, and even should she do so, he had no guarantee she would read it with any intention of believing his word. It was hardly a fool-proof plan, yet he had no other. Thus it was that the letter would be written and without delay.

Elizabeth closed the door as the servant turned away, her attention with the crumpled letter that had been discovered in the pocket of her coat.

She frowned as she straightened the pages. The maid had been adamant that these two sheets were all, yet Jane had on this occasion run on to a third.

The only likely answer was that she had left it behind in the copse, for she had been perusing that very page when Mr Darcy had first disturbed her. With a sigh, Elizabeth laid the pages aside and walked over to the window. The storm had long passed over, and a brisk breeze hurried the clouds across the sky. Slipping into a pair of dry shoes and grabbing a shawl from the end of the bed, she let herself out of the chamber and made her way quietly out of the house, determined to locate the missing page before the wind could take it beyond her reach.

Dusk was falling over Rosings Park. The day that had begun so inclemently was blessed with the beauty of a sunset quite lost upon the occupant of one dimly lit room where the fire had long smouldered in the grate, and the only candles that had been lit burned low in their holders.

Darcy dipped his quill into the ink-well one final time, and then paused before placing the tip of the pen on the page. How to close the most difficult letter he had ever had occasion to write? He hesitated, then wrote, *"I will only add, God bless you,"* followed by his name. Blotting the words firmly, he then folded it precisely and reached for a roll of wax and one of the candles. It was done, and all he wanted was to rid himself of it, that it might aid him in shedding once and for all his past hopes and dreams.

That thought propelled him from his chair, and he strode over towards the washstand. Having splashed some water over his face, he turned to survey the room where he had been closeted these past hours. It was time; he must find a way out of the building without being perceived and whilst the Collinses remained at Rosings.

Having retraced her steps, Elizabeth had soon returned to the copse, the errant page easily detected lodged in a briar near the stone bench. Little remained legible of her sister's hand but content to have it once more in her possession she secured it in her pocket and hastened to leave the scene. Yet even as she made her way back along the sheltered stone path, the powerful memory of being held in the gentleman's arms and the notion that he desired to kiss her returned.

Elizabeth felt the heat steal into her cheeks. What would she have done if Mr Darcy had acted? What would her response have been? Outrage, of course, she berated herself quickly. How else could one react to such a deed, and even more so in someone one hated as much as she did Mr Darcy; she would have been repulsed, most surely.

Tentatively, almost against her volition, Elizabeth pressed her fingers to her lips. What was it like to feel someone's mouth against one's own? What sensations or emotions might it arouse? Conscious of the direction of her thoughts, a wave of embarrassment swept through her. What was she doing, thinking such thoughts about a man she could not, *would not*, like?

Emerging into the open, she drew in a deep breath of the cool, early evening air before turning her steps towards the lane that would lead her back to Hunsford, determined to dwell on it no longer.

As Darcy neared Hunsford, the restraint he had upon his emotions slipped slightly. He had given no thought to how he would deliver his letter or whether Elizabeth would even permit him an audience — yet now, as he slowed his horse from a gallop into a canter the notion of facing her struck him once more.

He pulled on the reins, causing his mount to slow further. His heart was in no fit state for another onslaught from the lady, but how was he to merely drop off the letter and leave, knowing their paths would likely never cross in future?

With a rush of sensation, he was consumed by the feelings he had repressed that afternoon as he had dwelt upon her rejection and poor opinion of him. How was he to make his way forward in life and never lay eyes upon her again? Would he ever hear word of her, learn what life had lain before her?

Lost in such futile speculation, it was a moment before Darcy discerned a figure up ahead, moving along the lane: Elizabeth! Swallowing hard upon his trepidation, he urged his mount forward, unsurprised when his approach was detected. The wariness of her countenance struck him forcibly, but he reined in his horse and slid to the ground, flinching as his feet struck the gravel lane.

They stared silently at each other for a moment before he recalled himself and his purpose and, holding the reins loosely in one hand, he reached into his pocket for the letter.

# Chapter Three

THE SOUND OF HOOVES pounding the lane roused Elizabeth from her stupor. Barely conscious of Mr Darcy's departure, she had remained lost in the sensations caused by his parting gesture of pressing his mouth to her hand, his gaze never leaving her face. Now, she turned to peer down the lane towards Rosings, unable to discern more than a fleeting shadow in the dusk as both horse and rider disappeared from view.

Elizabeth glanced down at her hand. Before raising it to his lips, Mr Darcy had pressed a letter into her palm and closed her fingers over it. Turning back, she resumed her walk along the lane towards the parsonage, staring at her name, written in a firm, elegant hand. What was his purpose? He had claimed that he wished to defend himself against her accusations, but what possible explanation could persuade him of the necessity to address her so?

To be certain, it must be destroyed rather than read, for what could he say that could negate his cruelty to Wickham or repair the hurt and distress of her sister? If she broke the seal – if she did him the honour of reading it – was she not being disloyal to those whose misfortunes she defended? With a frustrated sigh, she shoved the letter deep into her pocket and hurried on.

Barely was she ensconced once more in her room, when there was a sudden disturbance – the sound of doors banging and voices – alerting her to the return of her hosts. Pulling Mr Darcy's letter from her pocket, she studied it thoughtfully. Whilst she could not yet bring herself to destroy it, nor could she contemplate reading it and, conscious of the sound of footsteps approaching, followed by a tentative knock upon her door, she quickly placed it beneath her pillow before bidding her friend enter.

Often silent and morose during his annual sojourn at Rosings, Darcy's distraction that evening appeared to excite no special attention from either his aunt or his cousin, Anne. Yet that which would escape the attention of the ladies made a powerful impression on his other cousin.

Colonel Fitzwilliam understood sufficient of Darcy to comprehend that he was exceedingly troubled. As a military man, the Colonel was a keen observer and had not failed to note the peculiarity of Darcy's behaviour during this visit – nor was he blind to the coinciding factor of the alteration in the local neighbourhood.

Darcy's somewhat erratic conduct over recent weeks – merely a source of covert amusement until now – had culminated earlier that day with his absence from the Collins' invitation to tea at Rosings and instead disappearing from the house when rather inclement weather threatened. The Colonel had watched Darcy as he strode with noticeable purpose towards the stables – what had possessed the man? Furthermore, upon his return, he had closeted himself in his rooms for the remainder of the day, and now this. His air bespoke not merely distraction of mind, but more an element of despair.

It would take a man far less observant than the Colonel to remark the other coincidence in all this: Miss Elizabeth Bennet had also declined the invitation to afternoon tea. He frowned as he took a drink from his wine glass. Mrs Collins claimed that her friend had pleaded to be excused, citing a minor indisposition; yet the Colonel, who had had the pleasure of encountering the lady on a walk earlier that day, believed none of it.

Inquisition was another of Colonel Fitzwilliam's indulgences, and he had felt perfectly entitled – upon perceiving that no amount of tapping and ultimately hammering on his cousin's door would rouse him – to interrogate the stable boy, who had willingly confirmed that the gentleman had driven off with a curricle in the direction of Hunsford and that it was now safely returned to the coach house.

It did not take a military mind to conclude that an encounter may have taken place between Miss Bennet and his cousin, yet he failed to understand why this might cause Darcy such disturbance of mind, for they had both frequently met with the lady in the park over recent weeks, sometimes together, oft alone. What could possibly have occurred?

The Colonel shrugged. He was a patient man, and he knew the value of luring his prey into a sense of security, to seize the most opportune moment, the element of surprise if you will, before launching his attack. Further, he mulled with some satisfaction on the weapon in his aunt's study (a rather fine

French cognac that was nigh on hard to acquire in these unstable times) that he had every intention of wielding upon his cousin when they separated from the ladies.

Dining in company proved more challenging than Darcy had anticipated, and his hope of distraction in company came to naught. He was haunted by Elizabeth. If he pushed aside her angry voice, then his mind was filled with her presence – the weight of her in his arms, the pressure of her body against him, the beauty of her eyes as they stared into his, and finally the warmth as he had possessed himself boldly of her hand before pressing his lips to her smooth skin…

With a clatter, Darcy's fork slipped from his hand onto his still laden platter. He blinked, attempting to rid himself of such thoughts, and glanced about the table, relieved to note that his aunt remained oblivious, unlike the Colonel, whose eye seemed firmly fixed upon him.

Darcy returned his gaze to his setting. He was familiar with the look on Fitzwilliam's face and, if he was not mistaken, there would be a need for evasive action after dinner to avoid a grilling. He took a fortifying drink from his glass and tried to feign interest in his aunt's monologue, little though he desired her approbation. Yet his attempt at distraction was to no avail. Lady Catherine's wearisome tone held Darcy's attention even less than his plate of food, and within seconds his mind travelled back to his more recent encounter with Elizabeth.

*For some seconds they had merely stared at each other. She had raised her chin slightly as she looked up at him - a gesture of defiance, he had assumed, yet it had failed to distract him from drinking in the charming picture that she made, her hair loosely tied and somewhat unattended since her earlier drenching...*

Darcy cleared his throat quietly and took another sip of his wine. He dared not glance in his cousin's direction, and his recalcitrant thoughts soon dragged him back to that moment.

*A formal greeting after such a delay and in such circumstances had seemed pointless, and he had pulled the letter from his pocket and held it out towards her.*

*"Will you do me the honour of reading that letter?" he had said, his voice sounding rough to his own ears, as if he had lost the use of it.*

Darcy's insides twisted uncomfortably as he recalled the moment: the anticipation, the anxiety, the aching within, and closing his eyes he drew in a deep breath.

Across the table, Colonel Fitzwilliam eyed his cousin thoughtfully. Something was seriously amiss, and as he turned his attention to clearing his plate, his mind began to dwell upon his strategy for discovering the cause.

Despite Charlotte's attempts at persuasion, Elizabeth remained in her chamber. The pain in her head she had pleaded earlier was no longer a pretence, and her pale visage and uncharacteristic discomposure of spirits soon convinced her friend that her need for solitude was genuine.

Yet left with aught but her own company, Elizabeth's mind remained disturbed and, unable to conquer her wayward thoughts, she continued to amble restlessly about the room.

Her frustration at being so affected by her newly aroused consciousness of Mr Darcy troubled her. She wished to overcome the effects of the day's unforeseen events and purge the inexplicable thoughts of him from her mind. How dare he disturb her so? This was *all* his fault. His unsolicited attentions, his arrogant interference in the affairs of others were all of his own doing, and as the man who had caused such turmoil, he warranted far less notice than this.

She pushed aside the small voice that attempted to remind her of her culpability, that her own pride had led to the physical encounter that might well account for some of her current distraction of mind.

With sudden determination, she marched over to the bed and retrieved Mr Darcy's letter from under her pillow. Should she read it or destroy it? Walking over to her nightstand, she took a taper and lit a candle. Slowly, Elizabeth sank into the fireside chair, placing the candle on the side table. She weighed the letter in her palm, forcefully rejecting the memory of the feel of Mr Darcy's touch against her skin. What would haunt her more? Never knowing what he had to say, or permitting him to defend himself when she could anticipate no justification for his actions?

With a sigh she succumbed to the inevitable and, before further doubt could ensue, she purposefully broke the seal and unfolded the letter.

Darcy reached for the water jug, attempting to ignore his despair. That Elizabeth might not accept the letter had filled his mind throughout the writing of it. Indeed, he could hardly blame her, for to address her in such a way was nothing if not irregular.

Oblivious to the clearing of the table around him as dessert was served, his mind continued its ceaseless replay of their last meeting.

*The silence between them had stretched painfully; her eyes had moved from his face to his letter, a frown upon her countenance. His mind urged her to accept it, his heart begged her to want to understand him, but when she failed to reach out and take it, Darcy felt he understood her wariness of its content.*

*Forcing himself to speak, he had made an attempt at reassurance but his voice sounded distant, as though belonging to another and spoken aloud, his reasoning had sounded little more than trivial.*

*Conscious of the futility of their encounter, he had stepped closer to her; her eyes had widened but she had not retreated. Reaching out, he had taken her gloveless hand in his, savouring the feel of her skin as he pressed his letter into her palm and closed her fingers over it.*

*Elizabeth had spoken no words; her eyes had remained locked upon his, a light blush staining her cheeks, and he had fought the desire to reach out and touch her face. Almost forgetting to breathe, achingly aware of her fingers under his and drinking in her features for the last time, he had raised her hand and rested his lips against the smooth, warm skin. Then, he had released her, turned on his heel and mounted his horse, refusing himself the indulgence of even a backward glance.*

Darcy stirred on his chair, conscious of the table being cleared. Seeing the coffee cup being placed before his cousin Anne, he realised he had missed the remainder of the meal, and he cast a wary look in Fitzwilliam's direction, noting with relief that he was no longer in his seat.

Excusing himself abruptly, he rose and left the dining room, but ventured no further than the hallway as the heavy doors closed behind him. He leaned back against them and closed his eyes, breathing deeply. How he was to pass the more than four and twenty hours before departing for London he knew not; he suffered no illusion but that this was to be the most difficult night of his life. He wondered bitterly what would be the better fate: that sleep would evade him entirely and he would pass the long hours until dawn drowning in the memories of this dreadful day, or that he would sleep but dream – and who knew where the depths of his subconscious might take him.

A hand gripped his shoulder, and Darcy's eyes flew open only to encounter his captor's assessing gaze.

"I know not where you tarried this past hour, Darcy, but I am certain of where you are going now!"

Darcy studied Fitzwilliam's amused countenance with narrowed eyes. Then, with a heavy sigh, he acknowledged his surrender. There would be no escape from this ambush, and all Darcy could hope for was sufficient wit about him to deflect any attempt to draw him out and that the brandy would be sufficient to make it bearable.

The separation of the parties at Rosings had become permanent, and the tolling of midnight on the ornate clock in the library was noted with appreciation by both gentlemen, but for contradictory reasons.

Darcy felt a little hazy, but believed he had survived his captivity relatively intact and mulled with some satisfaction on his improved ability to counter his cousin's tactics. Feeling confident that he had revealed little of the day's events, he raised his glass to his lips to drain it, failing to register either the lack of liquid within, or that he had repeated the same gesture three times in as many minutes.

Colonel Fitzwilliam, meanwhile, reflected with satisfaction on a campaign well run and savoured his victory as he swallowed his last mouthful of liquor. Admittedly, his cousin had put up as good a fight as ever, but the Colonel had managed to play upon a weakness in his defence that Darcy had failed to consider – his empty stomach. The effects of alcohol on such never failed to deliver results, and as the man had merely toyed with his breakfast and seemed unable to consume his dinner, his capitulation was assured.

*Unfathomable to pass a day in such neglect of one's digestion,* mused the Colonel, who had a healthy appreciation for his food that little could impede.

Despite the collaboration offered by Darcy's empty insides, it had, nevertheless, taken the Colonel much patience and the valuable support of their aunt's finest cognac before Darcy had yielded. His cousin had not been an easy opponent – not that the Colonel had anticipated otherwise – and at first he had let Darcy steer their discourse towards his sister, Georgiana. Indeed, after the first cognac had been sipped reverently in appreciation of its quality, Darcy had almost seemed content. The rigidity in his frame had begun to ease, and by the end of his second glass he was even smiling slightly as he recounted an anecdote from his sister's latest letter.

Yet as time passed and the contents of the decanter diminished, the Colonel's fortitude was rewarded. His carefully interspersed remarks that slowly but surely brought the conversation around to the enhanced company to be found at Rosings this year were followed equally stealthily by the occasional mention of Miss Elizabeth Bennet herself. It had only taken the passing observation that he assumed his cousin had called at the parsonage during the afternoon to enquire after the lady's welfare (an aside that had earned him a disconcerted glance from Darcy), followed by the Colonel's polite enquiry into how she fared, before Darcy's head dropped into his hands and a long silence ensued.

But Darcy's comment, uttered as if the words were torn from him: *"How is she? She is everything... everything..."* had finally led him to put together the pieces of the puzzle; his cousin had fallen at last. The only thing not apparent to the Colonel was why Darcy was so ill-affected by the realisation of his condition.

He squinted over towards his cousin now, slumped in his armchair and staring morosely into the dying flames of a fire that had been neglected by them both as the evening waned.

Darcy's repeated avowal, the only words he had uttered thereafter, despite considerable goading – that she despised him – the Colonel put down to the effects of alcohol, and as he had been unable to draw anything further from him once Darcy had sunk into his seat and refused to say another word on the matter, he was left to draw his own conclusions.

For many years, the Colonel had observed his cousin at the mercy of society, fully cognisant of Darcy's lack of interest in the parade of young women all more intent upon becoming *Mrs Darcy of Pemberley* than to be his wife.

Never had he seen him thus affected, and never had the Colonel imagined witnessing such emotional despair in a man who prided himself on his self-control. Something would have to be done, and without delay.

Just then, Darcy hauled himself to his feet, and the Colonel watched as his cousin appeared to adjust his gaze a little, then set off purposefully across the room. He bit back a smile, trusting that he was not going to have to wrestle the decanter from him. Darcy had definitely downed sufficient liquor for one evening and was no doubt going to have the devil of an ache in the head to show for it in the morning.

Darcy, meanwhile, was a little disconcerted to find that, though he had set off in the direction of the drinks table, it seemed to have moved. When he eventually fetched up next to an armchair instead, he stopped, frowned, then looked to his right. *There* it was! Reaching out he very carefully placed his empty glass on the silver salver, raising a brow at the unexpectedly loud noise it made.

Then he headed for the door; he needed his bed — except he was not entirely sure how to find it.

Colonel Fitzwilliam grinned as he watched Darcy's progress towards the door. In general, his cousin was well able to hold his liquor — though he knew how to appreciate a fine wine, he made no habit of turning to spirits to make his way through life's difficulties. Yet this evening he had required little persuasion to have his glass filled repeatedly.

The Colonel stood up, savouring the remaining drops in his glass before placing it on the tray as he passed. Darcy had managed to fetch up by the door, but now leant his head against it, eyes closed and, if the Colonel was not mistaken, not far from falling asleep.

"Come along, old chap!" he encouraged as he joined his cousin. Darcy's head shot up, and he blinked rapidly. His eyes appeared to be trying to focus on something, anything. "Let us retire for the night, for in the morning the campaign must begin, my friend, and you should be fully rested so that you are prepared!"

Darcy, having finally realigned his vision into some semblance of order, peered at his cousin in confusion. He had no idea what Fitzwilliam was rattling on about, but no doubt it was down to the fact that his military cousin had consumed far too much alcohol for his own good. Darcy grunted rather than try to formulate a response and allowed the Colonel to steer him out of the room.

# Chapter Four

THE WEAK SPRING SUNSHINE of a new day filtered through the drapes at Hunsford Parsonage, rousing the inhabitants from their slumber.

Drained of emotion after a sleepless night, Elizabeth lay on her bed staring at the canopy. If she had thought that reading Mr Darcy's letter would ease her troubled mind and allow her to put the man out of her thoughts once and for all, she could not have been more mistaken.

The letter had been read and re-read, yet she could not discard it. Even now, it remained clasped in her hand. How poor had her judgement been? Flattered by Wickham's attentions and slighted by what she had perceived as Mr Darcy's disapproval, she had been blinded by her own vanity into accepting the attentions of a cad and wounding a man of good character. Ashamed of her behaviour and appalled at her poor discernment, she could have wept over her stupidity.

Elizabeth sat up wearily. How fortunate that she would never have to cross paths with Mr Darcy again, for how could she ever look the man in the eye?

*Look him in the eye…* For a fleeting second, the remembrance of being held against him flooded her senses, but she shook the disturbing memory aside and swung her legs off the bed. The morning would be long past if she did not make some effort to ready herself, and placing the crumpled letter on the bedside table, she hurried over to the dresser.

The maid had left a pitcher of fresh water, but as Elizabeth poured some into the basin she caught sight of herself in the mirror above the washstand. A pale face and solemn eyes stared back, the person in the reflection a stranger to her.

Uncomfortably, she lowered her gaze. The letter had revealed things about both Mr Darcy and herself, all of them most unexpected. Not only did she have to revise her long-held opinion of his unworthiness, but she had to credit herself with that very characteristic. Once again, a feeling of shame swept through her, but she ruthlessly pushed it aside and forced herself to look up and face her own likeness again. She would overcome this; she had to. Besides, poor though her judgement may have been and improved though her opinion of him was, there was no denying that not all Mr Darcy's supposed transgressions were justifiable.

That he had acted with arrogance and a blatant disregard for the feelings of either remained a truth that Jane and Mr Bingley would no doubt suffer from for no little time. That his proposal to a woman he professed to love could be couched in such terms as his had been was unfathomable.

Such was the pattern of thought that ebbed and flowed through Elizabeth's mind as she prepared herself for the day. Her guilt and embarrassment warred with her indignation, yet she could not deny that she also felt for Mr Darcy and wished that she had not thrown such unfounded accusations at him. She regretted little over her actual refusal other than its delivery, for her long held ill-opinion of him was too ingrained to be swept away in an instant. Even so, her behaviour of the previous day did not sit well with her.

Nor did she have much tolerance for her recalcitrant memory, which would persist in recalling with vivid clarity the intensity of their unexpected embrace.

Colonel Richard Fitzwilliam greeted the new day with optimism. Admittedly, his head was a little less clear than he would wish but a strong cup of tea and a platter of hot food would soon set him to rights and remove any lingering remnants of last night's indulgence.

With a bounce to his step, he left his room and made his way along the landing, pausing briefly outside his cousin's chamber to discern if there was yet any sound or movement within. The silence that greeted him was reminiscent of the previous day, and the Colonel's expression sobered as he continued on his way downstairs.

Recalling Darcy's demeanour yesterday, he wondered at the depth of his turmoil – could this intense reaction be due to the shock of finding his emotions engaged? Darcy had never so much as hinted at any expectation of making an alliance of affection. The Colonel knew from personal experience the pressures from family to make a suitable marriage, both in terms of fortune and connections.

He had reached the hall, yet despite the tempting aromas drifting along from the breakfast room, he paused by one of the tall windows and stared out over the manicured grounds.

Darcy could not have anticipated making the acquaintance of a woman, in the Colonel's opinion, as suitable as Miss Elizabeth Bennet. She would be a fine sister to his young cousin, Georgiana. Her lively spirit and her refusal to be intimidated by the likes of their Aunt Catherine indicated a temperament that could only complement and benefit the reserved manners of both Darcy siblings.

From his understanding, she brought no increase of fortune to the Darcy coffers, but it was hardly as if it signified. She was a gentleman's daughter, that he did know, so there could be no other objection, and he was keen to encourage Darcy to put aside his reservations and grasp his chance of happiness.

With a sigh, the Colonel turned towards the breakfast room. Darcy clearly needed help. He must be debating with himself over the lady's suitability or otherwise, and his sense of duty was in conflict with his heart.

Nodding at the footman to open the doors for him, Fitzwilliam entered the room, his brow creased in thought. His cousin's repeated mutterings last evening that the lady loathed him, he negated. Darcy had doubtless interpreted her lively manner and her confidence in challenging him, her failure to fawn upon him as was other ladies' wont, as disinterest. But dislike? Impossible. There was no finer person than his cousin Darcy – a true gentleman, a loyal friend, devoted brother and much esteemed master, both on his estate in Derbyshire and in his London home.

With a grunt, Fitzwilliam threw himself into the nearest chair and immediately beckoned a servant to fill his platter. It would seem it was down to him to improve the situation.

Tucking into his breakfast, he reflected on how proud his mother would be of him, for who could have foreseen that he would turn a maker of matches, and for all people, his Cousin Darcy?

Finally dressed, Elizabeth turned to survey the room, her eyes drifting against her volition towards Mr Darcy's letter. She walked over and picked it up, smoothing out the creases and putting the pages into order. So engrossed was she in her task that she failed to discern the knocking on the door, and she spun around startled to perceive that Charlotte had come into the room.

"Dear Lizzy. I was concerned and could not rouse you…" Charlotte let the sentence hang in the air between them.

Forcing a smile, Elizabeth instinctively put the hand holding the letter behind her back.

"How are you this morning?"

"I am much revived, Charlotte," Elizabeth lied, knowing full well that her tired and pale complexion would not escape her friend's notice.

"Hmmm," Charlotte frowned. "Whatever was ailing you seems to linger yet."

"I am well, truly I am." Elizabeth crossed the room and placed the letter in her writing case, turning the lock and pocketing the key before turning to face her friend.

"You look unhappy. Have you been dwelling on Jane's situation? I know her letters have brought you little comfort."

Thankful for Charlotte's misconception, Elizabeth was quick to reply. "I was just re-reading something… suffice to say, it has affected my mood, that is all."

Charlotte shook her head. "You should not distress yourself so, Lizzy. Jane will overcome her disappointment, you will see, as will you on her behalf."

Elizabeth summoned a smile. Then, she realised that Charlotte held something out to her, and with a start she saw it was another letter.

"I am certain that as the postmark is *'Cheapside'*, you are soon to have your anxiety relieved."

"Dear Charlotte," Elizabeth said as she took it. "Pray forgive me. I promise you most faithfully, whatever news my sister brings me, that I will join you in the parlour directly, and I beg you would excuse my poor manners of the past four and twenty hours."

Charlotte shook her head. "I am only relieved to hear that you are in better spirits", and she left her to read her correspondence.

Darcy awoke to a pounding head that momentarily distracted him from his depressed mood. He passed a weary hand across his eyes and groaned. Against his expectations, he had neither lain awake wrapped in memories, nor slept encompassed in his dreams – it had been an abyss.

His recollection of the previous evening was poor, yet he remained confident that he made no confession to his cousin; his failed proposal, his summary rejection and the associated humiliation and despair were his alone to bear – though he could distinctly recall having no small difficulty negotiating the staircase.

Raising his head from the pillow, Darcy squinted about the room. The glare of daylight through the gap in the heavy brocade drapes hinted at the progression of the morning, and the sounds of a bath being prepared in his dressing room confirmed that it was time to rise and face the day. Rubbing a hand against his aching forehead, he slowly eased himself to the edge of the bed and surveyed the room.

The sight of Thornton, his face a study of resigned disapproval, righting an overturned chair, along with the fact that Darcy appeared to still be attired in last night's shirt and breeches, stirred a vague memory of his cousin hauling him off the floor and dropping him with little ceremony onto the bed, but beyond that he could recall nothing.

Standing a little unsteadily, he walked purposefully towards the door to his dressing room, relieved to see Thornton heading for the small medicinal cabinet where he kept restorative powders.

Upon entering the dining room some time later, Darcy's confidence faltered as he encountered Fitzwilliam's smug expression as he greeted him jovially. Had it not been for the pain in his head and the queasiness in his stomach, he may have questioned what it was that had given the Colonel his air of complacency. As it was, he was more intent on holding his hand steady as he attempted to consume a much-needed cup of tea.

Her heart lightened by her letter, Elizabeth was true to her word and soon joined Charlotte in the parlour.

"So you are to leave me a week earlier than planned, Lizzy. I shall miss your company most sorely." Charlotte busied herself preparing the tea as she spoke, and Elizabeth chewed her lip as she studied once more the letter in her hand.

"I am sorry to desert you, Charlotte. Much as I am relieved to perceive the improvement in Jane's spirits, and anxious as I am to see her, I would not have curtailed my visit had it not been at my aunt's particular request."

Charlotte straightened up, offering a cup to her friend.

"Do not concern yourself. One must bow to the dictates of family, and I am sure that there are few occasions when your Aunt Gardiner has been obliged to make a demand of you."

Elizabeth nodded, thankful for her friend's understanding, and the two girls settled themselves down to their tea.

"So tell me," Charlotte continued, "How does Jane fare? Is she much improved, for you seem well pleased by her letter?"

"She seems in good spirits, and it appears my company is required because of the presence of our aunt's Godson. You recall Mr Nicholas Harington, do you not?"

Charlotte laughed. "Who could fail to remember Mr Harington? So it is he that lightens the spirits. Or is my assumption too reminiscent of your mother not so many years back?"

Elizabeth smiled. "Indeed; who could forget Mama's attempts to match either Jane or myself with Nicholas? Fortunately, he escaped her clutches, much to our relief, such a friendship as we have always had! I am sure he has done much to help Jane rally, for she reports that he has kept her and my aunt and uncle well entertained. I must own that I am eager to see him."

"Well, then," Charlotte added more tea to Elizabeth's cup, "You have but two days to endure before you head for the gaiety of London and the renewal of old friendships. We must make arrangements for your journey thither."

"It is done! My uncle feels the obligation, as it is at their request that I join them earlier; thus he sends a carriage on Wednesday."

Charlotte smiled. "Then it is all settled. I am pleased you are well once more and that you have something more exciting to look forward to than merely a return to Longbourn! We shall be a sorry party here once all the visitors are gone, for Mr Darcy and the Colonel depart on the morrow, do they not?"

Elizabeth's smile faltered for a moment. "I believe so."

"Though," her friend continued with a smile as she got up to give the fire a prod with the poker, "their continued presence is, by all accounts, unprecedented, for I understand from Mr Collins that Mr Darcy has twice postponed his departure this year."

Elizabeth's cup rocked as she placed it rather quickly back onto its saucer as Charlotte returned the poker to its resting place and resumed her seat.

"Lady Catherine has been expressing her satisfaction to Mr Collins – she believes it indicates her nephew's growing preference for Miss de Bourgh's company. It is perhaps impolitic of me to say so, but I confess I do not envy Mr Darcy should he formalise the anticipated arrangement."

Struggling for the appearance of disinterest, Elizabeth shrugged her shoulders. "Perhaps he has no intention of being persuaded to his aunt's way of thinking."

"What, then, might be the attraction that causes Mr Darcy to linger in Kent? With the entire *ton* at his disposal, one must wonder at his sense of duty towards his aunt and cousin."

Elizabeth sighed. The constant allusion to Mr Darcy incited a pressing desire to excuse herself and return to the sanctuary of her room, and with that in mind, she stood up.

"Pray excuse me for a moment, Charlotte. I – I," she hesitated, then with relief her eyes lighted upon Jane's discarded letter. Snatching it up from the table she waved it vaguely in the air. "I must away and respond to Jane's letter, so that my aunt and uncle know that I expect the carriage. I should not delay, or my letter will not reach them beforehand."

"Of course; it will put everyone's mind at ease." Charlotte returned her attention to the tea tray, and with a poorly concealed sigh of relief, Elizabeth turned towards the door.

"Oh, and Lizzy?"

Elizabeth glanced over her shoulder.

"You will be delighted to know that we are invited to dine at Rosings this evening – it will be an opportunity for us to farewell the gentlemen."

# Chapter Five

DARCY'S BELIEF THAT THE lateness of the hour would secure him solitude at the table was mistaken. Though it was apparent that the others had broken their fast without him, not one made a show of rising, and before he had swallowed his first mouthful of hot tea, his aunt had launched into an invective on his failure to return to the drawing room on the previous evening. From the way she gestured at a servant to refill her cup and pulled herself up in her seat, Darcy knew she had no intention of letting him off lightly this morning.

He nursed his cup in his hands, conscious that Fitzwilliam had taken advantage of Darcy's appearance to request a fresh serving. Unlike his cousin, he had little appetite. Now that the pounding in his head had begun to recede, the ache in his breast had intensified. The pain of his rejection, combined with Elizabeth's poor opinion of his character, hurt his sense of his own self-worth, and yes, his pride – though he shied away from the word as it crossed his mind.

"You must come, Darcy. And bring Georgiana – I insist upon it."

There was little at present that could draw Darcy in, but hearing his sister's name, he directed his gaze towards Lady Catherine.

"Come whither, Aunt?"

"Whither? Surely you recall our conversation at dinner?"

Darcy looked at her blankly.

*"Well?"* she snapped, her narrowed gaze fixed upon him.

He raised a brow, determined to stare her out, despite the increased pain in his head, but before a silent battle could ensue, Colonel Fitzwilliam spoke up.

"Aunt, I believe Darcy has commitments in Town that would prevent him joining you and Anne on your visit to Bath. Is that not so, Darcy?"

"Fitzwilliam is correct. My apologies, Aunt. I trust your stay will be beneficial, Cousin." He glanced briefly in Anne de Bourgh's direction, surprised to note that she had raised her head to stare at him quite fixedly.

"What nonsense, Darcy!" his aunt snapped. "I will not be gainsaid. It is long overdue for Georgiana to spend some time with Anne, and what finer place than Bath at this time of year? You are too selfish!"

Darcy flinched; his wounds were too fresh to take another pounding, albeit he cared little for his aunt's approbation. Putting down his cup, he leaned back in his seat as she extolled the benefits of Bath for Anne's constitution. Had she but left the matter there, he would have wasted no further breath on it; yet Lady Catherine was not finished.

"What a fine opportunity for Georgiana," she announced. "She is *far* too introverted, Darcy. She is but a season from her coming out, yet her shyness consumes her. This would be an excellent opportunity for her to experience some smaller social occasions not under the eye of the *ton*, as well as for the furtherance of her intimacy with Anne. Social skills must be practiced like all accomplishments, if she is not to disgrace the Darcy name."

Conscious that Georgiana's palpable timidity in front of her aunt was solely down to that lady's intimidating manner, he suppressed the desire to tell her so, merely saying in a biting tone: "Georgiana is making excellent progress in all aspects of her education; removing her from ease of access to her tutors in Town will hardly be conducive to her improvement."

Lady Catherine eyed him beadily, but before she could respond, Darcy drained his cup and rose from the table.

"You will excuse me, ladies – Fitzwilliam. I will see you at dinner," and tuning out his aunt's voice as she began to protest, he left the room.

Darcy had perhaps climbed three stairs when he became conscious of someone behind him, and without turning or pausing in his ascent, he said wearily, "What is it, Fitzwilliam?"

The letter to Gracechurch Street soon dealt with, Elizabeth felt some reluctance to return to the parlour and lingered at the writing desk. The chance of tendering an apology to Mr Darcy she had initially negated, but now she had cause to consider whether such an opportunity might present itself that evening. Yet how could such a delicate matter be addressed in company, and how would it feel to face the man she had so recently rejected?

The reminder of the proposal was most unsettling, all the more so as the shock of Mr Darcy's making such an application diminished. Elizabeth sighed as she acknowledged what troubled her – the gentleman had asked her to be joined to him in matrimony; he desired her as his wife and, try as she might, she could not negate thoughts of all that it entailed. A deep blush infused her cheeks as she recalled the intensity of his declaration, followed by the memory of their embrace, and glancing at the open writing case, she vividly recalled the words of his letter where he confessed that it was the *'utmost force of passion'* that had led him to override all his apprehensions about the match

With a groan of frustration at the turn of her thoughts, Elizabeth got to her feet. Pocketing the letter to her aunt, she quickly locked the case before she could give in to the temptation to take Mr Darcy's letter out and peruse it once more. How foolish her presumption that reading it would rid her of such thoughts. The notion that she could dismiss him was a fallacy. Little had she foreseen that, with much of the reasoning behind her dislike blown to nothingness, there were few obstacles against her growing interest in the man. Worse than this, the treacherous memory of how it felt to be held against him was no longer safe-guarded by her disgust, and without the protection of her former animosity, she felt both vulnerable and very young.

Colonel Fitzwilliam paused as he crossed his room to collect some papers from the desk. Something had caught his eye and, moving over to one of the windows, he saw Darcy riding at speed across the park towards the open countryside that spanned the area between Rosings and the nearest town of Coxheath. Not a man to alarm easily, the Colonel nevertheless winced as Darcy took a fence at a reckless pace, though he knew his concerns were groundless – there were few men with a better seat on a horse than his cousin.

Settling himself at his desk, prepared to suffer an hour or two of military business, Colonel Fitzwilliam reflected on his brief discourse with Darcy after breakfast. His suggestion that they tarry another week in Kent had been greeted with silence as they mounted the staircase. A curt negation had followed, with Darcy refusing to be persuaded from either leaving the next day or from taking a long and solitary ride now.

With a sigh, the Colonel tossed the papers back onto his desk; he could not concentrate. He did not appreciate being thwarted, and he had relied upon encouraging Darcy to extend their stay further – or at the very least to making the most of this last day – but the futility of the scheme was now clear. With Darcy absent on a solitary ride in the opposite direction to those walks where they had often encountered the lady, the Colonel needed a plan.

He was thus gratified to learn later from his aunt that, as a mark of respect for his and Darcy's final night of their stay, the company from the parsonage had been honoured with one final invitation to dine at Rosings and, rubbing his hands together in glee, the Colonel took himself off for a walk about the park, confident that the evening would deliver ample opportunity to further Darcy's cause.

As the afternoon faded, Elizabeth found herself once more sharing the parlour with Charlotte as they both worked on their needlepoint, though her progress was lamentable.

"I do not wish to go, Charlotte. I cannot believe that such an intrusion on the family's last evening would be either welcome or required."

"That is as may be, Lizzy, but Lady Catherine has taken it upon herself to extend the invitation, and you know full well that it is more by way of an order."

Elizabeth rose quickly from her chair, discarding her tangled work, and began to pace to and fro before the fire. Despite her desire to apologise, her heart quailed at the thought, perceiving disgust in his expression, the admiration she had failed to detect having turned to dislike. How could it not in the circumstances? *"I cannot... I simply... I simply cannot..."*

"Cannot *what?*" Charlotte's question brought Elizabeth's pacing to a halt, conscious that she must have uttered the words aloud.

"Believe that Lady Catherine would extend yet another invitation to our party." She hesitated. "Must we accept?"

Charlotte frowned. "Lizzy, think! How will it appear if you do not accompany us, after excusing yourself yesterday? I know you have little patience for my husband, but he was beside himself with what he perceived as an affront to his patroness. If you fail to attend her this evening, he may well write to Mr Bennet," Charlotte paused for a moment. "And I believe you love your father too well to wish him the recipient of a long letter of censure from my husband?"

Elizabeth chewed her lip; she was trapped. Her own sense of duty meant she could not pay Charlotte the disservice of refusing the invitation. Her father's opinion she disregarded, not out of disrespect, but because she knew full well that he would merely laugh at the absurdity of Mr Collins' turn of phrase and await his daughter's own version of events.

Throwing herself back onto the couch, she met Charlotte's steady gaze with a shrug.

"Then we must trust that the gentlemen do not object to the intrusion."

"The gentlemen?" Charlotte laughed. "Come, Lizzy. The Colonel clearly enjoys your company, and since when did you either care for Mr Darcy's opinion or his enjoyment or otherwise of an evening?" She shook her head and returned her attention to her needlepoint.

Elizabeth stared at her friend, unable to muster a response. Then, attempting nonchalance, she too picked up her discarded work and tried to focus on choosing a new thread, determined to push aside any thought of the impending evening.

Darcy returned to Rosings weary and saddle-sore. He had not intended to venture quite so far when he had set out, and he was desirous of nothing more than a solitary evening in his quarters and a rapid departure for Town.

He knew it to be a fruitless wish, and he closed the door of his rooms with a snap and leaned against it, a posture reminiscent of earlier that day, after Fitzwilliam had suggested staying a further week. His instinctive response should have been to laugh bitterly at such a notion, yet he had been struck dumb momentarily by the surge of hope that had swept through him at the thought of spending just one more precious week in the same environs as Elizabeth. It mattered not for that brief moment that she hated him. The certainty of his never laying eyes upon her again had been tearing him apart, and the desire to look once more upon her face a temptation he was ill-prepared to suppress.

The one consolation he had drawn was that he was secure in his belief of his cousin knowing nothing of the previous day's events, or he would not suggest such a thing. The failed proposal and his subsequent humiliation were his alone to bear.

Yet his long ride had been beneficial. Aside from losing the ache in his head from his indulgence in the fresh air, he had succeeded in convincing himself that he was relieved that he need never meet with Elizabeth again – pained by it, but relieved. If she was lost to him, then let her be gone, that he could attempt to heal his wounds and face his future with no further reminder of her distaste for his society.

With determination, Darcy pushed himself away from the door and strode with purpose towards his dressing room, where he encountered Thornton busying himself putting the finishing touches to the packing.

"Good evening, Sir," Thornton straightened from his task and bowed politely.

"We are to depart at first light," Darcy announced as he shrugged out of his riding coat, waving away his valet's attempt to assist him. "Was the *Express* to Mrs Wainwright despatched?"

"As you wished, Sir," replied Thornton bluntly.

Darcy smiled slightly at his valet's tone. "Yes, yes – Mrs Wainwright will have the house in all readiness with no need of forewarning. The point is taken."

Thornton bowed and pulled the bell rope to summon the servants with hot water.

A bath revived Darcy somewhat, and as his valet put the finishing touches to his attire, he ruminated upon the return to Town and being reunited with his sister. He had tarried too long in Kent, extended his stay more than once, and…

"You are ready, Sir."

Darcy cleared his throat. "Err, thank you. Is dinner as usual?"

"Eight o'clock, Sir, but her Ladyship requests you attend her at half past seven," and at Darcy's raised brow added, "Lady Catherine desires your presence in the drawing room beforehand."

Darcy acknowledged Thornton's aid with a nod of his head, and turned on his heel and headed for the door. No doubt another dressing down and a further attempt at persuading him to journey to Bath were pending.

He reached the foot of the stairs as the hall clock chimed the half hour and set off across the marble floor towards the doors that led into the impressive, over-ornamented drawing room, nodding at the footman to open the door for him.

As the servant stepped forward, Darcy discerned the murmur of voices from the room beyond, and his steps slowed. With a jolt of despair, he realised in an instant what he was about to face: the party from the parsonage was in attendance! As if to reinforce it, the sound of *her* voice drifted towards him as the footman swung the doors open. His heart pounding painfully in his chest, Darcy found himself frozen to the spot.

*"I cannot go in,"* he thought frantically. *"I can face neither her dislike nor her pity."*

He was about to turn back and seek the sanctity of his room when a hand thumped him unceremoniously between the shoulder blades and with a jovial shout of "There you are, Darce! Where have you been riding to all day, man?" Colonel Fitzwilliam propelled his cousin firmly forwards into the drawing room.

# Chapter Six

BY THE TIME THEY SET out for Rosings, Elizabeth's spirits had calmed. The encounter would prove challenging, without doubt; in truth, any evening passed in a country house under Mr Darcy's disparaging eye could be so, without such added complexity. Yet, conscious that he was blatantly the more injured party, she could only imagine that his torment must be of stronger nature than hers.

Though the manner of his leave-taking when delivering his letter did not indicate he held her in contempt, she struggled to reconcile her behaviour towards him whilst simultaneously retaining his good opinion. As this led her to wonder why she even wished this to be so, her confusion was great indeed.

All the way across the park Elizabeth ruminated thus, bewildered as to why she should care one way or the other, but it was not long before they were ushered into the drawing room and, her cheeks bearing a colour that was not merely induced by their walk, Elizabeth steeled herself for the encounter, only to find that the gentlemen had yet to appear.

Her agitation had little time to resurface though, for there was ample diversion in deflecting Lady Catherine's asides from across the room whilst attempting to converse with Charlotte, who sat opposite her upon an elegant but overstuffed sofa. Thus, she was barely conscious of the doors opening, heralding the arrival of further company until she realised her friend's attention had left her.

A quick glance over her shoulder confirmed the entrance of both gentlemen, and Elizabeth stood, unable to restrain the flow of warmth into her cheeks as their eyes met across the room, and she held Mr Darcy's gaze for a moment before hurriedly dipping her head and curtseying. For an instant, her composure wavered for she realised from his countenance that he had received no prior warning of her presence.

Unable to articulate a sound, Darcy greeted the company with a short bow and made his escape to the far side of the room. His heart raced in his chest and heat permeated every pore of his body. The shock that had been thrust upon him had yet to abate, and instinctively he felt that his best option for survival of this tortuous evening would be to keep as far as possible from the source of his distress. By return, it was the least he could do to alleviate Elizabeth's certain disquiet in the circumstances.

Without conscious thought, his gaze had fastened upon her even now, and he forced his eyes away only to meet instead the enquiring look of the Colonel across the room. Darcy swallowed in an attempt to relieve the sudden constriction in his throat and turned to face the window – a pointless exercise, as outside dusk had fallen and all he could determine was his own reflection and that of Elizabeth's profile beyond him where she had retaken her seat.

Colonel Fitzwilliam stationed himself in what he felt was a strategic position for surveillance of the territory. He was opposite Elizabeth, and next to Mrs Collins – upon, it must be acknowledged, the most uncomfortable seat he had ever had the misfortune to be afforded – the perfect base for both observing his cousin whilst conversing with the ladies, for Darcy remained fully in his vision.

Yet despite his good intentions, the Colonel's mind was troubled. The first hint of disquiet had struck him earlier that day when trying to focus on business matters but had easily been pushed aside, for it was not uncommon for his subconscious to seek random reasons to procrastinate when there was tedious paperwork to deal with.

His pleasure in realising that his cousin had secured a further evening in the lady's company and his stroll around the park had driven away any niggling thoughts that there was something escaping him in all of this situation with Darcy. Yet now, as the conversation typical of any pre-dinner gathering flowed around him, he was once again revisited by that concern, and...

"Colonel?"

He gave a self-deprecating smile. "Forgive me, ladies; what poor manners. As penance, I shall converse upon any matter that you may choose."

Mrs Collins lips twitched, and Elizabeth laughed, and the Colonel leaned back against the brocade cushions, attempting to find a more congenial position.

"Any matter, Colonel?" said Elizabeth. "Surely not! For what would you have to say of lace or bonnets?"

"I would welcome your educating me in such fineries, for my understanding is limited, and I would far better serve my cousin, Georgiana, when I seek a gift for her on my travels if some generous-hearted ladies would be so kind as to instruct me."

"You flatter us, Colonel, by asking our advice," Elizabeth smiled at him. "But I am certain the ladies of the *ton* would have more usefulness to offer than those of us who hail from the depths of Hertfordshire."

Fitzwilliam frowned briefly as the nagging doubt tugged once more at his subconscious but he pushed it aside. "Ah yes, never under-estimate the ladies of the *ton* when it comes to fashion! Yet," he leaned forward slightly, lowering his voice conspiratorially, "their rapacity for assisting me would be terrifying to behold. Their desire, ladies, to be of use to such a close relative of Darcy's – should I be foolish enough to share my purpose – would surely overwhelm a man less robust than myself."

As his companions expressed their amusement, the Colonel noted with resignation the stiffening of Darcy's back over by the window and, determined to display his cousin in the best possible light, he ruminated upon the means. As they had touched upon the shallow group of ladies who could be the bane of Darcy's life, he felt now might be an opportunity to regale Elizabeth with some examples of how his cousin was put upon, and as Mr Collins came at that moment to secure his wife's attendance, he turned to the lady intent upon his purpose.

Drawing his reserve about him like a cloak, Darcy had at first withdrawn, striving to shut out the conversation that ebbed and flowed around the room, but his acute awareness of Elizabeth's presence, the pleasing tone of her voice, her laughter, all conspired against him.

Shifting his weight restlessly to his other leg, Darcy stared unseeingly out into the darkness that shrouded the grounds. Foremost upon his mind was whether or not Elizabeth had read his letter. Her reluctance to take it from him had left him in no doubt that she might not. Indeed, had he not debated that very point to himself when making the decision to write to her? And here he was, neatly caught in a dilemma of his own making: not knowing if she had generously allowed him to address her so and, if she had acquiesced, what her reaction towards its content might be.

With a suppressed sigh, Darcy reflected upon the perverseness of Fate. Though he had believed he might never see Elizabeth again, and whilst he neither anticipated nor desired any particular attention from her, he fought to resist the temptation to place himself where he could overhear her conversation and rest his gaze once more upon her features.

Shifting his position slightly so that the window afforded a better view of Elizabeth, he frowned at the reflection. Finding his cousin deep in conversation with her was unexpected, for he had thought that Mrs Collins was in company with her friend, yet she now appeared to have been commandeered by his aunt.

Darcy narrowed his eyes. His cousin clearly enjoyed himself, but Darcy was not foiled by Elizabeth's performance. Though she appeared to maintain her end of the conversation with a smile, her air and countenance bespoke a mixture of discomfort and challenge. Darcy shook his head. How could he profess to know her so when he understood nothing of her dislike of him? How blind love had made him.

*Love…* Darcy acknowledged the ache in his breast as it intensified. Never had an evening at Rosings stretched before him so interminably. He realised, however, that to remain aloof he needed a purpose, and he reached for a book that lay on a nearby table, opening it randomly. It was the perfect foil as he resigned himself once more to closing out the sounds around him and allowing his thoughts to drift.

A short while later Elizabeth released a relieved breath as the Colonel took his leave of her. Innocent though he was of the implication of their recent banter, it did little to assuage her flustered spirits, and she only hoped that Mr Darcy had heard none of it.

Recalling that she had neither seen nor heard aught of that gentleman since she had retaken her seat, Elizabeth frowned, but with a slow and considered turn of her head, she immediately espied his presence over by one of the tall windows. She bit her lip in contemplation. This was likely her sole chance to offer an apology for the slurs she had made against Mr Darcy's character and, much as he understandably desired none of her company, she *would* speak to him.

Rising from her seat, she made her way around the back of her chair before she lost her nerve. Conscious that to approach him directly might attract unwanted attention, Elizabeth hesitated before crossing over to the pianoforte and pretending to look through the music scattered thereupon. Once she was satisfied she had provoked no interest in the remaining company, she raised her eyes to peer over towards Mr Darcy. He still maintained his position at the window, albeit he now held a book listlessly in one hand. Yet the rigidity of his stance and the fingers of his left hand, drumming repeatedly upon the sill led her to believe that it held little sway over his thoughts.

Elizabeth returned the sheets of music to their original position and straightened her shoulders; then, hands clasped in front of her, she approached Mr Darcy's back with purpose.

The sounds in the room behind Darcy had faded so far as to be hardly detectable, the conversation now a low, persistent humming that failed to intrude. Staring at a page that held none of his attention, it was a moment before something alerted him to someone's presence nearby, and he looked up, searching the mirrored room behind him. His cousin appeared to be joining his aunt, and Elizabeth's former seat was empty...

With a jolt of something akin to panic, he was assaulted by a waft of the very scent that he always associated with Elizabeth, and he strove to modulate his breathing.

"Darcy!"

Lady Catherine's strident voice came as a surprise to more than just Darcy. He blinked rapidly before turning to face the room. Elizabeth was not six feet away, her reflection having been concealed behind his own, and she, like everyone else, had turned towards his aunt on the opposite side of the drawing room.

"I need you here this instant. I *insist* upon it. You have tarried too long at that window!"

Conscious that his heart raced and that every head was now turned back in his direction, Darcy replaced the book in its former place, bowed briefly in Elizabeth's direction and made his way across the room towards his aunt.

The Colonel had refreshed his glass before settling himself into the chair vacated by Mrs Collins who, having been released from his aunt's company, resumed her former seat. From his new position, he was able to scrutinise the whole terrain with ease. Having observed Elizabeth's approach towards his cousin and Darcy's palpable relief at having successfully evaded her, he had to admit to being extremely baffled. Why, even if unprepared to act upon his feelings for her, would he vigorously avoid Elizabeth's company? Clearly her presence had been unexpected, but he knew Darcy to be made of sterner stuff than to be overcome by such a trifling matter.

The lady seemed intent upon seeking him out, belying Darcy's foolish notion was that she held him in disfavour. Indeed, the spirited conversation he had just enjoyed with her only proved her suitability as the perfect choice for his cousin. The Colonel grunted to himself, and fidgeted in his seat – *damn it, if this seat was not as uncomfortable as the last.* Pushing his back into the hard cushions, he nodded at Darcy as he took the chair on the far side of his aunt, before turning to observe the ladies who had resumed their earlier positions.

The niggling concern that had assailed the Colonel earlier returned, but this time more pronounced. There was more to this than met the eye. Something prevented Darcy from furthering his cause and having observed the depth of his cousin's despair and despondency these past four and twenty hours, the Colonel was determined to fathom it out. Clearly there was some sort of impediment, and if Darcy was prepared to neither confess it nor overcome it, it behoved Fitzwilliam himself to determine what it was and take whatever steps were required to remove it.

Meanwhile, he was determined that Darcy spend some time in company with Elizabeth, and with that intent firmly in mind, he stood and excused himself to his present company, heading for a further much needed top up of his glass.

Realising all of a sudden that Elizabeth had re-joined her and had spoken, Charlotte gave her friend an apologetic smile.

"I do beg your pardon, Lizzy, my thoughts were a-wandering."

"Then perchance they met with mine? I must own to having lost them just now!" the two friends exchanged a warm smile. "I merely remarked that we must be close to being called to table – I perceive Mr Collins is on his feet in anticipation!"

Following her friend's gaze, Charlotte noted with resignation her husband, pacing with importance to and fro before the imposing double doors to the drawing room, and consulting his pocket watch with irritating regularity.

"I suspect he takes that position in order to anticipate the approach of the footman. That way he can be the first to advise her Ladyship of his imminent arrival. 'Tis not the first time I have seen such a manoeuvre." Charlotte's tone was staid, but the glimmer in her eye hinted at her amusement.

Elizabeth laughed. "It is fortunate, then, that the doors open outwards, for I would otherwise fear for his well-being!"

Thus it was that within moments of this exchange, the anticipated event occurred, with Mr Collins removing rapidly to his patroness' side even as the footman entered to summon them all to table.

# Chapter Seven

HAVING RISEN FROM HIS seat more slowly than the rest of the company, Darcy waited until everyone had passed through the doors before turning to follow them. He kept his distance as they made their way to the dining room, envying his cousin's easy banter as he escorted Mrs Collins across the hallway. Any attempt at pleasantries was beyond his reach at that moment, Elizabeth's very presence a severe distraction that destroyed any remaining equilibrium.

His tarrying cost him dear, however; by the time he joined the remainder of the party at table, there was only one seat remaining, and, as Fate would have it, by Elizabeth's side.

Seated at last, Darcy reached quickly for the water jug. Normally a man in full control of his life and his emotions, he knew not, in such circumstances, how to behave – doubtless he should be striving to act as if nothing untoward had passed between them but he knew it was beyond him to do so.

Taking a welcome gulp from his glass, he strove to relax and let his eyes drift about the table, taking comfort from everyone seeming suitably distracted, his cousins engaged in a low-voiced dialogue and his aunt addressing herself loudly in the direction of both Mr and Mrs Collins. He glanced towards that end of the table: Mrs Collins appeared to be paying polite attention, as her husband attempted to bow and listen at the same time, putting him in serious danger of dipping his ear into his soup.

Darcy leaned back in his chair slightly as the servant finally arrived to serve him, and chanced a quick glance in Elizabeth's direction. She sat sedately, her hands in her lap and her head bowed – it was a position more reminiscent of his cousin Anne than the Elizabeth Bennet he knew, and he was filled with regret at being the cause, struck anew with the futility of this further encounter. She hated him, wanted nothing more to do with him, and this enforced closeness must be a sore trial to her.

Sitting forward once more, he made a pretence of applying himself to his soup bowl. The fact remained that his company brought her no pleasure, nor had it ever, and the sooner he relieved Elizabeth of his presence the better for them both.

Staring at her hands, Elizabeth frowned. Her mind was in conflict over Mr Darcy. Though his avoidance of her company did not surprise her in the circumstances, she was disturbed to discover that the loss of his regard saddened her. Yet if his fine opinion of her *had* gone why should she care? She had neither sought his estimation nor anticipated his proposal.

And how was it that the man affected her so? Nothing could have prepared her for the onslaught of feelings that had coursed through her when held against him, and now she seemed destined to be haunted by those self-same sensations whenever they locked eyes.

Raising her head, Elizabeth looked about the table. How she despised this weakness in herself. Admittedly, no man should have to deal with such humiliation as this evening provoked, but her own vulnerability towards Mr Darcy unsettled her. It was an opportune moment to recall that some of his actions deserved no such attention as an apology from her, and deliberating thus, she determined not to be cowed by their present situation.

Elizabeth turned her attention to her cooling soup, though she had little appetite for it, but then her eye caught a movement to her left, and she observed Mr Darcy's hand as it lay upon the table. His spoon rested loosely in his fingers, his thumb stroking the handle as if he was unaware of doing so; he appeared to have made no attempt to place it in the contents of the bowl.

Staring at his thumb as it moved to and fro, Elizabeth found the all too familiar heat invading her cheeks. Fighting a powerful urge to reach over and still his movement, and frustrated again at the conflict in her emotions – that she could be both angered by him as well as entranced – she sought refreshment and reached for the water jug. Unfortunately, the combination of the fullness of the pitcher and its heavy crystal ware made it cumbersome for her slender wrist, and her hand shook as she endeavoured to lift it. Without a word, the jug was taken from her grasp and a glass of water poured for her before she could catch her breath.

Ignoring the sensation engendered by Mr Darcy's fingers brushing against hers, yet aware she should acknowledge his assistance, she sat back in her chair and murmured, "I thank you, Sir."

Sensing his quick glance towards her, she suspected his intention had been to look away again immediately, but it appeared that once their eyes met, he was as unequal to the task as she. For a long moment they stared at each other, both equally expressionless. Then, with a quick nod in her direction, he returned his gaze to his setting.

Silence continued to reign over them as the opening course was cleared, though conversation amongst the remaining guests continued apace, accompanied by Lady Catherine's terse instructions to the servants and the occasional snippet of advice thrown in the direction of Mrs Jenkinson, who sat silently in a corner, awaiting her charge's dismissal.

Elizabeth chewed her lip, then bestirred herself. If she really hoped to secure the opportunity to speak with Mr Darcy, then the deed must be done this evening, and as they were such a small party at table, leaving little opportunity for completely private discourse, she must diffuse his apparent desire to avoid her company after dinner.

Recognising that much of their interaction before now – in Hertfordshire and Kent – had stemmed from her determination to provoke him, she realised this might be the best way to return them to a familiar footing; confrontation had, after all, served them well in the past.

Straightening in her seat, she said softly, "Mr Darcy," and when he sent her a startled look, summoned a smile. "I believe that we must have some conversation, Sir. To sit here in silence will, perhaps, draw attention we neither seek nor desire."

Elizabeth held his gaze for a moment before he gave an almost imperceptible nod, but speech seemed at that moment beyond him, and she sighed. Have some sympathy for him she may, but he could frustrate her as no other. She only hoped that her instinct served her well and that taxing him might restore some of his equilibrium.

Darcy felt some conflict of emotion. Why Elizabeth had attempted to approach him before dinner he knew not, but upon reflection he did not think it unreasonable that she might be intending to reproach him for some further aspect of his behaviour on the previous day.

Yet this protracted silence between them had been growing into an obstacle that was beyond his means to conquer, and his head seemed full of subjects upon which there lay an embargo: his sister, her sister – indeed, anything that touched on any of their relations – their encounters in Hertfordshire, her enjoyment of her time at Hunsford were all a potential stumbling block to fluid conversation, and all likely to raise associations that would be uncomfortable for them both.

But converse they must. Darcy resisted the urge to take a drink from his glass and, his eye caught momentarily by Fitzwilliam and Mrs Collins deep in conversation, said with relief, "Mrs Collins – she must have enjoyed your companionship these few weeks; I am certain that you have missed her since she moved away?"

"Indeed I have, for in Hertfordshire, with so confined and unvarying a society, the loss of one friend is sure to be keenly felt, would you not agree, Mr Darcy?"

Darcy threw Elizabeth a sharp glance. Was he mistaken, or was she hinting at a conversation from earlier in their acquaintance? Meeting her steady gaze, he cleared his throat, deciding that perhaps Mrs Collins was also a subject he had best avoid and glanced quickly about the room, seeking further inspiration.

"I believe you informed my cousin that you hope to travel to the Lakes this summer?"

Elizabeth admitted that it was so. "I will be accompanying my aunt and uncle," she paused briefly. "My relations from Cheapside, Mr Darcy – I am sure you must have heard them mentioned?"

He narrowed his gaze and studied her thoughtfully. Her chin was raised in a way that was not unfamiliar, and her eyes glimmered with what he surmised might be growing humour at his expense, but he refused to bite.

"And have you travelled to the Lake District before now?" Darcy observed Elizabeth's raised brow as she acknowledged his evasion.

"I have not; did not Mr Bingley and his sisters visit there last year? I am certain I heard it mentioned during my stay at Netherfield."

She cast him a sidelong glance, and Darcy suppressed the sudden urge to laugh. It would seem that whilst he desired to avoid almost every possible topic of commonality between them, Elizabeth felt the contrary. What had she said to him that entertained her? The follies of people, their whims and inconsistencies – and now it appeared he was to be her sport.

"You refer perchance to Miss Bingley's mention of visiting Windermere and her suggestion that perhaps a stroll around a lake of such significance might sufficiently curb your hunger for a good walk?"

Elizabeth smiled, a genuine smile of amusement and Darcy's breath caught in his throat. "Ah yes, Miss Bingley's desire that I walk Windermere, the largest lake in all the land!"

Wrapped in both the memory of the conversation at Netherfield, and their unexpected shared amusement, their eyes met and once again they neither seemed able nor willing to disturb the connection. Sadly, no such compunction affected their hostess.

"What is this I am hearing, Darcy – Bingley? *Windermere*? I thought Bingley's new residence was further south. What would induce a man to take an estate in a place so remote as the Lakes? You must advise him accordingly, Darcy. He relies upon your esteemed counsel, as well you know, for you have never guided him ill. What purpose is there for a gentleman to be situated so inconveniently for Town?"

Observing instantly the change in Elizabeth's expression, Darcy turned impatiently towards his aunt, but his embarrassment at her discourteous interruption and her inference of his power over his friend rendered him silent as she continued to loudly voice her opinion, and within seconds his mind had drifted, consumed once more with despair over the situation.

Colonel Fitzwilliam frowned. The gnawing at the edges of his subconscious had grown in intensity, and he would be damned if it was not starting to affect his interest in his repast – most singular.

Yet the uncomfortable look exchanged between Darcy and Elizabeth upon his aunt's mention of Bingley had not escaped him. Mystified as to the reason, the Colonel tried to recall what his cousin had said lately of his friend. He had been in love again, and Darcy had been of assistance in extracting him from the potential of an alliance with an unsuitable family. But where had Bingley met this woman? Had it been in London, or out where that new estate of Bingley's was – he was certain his aunt was mistaken and that it was nowhere near the Lakes.

He frowned at the platter in front of him.

"Fitzwilliam!" his aunt's strident tones bestirred him, and he looked up. "Is something amiss with your food?"

The Colonel stared blankly at Lady Catherine for a moment, still frowning.

"Your food, Fitzwilliam. You are glowering at it as if it does you a disservice. Do you wish a fresh platter?" Lady Catherine motioned a footman towards the Colonel as she spoke, then began to launch into a monologue on how solicitous she was of her guests and their constitution.

With resignation, the Colonel sat back in his chair whilst the bemused footman removed his full platter and replaced it with a clean one. The servants lined up to offer meat, vegetables and gravy once more, and the Colonel shrugged before helping himself to the food on offer. There was little he could do to solve the puzzle in the interim, and sitting forward now that his plate was filled, he picked up his implements and set to.

The suggestion of Mr Darcy's influence over his friend piqued Elizabeth, but despite the gentleman's attention seeming no longer with her, she had little intention of them drifting back into silence, and before such recollections could influence her mood, she attempted once more to engage him in conversation.

"Do you leave particularly early for Town on the morrow, Sir?" Elizabeth glanced at him, wondering if he would even hear her, so deep in thought did he appear to be. The sudden turn of his head in her direction was thus unexpected, but as her eyes met his and she absorbed the anguish and pain blatantly expressed upon his features, her insides lurched and for some inexplicable reason, she felt the pricking of tears behind her eyes. Concerned as she was over her own vulnerability, she had failed to consider his until seeing it openly displayed before her. Swallowing hard on an inexplicable constriction in her throat, she turned back to the table and grasped her wine glass, raising it a little unsteadily to her lips.

"Yes -" her gaze flew back to him as he spoke. "Yes, I must depart at first light. I have tarried too long in the country…"

His voice seemed to fail him, and with deliberation, Elizabeth placed her glass back upon the table and, stifling her original intent to antagonise him, responded neutrally, "Time away from one's affairs can bring tiresome results, can it not? I do not envy you the responsibility, for I see my father suffer for it often, even with an estate the size of Longbourn."

"Darcy, do you sicken for something?" Lady Catherine's sharp enquiry prevented the gentleman from responding to Elizabeth's overture. "Your air is quite distracted, and you are by turns pale as can be, then flushed with colour, and I confess I have yet to see any food pass your lips these four and twenty hours. What ails you? I must know it!"

Throwing a quick glance at the man by her side, Elizabeth returned her gaze quickly to her platter. The tightening of Mr Darcy's jaw as he glared at Lady Catherine did not auger well.

"I am perfectly well, Aunt."

"Nonsense, Darcy. You most certainly are not. I insist that you reconsider and join us in Bath. The waters there will be the perfect restorative for your malady."

"I assure you they will not."

Lady Catherine ignored his response, and attempted to engage the support of the Colonel. Elizabeth, feeling all the awkwardness of being privy to such a display, glanced across the table and shared a small smile with Charlotte. With relief, she observed the entrance of the servants once more, signalling the arrival of dessert and coffee, and knowing that the separation of the parties was imminent, she heaved a thankful sigh.

Their hostess, also remarking the clearing of the table, glared pointedly at Mr Darcy once more, before directing her attention to ordering her staff in duties that they knew full well how to perform.

# Chapter Eight

AT THE EARLIEST POST-DINNER opportunity, Mr Collins hurried to the library in an attempt to discover a book advocated by his patroness. The volumes on horticulture had all been relegated to a shelf befitting their level of interest, and the only conceivable way for him to read the titles in this gloomiest corner of the room was to take a candle and recline at floor level as he read the spines.

As such, concealed by furniture, his presence went undetected by Darcy and Fitzwilliam as they entered some two minutes later.

The Colonel headed for the drinks tray and poured himself and his cousin a generous helping of port, but upon turning to hand over the second glass he found Darcy had not followed him. Instead, he leaned against the ornate mantelpiece, absent-mindedly kicking the fender.

Fitzwilliam sighed and walked over to join him. His cousin and Miss Bennet had entered into what appeared a quite lively exchange before his aunt's interruption regarding Bingley. He remained mystified as to how that gentleman could be of any relevance in all this, but was conscious that his own disquiet had increased at the mention of his name and the reaction it invoked.

"Darcy?" the Colonel held out the glass, unsurprised when his cousin gave a visible start, and suggested they sit, and they had soon taken up the same chairs they had possessed on the previous evening.

"How fares young Bingley, Darce? When last we talked of him, he nursed his wounds, did he not?" The Colonel watched his cousin closely, but gleaned no specific reaction, Darcy's gaze being intent upon his booted feet. "And where did he meet this love of his life? In Town, or down near that country estate of his – wherever that is?"

"I have no wish to discuss Bingley further with you, Fitzwilliam," Darcy raised his head and leaned back in his chair.

The Colonel shrugged. "As you wish. I am merely curious – I had an inkling it was nearer London – his estate."

Darcy closed his eyes whilst Fitzwilliam talked, but the grip he had on the stem of his port glass and the shadow that crossed his features bespoke the touching of a nerve. Knowing his cousin would need some serious provocation to confess what really troubled him, the Colonel decided to change tactics.

"I had an enlightening discussion with Miss Bennet before dinner."

Darcy eyes flew open, his gaze snapping to his cousin's. "You did?"

"Indeed," the Colonel nodded. "She is a most lively conversationalist, is she not?"

Gaining no reaction other than a narrowing of his cousin's eyes, the Colonel took a sip of his port. "We were discussing, amongst other things, marriage."

Darcy, having just taken a fortifying gulp of his own drink, almost choked upon it.

"*What?* Fitzwilliam, have you taken leave of your senses?"

The Colonel raised a brow. "I think not. It was most informative."

Darcy placed his glass on the side table, then fixed his cousin with a piercing look. "You know full well my point, Fitzwilliam. It is hardly an appropriate subject."

The Colonel shrugged. "If the lady raised no objection, I cannot see what there is to protest. Indeed, I extolled the pressures upon you," and at his cousin's look of abject distrust added, "No, seriously. I was most assiduous in letting Miss Bennet know what a trying time you suffer whenever you are in Town, at the mercy of all those aggressively matchmaking mamas and their socially aspiring daughters."

Seeing that his cousin had become progressively paler, the Colonel pressed on. "She evinced some interest in the matter. She was most curious about how the mamas of high society behaved and seemed particularly surprised to hear how vulgar their machinations could be for their offspring. Indeed, we conversed for some minutes on it, which ultimately led to a consideration of how so many settle for a match of convenience – but I was interested to learn one thing, old man."

Conscious that his cousin's unwavering gaze was fixed upon him, the Colonel drained his glass.

"Miss Bennet implied that nothing but true affection would tempt her into matrimony. An honourable intention, as I observed to her, but she was quite adamant…" the Colonel broke off as Darcy pushed himself out of his chair and began to pace to and fro in front of the fireplace. He felt some guilt for pushing him so by making the lady the topic of conversation, but could not help but derive some satisfaction from finally getting a rise out of his cousin. Another two hours of Darcy skulking about the drawing room like a shadow, trying in vain to sink into the wall coverings, was more than he was prepared to tolerate.

"You overstep the mark, Fitzwilliam," Darcy bit out as he turned on his heel and paced back again. "What possessed you to spout forth on such matters?"

The Colonel shrugged and got to his feet as Darcy picked up the poker and gave the logs a fierce prod. "One has to talk of something," he muttered as he walked over to the drinks tray, his empty glass in his hand.

Neither of them heard the muttering from behind a nearby chaise of "pestilence… pestilence… pestil… a*ha!*"

As the ladies settled themselves back into the drawing room, Elizabeth felt all the relief of the respite from the tensions of the dinner table, though the separation of the sexes would be of short duration, she did not doubt, for Lady Catherine had been most insistent upon it. Elizabeth suppressed a smile as she recalled that lady's comments and the resigned expression on the Colonel's face.

"Miss Bennet!" The piercing voice interrupted her reverie, and she turned her attention towards the lady with an enquiring look.

"Lady Catherine is expressing an interest in your return to Longbourn, Lizzy," Charlotte interjected.

"You will be fetched, I assume, Miss Bennet. A gentleman's daughter must not travel by Post; your father's conveyance will come for you." Though a statement rather than a question, Elizabeth chose to answer it all the same.

"My uncle is sending his carriage, Ma'am."

"Your *uncle?*" Lady Catherine frowned, and then peered suspiciously at Charlotte. "Your husband indicated that Miss Bennet's uncle is a country attorney. How is it that he affords a carriage and is able to finance the sending of it all the way to Kent merely to retrieve his niece?"

Elizabeth spoke quickly, resenting Lady Catherine's tone in so addressing her friend. "I have two uncles, your Ladyship. My uncle in Town is sending the carriage for me, for I am to pass some days there before my return to Hertfordshire." Here she paused for a moment, knowing that her early departure must be revealed, but Charlotte spoke before her.

"Miss Bennet departs for Town the day after next and shall be sadly missed."

Lady Catherine's narrowed gaze moved from Elizabeth to Charlotte, and she pursed her lips. "Why was I not made aware of this? I insist upon knowing the comings and goings of guests at the parsonage. How was I not informed sooner?"

Leaving her friend to placate the lady as best she could, Elizabeth rose from her chair to take a turn about the room. She felt Wednesday could not arrive a day too soon – her stay in Hunsford had out-stretched all her wildest imaginings and if she could but secure her intention of delivering an apology to Mr Darcy, and thus absolve herself somewhat of her present guilt, she was convinced that she would leave for London with few regrets.

In the library, the hands of the ornate clock on the mantel indicated that the gentlemen's period of respite neared its end. The Colonel, however, continued to discuss Elizabeth, pleased that it drew Darcy's attention if nothing else.

"As you would expect, our conversation on wedlock raised some interesting points." He took a sip from his replenished glass. "What think you the odds of a woman turning a fellow down, Darce?"

"*What?*" Colour flooded Darcy's until now pale cheeks.

"Calm down, man, calm down. For 'tis merely a question," the Colonel had not returned to his seat after refilling his glass and they both now eyed each other from opposite sides of the fireplace. Fitzwilliam assumed an innocent expression, masking his avid interest in the emotions playing across Darcy's face.

"Specifically, we talked of how matrimony involves an element of choice, but the majority rest with the man: he has all the preference of where to make his offer, the woman merely has that of acceptance or refusal."

A slight squeak and a shuffling noise from the far side of the room caused him to pause and glance over his shoulder, but detecting nothing untoward he made a mental note to talk to the housekeeper regarding mice in the skirting boards and turned back to face his cousin's disbelieving stare.

Darcy walked over and regained his seat, dropping his head into his hands. "I cannot believe you, Fitzwilliam. What possessed you to stray into such an area?"

The Colonel shrugged. "I did nothing. Conversation has that tendency, you know, to divert itself all on its own. You should try it, my friend."

"I am in no humour for your jokes," Darcy muttered.

"No, indeed. You are in no humour at all! But I digress, and as such illustrate my point perfectly!" The Colonel grinned at Darcy's grunt. "Where was I? Ah yes, a woman's capability to deny we poor gentlemen. It evolved, since you wish to know its origins, from a discussion on dance partners to be precise, and the dilemma of a young woman who, once she has rejected an application for her company for a movement or two, is then obliged to sit that dance out. Naturally –"

"Naturally?" Darcy interjected, raising his head to stare at his cousin. "For heaven's sake, Fitzwilliam, what is there of naturalness in all of this?"

The Colonel laughed. "A fair point, my friend! Yet I must resume…"

"Must you?"

"Yes, indeed. Now do stop interrupting, you are becoming almost loquacious, yet your timing is not opportune. Where was I? Ah yes, somehow – I know not how, so do not ask – this led into a discussion about rejection. I waxed lyrical about us unfortunate men and how it feels to be turned down once one has summoned the courage to cross the floor to approach a lady…" the Colonel paused briefly to sip his drink, noting Darcy's expression with interest. "I must own that Miss Bennet did seem to desire a change of subject at this point – no doubt she has often cast off a budding suitor at an assembly and wished to spare my feelings! But I managed to retain a foothold, for I jokingly suggested that the weapon which women wield upon the dance floor would be but rarely utilised regarding the weightier issues in life – an offer of marriage, perchance."

"Is – is that all?" Darcy rasped out, the hoarseness of his voice surprising the Colonel.

Fitzwilliam glanced at the clock and nodded at it to indicate to Darcy that they should make a move to re-join the ladies. "Actually, not quite."

He turned to deposit his glass on the sideboard, disappointed that any progress he had made in stirring his cousin had so far come to naught.

"Miss Bennet warned me not to underestimate the power of refusal! Was there ever such a woman, Darce?"

The Colonel turned about but found his attention arrested by the sight of Mr Collins as he emerged from the shadows with dusty knees, clutching a large book on pest control, and wearing a look of abject mortification on his face.

In one of the ornate guest chambers, engrossed in his preparations for an early morning departure, Darcy's valet, Thornton, secured the leather fastenings on his master's trunk and straightened up, stretching awkwardly for his joints were not what they were. Turning towards the dressing room, his ears picked up the faint tingling of the carriage clock on the dresser, indicating the lateness of the hour and reminding him to hurry.

Gathering the few remaining items from the writing desk, Thornton entered the dressing room and approached the small travelling case that contained Mr Darcy's personal possessions. Carefully, and with reverence, he placed the various items into their respective drawers, locking them with the small keys he kept on a brass ring. He then reached over to pull the outer casing up, but paused. Hesitantly, he established the correct key and opened the small compartment in the centre of the case.

Thornton sighed; it was still there. Then, reaching out, he picked up the small circular leather case and lifted the lid. Nestled inside on its velvet bed, glowing in the light of the nearby candelabra, was the ring that had adorned the finger of the late Anne Darcy; a dark emerald surrounded by tiny seed pearls and diamonds, and Thornton had known, as soon as his master ordered it retrieved from the safe, that Mr Darcy was going to make an offer for Miss de Bourgh.

That his master had decided it was time to act did not surprise him. Mr Darcy was, after all, eight and twenty and – in Thornton's humble opinion – of an age long in need of a wife. The only problem was, Miss de Bourgh was not the wife he felt his master was in need of.

Yet here they were, on the evening of their departure and the ring remained fingerless. Thornton harrumphed at his thoughts. He was somewhat mollified, as his heart had sunk on more than one instance during this extended visit. He had at least twice known the ring had been removed from the travelling case, and what relief he had derived from seeing it returned – one of those occasions being only yesterday.

Shaking his head, Thornton replaced the box, sealed it safely into its compartment and turned the locks of the case, before pocketing his precious keys. Relieved though he was that his master remained free of any commitment to his cousin, his heart felt for the man, for no one knew as well as he the loneliness of much of Fitzwilliam Darcy's life.

# Chapter Nine

ON THE GROUND FLOOR corridor of the west wing a heavy silence reigned as the three men walked purposefully back towards the drawing room.

Mr Collins, taking an occasional skip in his attempts to keep apace with the gentlemen, had forgotten all about the precious volume he had scoured the library shelves for, despite the fact that it remained clasped to his chest. It may have taken him a while to pick up on the nuances of the discussion taking place between Lady Catherine's nephews, but once he did, he felt it incumbent upon himself to reveal his presence and apologise most profusely for Cousin Elizabeth. Indeed, he had been most anxious, upon discerning the content of the Colonel's dialogue with her, to explain how he, William Collins, had been fortunate enough to be the recipient of his cousin's manipulation of the "power of refusal". In sharing the concern he felt over his cousin's manner in general, he hesitated not to reveal that she was as headstrong as such a comment implied and how he rejoiced in his narrow escape, for his noble patroness would surely have been unable to tolerate such impertinence in her parson's wife.

The Colonel kept apace with his cousin as they crossed the entrance hall, for once sharing his companion's desire for silence. It would seem that Miss Elizabeth Bennet was as good as her word and that she had indeed turned down an offer of marriage. The Colonel could only breathe a sigh of relief on her behalf that she had spared herself such an end. With a grimace, he recognised his own folly in allowing his earlier conversation with the lady such free rein, but had to acknowledge that yet again she had risen in his estimation. There was not one single woman of his entire acquaintance who could have maintained their composure so well in like circumstances.

Darcy passed a weary hand across his forehead as for the second time that evening he neared the closed doors to the drawing room. What had just occurred in the library had successfully obliterated, for the time being, not only his cousin's dialogue with Elizabeth but also the tensions engendered by this unexpected evening in each other's company. Mr Collins' grovelling apology for what he deemed as Elizabeth's impertinent behaviour had caused Darcy to do little more than raise a brow in disdain and wonder at the nerve of the man for concealing his presence, but then... *then* his attention had been caught in a way he could not have imagined. Collins had offered for her – for Elizabeth!

Darcy's pace slowed, and he observed Fitzwilliam waving the footman forward to perform his service. Coming to a halt, he watched as his cousin walked into the room, followed closely by the almost running Reverend. Shaking his head briefly at the servant, the doors closed softly.

Walking across the hall, Darcy sat heavily on a bench against the wall, his mind full of this new information. So, he and Collins shared a particular fellowship – that of being rejected suitors of Miss Elizabeth Bennet. Darcy flinched at the association. His imagination struggled with such knowledge – did Elizabeth summarily reject all proposals? Were he and Collins just two of many, the landscape of southern England littered with her discarded beaus? Pushing this absurd notion aside, Darcy cast a regretful look at the staircase, wising he could seek the privacy of his rooms.

He sat forward, his elbows resting on his knees and stared at the marble floor, unsure whether he felt better for not being the only eligible man turned down by Elizabeth. Yet his mind would struggle with this thought: if he was the last man she could ever be prevailed on to marry, it meant she found the Reverend Collins a more viable proposition than himself – that ridiculous man had had more chance of being accepted than he, Fitzwilliam Darcy of Pemberley. Never, in all his born days, had he felt so bewildered and so humbled.

Elizabeth had strolled slowly round the drawing room, attempting nonchalance as she eyed first the pianoforte, then the harp – neither held much appeal. If Lady Catherine found her skill on the former wanting, she would likely take ill to hear her on the latter, but before she could deliberate this further, she realised the doors had opened.

Mr Collins, looking rather flustered and carrying a large tome, scurried through the entrance and perched himself reverently on a seat close to Lady Catherine's armchair, but as that lady presently arose from her place, he was unsuccessful in his attempt to catch her eye.

The Colonel, after bowing to his aunt, took a place near Charlotte and appeared to be settling in for a long sojourn, if the way he pummelled the cushions was any indication.

Yet to Elizabeth's surprise and disappointment, Mr Darcy did not accompany them. Frowning, she continued her walk. Surely he would not stay away for the remainder of the evening?

"Miss Bennet!"

She turned towards Lady Catherine who, she now observed, had returned to her place having apparently completed her instructions for the serving of coffee.

"Yes, Ma'am?"

"My curiosity demands satisfaction; pray, come hither."

Much against her inclination, Elizabeth crossed the room to take the seat indicated by Lady Catherine's pointed flick of her fan.

"I am not at all reconciled to your imminent departure for Town. What purpose could there be for your relative to request you alter your plans at such short notice? You should not inconvenience your hosts in such a way, Miss Bennet, it is not the mark of good manners."

Elizabeth stifled the temptation to enquire how her Ladyship could possibly understand the concept of good manners and, reminding herself of her friend's difficult situation, she forced a smile.

"I trust that Mr and Mrs Collins will forgive my early departure, Ma'am. My aunt requests my presence because her Godson is in Town, and she is desirous that I pay him my respects before he is obliged to return to the country."

"Your aunt's Godson, you say – yet he cannot be a man of importance, for I understand from Mr Collins that your connections are of little consequence."

Elizabeth threw a brief but pointed glance in her cousin's direction, who had the grace to lower his eyes.

"With all due respect, your Ladyship, Mr Collins has only recently renewed his family's acquaintance with ours, and thus cannot be considered familiar with all our connections."

"Yes, yes, that is all very well," Lady Catherine waved an impatient hand, "but how is he of such significance that his claim for your attendance must disrupt your present situation?"

"He is a dear friend of the family, Ma'am, and the favourite of my aunt. Indeed, his mother and my aunt have been the closest of friends these many years."

"Do not evade the issue, Miss Bennet. His value to you personally is of little interest to me. You know full well that I wish to know of his consequence to the world in general."

Elizabeth's eyes sparkled with suppressed emotion, but just then the servant arrived to pour more coffee. Diverted for a moment, that lady observed the room in general with a narrowed gaze then snapped, "Pray, where is Darcy?"

Lady Catherine turned her frowning countenance on her other nephew.

"He will return directly. He is no doubt checking on the preparations for our departure."

His aunt's frown intensified. "He had better return forthwith or I shall be most seriously displeased!" She returned her gaze to Elizabeth, who met her glare with a composed expression that belied the amusement she felt at realising she was, for the first – and possibly only – time, actually in agreement with Lady Catherine.

"Now," that lady continued, "where was I? Ah, yes; who is this Godson, that his presence claims your attendance so precipitously?"

"He is Mr Nicholas Harington, Ma'am."

"Harington? Harington… I do not recall the name, but then I did not expect to. From where do these Haringtons hail?"

"Sutton Coker, your Ladyship, in Somerset."

"Somerset…" Lady Catherine paused before a slightly surprised expression crossed her face. "*The* Haringtons of Sutton Coker House?"

"Indeed, Lady Catherine, the very same. Are you perchance acquainted?"

"We are not, but the estate is well-known; they will be well aware of who I am." Lady Catherine raised her chin imperiously and looked down her nose at Elizabeth. "How old is this Mr Nicholas Harrington? Is he the heir?"

Elizabeth strove to hide her indignation as such intrusive questioning. "He is the second son, Ma'am, and of an age akin to my eldest sister."

"Hmmm," Lady Catherine settled back against her chair. "It would be a fair prospect for you, better than you should really hope for or expect, your circumstances such as they are – oh yes, I know it all. Mr Collins has explained the deplorable situation of your mother's family and their poor connections; with the further hindrance of the entail and such small dowries from your father's estate, I believe you will be fortunate to secure *any* offer."

Elizabeth's eyes flashed in response to this, and she wondered briefly how Lady Catherine would react should she choose to reveal exactly how erroneous her opinion was. Yet, she merely replied, "Optimism reaps its own reward, Ma'am."

Conscious that Mr Collins had paled significantly during this exchange and was practically on the edge of his seat in his eagerness to divert Lady Catherine's attention, Elizabeth took the opportunity to excuse herself before the matter could be pursued further. Rising from her seat she curtseyed politely and resumed her assumed activity of a post dinner turn about the room, thankfully ceding the ground to Mr Collins and his book.

Taking advantage of the movement around him, Colonel Fitzwilliam grasped the opportunity to excuse himself from Mrs Collins and headed for the tray of spirits with his recently refilled coffee cup.

The Colonel had a strong ability to engage in conversation with one part of his brain whilst the other remained free to pick up on the nuances that floated around him. Thus it was that though ostensibly talking with Mrs Collins about the merits of spring in the country versus Town, he had been perfectly sensible of the conversation taking place between his aunt and Miss Elizabeth Bennet.

Adding a few drops of whisky to his cup, the Colonel reflected on his aunt's words. So it appeared that the Bennet family lacked connections of any value in the eyes of society and that their financial security was tenuous at best – could this be the impediment for Darcy? The Colonel was well aware of the expectations placed upon the master of Pemberley. Though he could never be classed as mercenary, Darcy, like many a gentleman of his standing, had been raised to conform to society's expectations. Yet Darcy would likely have never anticipated that he might fall for a lady perceived as being outside his own sphere. The Colonel shrugged. If this was the obstacle, he felt confident he would have little difficulty in persuading Darcy to overcome it.

Each moment spent in Elizabeth's company increased the Colonel's belief that she was the perfect foil for Darcy – her intelligence, compassion and spirit were everything he needed in a partner in life, and his admiration had only increased upon determining these new things about her: a gentleman's daughter she may well be, but clearly she was in need of securing a situation. Knowing as he now did that she had rejected a feasible offer of marriage, it also supported her earlier avowal of seeking a match of mutual affection over financial security or gain.

Just then, the doors swung open and Darcy entered the room, and the Colonel's gaze narrowed as he studied his cousin's countenance. Was this news to Darcy, though? Had he, in fact, known that the lady had turned down a sound offer of marriage, and was that the reason for his rather strong reaction to Fitzwilliam's topic of conversation with her?

"Darcy! There you are!" announced Lady Catherine. "It is above time. Your company has been sadly lacking these past days, and I must insist upon you fulfilling your duty this evening."

The Colonel suppressed a smile and drained his cup as he observed the resigned expression that crossed his cousin's face and truly empathised. Leaning back against the ornate marble-topped table that held the drinks tray, he surveyed the room thoughtfully. Elizabeth's amble about the drawing room had come to an abrupt halt upon Darcy's reappearance, and she seemed to be watching his cousin, unobserved by the man himself as he pulled out a chair for their aunt at the newly erected card table. Then, the ever-present Mrs Jenkinson shadowed Cousin Anne as she led her over to the seat beside her mother.

Several servants milled around trying to respond to his aunt's rapped out instructions, constantly getting under each other's feet and as a result drawing their mistress's wrath down upon their heads.

With a smirk, the Colonel beckoned one of them over and accepted a refill to his cup, requesting at the same time another be brought for Mr Darcy.

Left alone again, he realised the Reverend Collins had moved rapidly to take one of the vacant chairs, leaving only one spare and, determined to prevent Darcy from being trapped at the card table for the remainder of the evening, the Colonel stood up, about to intercede, but was forestalled by the fortuitous sight of Mrs Collins seating herself at the only remaining place. Accepting the additional cup of coffee from the servant, he raised it in Darcy's direction and beckoned him over.

# Chapter Ten

WITH ONLY HERSELF, Mr Darcy and the Colonel not secured around the card table, Elizabeth realised that any pointed movement in Mr Darcy's direction would be more than apparent; besides, how was she to remove him from his cousin?

Thwarted but still determined, she walked over to where the small group of players sat and positioned herself between Charlotte and Mr Collins, where she could ostensibly appear to be interested in the game and actually observe the gentlemen in the hope that they might separate.

Unfortunately, by placing herself at such an advantage, she had the misfortune to be stood directly in Lady Catherine's line of vision whenever she removed her attention from her hand of cards, and within moments of taking up her position found herself once more addressed on the topic of her departure.

"I am struck with a notion, Miss Bennet, for it is always my way to bestow my generosity upon those less fortunate than myself wherever possible."

Elizabeth said nothing to this.

"My nephews depart for Town on the morrow; if you are to remove from Kent earlier than planned, then you shall travel with them in Darcy's carriage. I will send a maid with you for your convenience." With a dismissive nod, Lady Catherine returned her attention to the game.

"Your Ladyship," Elizabeth began, "I thank you for the attention, but I must refuse your generous offer."

Lady Catherine's head snapped up, and Elizabeth straightened her shoulders and met her sharp eyes steadily. She would not be swayed on this, and if need be she would invoke Mr Darcy's support, for she could think of nothing they both desired more than to be once and for all out of each other's company, and sharing a morning's ride in the close confinement of a carriage was not to be borne in the circumstances.

Yet as it happened, Lady Catherine herself turned to the man in question.

"Darcy! I insist upon your taking Miss Bennet with you to London!"

With a suppressed groan, Elizabeth closed her eyes briefly, opening them to find that Mr Darcy and the Colonel were approaching the card table, and Elizabeth hurried to explain the matter.

"Your aunt is all politeness, Sir; she has learned that I depart Kent earlier than planned, in but two days' time, hence her suggestion. But I have declined her offer."

Darcy frowned. "You are for London, then, not Longbourn?"

"I am, Sir,"

"Miss Bennet is too presumptuous!" interjected Lady Catherine. "It was not an invitation but an order. You have ample room Darcy, and I am most disinclined to have carriages going hither and thither carrying one person here and two there, all on the same route, merely a day apart; such a waste of resources."

Elizabeth threw Mr Darcy a beseeching look, silently willing him to understand her and intercede. He held her gaze for a moment, and then turned to face his aunt.

"If Miss Bennet is to curtail her visit with her friend, then surely they will cherish these last few days in company? Leaving so precipitously would rob them of those moments, would it not, Aunt? I know you are too considerate of the well-being of those dependent upon you to cause such deprivation."

Feeling the need to contribute further, Elizabeth added, "My aunt and uncle do not expect me yet, Lady Catherine, and I will not be able to forewarn them of an earlier arrival."

"It is clear that someone must be inconvenienced by your change of plans, Miss Bennet; better that it is your relatives than myself, for they are family and more disposed to make allowances." Lady Catherine paused for a moment. "But I accept your point, Darcy, vexing thought it is!" She eyed the people at the table, who had been obliged to halt their game whilst this conversation took place, and then suddenly returned her gaze to her nephews where they stood by her chair. "But I have the answer! Darcy, Fitzwilliam, you will delay your departure and leave here on Wednesday with Miss Bennet. There. That is the matter determined," and with a rap of her fan on the table she indicated to her daughter to commence playing.

"Aunt Catherine!" Mr Darcy's voice drew every eye, and his glance flickered across the faces staring at him before he returned his gaze to his aunt. "Miss Bennet will travel as planned on Wednesday, and we will depart at first light on the morrow. It is neither practical nor convenient for Miss Bennet to change her plans so precipitously, nor can we delay our departure – I have pressing matters of business to attend that cannot be delayed further, and there is the end of it."

"Business, Darcy?" Lady Catherine boomed indignantly. "For what purpose do you keep a steward, a butler, a valet and all manner of servants? One should not keep a pack of hounds only to hunt the fox oneself. I never heard such nonsense!"

"It is not nonsense, Aunt, but fact. We leave in the morning." Darcy bowed in general to the company and turned on his heel, returning to his position by the drinks table. Elizabeth followed him with her eyes, noting that he had picked up his cup again though he made no attempt to drink from it. Then, she returned her attention to those around her and, meeting the Colonel's gaze, she smiled at him. Rolling his eyes at her with a sideways glance at his aunt, he grinned before bowing in general to the table and taking his leave.

Lady Catherine pursed her lips, her eyes flashing and then turned to look at Elizabeth, who assumed as blank an expression as possible.

"Very well. As it is Darcy's specific wish, I shall not insist upon having my way. Now, Miss Bennet, you have interrupted our game long enough. Find yourself some amusement and leave us to concentrate," and with a dismissive wave of her hand in Elizabeth's general direction she turned her attention back to the table, and snapped, "Play!"

Darcy leaned against the table, realising that his altercation with his aunt had revived him somewhat, and he now felt calmer than he had either before or during dinner. Balancing his cup in one hand, he reached for his pocket watch and checked the lateness of the hour, before replacing it thoughtfully. There would be less than an hour left to tolerate – but was it endurance, or a secret indulgence?

"Mr Darcy?"

He started and hurriedly placed the cup on the table before turning around.

"Miss Bennet."

Conscious that Elizabeth had thrown a quick glance in the direction of the card table and that her colour was high, he frowned. Then, he recalled her attempt to approach him before dinner: she had something to impart and, observing his cousin, the only other person not seated at the card table, perusing some sheets of music on the pianoforte, he determined that to walk slowly about the room would likely draw less attention than if they stood for some time in conversation together.

With that in mind, he raised his hand by way of illustration and said, "Shall we take a turn?"

She nodded quickly, and they set off across the heavily patterned rug. Conscious that she had approached him, Darcy made no endeavour at first to attempt a dialogue, assuming that she would open the discourse with whatever troubled her.

However, as they made their way past the pianoforte, he remembered her words at the dinner table and, determined this time to be the one to break the silence between them, he glanced at her before saying, "I trust you were in accord with my decision regarding your departure for Town. I would not want to speak for you, but I was under the impression that you did not wish to curtail your visit further by departing on the morrow?"

"You surmise correctly, Sir, for I am shortening my stay by several days as it is." She glanced up at him and quickly looked away again. "I must express my gratitude for your intervention."

He negated her thanks with a shake of his head, wishing she would reveal to him why she was to be in Town, what her purpose was and how long her sojourn would be, for he could not in good conscience push for the confidence; yet even as the thought crossed his mind he realised the futility of it. What would be the sense of gleaning such information from her? She had no wish to further their acquaintance wherever they were in residence, be it London, Hertfordshire or Kent.

Gradually, they made their way around an assortment of small tables and ornate gilded chairs bearing legs far too spindly for their professed purpose. Elizabeth glanced up at him a couple of times, and he turned to look at her.

"Mr Darcy, your letter," she looked down at her hands for a moment, and then raised serious eyes to his. "I must tell you…"

"What are you and Miss Bennet talking of, Darcy? What does Miss Bennet say to you?" Darcy drew in a frustrated breath as his aunt's piercing voice reached them. If it were not for the implications upon Elizabeth, he was seriously tempted to tell her, convinced it would silence her for some considerable time, but instead he resigned himself to prevarication.

"We are discussing the art of penmanship, Ma'am" he volunteered, his eyes still fixed upon Elizabeth's face as they both tried to put a little distance between themselves and the card table, but as his aunt continued to intrude, he felt obliged to halt their progress and turn in her direction.

"Calligraphy, you say? I am, of course, a renowned proficient with pen and ink. No one has a finer hand than I. And Anne would be equally lauded, had she the strength to hold an implement for such time as would be required to fully display her talents."

Lady Catherine continued thus in a monologue of self-satisfaction, and Darcy turned back and indicated to Elizabeth that they continue walking, ruminating with some discomfort upon what she had been about to say.

"*Your letter...*" Your letter *what?* Was an affront? Ill-judged? Destroyed the moment you turned your back? He tried to interpret her expression as she turned and joined him, but there was no hint as to her intent upon approaching him. Yet he had wished to know, had he not, whether she had read it, whether she had paid his words any credence? Drawing on his courage, he decided to try and forestall any further reprimand.

"I must beg your forgiveness for demanding your attention in such an unorthodox manner, but I had not envisaged our being in company again and felt a compelling need to defend myself. With hindsight, I am not certain that I should have succumbed to the temptation."

Unsure whether she would join him in his self-censure, Darcy met her gaze with troubled eyes. It was some comfort to note that she did not look as if confrontation was her purpose, and when she spoke her voice was subdued.

"I am mortified, Mr Darcy, by what I accused you of, and... and to have been so foolishly blind."

"Please, Miss Bennet," involuntarily, Darcy reached out a placating hand towards her, then realising what he was about, withdrew it quickly. "You should not blame yourself for being taken in by that man. He is a true proficient at deception, as I know to my cost." Try as he might, he could not prevent the bitterness of his tone.

"And your sister, Sir? Is she – is she well?"

Feeling all the awkwardness of the situation, Darcy slowed his pace, staring at the floor for a moment before returning his gaze to hers.

"She is not as recovered as I would wish. It is but months since her... disappointment, and she has had to overcome a dual assault upon her emotions."

Darcy had come to a halt now and passed a weary hand across his eyes. How bittersweet it was to talk with Elizabeth about this; how he had dreamed in recent months that this was the sort of burden he would be able to share with her; how he had longed for her counsel, her kindness, her concern. Unable to look on her face, suspecting the compassion he would read there, he lowered his gaze once more to the floor.

"A dual assault, Mr Darcy?" Elizabeth's voice prompted gently, and he knew he could not resist her.

He ran a hand through his hair distractedly, then raised his head and met her troubled gaze.

"Yes – her disappointment was two-fold, firstly on the count of respect and secondly of love. Not only had she deceived herself over someone she had long esteemed, in that he did not value her character at all, but also she has had to accept that she bestowed her heart where there will never be reciprocation. She has suffered the pain of unrequited love."

The similarity between his sister's disappointment and his own did not escape her, and Elizabeth quashed an irrational urge to reach out to Mr Darcy as the portent of his words sank in. They stared at each other for some moments, oblivious to the room and its occupants. Mesmerised, she watched the emotions playing across his face, the anguish in his eyes, recalled again his declaration of loving her and then caught her breath as she saw him glance fleetingly towards her mouth, his eyes returning immediately to hers. Was she not mistaken then? Had he really desired to kiss her yesterday, and was that even now upon his mind?

"I cannot but wonder what it is, Darcy, about handwriting that could bring such a colour to Miss Bennet's cheeks."

Elizabeth started and took a step backwards, conscious that Mr Darcy had blinked rapidly at the intrusion, his gaze returning to hers before responding bluntly, "I am sure you cannot." Yet he seemed to detect the discomfort upon Elizabeth's face now they had once again attracted his aunt's attention, and he threw her an apologetic look.

"Perhaps we should continue," he once again lifted his hand to indicate that they should resume their walk, and Elizabeth thankfully fell into step beside him, disturbingly conscious of his presence at her side once more as they put a little distance between themselves and Lady Catherine.

# Chapter Eleven

THERE WAS SILENCE BETWEEN them for a moment; then, Mr Darcy spoke:

"I cannot tell you how gratified I am that you accept my word. Having made the decision to set before you all that man's dealings with my family, I very much hoped that you would hear me out, but to know for certain that you now understand his true character and will thus no longer fall victim to his artifice is of no little comfort."

Mr Darcy paused, and Elizabeth felt all the shame of her misapplied accusations well up inside; she looked away, blinking back a rush of sensation about her eyes.

"Miss Bennet?" the concern in his voice caused her to swallow painfully before turning back towards him, conscious that her eyes might be a little moist and praying that he would not notice.

"I hope – I hope most fervently that you soon recover from your disappointment."

Elizabeth frowned, unsure of his meaning; then, suspecting he thought her enamoured of Mr Wickham – and why should he not, following her defence of him yesterday – she opened her mouth to speak, to assure him she was not personally injured by hearing of his true character, but the words were never spoken, for Colonel Fitzwilliam had materialised by his cousin's side, and Lady Catherine's voice once more intruded.

"Really, Darcy, I must insist upon your stopping this tiresome pacing, it is most distracting. I think Miss Bennet has taken ample exercise for this evening. Her colour is too high."

It seemed to Elizabeth that Mr Darcy could not find an immediate response this time, but his loss of words mattered not for the Colonel stared thoughtfully at her before saying over his shoulder,

"That is because I am badgering Miss Bennet to play for us, Aunt," he turned back to face her, smiling as he spoke. "And of course, her modesty is objecting to the rather copious praise I am bestowing upon her in an attempt to persuade her to delight us once more."

Elizabeth returned his smile gratefully, thankful for his intervention, but hoping very much that he had not overheard their dialogue. At Mr Darcy she dared not look. Though relieved that some of her regrets had been expressed, she did not think she could have handled the intensity of their discourse for much longer. Perhaps if they had been able to have the exchange some time in the future… but just now, it was all too raw, too fresh and if she felt thus, she could not imagine how much worse it was for him.

Before she could make her way towards the pianoforte, though, they were joined by none other than Lady Catherine herself.

"Darcy, Fitzwilliam, fetch me some fresh coffee. I wish to speak with Miss Bennet."

The Colonel snorted. "Good grief, Aunt, whatever happened to the belief that *'one should not keep a pack of hounds only to hunt the fox oneself'*? Are there not sufficient hounds here to pour the coffee?"

Lady Catherine glared at him. "Surely it is not much to ask, that my nephews might bring me some refreshment?"

Mr Darcy glanced over to the rest of the company as they rose from the card table. "Should you not return to your game, Aunt? They appear to be restless without you."

"I am no longer disposed towards playing cards. Mr Collins has been instructed to tidy all away. I wish to have my part in the conversation."

The Colonel grunted. "Come then, Darcy. It falls to us to know our place. Let Aunt Catherine converse with Miss Bennet."

With a swift glance in her direction, Mr Darcy turned towards the nearby table housing the coffee accoutrements, accompanied by his cousin, who could be distinctly heard making a yapping noise not dissimilar to that of the hunting dogs at Longbourn.

Biting back a smile, Elizabeth faced Lady Catherine, who wasted little time in coming to her point.

"Remind me how it is that you are acquainted with my nephew, Miss Bennet. I fail to comprehend how your paths could have crossed sufficiently to claim an acquaintance."

"It was in Hertfordshire, Ma'am."

"Hertfordshire? What would Darcy be doing in Hertfordshire, of all places?"

"He was a guest of his friend, Mr Bingley, your Ladyship." Conscious that the Colonel had turned suddenly in her direction, Elizabeth caught his eye briefly and frowned at the strange expression that crossed his face. Pushing it aside, she looked expectantly back at her companion, unclear where the line of questioning was going.

Lady Catherine's gaze narrowed and then she nodded. "Ah yes, Darcy's very close friend. He takes such prodigious good care of him, for his fortune is newly acquired, and he requires much direction and, indeed, protection. So Hertfordshire is the location of his estate, not the Lakes. I am better pleased with that choice, for all the County has little to distinguish it by."

Elizabeth was all but ready to launch into a defence of her own little corner of England, conscious that the recurrence of the insinuation of Mr Darcy's ability and desire to control Mr Bingley caused her no little agitation, but she was forestalled before she could speak.

"You would, of course, be but little known to Mr Bingley. Though I can understand how, being a gentleman's daughter, you may have contrived some form of introduction during their stay in your country, it could be little more than that of a passing acquaintance."

She turned to take her coffee cup from Mr Darcy as he re-joined them.

"Indeed, your Ladyship, you are mistaken. My acquaintance with the Bingleys was not 'passing'."

Lady Catherine returned her gaze to Elizabeth, narrowing her eyes as she did so.

"Yet they can be nothing to you, Miss Bennet. Though their family's position in society is not of long standing – indeed, it is nothing to the Darcys, the Fitzwilliams or the de Bourghs – they are reasonably well-endowed financially and will –"

"Aunt! That was not what you said when I was last in company with you. You claimed young Bingley was just some upstart clinging to Darcy's coat tails in the hope of social ascension." The Colonel was unable to contain his amusement as he handed a cup to Elizabeth.

Lady Catherine's mouth snapped together in a rigid line as she glared at her nephew.

"Fitzwilliam, you overreach yourself!" Turning back to Darcy and Elizabeth where they stood, she eyed them carefully for a moment before raising her chin, "So – as I was saying, Miss Bennet. The Bingleys, though not of the same standing as ourselves, would move in a different circle to your own family – and indeed that of Mrs Collins," here she gave a dismissive nod in Charlotte's direction.

"You are under a misapprehension, your Ladyship." Elizabeth could feel the heat in her cheeks. "I was in company with both Mr Bingley and Mr Darcy on several occasions during their sojourn in the neighbourhood." She drew a breath to calm her indignation. "Thus we are most certainly fully acquainted."

A coughing sound from her right distracted Elizabeth slightly, but realising the Colonel had merely choked a little on his drink, she returned her gaze to her inquisitor.

The elder lady drew in a hissing breath, but Elizabeth was unimpressed.

"Mr Bingley's estate is but three miles from my father's and we frequented the same gatherings as he and his party," here Elizabeth threw a lightning glance in the direction of Mr Darcy. "I also passed several days as a guest in his house when my sister was taken ill there."

Colonel Fitzwilliam's head reeled. Observing his aunt's tightly compressed lips, effectively silenced as she was for a moment, he excused himself and took his coffee cup over to the tray of spirits, this time adding a hefty dash of whisky into his cup before taking a fortifying sip.

So Hertfordshire was the connection, the reason for the niggling doubt in his mind these past four and twenty hours – both Miss Elizabeth Bennet *and* Bingley hailed from that same county! Notwithstanding that coincidence, it now transpired that they were acquainted.

Fitzwilliam stifled a groan. He had shared some delicate information with her that he had suggested related to Bingley as they walked in the park on the previous day, and later the lady had pleaded an indisposition.

He turned around to face the room, leaning back against the wall next to the drinks table. His aunt had returned to her seat and was once more holding court with the Collinses. Darcy had taken a chair removed from the remainder of the company, his gaze resting fixedly upon Elizabeth, who had finally taken a seat at the pianoforte. Fitzwilliam eyed her full of guilt: what had he done?

Taking another hefty draught that almost emptied his cup, the Colonel was assailed by the implications of his ill-fated words. How naïve of him to speak so of Darcy's closest friend.

The Colonel looked from Elizabeth to Darcy, then over to Mrs Collins. Yet there remained the mystery of the woman Bingley had fallen for, the alliance that Darcy had claimed he rescued him from. Wearily, the Colonel passed a hand over his eyes. It now struck him that there was every likelihood that either Mrs Collins or her friend knew the family concerned. Given Elizabeth's dissatisfaction with Darcy's actions when he revealed them, her challenge of his words and her later indisposition... Good heavens, there was even a chance she was acquainted with the young woman herself!

Well, there was nothing for it. He had a duty to ascertain the truth of it. Placing his empty cup on the tray he made his way across the room to join Mrs Collins and requested permission to join her.

"Your friend appears in better health this evening, Mrs Collins. I trust she is recovered from her indisposition?"

"I thank you for your concern, Colonel. I do believe she is well enough." She smiled at the Colonel. "Lizzy has a very loving heart; she has been dwelling too long and too deeply on a disappointing situation that arose in Hertfordshire and has suffered some disturbance of her natural spirits, but I am pleased to see that she is improving."

A disappointing situation? *I hope most fervently that you soon recover from your disappointment.* Darcy's own words that he had overheard not moments earlier burnt a trail through his mind, and a sickening realisation began to dawn upon the Colonel. It all made so much sense, and if what he surmised was true, he could comprehend the rightful grounds for Darcy's despair and conflict of mind.

Determined to confirm the matter, he launched into speech.

"Miss Bennet's family – I understand she has several sisters?"

Charlotte smiled. "Yes, Colonel. The Bennets were blessed with five daughters, and each is as different from the next as could be!"

He forced a laugh, and tried to settle himself more comfortably against the cushions. With stealth and skill, he gently led Charlotte into a conversation about her home town of Meryton and the interests in particular of the local populace.

He suspected she was not a woman prone to or influenced by gossip, yet it was evident that Mrs Collins relished the opportunity to recall her friends and home and reflect upon their day to day lives and, as anticipated, the Bennet family were frequently mentioned. Though Mrs Collins was perfectly polite about her neighbours, sufficient was emerging to paint a picture of the Bennets, the family matriarch in particular.

Racking his brains the Colonel tried to recall what his aunt had been bemoaning upon their arrival in Kent: Mrs Collins' friend came, she had advised them, from a family where there had been no governess, leaving the upbringing of five daughters in the hands of the mother – daughters who were all out, despite their young age and the elders being unspoken for.

The Colonel sat up straight and slapped his head as comprehension dawned.

"Are you quite well, Colonel?"

"Forgive me, Madam. Pray, do continue – you were mentioning an assembly?"

Leading her carefully back into her monologue, the Colonel leaned back against his seat, impervious to the knobbly cushion digging into his back. Combined with his understanding of Miss Elizabeth Bennet's lack of good connections or dowry, this must be the unsuitable family!

Conscious that Mrs Collins studied him curiously, he roused himself and apologised.

"My dear lady, please forgive an old soldier's poor concentration. May I fetch you some more coffee?"

Relieved at her acceptance, the Colonel excused himself and headed for the refreshment table, waving away the ever-hovering servant. Barely conscious of his actions, he poured coffee into two fresh cups and absent-mindedly added a liberal dash of whisky to both, and then paused as he held the cream jug over one of them. So this was the impediment revealed at last. His guilt over his indiscretion receded in a wave of anger towards Darcy. How could he? How *dare* he?

Darcy had, by his own admission, saved Bingley from the inconvenience of a most imprudent marriage – a young lady of unsuitable background with whom Bingley believed himself in love. Elizabeth was not only acquainted with the woman, she *was* the woman. His cousin, enamoured of Elizabeth himself, had separated a couple who shared a mutual regard and was now in the unenviable position of being unable to offer for her, not because of her unfortunate connections and unsuitable family, but because of his close friendship with Bingley, whom he had persuaded away from the very same alliance – an impediment indeed.

Adding liberal amounts of sugar to both drinks, the Colonel turned to face the room again, a cup in each hand. Elizabeth continued alone at the pianoforte, her head bowed in concentration; Darcy's gaze was fixed upon her, a surfeit of emotions playing across his features. With a grunt of annoyance, Colonel Fitzwilliam replaced his cup on the table and walked with determined steps towards Mrs Collins, to whom he offered the remaining one before excusing himself.

Darcy was so engrossed in his thoughts that he did not immediately discern his cousin's approach. This stolen evening was at its end; Elizabeth would be leaving with the Collinses at any moment, and he would likely never hear word of her hereafter. The ache in his throat intensified as his eyes devoured the sight of her at the pianoforte, the pain in his chest forming a physical band across his rib cage.

In the soft light of the candelabra, her dark hair shone and though she had not raised her eyes from the keys since she had started to play, he could picture well enough the glimmer that would be reflected in them should she do so. He could not tear his gaze away. He found her profile beautiful: long lashes resting on her cheeks, the sweep of her nose, her full lips… how could he let her go?

With an impatient sigh, Darcy stirred restlessly in his seat. She was not his to let go and never had been. He must accept that fact and, even more so, that one day she would belong to another…

"Darcy!"

With a start, he looked up to observe his cousin standing in front of him with a rather forbidding countenance.

"Come, I would speak with you," and when Darcy did not immediately react, "*Now*, Cousin!"

Darcy rose from his chair. "What is it? Can it not delay?"

"No, it cannot. Now *come!*" and the Colonel set off towards the drawing room doors at a rapid pace.

Darcy looked on in bemusement, but fully conscious that the present direction of his thoughts was a self-indulgence he could ill afford, he slowly followed in his wake. At the door, Darcy hesitated, casting one last, lingering look towards the pianoforte, and then caught his breath. Elizabeth had raised her head and turned in his direction. Meeting her eyes for the last time he took one step towards her and bowed deeply before turning on his heel and leaving the room.

# Chapter Twelve

THE LIBRARY AT ROSINGS PARK was one of its few master rooms that retained an aura of natural grace and style. Essentially a masculine domain, Sir Lewis de Bourgh had established his reign over it and in the process had refused any over dressing of its space. As such, it retained an elegance and simplicity that the remainder of that great house could not pretend to emulate. There were no garish murals here, nor heavily ornate mirrors or chandeliers. Indeed, the walls were somewhat sparsely furnished with a small selection of watercolours of various sizes and subjects, one of which was a simply framed study of Anne de Bourgh whilst still an infant that had been commissioned by her father.

The baby Anne, swathed in pastel cloth and tended by a host of delicately drawn angels, had a skin tone far healthier than her sallow complexion in life, a specific instruction to the artist, for Sir Lewis had been advised that his only child was not long for this world. That he had sought to have her likeness captured as soon as was practicable, for fear there might come a day when he would fail to recall her face, served him little; within a twelve month of the finished painting being hung in the library it was the father who had succumbed, not the daughter.

In more recent times, due to the inclinations of the present occupancy at Rosings, none of which demonstrated much interest in reading, the library was but rarely in use except when Lady Catherine's nephews were in residence, when it became so often engaged as a refuge that below stairs it had been renamed *"the Sanctuary"*.

Thus it was that the servants, who had been dispatched to tidy the room after the post dinner indulgence by the gentlemen of the party, had all but finished their preparation of the room for its anticipated further usage. The fabric of the seats had been brushed, cushions plumped, the decanters replenished and the used crystal ware banished out of sight to the kitchens.

Having re-stoked the fire and checked the candles for their life span, the last of the retainers disappeared through the servants' access door concealed in the wooden panelling not a moment too soon.

Conscious of the ever-present footmen in the hallways, Colonel Fitzwilliam and Darcy made their way to the library in purposeful silence, each deliberating upon the other's rather singular behaviour. On entering the room, Darcy hovered just inside the doorway, watching in confusion as his cousin peered behind two elegant sofas and a particularly large desk before heading for the newly refreshed tray of spirits.

"Fitzwilliam, what are you about?"

The Colonel turned to face his cousin, responding rather shortly: "I would have thought it apparent. I have no desire for this conversation to be overheard. Whilst I do not consider Collins to be an illusionist and thus in two places at once, I wish to be confident our privacy is assured."

Observing his cousin still standing near the doors, his air and countenance bemused, the Colonel sighed impatiently. His ruminations over the past four and twenty hours had not anticipated such a source for Darcy's lowness of spirit, and he felt momentarily forestalled over how to proceed.

"Whatever this is, surely it can be delayed until we are on the road." Darcy paused and cast a glance over his shoulder towards the door. "We cannot fail to farewell the guests."

"We can, and we most certainly shall. *Darcy!*" Noting that his cousin had half turned away as if seriously contemplating a return to the drawing room, the Colonel realised he had little option but to launch his attack, and allowing his anger full rein he snapped out, "I no longer wonder as to your supposition that Miss Bennet despises you. From what I have ascertained, she may well have just cause."

Fitzwilliam's words had the desired effect, for Darcy's body stiffened noticeably, and slowly he turned back towards him. Yet he had not anticipated the powerful emotion that would be writ upon Darcy's face, and indignant though he was over his cousin's inexplicable behaviour, Fitzwilliam could not help but feel for him in such untenable circumstances.

Darcy met his cousin's steely gaze with a combination of shock and hurt. Having so recently been engaged in a conversation with Elizabeth that, whilst difficult, had also been strangely comforting, the stark reminder of how the situation really stood was not only unwelcome but also intensely distressing, and he walked over and sank into one of the armchairs by the fireplace. Leaning his head back against the leather, he closed his eyes, willing the tightness that had suddenly gripped his chest to subside. Whilst Darcy had been in no doubt since yesterday of Elizabeth's feelings for him, it was agonising to have her dislike of him confirmed by someone else.

The sound of ice and liquid against glass informed him of his cousin's actions, and he was not surprised a few seconds later to open his eyes to the sight of a crystal tumbler filled with amber liquid being held in front of him. Accepting it, he took a fortifying drink as his cousin settled himself in the chair opposite.

Allowing the liquor to warm him, Darcy stared thoughtfully at Fitzwilliam. What had led him to say such a thing? It was evident that his temper had been roused, but over what remained yet unclear, and Darcy raised a brow as the Colonel suddenly pushed himself out of his chair and began walking up and down in front of the hearth, his glass dangling precariously from one hand.

"I have discovered what you have done." The Colonel threw him a stern look, then continued his pacing.

For a split second, fear gripped Darcy as he struggled to comprehend what, of the many things he wished to conceal, Fitzwilliam might have learned.

"It is unconscionable! I would never have expected such from you. Admittedly, I can appreciate the inducement that would tempt you to act so – but that you did? I can hardly credit you with such behaviour!"

Following Fitzwilliam's progress as he marched to and fro across one of Rosings' finest hearthrugs, Darcy's eyes narrowed. Was his cousin referring to Darcy's decision to offer for Elizabeth? Being such a liberal thinker, Fitzwilliam's attitude was, to say the least, unforeseen and more the sort of reaction he would have anticipated from their aunt.

With a frown, Darcy studied the glass he now cradled in both hands, then shook his head.

"I have not the pleasure of understanding you, Fitzwilliam. What is it that I am supposed to have done?"

"This so-called act of loyalty towards a friend – Bingley, I had assumed."

Darcy enjoyed a moment of relief, but then he stared at his cousin in confusion. "But that is old news, Fitzwilliam – we spoke of it some time ago."

"But not of the lady."

As realisation dawned, Darcy blew out a breath. *Of course.*

"I am struggling, Cousin, to reconcile the man I know you to be with someone who would wilfully separate a couple who loved each other and thus expect to gain some peace of mind. How could you think taking such a step would secure the happiness of anyone concerned? And what of Miss Elizabeth Bennet? I understand that your feelings are engaged, but so it would seem are hers, and distasteful though that is to you, you cannot discount it."

"Damn you, Fitzwilliam! Are you playing my conscience?" Darcy dropped his glass onto a side table and pushed himself from his chair, meeting his cousin half way across the rug. "Why do you persist in this? I have no desire to discuss Bingley further with you, as I told you earlier, and even less to talk about Miss Elizabeth Bennet and where her affections lie." This unwelcome reminder of her interest in Wickham combined with her obvious disappointment earlier over the revelation of his true character caused sufficient turmoil in Darcy's mind that he failed to wonder how his cousin might have acquired such intelligence.

For a moment the two men glared at each other, then the Colonel resumed his pacing. Darcy ran a hand through his hair before rubbing his eyes, his anger dying as quickly as it had come. He had no taste for a conversation that centred around any of his Hertfordshire acquaintance, yet he knew there was little point in resistance. His cousin was unlikely to let drop whatever troubled him, and no doubt all would reveal itself soon enough. With a weary sigh, Darcy resumed his seat and reclaimed his glass, nursing it in his lap resignedly.

Much as anticipated, Fitzwilliam turned on his heel to face him, shaking his head from side to side as he studied Darcy intently. "I have no wish to quarrel with you, man – but it angered me to see you err in such a way. If there is some justification for what you did…" he paused for a moment. "Do you wish to explain?"

"You imply I have some choice in the matter."

"I am all ears, Darcy."

"I must disagree. You use your mouth to much effect, Cousin."

"Well, one of us must be prone to garrulousness – how else might we ever hold a conversation?"

For a moment both men observed each other in silence; then, Darcy sighed. "Might I enquire how it was that you found out?"

"A series of conjectures. Mrs Collins has just supplied the final clues to the riddle, of course, but I had noted that Miss Bennet suffered a lowness of spirits during our recent walk, and was indisposed thereafter– it merely took until this evening to discern that my indiscretion yesterday was likely the cause."

Darcy sat bolt upright. "Indiscretion? Fitzwilliam, what have you done?"

For the first time since they entered the room, the Colonel looked defensive, and he took a hefty swig from his glass that left it imminently in need of replenishment.

"I told you – I met with Miss Bennet whilst taking my usual tour of the park and turned back with her to escort her as far as the parsonage gate." He hesitated, running a hand through his hair. "During our walk, in an attempt to show you in a better light, I advised her of the recent service you rendered a friend, whom I supposed to be Bingley. Of course, at the time I knew not the identity of the lady in question."

Darcy sank back into his chair as he realised both the significance of the knowledge imparted and its timing, then shook his head at his cousin.

"For a military man you are extraordinarily loose with your tongue, Cousin."

Fitzwilliam held out his hand indicating Darcy's half-empty glass, and he drained it before handing it over. As the Colonel walked over to the drinks tray, he addressed Darcy over his shoulder. "Then you are not too cross with me? It was not my intention to reveal such distressing news to someone so closely connected with it. Indeed, in all honesty it was an attempt to illustrate the goodness of your character."

Darcy let out a bitter laugh. "Then you would have better saved your breath. Nothing could have demonstrated the opposite further than to have confirmed to Miss Elizabeth Bennet the depth of my interference with Bingley and the object of his affections."

The Colonel glanced somewhat sheepishly over at Darcy before returning his attention to their glasses. "She seemed quite out of spirits with your good deed. With hindsight, I begin to see why."

Darcy nodded thoughtfully. "I do not doubt that she had her suspicions."

Their glasses now replenished, the Colonel resumed his seat.

"I must own that my attempt to sketch your character ultimately led to my anger over your behaviour. I struggle yet to approve your actions, but what is done is done. The question that remains now is this: what are you going to do to put things to rights?"

"What is there to be done?"

"But you cannot leave things as they are! The happiness of people who are dear to you is at stake, and if you cannot take into account your friend, then at least consider Miss Elizabeth Bennet. She has rejected a proposal of marriage from the vapid Collins to await one that now will never come!"

Gripped by the strength of his emotions, Darcy rose purposefully from his chair and walked over to the fireplace before turning to face his cousin.

"You astound me, Fitzwilliam. Surely even you can comprehend why I had to intervene."

"What? Because you could not have her, you would not let anyone? You claimed only yesterday that she is everything to you, yet this is how you serve her?"

Assimilating his cousin's words, Darcy nodded slowly. "So that is what I revealed. I did wonder…"

The Colonel let out a huff of breath. "Well, to little avail, it would seem. You cannot hold her in true esteem, man, for if you did you would never destroy her happiness in such a manner."

Darcy brought his fist down upon the mantel and then turned to face his cousin, his expression one of incredulity.

"You mean to say, knowing all his evil tendencies, his proclivities, you would have me not disabuse her of them?" Darcy stared at his cousin in disbelief. "That is what you call acting to destroy her happiness?"

"*What?* Evil … his proclivities? Bingley?"

"Bingley? I speak not of Bingley, Fitzwilliam. There is more than him in all of this!"

"How can that be, when he is the origin of both your loss and your most singular behaviour? You alleged Miss Elizabeth Bennet's indifference to him, but her affections are clearly engaged."

"What?" Darcy passed a hand across his eyes, trying to digest this. Then, he shook his head. "You are mistaken, Cousin. Bingley is not the recipient of her affections."

"No longer, that is as may be, but down to your actions alone."

Darcy frowned. "Bingley is not, now or ever has been, enamoured of Miss Elizabeth Bennet. Nor she him. I cannot comprehend why you would think so."

Colonel Fitzwilliam stared at him, his mouth slightly agape. Then, he rose from his chair and came to stand opposite Darcy.

"Then I will own to being somewhat confused."

"In that you are not alone." Darcy sighed. "What exactly is it that you would have me guilty of?"

The Colonel shrugged.

"You told me yourself that you saved a friend from a most imprudent marriage – I assumed all along it was Bingley, for he is the sort to get into a scrape of that kind, and you were together all of last winter. And everything I discerned this evening pointed to the woman being Miss Elizabeth Bennet."

Darcy expelled a slow breath as he absorbed this. "And they let you lead young men into battle, Cousin? I trust you secure the veracity of your evidence more thoroughly on the battle field than you do in the drawing room before launching your assault."

"Very funny, Darce. But tell me, if not she, then who?"

"Her sister."

Fitzwilliam frowned. "Which one? There are several, are there not?"

"The eldest, Miss Jane Bennet."

"Ah. So it was she who was indifferent to him."

There was a pregnant pause as they observed each other, the only sound being the crackling of the logs in the grate. Then, the Colonel shrugged his shoulders.

"I must tender my apologies, Darcy. I confess to being rather shocked by my own surmises – it is not behaviour that I could comprehend coming from you, and I should perchance have fixed upon that before drawing my erroneous conclusion."

"You forget, Fitzwilliam, that I am well versed with your impetuosity."

Darcy found that he could rouse no anger, for he was struck forcibly by the fact that his cousin's displeasure with him was nothing to Elizabeth's, in either depth or longevity. Beyond this he struggled to think, having neither the energy nor the inclination for further debate.

"Apology accepted; let us drink to having cleared up our misunderstanding."

# Chapter Thirteen

LEAVING DARCY TO FRESHEN their glasses, the Colonel prodded a recalcitrant log with his boot to encourage it into the flames. "I have been on the wrong trail entirely. But wait! Is this not excellent news?"

"How so?" Darcy glanced over his shoulder at his cousin.

"If you are not guilty of separating Miss Elizabeth Bennet and Bingley, as I supposed, and the lady is thusly not harbouring feelings of rejection and resentment, then your path is clear."

Darcy let out a noncommittal grunt at this and turned his back again to pick up the decanter, trying in vain to shut out his cousin's voice.

"You have acknowledged to yourself the depth of your feelings; you must act! What do a lack of prominent connections and a minimal dowry mean to you, and as for the family's conduct – good Lord, Darcy, Hertfordshire and Derbyshire are sufficiently distanced for it to be irrelevant, and who are we to judge others on their ill-mannered relations? Do you fear rejection?"

Darcy winced as the decanter stopper slipped from his hand onto the tray, but his cousin continued.

"No woman is going to turn *you* down, old man. You have been the catch of the season since... well, since you left the womb!"

Staring at the drinks he had just poured, Darcy concentrated on breathing slowly, evenly. Emotions that stemmed from the very depths of his being had been wrung from him these past four and twenty hours, and he was all but drained. He knew full well that he could retire for the evening, keeping his awful secret safe, but Fitzwilliam was akin to a hound after a fox once onto the scent of something, and Darcy possessed intelligence that could silence his cousin forever on the question of Miss Elizabeth Bennet – and the time had come to do so.

Straightening his shoulders and taking a glass in each hand, he turned to face the Colonel.

"Miss Bennet would not have me."

"Yes, yes, very droll, Darcy. I respect Miss Elizabeth Bennet more highly than I do any other young woman of our acquaintance, but rejecting the ridiculous Collins is hardly the test of one's resolve in earnest. Come man, think! Nothing would induce a woman of her good sense and intelligence to be bound to such a man. There is no comparison between the two offers; one is infinitely superior to the other."

Darcy threw Fitzwilliam a look of sheer exasperation as he walked over and thrust one of the glasses at him, resisting the temptation to pour it over his cousin's head. How was it none of his regiment had sought him out before now and murdered him in the still of night?

"You misunderstand me. It was-"

"So where is the impediment?"

Darcy stared at his cousin. "I beg your pardon?"

"The impediment!"

"Impediment?"

"Yes – the obstruction, the encumbrance, the…"

"I do not fail to know its meaning, Fitzwilliam!"

"Then why the repetition?" The Colonel shook his head, "You are beginning to resemble a parrot, Darcy. It does not bode well."

Darcy bit back an expletive and turned his head aside in frustration before returning his gaze to his cousin. "Fitzwilliam!" he paused, then stated slowly and clearly, "Please explain your meaning."

The Colonel shrugged his shoulders, raising both hands to emphasise the point, as they returned to their chairs on either side of the fireplace. "I assumed there was some obstacle to offering for the lady. Why is it that you deny yourself the opportunity to secure her?"

Leaning his head back against the leather of his chair once more, Darcy observed his cousin waiting expectantly for a response and wondered just how much longer he could endure this farce of an evening.

Suddenly, Fitzwilliam raised his chin, and then he nodded. "Ah. I see."

Darcy sighed. "What do you see? No doubt it is several furlongs distant from what is actually in front of you."

"The lady's desire to seek a match of mutual regard – she must harbour tender feelings for someone else. Mrs Collins did hint at a recent disappointment, yet I had assumed it to be Bingley. If not he, I wonder who this fellow might be?"

This reminder of Wickham's place in Elizabeth's affections was sufficient to force Darcy from his seat once more. In an attempt to conceal his agitation, he grabbed the poker and rammed it into the strongly burning logs, causing them to spark and hiss. He was about to repeat the action when the poker was taken firmly from his grasp and restored to its usual resting place.

"Am I to assume from your vigorous attack upon that poor innocent log that you know the gentleman concerned? I am sorry, man. It is an impediment indeed." The Colonel rested a comforting hand on Darcy's shoulder, but he shook it aside and straightened up before meeting his cousin's eye.

"Wickham."

"I beg your pardon?"

"It is Wickham."

"I do not follow, Darce. What in the name of God could that bastard have to do with all of this?"

"He was in Hertfordshire when I stayed with Bingley. I saw little of him, fortunately, but apparently Miss Bennet experienced the contrary. Indeed, it would seem that Wickham indulged in his favourite pastime of late, besmirching the Darcy name, slandering me by deed and character."

"Good Lord, man. I am so sorry. And Miss Bennet – surely you do not believe her affections engaged by that scoundrel?"

"I have every reason to suppose it is so, and all I have heard or seen of late substantiates my suspicions. Indeed, I thought that was what you were implying earlier. How intimate they are I know not, but they must be very well acquainted, for she defended him staunchly to me not only back in Hertfordshire, but further – and with great passion – only yesterday."

"Yesterday?"

Darcy nodded.

"When you took a rather singular drive in a threatening storm?"

"Precisely."

"Ah." The Colonel nodded too. "I begin to understand the disturbance of your spirits last evening." He eyed Darcy closely. "Is that all that you base your supposition upon?"

Darcy dropped his eyes to his booted feet. "No – no, it is not." The direction of this discourse was painful yet also liberating to be able to share it with another, in particular someone who so well understood the blackness of Wickham's character and therefore would support his intentions of protecting innocent people from him.

"Darcy?"

Raising his head, he met his cousin's concerned gaze. "Miss Bennet was quite distressed earlier. She concealed it as well as she could, but it took little difficulty to detect her unhappiness over discovering the truth about her favourite. Indeed, though I could not fail to express my concern over her disappointment, I perceived how close to tears she came." Darcy swallowed in an attempt to ease the constriction that had returned to his throat. "It grieves me to think of her suffering, but over such a cad – how could I not disabuse her of her belief in his character?"

The Colonel frowned. "How were you able to do that? Surely it was not achieved throughout the course of the evening?"

Darcy knew the time had come to reveal what his absence today on his long ride had prevented.

"I wrote to her after our... meeting yesterday."

"You addressed her by letter? Heavens, man, what were you thinking? What must *she* be thinking?"

"I needed to set before her my dealings with Wickham. There was no opportunity to speak with her; I had no expectation of ever being in company with her again, and it seemed my only recourse. And there is something further that I had intended to advise you of," Darcy paused and lowered his gaze for a moment, then looked back at his cousin. "I confess that I have told her all that relates to Georgiana."

"You *told* her about Wickham's designs upon your sister?"

"I had no choice – did you expect me to sit back and see her throw herself away on that man? Had he been of decent, upstanding character I would have had to stand back, but to see her deceived as much as Georgiana was, know what her fate might be – never!"

The Colonel stared into the fire for a moment, his expression serious.

"You should not fear, Fitzwilliam. I have no doubt whatsoever that Miss Bennet can be trusted with such confidential information."

The Colonel grimaced. "Over that I have little concern. I had recently felt her to be the perfect sister for Georgiana – how ironic that they both fell for the charms of such a man." He rubbed his fist across his forehead. "There is some comfort in knowing they are now safe from the bounder, but I perceive it is little consolation in your circumstances." He paused again. "I

A FAIR PROSPECT: VOLUME 1

take it, then, that this is the reason you surmise Miss Bennet would not have you if you offered?"

Darcy took a long draught from his glass, letting the fiery liquid burn a path down his throat before responding.

"I do not surmise, Fitzwilliam, I speak with veracity. It is an irrefutable fact."

"What? You *did* it? You offered for her?"

"Indeed."

"And she did not accept you?"

"What do you think, Fitzwilliam? With all this evidence before you to support her distaste for me that you admitted earlier to not only understanding but almost sharing."

"I am so sorry, Darcy." The Colonel frowned. "But when did this take place?"

"Yesterday."

"Good Lord, Darcy, what a singular day you had! What dashed ill-timing. And to think I have been struggling to understand why you would not tender a proposal."

"Then I am pleased your struggles are over. The offer was made; she would not have me."

"Because her affections are engaged."

Darcy winced; the suggestion was painful to him and the reality of his situation had begun to hit home. "I believe that might be the least of her objections to the match."

"Come now, Darcy, it cannot be as bad as all that. It is indeed unfortunate that you have encountered perhaps the one woman in all of England who would turn down the hand of Fitzwilliam Darcy of Pemberley, but her reasoning must be respected. Yet all is not lost; she does not seem to resent you, for she quite clearly approached you tonight to engage you in conversation, and this inclination for Wickham will pass. I know your early hopes have been disappointed but –"

"Disappointed? *Disappointed?*" Darcy paced over towards one of the tall, unadorned windows and stared out into the darkness that had enveloped Rosings Park. "Fitzwilliam, you have no idea what my hopes have been, nor what I am feeling. Do you really wish to know why she found my offer so unacceptable?" He turned to face his cousin who made no response other than a shrug of his shoulders. "We argued – heatedly. She knows full well that

87

I destroyed the happiness of her sister, and she believes the very worst of my character."

With a frustrated sigh, Darcy walked back towards the fireplace. The merest hint earlier from Elizabeth that she had accepted his word on Wickham had been an unexpected balm to his present anguish; yet acknowledging aloud their troubled past, it was but small consolation.

"Wickham may have done his worst in blackening my name, but Miss Bennet has other reasons for believing herself perfectly justified in her decision. I have not treated her with the respect she deserves, nor given her wishes or her feelings any consideration. I have been vain and arrogant in my assumptions. Her affection being engaged elsewhere is a blow and that it is for that scoundrel... I cannot even begin to think on it. But beyond all these things, these impediments if you will, the disappointment is all with myself."

Darcy lowered his eyes and stared into the flames as he openly acknowledged these words. He felt his cousin's consoling hand upon his shoulder and fought the overwhelming desire to give in to his pain. Then, he straightened up and faced his companion.

"You were right, Fitzwilliam. She does despise me and has done for some time, and I have compounded that distaste by not only being the person who has destroyed her hopes of happiness in marriage but also by making my own offer to her in such a way that she was both insulted and angered by it. I have been selfish beyond belief, and now I reap my just reward."

"Gracious, Darce, that is a litany of fine proportions!" The Colonel gave his cousin's shoulder a reassuring squeeze before releasing it. "I had no idea your acquaintance with her had been so plagued. You did not stand a chance."

Darcy swallowed, hard. The constriction that had gripped his throat on more than one occasion this evening threatened to overwhelm him to the point whereby he would be unable to utter another word.

"No – no, I did not." Darcy winced over the concern evident in his cousin's face; his compassion was almost more than he could bear. "I can talk of it no further, Fitzwilliam; please excuse me." And turning on his heel, Darcy headed purposefully for the door.

Having bid goodnight to Charlotte, Elizabeth slipped inside her chamber and closed the door with a sigh of relief. She crossed quickly to the fireplace and gave the glowing ashes a hopeful prod with the poker, stirring a little further heat from the embers, then turned to survey the room.

There was ample evidence of the distraction of her thoughts prior to their departure for Rosings earlier that evening, for the bed was littered with discarded towels, a selection of ribbons and several hairpins, and some of Jane's more recent letters were liberally strewn across the table along with that of Mr Darcy. Her journal, which normally claimed her full attention when her mind was troubled, lay open where she had discarded it on the desk under the window, the quill caked in long-dried ink.

Extricating herself from her shawl, she threw it across a chair. How could she could feel so conflicted? Her relief that the evening had ended was understandable; her regret was not.

Elizabeth shivered and, conscious that the warmth of the room was rapidly receding, she made haste to prepare herself for the night. Within moments, a further shawl wrapped warmly over her nightgown, she was perched on the edge of the bed plaiting her hair, but her hands stilled in their action as she reflected on the evening.

She felt somewhat comforted by having let Mr Darcy know that she regretted her stupidity in falling for such a tale as Wickham's. The fact that he had understood her regret gave some ease to her conscience, and the generosity with which he had absolved her merely reinforced her imprudence in putting her faith in the wrong man in the first place.

Recalling her suspicion that Mr Darcy seemed to think her attached to Wickham, Elizabeth stirred restlessly on the bed. Why should he not, for had she not set herself up as his champion? More fool her for allowing her pride to blind her to both men's true characters; but in all honesty, could she say that she had been truly attached to the cad?

Shaking her head, she owned that she had found Wickham all that is charming and attractive, and his attentiveness had been gratifying. Yet thankfully, her heart had not been fully touched by him. This revelation of his true nature had shocked her – how could it not? It had humbled her, yet her overriding emotion was not sorrow for what might have been, but shame for what had.

She pushed this unsettling truth aside and turned her mind instead to her sister. Try as she might, Elizabeth could not see a way to absolve Mr Darcy of his actions in this quarter. His loyalty to his friend notwithstanding, misplaced though its application was, he had still made an arrogant assumption about Jane's feelings, and whilst she began to accept that perhaps their own family had been a significant contributor to her sister's disappointment, Mr Darcy's interference could be neither overlooked, nor forgiven.

With a lowness of spirit that she was too weary to examine, Elizabeth stood up and stretched, before turning to sleepily survey her dishevelled bed. Stifling a yawn, she removed the detritus from the counterpane and threw back the covers before tumbling wearily onto the bed and letting her head sink into the pillows. She knew she was too tired to fight her own thoughts and as such let her mind take her where it would and, much as anticipated, it drifted swiftly down the stream of her subconscious towards the gentleman who had occupied most of her attention that evening.

Her sleepy reflections acknowledged that, relieved though she was that he was leaving Kent the next day, she regretted she had not understood his character better throughout their acquaintance. It was fortunate that this thought, upon which she closed her eyes, was soon lost to her in the realm of sleep, for had she retained it, she might have wondered at it.

# Chapter Fourteen

THE FAINT LIGHTENING of the sky that precedes the break of dawn roused Darcy from where he sat near the window of his chamber. He had passed a restless night and, once he had become aware of Thornton's movements in the adjacent dressing room, he had given up on his fruitless search for rest and had taken a shallow bath before dressing to face the day. Since that time, he had done nothing further than take up his present position. Now, however, he bestirred himself, leaning back in his chair for a moment, his eyes moving restlessly over the ornate pelmet and drapes that framed the window.

Returning to his chambers the previous evening, Darcy had been drawn to this window by the sound of hooves on the gravel driveway, yet the sight of the conveyance that had recently restored the visitors to Hunsford had been of little comfort.

During his sleepless night, Darcy had had ample time to reflect on the state of his own feelings. His anger on Sunday had been so fleeting compared to the emotions that had subsequently gripped him, he could scarce recall it; the shock of his rejection had soon been superseded by a painful sense of loss and an ensuing inner turmoil beyond his experience. Considering now the emptiness of a future that he had recently been imagining as full of every possible gratification by securing Elizabeth as his wife, he fought to see his way forward.

Darcy shifted his position slightly as the carriage clock on the mantel chimed, indicating the passing of the hour. It was time to depart, yet he struggled to shed the oppression of his thoughts and motivate himself. The hollowness that consumed him had an all too familiar resonance, and he knew whence it stemmed. He could liken it, without doubt or hesitation, to the emptiness that shrouded him on first his mother and then his father's passing. Elizabeth remained as lost to him as they, and accepting that truth had been something he had forced himself to own in the cold emptiness of his interminable pre-dawn vigil.

Darcy dropped his head into his hands for a moment and closed his eyes, squeezing them tightly shut for a few seconds. Then, he raised his head. This would not do. He sat upright in the chair, then got quickly to his feet. Inactivity was an indulgence he could ill afford; it would not serve him well. The ache within his breast portended some permanence, and he would have to bear it.

Taking a last look about the room, Darcy walked over to the bedside table to collect his pocket watch, money clip and hip flask, weighing the heavy silver canister in his hand for a moment. Then, pocketing the other two items, he left the room.

Walking swiftly along the landing and down the stairs, Darcy encountered no one. His pace did not cease until he reached the door to the library and, pushing it aside, he headed for the tray of spirits. It took merely a few seconds to fill the small flask with brandy and, tightening the stopper, he turned to survey the room for a moment, unable to prevent thoughts of the previous evening filling his mind.

Though the sun had yet to rise fully, the lack of drapes permitted a soft light to grace the room, and as he walked back towards the door, Darcy's eye was caught by the watercolour of his cousin Anne. He crossed over to study the painting, registering not its subject but its intent; then he dropped his gaze to his feet. He had nothing of Elizabeth to comfort him in his loss; there was no miniature for him to secretly cherish, that her features might never fade from his mind.

Memories of the previous evening swept over him – the awkwardness of their meeting; their silence when first at table; Elizabeth looking up at him with large, serious eyes as she informed him of the effects of his letter; Elizabeth restraining tears over Wickham's deceit…

Releasing a slow breath, Darcy raised his head and stared at the painting for a moment before turning on his heel to leave the room.

As the first rays of light whispered across the countryside and the birds began their morning ritual of heralding its arrival, Hunsford parsonage began to awaken. Maisie, the house maid, busied herself laying fires in the grates and Cook stoked the oven in preparation for a morning's baking.

Upstairs, Elizabeth tossed and turned in her bed, the tousled covers testament to the disturbance of her slumber, her eyelids flickering but not with the movement that precedes awakening.

*The rain fell; it fell so very hard that every sound was eclipsed by the pounding of the drops on the leather hood above. She knew she travelled at speed, yet though in some form of conveyance, her breath came in rapid gasps, as though she laboured on foot.*

*Despite the protection the hood ought to offer, she felt cold, wet and exposed to the elements. Then, the carriage lurched as it rounded a curve in the road, and she threw her arms out to purchase some balance, but her hands grasped at nothing but air, and she found herself falling…*

Conscious that dawn had finally broken, Colonel Fitzwilliam studied his pocket-watch and then spoke to the footman before returning inside the house in search of his cousin.

He knew that Darcy had risen early, though there had been no sign of him at breakfast, and Fitzwilliam made a methodical check of all the principal ground-floor rooms, coming finally to the drawing room. He stood in the doorway for a moment, his eyes struggling to pierce the dim light that filtered through the drapes. He detected no movement, the room shrouded in a grey stillness that bespoke emptiness, yet instinctively he sensed someone's presence.

Slipping inside, his eyesight adjusting, he soon espied Darcy. He sat at the pianoforte, one slender-fingered hand resting on the ivory keys but making no movement and thus no sound, the other across his eyes, his head bowed as if in silent prayer.

Moved more than he cared to own, the Colonel walked slowly towards his cousin. He understood Darcy's pilgrimage, for he had seen it often with men under his command. He paid tribute to the last sighting he had had of someone dear to him; his grief was palpable.

Placing a hand upon Darcy's shoulder, the Colonel said gently, "Come, Friend. We must depart."

*With no air left in her body to breathe, Elizabeth found her fall had been precipitously halted, and she now rested in the strong embrace of a man. Arms held her close to his body, and a steadfast gaze held hers enthralled. Oblivious now to the still pouring rain and the rumbles of protest in the heavens, she struggled to regain her breath, unable to break eye contact, and as she saw his glance dip to her mouth she swayed towards him as*

*her lips were caught by his in a rough, passionate kiss. No gentleness was expressed, only a raw, angry need. Feeling the heat sear her skin at such intimacy, she clung tightly onto the only thing she could – his shoulders beneath her hands. The closeness seemed unsurprising, as though wholly familiar to her, and when he broke away, breathing heavily, she retained her grip upon him to maintain her balance.*

*Meeting his now troubled gaze, she could feel her embarrassment mounting, but she could neither look nor step away. She was captivated by this most intimate of moments: his scent, his strength and the expression in the depths of his eyes. Tentatively, she reached out and caught a raindrop as it fell from his wet hair to roll slowly down his cheek. His eyelids flickered slightly, then he placed his hand – which felt cold upon the heat of her skin – against the side of her face and stroked his thumb across her bottom lip, slowly, sensuously.*

*She knew he would kiss her once more but that somehow, this time, it would be different. Closing her eyes in anticipation, awash in the sensations he aroused in her, she waited. A ghost of a touch passed her lips, the lightest pressure, then another, and another. Letting out a sigh, she instinctively pulled him closer, and his mouth met hers fully in a soft, persuasive kiss of such gentleness that she felt tears prick her eyelids. It was a gesture full of love, and desperate to see the look in his eyes once more, she opened hers – to find herself alone, grasping onto nothing but air as the storm raged about her.*

Waking with a start, gasping for breath and flushed from her toes to the top of her head, Elizabeth sat up. Startled and disorientated, her gaze flickered restlessly about the room as she became conscious once more of her surroundings and the dream began to recede. Throwing herself back on her pillows with a sigh of relief, she stared at the canopy of her bed. She did not need to put a hand to her face to know that her skin was warm; too warm.

Breathing slowly, she tried to steady the beat of her heart; then, she tentatively raised her hand and pressed the back of it to her mouth. How could a dream of something she had never experienced feel so… *real?* Her eyes drifted closed as she attempted to regain the sensations she had awoken to; then suddenly, she realized what she was about. She lay abed, still warm from the memory of being kissed – and if she were totally honest, *kissing* – Mr Darcy.

With a groan, she flipped over onto her stomach, burying her face in the pillows. That she should dream of such a thing was unconscionable; that she would wish to relive it unfathomable. More disturbingly, her feelings upon waking were not repulsion, of him or their behaviour, but an inexplicable sadness that he was gone from her life.

Colonel Fitzwilliam watched Darcy staring out of the carriage window as Rosings Park receded into the distance. Within moments, their conveyance passed through the main gates and turned westwards onto the lane towards the London turnpike, a direction that would cut through the hamlet of Hunsford, and Darcy shifted his position, turning his back upon the hedgerows, only to meet the solemn gaze of his cousin.

The Colonel studied his companion thoughtfully for a moment, observing the shadows beneath his eyes and the set of his jaw that bespoke both a disturbed night and a determination not to be drawn into conversation. The restless movements of Darcy's hands were sufficient indication of his present state of mind, yet he knew his intent would be to allude no further to its cause.

A man of action by nature, Richard Fitzwilliam tried to suppress the innate urge to shake some sense into his cousin and demand that he do something to alter his present circumstances, though he must concede he was somewhat confounded over what exactly Darcy *could* do: curing Miss Elizabeth Bennet of her affection for another - worthless though that man was – *and* turning her disapprobation of his cousin into admiration could prove an uphill struggle, and there was no guarantee of success at the summit. But what was an obstacle in life if not to be overcome?

With a frustrated grunt, Fitzwilliam's gaze drifted to the scene outside the carriage, but the realisation that they now skirted the walled garden of Hunsford parsonage caused him to quickly look back over at his companion. Meeting Darcy's glance briefly, it was no surprise when that gentleman pointedly turned to stare out of the opposite window as the carriage rumbled past the home of the Reverend and Mrs Collins.

Having splashed cold water over her face, Elizabeth pressed a soft towel against her closed eyes but just then heard the unmistakable sound of a carriage and horses coming along the lane. Her eyes flew open as the towel fell unheeded to the floor, yet she willed herself to withstand the temptation to cross to the window. There could be no doubt that it was Mr Darcy's carriage, for no other would be in the lane at this hour. She held her breath, then let it out in a rush as the rumble of wheels on the dirt road faded into the distance.

Walking over to the window, she pulled the drapes aside and stared out into a morning that was far from old. Dust disturbed by the passing wheels continued to settle upon the ground, and mist still rose from the fields, yet the thinness of the haze across the newly-risen sun portended a warm day to follow, and suddenly eager for the outdoors, Elizabeth let the curtain fall back into place. Hurrying to complete her toilet, she made haste to dress herself, paying little attention to her hair, for which she only had patience to tie back with a piece of ribbon.

Scribbling a hasty note for Charlotte, her eye was caught by the mound of parchment on the table and, realising Mr Darcy's letter lay amongst it, she quickly snatched the papers up and stuffed them into her case. Having sealed the lock, she slipped the key into her pocket, picked up her shawl and left the room, bent upon restoring her equilibrium in the morning air.

A few miles into their journey, the Colonel detected Darcy's growing irritation and as such was little surprised by the sudden turn of his cousin's head as he snapped, "Must you persist in staring at me, Fitzwilliam?"

"There is little else to divert myself with. The scenery is much of a muchness, having travelled this way before; whereas with you, my friend, there is much to ponder."

Darcy rolled his eyes and pointedly turned his head to stare once more out of the window, a fruitless action, as Fitzwilliam well comprehended, for the London road out of Kent was predicable in all it had to offer by way of diversion, with as little on this occasion to distract the eye as ever.

Yet Fitzwilliam was a firm believer in ousting the beast of burden to free one's wits and refused to let his cousin keep his counsel, for he believed it would serve him no favour.

"You are too prone to introspection, Darcy. You cannot suppress this, for it will do more harm than good; and consider Georgiana! You must shed this melancholy air, or she will fear something dreadful has befallen you."

Darcy turned and raised a sardonic brow at this, and his cousin rolled his eyes. "Yes, yes. I fully comprehend your point, as I am certain you do mine."

They stared at each other for a moment, neither one speaking; then, the Colonel leaned forward in his seat, arms resting upon his knees, and fixed Darcy with a firm stare. "Speak to me."

Darcy threw Fitzwilliam a look that clearly bespoke his frustration and, refusing to be drawn, he shifted his position, turning his face once more towards the window, albeit he clearly saw little of what passed.

The Colonel grunted. So be it. A change of tactics was clearly warranted, and if Darcy would not talk, then he would.

"I must offer you a further apology, my friend," he paused. Darcy had, despite himself, turned once more to look at him. "For relating the direction of my conversation with Miss Bennet last night. Of course, I knew not the implications at the time – but all the same, I can appreciate that the gist of our discourse must have been somewhat distressful in the circumstances. You know I would not intentionally have given you pain."

Darcy shrugged. "Do not concern yourself, though the sentiment is appreciated."

The Colonel stretched in his seat, settling himself more comfortably into his own corner. "If Miss Elizabeth Bennet really is determined to wed for nothing but mutual affection, I hope that she is not disappointed in her search. Marriages where the affection lies all on one side are not uncommon, even if not as widespread as those where there is none at all – and I do not know which might cause the most pain. All part of your reasoning with Bingley, was it not?"

Darcy threw his cousin an exasperated look, then leaned his head back against the cushions. "It was. Thank you for pointing that out. Ironically, it only serves to highlight my interference, self-deceit and hypocrisy."

The Colonel frowned. "Interference – well, yes - I will grant you that one; but self-deceit and hypocrisy? Are you not too harsh upon yourself?"

A long silence ensued as the carriage rattled its way along the road. Darcy rubbed his forehead, and Fitzwilliam observed him draw a ragged breath before meeting his cousin's gaze.

"Was it not self-deceit of the highest order that I presupposed Miss Bennet's immediate acceptance? Such was my arrogance..." Darcy tugged at his neck cloth as it if its restriction troubled him. "So convinced was I that she had understood my interest, that I expected no overt surprise from her upon receiving my addresses." He sighed. "And further consider that I managed to put aside all my objections to the Bennet family's condition in life, when I had used the very same against my friend."

He stared at his booted feet for a moment, and the Colonel held his tongue, his patience rewarded as Darcy raised eyes darkened with suppressed feelings to meet his cousin's gaze.

"And if that is not sufficient hypocrisy, consider that I sought that very condition you mention, the thing I strove to advise Bingley against – a marriage of unequal affection. If I am honest with myself, did I believe Miss

Bennet to reciprocate the depth of my affection for her? I cannot deny it; I never thought it to be so. Thus I am culpable of intending to secure for my wife a woman I have such strong feelings for that I negate her own in the matter. Entering a match of disproportionate affection has no place in my consideration because my own selfish needs are met."

The Colonel studied his companion thoughtfully as Darcy turned to stare out of the window once more. His cousin shouldered a heavier burden than he had supposed – clearly there was more to conquer than mere disappointment.

# Chapter Fifteen

EXITING HER CHAMBER, Charlotte Collins paused on the landing to peer out of the small casement window, squinting slightly as the bright sunlight pained her eyes. She could see her husband in his vegetable patch, the book he had spent precious time seeking in Rosings' library open upon the rug where he presently knelt in worship of its venerable counsel.

Smiling ruefully to herself, Charlotte set off down the staircase, ruminating that not only had she slept heavily, but also she had slept long, for Mr Collins' presence in his garden and the position of the sun both confirmed the lateness of the hour.

Seeing no sign of Elizabeth in the small dining parlour, she was about to head for the garden herself when she encountered Maisie in the passage, who handed her the morning post, along with the note from her friend. Thanking the maid and requesting a fresh pot of tea, Charlotte tucked the letters into her dress pocket and, opening Elizabeth's note, headed for her own private parlour.

Darcy shifted his position slightly as he discerned the outskirts of a small town, and by way of confirmation a milestone indicating that Bromley lay no more than a mile distant soon faded into the distance.

Yet though there was more to interest the eye as they neared civilisation, he struggled to pay attention to anything but his own thoughts, which, despite his best endeavours, would persist in considering questions for which he would ever have no answer: did Elizabeth wonder at the manner of his leave-taking? Had she found his swift departure at his cousin's hands a relief, or had she, like he, wished for an opportunity for further discourse?

With an impatient sigh, Darcy turned his back to the window, heedless of the carriage's vibrations against his shoulder. Was he some sort of fool, indulging in such thoughts? She believed the very worst of him, had been visibly distressed by their dialogue on the previous evening, and must surely have awoken this morning to nothing but relief at his removal from the neighbourhood.

He reached for his watch and flicked a glance at the time, but the gesture did not aid him, merely bringing unbidden the question as to whether Elizabeth might yet have risen, and if she had, what she might be doing. Having encountered her so often in the park around Rosings, he could not help but surmise that she might be out walking, and how he wished...

"Do we make good time?" Darcy blinked and threw his cousin a startled glance. For a moment he had forgotten his presence, but he nodded quickly. "Indeed. We should arrive in time for an early luncheon."

Fitzwilliam nodded his approval and in recognition of the hour striking on a nearby steeple as they passed, pulled out his hip flask and took a hefty swig. He offered it, but Darcy shook his head, patting his pocket to indicate that he had his own supply.

"I have been struck by a notion, Darce."

"Should we alert the troops?"

"Little point, old man. They know my habits well and are too ably trained – by myself, I might add. Now, no more interruptions, there's a good chap." The Colonel took another draught from his flask before sealing the stopper and returning it to his pocket. "Darcy, could you not consider furthering your acquaintance with the lady? Her disappointment over Wickham may be of reasonably short duration. Whilst her misconception over the man might well justify her original disregard for you, it must be overcome now the truth is out."

A sense of unease flickered through Darcy over the allusion to the origins of Elizabeth's dislike, but sensing Fitzwilliam's gaze upon him, he shook his head.

"There is more to it than Wickham. She held two charges against me on Sunday, both of equal resonance." Darcy stared at the floor for a moment, then raised solemn eyes to his cousin. "She will never forgive my interference over persuading Bingley to remain in London."

"But if her sister was indifferent to Bingley's attentions, then surely she would welcome his removal from the district? In that, you did them both a service, not just your friend."

Darcy fidgeted in his seat. He had all too easily convinced himself that he had acted altruistically, with no one but Bingley's welfare in mind, until

Elizabeth's passionate disavowal of his assessment of her sister's feelings had stripped away such pretence.

"Darce?"

"You do not understand."

"And thus it shall remain, lest you speak of it."

Darcy dropped his gaze to his hands for a moment, flexing them before interlacing his fingers, his sense of unease growing stronger.

"I may have erred."

"How is that so?"

He shrugged at his cousin. "It was conjecture, whether Bingley's admiration was returned. I saw no special attention from Miss Jane Bennet towards him, no openly-displayed affection and, as such, I chose to believe her indifferent to him."

"*Believe*? You *chose*? How could you act if there was uncertainty?"

"I... I..."

Darcy's voice failed him, as did his argument. Having such recent proof of his inability to comprehend the true state of a woman's feelings, a woman upon whom he had focused with such intensity during their every meeting, how could he honestly profess to comprehend Jane Bennet's?

"Darcy?"

With a groan of submission, Darcy sank his head into his hands, his elbows resting on his knees. When he finally raised his head once more, Fitzwilliam had likewise leaned forward and watched his cousin keenly.

"Removing Bingley to London was an act of preservation, protection."

"Protection?"

"Yes. And not only for him."

"Whom else were you protecting, man?"

Darcy sat back in his seat, then muttered, "Myself," before raising eyes raw with emotion to his cousin. "And in the process it would seem I have done irreparable harm."

There was a long silence, permeated only by the incessant sound of the wheels upon the road.

"I thought I acted for Bingley's well-being, yet I have worked against him. I have borne him ill will disguised as good." Darcy hesitated. "It – it was a sort of justification, yet I have failed to fully determine its true source until now. I admit I did question the depth of Miss Bennet's regard, and I cautioned Bingley so, especially in the light of her family, but I wonder now whether I would have acted had I not feared for myself also. I persuaded

Bingley to distance himself and remain in London, and thus I had no need to examine my own feelings." Darcy paused, running a hand through his dishevelled hair. "Elizabeth – Miss Elizabeth Bennet – she had become the focus of all my interest, consuming my notice. I felt such powerful stirrings, knew I was in danger and that I might soon be unable to walk away; yet I was convinced I could not offer for her." Darcy met his cousin's gaze with troubled eyes. "I genuinely believed Miss Jane Bennet indifferent at the time, because I had convinced myself it was so – yet whether for Bingley's sake or mine, I no longer know."

"And how is it that you now perceive yourself mistaken?"

Darcy glanced briefly out of the window, conscious that the carriage had slowed as they arrived at the watering stop for the horses.

"Miss Elizabeth Bennet. She gave me reason to understand that her sister not only received Bingley's attentions with pleasure, but that she returned them."

"But Darcy, is this not all a misunderstanding, much as the lady's believing Wickham's depiction of your character? Surely for all things there can be forgiveness."

Darcy moved to the edge of his seat as the carriage finally drew to a halt. "You have not heard the worst of it. Miss Bennet has recently been in London – calls were exchanged between the lady and Bingley's sisters, yet I joined them in concealing such a circumstance from Bingley."

"You hid it? How was such a disguise to be carried out?"

"Perhaps conceal is too strong a term. Let us say I chose not to reveal the intelligence. Whatever the expression, it was beneath me." He paused as a servant swung the door aside and lowered the steps. "So you see, Fitzwilliam, there is no misunderstanding, and thus no room for forgiveness, just my arrogance, conceit and selfish disdain of the feelings of others."

Darcy swallowed on the bitter taste in his mouth; then, as he stepped from the dimness of the carriage out into bright sunlight, he whispered under his breath, "I could not have put it better myself, Elizabeth."

Conscious of a desire to occupy her thoughts, lest they stray where she wished they would not, Elizabeth had turned her steps towards the church and had enjoyed no little time wending her way around the gravestones where they nestled cosseted by long grasses and wild flowers. She had taken much enjoyment from the cheerful birdsong and the beauty of the churchyard and had soon begun to feel the benefit of the fresh air.

Despite its lingering on the edges of her subconscious, she determined not to allow her dream any consequence. Her common sense assured her it was merely a trick played upon her mind born of the myriad singular events of the past few days. It was a common enough truth that dreams could take on a sense of the ridiculous, and she knew from personal experience that no matter its intensity on waking, the substance would soon fade like any other, so that come another day she would be hard pressed to recall its constituents.

After all, had she not, some years hence, suffered a recurring dream that Mama was a hen and they, her brood, all chicks? Admittedly, Jane had sported the finest golden feathers of them all, and Mary's beak had been permanently buried in a suitably tiny book – and she, Elizabeth, had repeatedly engaged in a quarrel with a passing swan – but clearly it had meant nothing, and the only reason she could still recall it was because she had been meticulous in keeping her journal at the time.

Thus it was that she knew her dream of Mr Darcy to be all a piece of nonsense, and she was quite resolute that she would pay it no further mind.

Having explored the outside to her satisfaction, she considered entering the church but the fairness of the day was too strong an inducement. Instead, she set off along the lane, unconscious of where her feet led her.

Unbidden, as she walked, a sudden vision of Mr Darcy's face as he expressed his feelings for her passed through her mind, and she felt her cheeks wash with colour as her step faltered. How could he admire her so? She had treated him with the utmost disdain since his arrival in Hertfordshire, believing without hesitation his maligned character and given no quarter over his protection of his friend's well-being. Further, she had persisted in her flippant manner throughout his stay in Kent, paid him no credence for offering his heart and his hand to her, and despised him for his honesty of address, when it spoke nothing but what she had long acknowledged regarding her own family's failings.

Agitated, Elizabeth increased her pace and, almost breaking into a run, she soon found herself skirting the woodlands of Rosings Park until, out of breath, she had to pause, resting her hands on her hips as she took in some welcome air. Did Mr Darcy relish his escape from a woman who had thrown his heart and his hand back at him with such cruelty, and furthermore, a woman whom, she suspected, he believed enamoured of a man whose very name was abhorrent to him?

She sighed, struggling to suppress the feeling of unease that such thoughts engendered. Then, Elizabeth straightened up and, seeing whence her feet had led her, she accepted the inevitable and turned her steps towards the stone path that led to the copse of birch trees.

Having completed her morning duties, Charlotte decided to follow the example indicated by her friend. A period of time passed in fresh air seemed an attractive proposition and as Mr Collins had removed to his study to make notes for that evening's prayer meeting, she felt quite at liberty to claim the garden for her own.

Conscious of the warmth of the sun upon her neck, Charlotte paused and looked about before heading for an old wooden bench tucked against the beech hedge that separated the lawn from the kitchen garden. With a sigh of contentment she seated herself and looked around, enjoying the pleasant vista of the parsonage, its aged and golden stone a true compliment to the verdant lawns and box hedges that encircled it.

She wondered where Elizabeth had walked, and how long it would be before she returned, for this was their last day together, and Charlotte new full well how much she would miss her friend's company come the morrow. Still, Elizabeth would no doubt soon be regaling her with letters full of the pleasures of Town, even more so now, in the enhanced company of Mr Nicholas Harington.

Such a recollection reminded Charlotte of the post that had been handed to her earlier, and slipping a hand into her pocket she withdrew the letters. Recognising the familiar hand of her sister, Maria, on one, she then glanced at the second letter – the hand was neat and clearly feminine and addressed to Elizabeth but the postmark was unfamiliar. Charlotte mused on who the sender might be as she tucked it safely back into her pocket, then turned her attention to her own correspondence. She would enjoy the solitude of this beautiful morning and read Maria's news from home; doubtless Elizabeth would soon satisfy her friend's curiosity as to who her correspondent was, and where in the country lay the place of its origin, '*Lambton*'.

# Chapter Sixteen

DARCY STARED UP AT the sign of the coaching inn on the outskirts of Bromley, shielding his eyes against the glare of the sun. Thankful for the opportunity to escape the confines of the carriage, as much to avoid his cousin's voracious interest as to take some air and stretch his legs, he welcomed the break in their journey.

He glanced over towards his carriage where his men still tended to the horses and his cousin had emerged to accept a draught of ale from a servant, then turned his back and walked across a small area of common land, stopping at one point to break off three long stalks of wild grass before heading for a nearby stand of young trees.

Resting his back against a relatively sturdy looking trunk, he placed one foot on an old stump close by and, running his hand along the length of the recently plucked stems to even them, he stripped the feathery heads with one sweep of his fingers and tied them at one end with the ease of familiarity. For a moment his gaze rested unseeingly upon his hand and its contents, then Darcy blinked suddenly and stared at the reeds as if he had only just realised he held them. *"Old habits die hard,"* he murmured under his breath, and accepting the inevitable settled himself more comfortably against the trunk and began to plait the reeds neatly along their length.

It was an old trait of his, yet one he had not practiced since a lad. In an attempt to still the agitation of his hands when experiencing emotion – be it anxiety or anger – he had long perfected the talent of plaiting wild grass stems as a way of occupying his constantly flexing fingers and, as such, had found himself soothed by the activity.

His task complete, Darcy held the slender stick up for inspection, his gaze narrowed as he assessed whether or not he still held his boyhood propensity for neatness, but his eye became distracted by movement across the road, and he lowered his hand, sighing impatiently. Who did he try to fool? No childish means for easing his spirits was proof against his present circumstances.

Casting the newly formed stick aside, he reached into his pocket for his hip flask. He took a mouthful of cognac, the liquid burning a slow trail down his throat, easing the rising tightness in his throat, an all too familiar sensation in recent days; then he dropped the flask back into his pocket. His cousin's persistence in drawing his confidence had been a sore trial to him, and his own growing comprehension of the veracity of Elizabeth's assessment of his character haunted him.

He closed his eyes, trying to prevent the memory from surfacing once more, but his lowered lids merely provided a backdrop for Elizabeth's angry face as the reverberation of her damning words began their relentless echo through his mind:

*...from the first moment of my acquaintance with you...'*

Darcy's eyes flew open. In his despair he had been consumed by her accusations; yet now he began to ponder upon the significance of these words. Memories of the Meryton assembly swept through his mind; that she had overheard his unthinking remark to Bingley he had long suspected, yet he had dismissed it with little regard for the implications. Recalling his demeanour throughout that evening, the reluctance with which he had attended all or any of the social occasions at which he had encountered Elizabeth thereafter, culminating in the ball at Netherfield, the feeling of unease that had filtered through him earlier returned with a vengeance.

That he had barely tolerated the local populace, he had made no effort to conceal. Nor had he made any attempt to respond to their overtures, even whilst partaking of their generous hospitality, something that must have been blatantly obvious to any who deigned to notice – and Darcy finally understood with piercing clarity that Elizabeth had.

Gripped by the dawning realisation that there was even more behind Elizabeth's dislike of him than he had originally surmised, Darcy straightened up and began to stride quickly back towards the inn. He could not think upon this now; he had only just begun to accept his own culpability over Bingley's present unhappiness. Anything further he felt ill-equipped to handle.

"Darcy! Come on, man!" His cousin hailed him, and Darcy looked over towards the carriage. Lifting a hand in acknowledgement, he paused near the door to the inn and took a draught of water from a servant before walking over to where his equipage tarried.

The journey resumed, and in an attempt to dissuade his cousin from further plaguing him, Darcy expressed his intention of resting his eyes, citing a disturbed night. Knowing that Fitzwilliam could hardly be surprised to hear that Darcy had not slept well, he was confident that the move would guarantee him some peace. Yet his success at silencing the Colonel's voice was hard bought, for the ones inside his head were more difficult to quieten. Thankfully, the weariness born of his lack of repose in recent nights and the movement of the carriage did lull him into a somewhat somnolent state; yet his mind was not at rest.

Having twice circled the copse, Elizabeth paused for a moment to gather her thoughts. It was all very well determining not to allow her dream any purchase, but she struggled yet to account for her inability to dismiss Mr Darcy himself from her mind.

As her steps led her once more past the stone bench where she had been seated on Sunday, she ceased her pacing and looked about the shaded enclosure. Perhaps it was the revelation of the depth of Mr Darcy's admiration for her; yet the shock of finding herself in his arms so soon after, and all the inherent sensations that had been aroused by such intimate contact were equally disturbing.

Shaking her head at the direction of her recalcitrant thoughts, Elizabeth contemplated the bench for a moment before laying her shawl out on it and sitting down. For a moment, she attempted to enjoy the peaceful scene, but the confusion of her thoughts soon came flooding back. *Mr Darcy…* how was it that she felt so piqued that just at a time when she felt the urge to discover more about the man, he had conveniently removed himself from her acquaintance? *"But I thought I did not like him…"*

*'Not* did *not like, Lizzy,* would *not. You would not allow him to be anything but disagreeable. Slighted by his insult of you and unimpressed by his unsocial, taciturn air you allowed your vanity to rule your common sense. Before now, you did not even perceive the man himself.'*

Pushing away this uncomfortable notion, Elizabeth stood up, retrieving her shawl and giving it a shake before fastening it about her waist and turning to walk down the path towards the park.

Instead of judging Mr Darcy, she now wished she had been given more time to appreciate him, and finally she accepted the truth she had battled these past four and twenty hours. She did quite like him. She was intrigued by the man, and now she could only regret that she would never know him further, never fully understand him, nor why he had developed such a depth of feeling for her.

Elizabeth emerged from the path deep in thought, but conscious of the position of the sun that hinted at the morning's progression, she quickened her pace, making her way up the bank of grass. Yet, with her eyes cast down to ensure a safe foothold, she could not fail to discern the wheel ruts cut into the turf, nor the dried out wheals of mud where the horses' hooves had dug into the hillside to retain some purchase. Acknowledging to herself that relegating Sunday's events to a distant memory was far from happening, she followed the trail of her curricle ride with Mr Darcy all the way back to Hunsford.

As the small towns that populate the outskirts of any large city gave way to busier thoroughfares, and the associated disturbance and noise penetrated the carriage, Darcy stirred in his corner and opened his eyes, blinking a couple of times as he sat up straighter against the cushions. Somehow he felt even wearier than when his lids had dropped, but he was thankful for the release from his thoughts.

In his drowsy state, his sub-conscious had taken full control of his senses, and a myriad of memories from his stay in Hertfordshire passed through his mind, culminating in a recollection of the ball at Netherfield where, struggling with the onslaught of unprecedented feelings towards Elizabeth – and railing against Wickham's presence in the neighbourhood – he had witnessed a display of coarse manners and inappropriate conduct from several members of the Bennet family.

Shifting his position, Darcy frowned at the memory. Prevalent in his mind was Mrs Bennet, her piercing voice lauding her daughter's good fortune and the benefit it would be for her family by raising them into similar company. Yet once more he recognised his failing. In his disdain for the local populace he had somehow managed to forget that he held the society in Town in equal regard.

Long before he had ventured forth into society, his father had cautioned him to be wary of the scheming mamas of the *ton*. What was their desire, but to make a good match for their daughters? What was he, Fitzwilliam Darcy, to them but a name synonymous with his estate, an estate that bespoke wealth, heritage and status? Wherein lay the difference between Mrs Bennet's desire to improve her family's lot and that of this society?

Darcy's gaze drifted to the slumbering form of his cousin on the opposite bench, before he lowered his eyes to the floor. With unbearable clarity, the difference became obvious: Mrs Bennet's purpose, vulgar though the expression of it was, at least had some basis in honesty. There was naught of disguise about her, whilst the ladies of the *ton*, mothers and daughters alike, were practised in concealing those very same intentions.

Darcy shuddered as the depth of his self-inflicted blindness struck him, and he whispered, *"You hypocrite."*

"What? Did you say something?"

He looked up, realising that his cousin had awakened.

"No. No, I did not. I was thinking aloud, nothing more."

Turning his head to look out of the window once more, Darcy hoped that Fitzwilliam would accept he had no wish to be swept into conversation, and for a while silence reigned in the coach as the conveyance made its slow way through the congestion of the London streets, heading for the quieter thoroughfares of Mayfair.

They were but minutes now from arriving at Darcy's town house, and though, judging by the hour, his sister would yet be engrossed in her lessons, it would not be long before they were in company. In this matter, his cousin had the right of it: nothing of his present melancholy must be evident.

Unbidden came the memory of the Colonel's words from the previous evening, of the irony that Wickham had managed to influence so easily both Georgiana and Elizabeth. Darcy grew cold at the thought of what might have been for either of them. If there was one thing he could be thankful for in all this misfortune it was that Elizabeth no longer stood any risk of being duped by that villain.

"Darce? Come man, you must rally, for you are as stony-faced as a marble bust and almost as pale."

Darcy threw Fitzwilliam a look of frustration. "You goad me beyond my endurance at times, Cousin."

"I aim to please, as you well comprehend."

Darcy blew out a resigned breath. "I am not ignorant to the service you have rendered these past four and twenty hours."

The Colonel looked somewhat discomfited and fidgeted with his cuffs for a moment, not meeting Darcy's eye; then, he raised an usually solemn visage to his cousin. "You are as a brother to me, Darcy. But above all else, you are my friend, and I would not see you suffer in silence, however much you might think it preferable."

Darcy forced a weak smile before turning once more to the window, albeit he failed to recognise aught outside the carriage.

*"I would not see you suffer in silence."* What had he done to his own friend – to Charles Bingley?

Having enjoyed the opportunity to read her sister's letter in peace, Charlotte had returned to the house, a little concerned over the length of Elizabeth's absence. It was thus with no little sensation of relief that she finally espied her friend in the road outside the parsonage, and she hurried out of the door and down the path towards where she stood, staring at the ground as if in intense reflection.

"Lizzy?"

Elizabeth started start as she addressed her, and Charlotte realised her suspicion was not far from the truth.

"Dear Charlotte! Forgive me, I have been gone far too long, but it is hard to forsake such a beautiful morning." Observing Elizabeth's uncharacteristically flustered demeanour as she turned to greet her, Charlotte's eyes narrowed for a moment, her gaze drifting briefly to the patch of disturbed ground that had appeared to capture her friend's attention; then, unable to account for such an absurd interest, and apportioning Elizabeth's enhanced cheek colour to her recent extended bout of exercise, Charlotte shrugged the thought aside.

"Come, I shall fetch some refreshments." She led the way up the path and back through the front door into the cool and dim interior of the parsonage, Elizabeth following in her wake. "I have news from Meryton; my sister writes – oh, I almost forgot…"

Charlotte paused as they arrived at the door to the parlour and turned to face her friend as she reached into her dress pocket. "This came for you," and she handed over the letter.

"For me?" Elizabeth's brow furrowed as she took it and studied the direction; then, she smiled. "Why, it is from Serena!"

As the clock on the mantel struck the hour, Darcy entered the dining room with a determined stride and, much as anticipated, he found his cousin tucking into his meal.

"Thank the Lord for a comfortable seat. I swear I have slept on better ground than aunt's furniture."

Not wishing to be diverted from his purpose, Darcy did not reply but walked up to the place normally occupied by his sister and placed a note upon her setting.

"Forgive me, Darcy," Fitzwilliam added. "My appetite got the better of me; I could await your joining me no longer."

Darcy shook his head. "Far be it from me to deny your stomach the satisfaction is craves, Cousin. Besides, I must beg you to excuse me for an hour or so."

The Colonel glanced at the note awaiting Georgiana and then eyed Darcy's outdoor attire. "But you must eat, Darcy! You made no time for breakfast and now you are negating a further repast!"

"I have a pressing matter to attend to, but shall return directly. Do not disturb yourself, Fitzwilliam, I am in no danger of wasting away."

Darcy ignored his cousin's snort, and turned on his heel, but as he reached the threshold he paused as Fitzwilliam called, "Where are you headed, that it cannot be delayed? We are only just arrived this past hour."

Darcy grasped the handle with purpose before saying over his shoulder, "I must speak with Bingley," and without a further backward glance, he left the room.

Fitzwilliam stared at the space where Darcy had been for a few moments, then reached for his goblet of wine.

"Damn it, I am not half bad when I put my mind to it!" he mused; then, raising the glass in a self-congratulatory toast, he drained it.

# Chapter Seventeen

DARCY'S DETERMINED PACE SLOWED as he approached the Pulteney Hotel on Piccadilly. Inevitable though the encounter was, he did not relish the impending revelation he must make.

Further, the walk had been sufficient in length for Darcy to fully consider the consequences of Bingley's potential connection with the Bennet family. If his friend were generous, nay rash enough, to one day forgive him his interference, Darcy would have to ensure he was unavailable to visit with him unless Bingley came to Town. To return to Hertfordshire and be repeatedly in Elizabeth's society, knowing that he was nothing to her and never could be, would be intolerable. Yet upon reflection, his own pain and pleasure he found himself able to negate. How much of a trial would it be for her? Their uneasy truce during that last night at Rosings had been bitter-sweet, but he had not been impervious to her embarrassment and unease.

Pushing these thoughts aside, he climbed the steps that brought him to the hotel's ornate portico and passed into the marbled interior, handing his hat and gloves to a porter as the manager hurried over, a welcoming smile on his face.

"Good day to you, Mr Darcy. Mr Bingley is presently dining. Would you care to join him?"

For a brief moment, Darcy cursed the resolution that had sent him on his mission at such an inconvenient time of the day. A public dining room would hardly be conducive to confession, which meant enduring no small amount of pleasantries before he could hold a private audience with Bingley. A fleeting temptation to say he would call again later, to postpone the inevitable, gripped him, but he shook it aside.

"Thank you, Winterburn. I believe that I shall." He turned towards the dining room, waving the manager aside. "It is no trouble, I will seek him out."

"But Mr Darcy, Sir, if you please? Mr Bingley is dining in his suite."

The manager looked somewhat discomfited, and Darcy frowned. Though possessed of an impulsive streak on occasion, Bingley was generally a creature of habit. He always resided in the same hotel if Darcy could not host him; he always took the same suite of rooms, and he always, without fail, took his meals at his customary table in the dining room. It had been carefully chosen overlooking the street, for there was nothing Bingley enjoyed more than to watch the passers-by in Piccadilly, his face bright with interest, the occasional chuckle escaping him as something absurd would catch his eye.

"Is Mr Bingley entertaining guests?"

"No, Sir."

"Has he made a habit of dining in isolation?"

Winterburn pursed his lips before responding. "He has yet to partake of a meal at his usual table during this stay, Sir."

Elizabeth walked slowly into the centre of the parlour at Hunsford, studying the letter's direction thoughtfully.

"I did not know Serena was in Lambton, for she was to pass the Eastertide at Sutton Coker."

"Is that not the Harington estate?" Charlotte addressed her over her shoulder as she opened the window to let some fresh air in.

"Indeed, for I had it from Jane in one of her letters. Serena has long been a favourite of Mrs Harington and has spent a deal of time there over the years." Elizabeth gave up her perusal of the envelope, which had ceded all possible intelligence and smiled at her friend. "Aunt Gardiner had the fortune to gain her half-sister within days of her closest friend yielding her own daughter, so they had a shared enthusiasm over both babes at the time."

Charlotte walked over to her friend, a frown upon her brow. "A daughter? I thought the Haringtons had but three sons?"

"Aye, three sons that survive, that is. Their only daughter was taken by the scarlet fever when she was but two years old, along with a new-born son. I do not recall the tragedy, being so young myself at the time, but my aunt has told us of it. It perhaps accounts for Mrs Harington's doting on Serena – I believe she soothes the ache of a daughter lost so prematurely."

Lowering her gaze to the letter once more, Elizabeth bit her lip thoughtfully. "I am at a loss as to how Serena has discovered my direction in Kent."

Charlotte patted Elizabeth on her arm. "Well, I am sure she will explain things to your satisfaction. I shall seek some refreshment for us and leave you in peace to enjoy your letter."

Elizabeth gave Charlotte a grateful smile as she left the room, before returning her attention to the letter in her hand; then, realising that she would sooner satisfy her curiosity by taking Charlotte's advice, she broke the seal and walked over to the open casement, settling herself upon the window seat to enjoy her friend's news.

Having been admitted by Bingley's manservant, Darcy preceded him along the hallway to the stylish drawing room, his presence as yet undetected by his friend.

Despite Caroline Bingley's assertion that Bingley stayed in a comfortless hotel when in Town, nothing could be further from the truth. The Pulteney was extremely modern and luxurious, as Bingley's regular suite of rooms attested. Little was she aware that her brother's desire to reside in a hotel had much to do with the fact that Hurst's house, whilst well situated in Grosvenor Street, was not overly spacious, causing Bingley far too little opportunity for distance from his sisters when in residence.

Bingley sat at a small, circular table, overspread with a heavy damask cloth and all the accoutrements that accompany a meal in a fine hotel. With his back to the window, he held his knife and fork listlessly in each hand, as if unsure of their purpose, and his meal remained untouched.

Darcy knew full well he had not left Bingley in good spirits when he had taken up residence at his hotel, leaving Darcy to prepare for his departure for Kent, yet at the time he had hardly given him credit for the lowness of his mood, assuming Bingley would rally.

Now he frowned as he observed the evidence to the contrary, acknowledging fully that the broken attachment had left after-effects that still had Bingley in their grip. Knowing now the pain of unrequited love in all its intensity, Darcy struggled to maintain his composure as he felt the weight of his previous actions collapse upon his shoulders. That he had willingly inflicted such pain upon his closest friend was indefensible.

Involuntarily, he cleared his throat, and Bingley looked up, the listless expression in his eyes fading in an instant, and with a wide smile he got to his feet, arms extended in greeting.

"Darcy! How splendid to see you. How fared your sojourn? Your aunt – she is in good health I trust? And your cousin, also?"

Darcy crossed the room to greet him and, at his invitation, joined him at the table. The waiter, who had been stood silently against the wall, stepped forward with a fresh glass and a hastily offered menu card, and whilst Darcy accepted the former, he waved away the latter, leaning forward to pour himself a helping of Bingley's wine.

"You are not hungry?"

Darcy cast a quick glance at Bingley's untouched plate. "In that it would appear I am not alone."

Bingley fidgeted a little under his friend's eye, and Darcy sighed. He shrank from the notion of discussing matters of the heart, yet his own culpability could not be denied, and too much time had been allowed to pass with his friend suffering unnecessarily. He was in the wrong, and he owed Bingley the truth and, distasteful though the process may be, it was a necessity.

"It truly *is* good to see you, Darcy. I must own that I am heartily sick of my own company and had begun to fear you might be detained in the country for the summer. So – what news from Kent? And shall I return to Mount Street with you directly?"

It was Darcy's turn to shift uneasily in his chair. He doubted such an invitation would be taken up once he had made his confession, and conscious he must forestall Bingley before he order his bags be packed, Darcy spoke. "Would you dismiss the servants?"

Bingley looked surprised, but nodded. "As you wish."

Within minutes the door closed behind the waiter and manservant, and Bingley turned to retake his place. "Is there some news you wish to impart? Good Lord, Darcy, you have not done it? You have not succumbed and made an offer of marriage after all this time?"

Darcy started, and hastily returned his wine glass to the table lest the tremor in his hand be detectable.

"I - I beg your pardon?"

"Your cousin. I know full well the pressure laid upon you and that it increases with every visit. But forgive me. I am impertinent."

Darcy shook his head.

"Do not concern yourself, Bingley. You could not be impertinent if you tried. But no – no, I did not offer for my cousin. Yet there is a purpose behind my desire for privacy."

He hesitated, realising with hindsight that in his determination to speak with his friend without further delay, he had taken no time to consider how he might begin such a discourse.

"There is something that I would tell you –" Darcy stopped, running a hand through his hair distractedly before readjusting his position on his chair. "I have not acted as a friend ought."

"You have not?" Bingley looked startled, and Darcy bit his lip.

"Indeed." He paused once more, tugging at his neck cloth as if it might somehow ease the constriction in his throat.

"Great heavens, man! Make haste, and tell me before I burst!"

Darcy released a pent up breath. "My apologies. I must tell you – you must know that I have served you ill, and in doing so I have caused both you and Miss Bennet uncalled-for unhappiness, and…"

"*What!*" Bingley sat bolt upright in his chair, his face awash with colour. "You have word of Miss Bennet? You have seen her?" He glanced quickly about, as if he expected the lady to emerge from behind the drapes, then turned his frantic gaze back upon his friend.

"No, I have not, I-"

"But she is here?"

"No. It was-"

"But then, how…" Bingley's voice tailed away as he stared at Darcy in confusion.

Darcy turned his head to the side in impatience with himself, then pushed his chair back and stood up, walking over to the window. Unsurprisingly, Bingley was more interested in news of Miss Bennet than what Darcy might be wishing to own. But it must be done.

With determination, he turned back to face the room. "I had the pleasure of renewing an acquaintance during my stay in Kent – with Miss Elizabeth Bennet. She – she led me to understand that I may have been in error with some advice I gave you," he flexed the fingers of his right hand, "with regard to Miss Bennet. Bingley, I am so sorry, but it appears I was mistaken. She was not indifferent to you. She –"

Bingley stood up so rapidly, his chair toppled over.

"What did you say?"

"I was wrong; completely and utterly wrong. Miss Bennet did return your affections. I am led to believe that she has suffered for my interference no less than you have."

Bingley's face paled, and his eyes clouded momentarily as if assailed by a distant memory, but then a slow smile touched his mouth, which grew into a wide grin.

Stepping forward, he grabbed Darcy's hand and shook it vigorously. "Thank you! Darcy, *thank* you for this."

Darcy stared at him, his hand still being pumped up and down by a beaming Bingley.

"You are *thanking* me? Bingley, did you hear what I just said?"

"The sweetest words I have heard these many months, my friend," and he clapped Darcy on the shoulder enthusiastically before turning back towards the table and refilling both their glasses with a flourish. "I cannot imagine how you might have come to discuss something so delicate but I am highly gratified that you did!"

Darcy suppressed a sigh. Perhaps by the time he had told Bingley all, his friend would see that Darcy had done him no favour. He accepted the wine from him, but before he could speak, Bingley began pacing to and fro, heedless of the glass in his hand.

"If you only knew, Darcy, what you have given me. After all this time – the despair, the sense of loss – you have given me hope. Can you imagine what it feels like to hear that your feelings might be reciprocated when you believed they were met with indifference? To know that you have been offered a second chance at a happiness you thought was surely lost for ever?"

The ache he bore within his breast sharpened momentarily, and Darcy turned to stare out of the window, clasping his glass with both hands in an attempt to still their agitation.

"Such hope you have brought me! The anguish of believing you have looked your last upon a loved one's face; expending futile hours wondering where they are, how they are, what they might be feeling or thinking – yet now to be at liberty to seek her out, that all my speculation might be answered…"

Darcy bowed his head as Bingley's voice continued to ebb and flow depending upon the direction of his pacing, but before his barely suppressed despair could surface once more he realised that Bingley had progressed from extolling his happiness at Darcy's news to thinking aloud. Turning his back upon the window, he faced the still pacing Bingley, keen to interrupt him and finally reveal the further depths of his interference, that his friend might know the full extent of Darcy's failure as his friend.

"Bingley, wait…"

"I shall return to Netherfield directly."

"Bingley, wait. There is more I…"

"I shall instruct Overton to pack my bags."

"Bingley, I have not yet told…"

"I shall need to send word to Grosvenor Street – or perhaps I should not? They may attempt to delay my return, or prevent it altogether, for Caroline was not enamoured of the Hertfordshire air… Darcy?"

Bingley ceased his pacing and looked expectantly over at his friend, his countenance bright with anticipation. "What do you think?"

"I think you should be still; you are causing my eyes to cross."

Bingley laughed. "Come, then, let us be seated," and he crossed the room, his glass still dangling from his fingertips. "And then you can tell me what I should do."

Darcy frowned as he walked back towards the table. "You are a glutton for punishment, Bingley. Would you wish for more poor counsel?" He resumed his place and reached for a piece of bread. The wine toyed with his empty stomach, and he had begun to feel quite light-headed.

"You have only steered me wrong once." Bingley placed his glass down before righting his chair and taking his place once more.

Darcy eyed him solemnly. "I understand that you are in high spirits, and I cannot tell you how pleased I am to observe it. But please permit me to finish what I have come here to tell you."

Bingley's smile faded as he seemed to take in the seriousness of Darcy's tone, yet the change in his demeanour could not be suppressed. Though his face assumed a more sombre expression, his eyes danced with a new light, and his unruly hair seemed to positively vibrate with his excitement as he nodded at his friend to continue.

"Miss Bennet may yet be in London."

Bingley's mouth dropped open a little before a smile once more graced his features. "Truly? How fortuitous! But wait... may *yet* be here?"

"Yes, you comprehend my meaning."

"She has been in Town – and you know of it? Did Miss Elizabeth Bennet...?"

Darcy shook his head, and Bingley frowned, "So how..."

"I learned of her visit long before I departed into Kent, though I did not see her. In divulging the source of my information, Bingley, I regret that I must do a further disservice to your family – to your sister. Miss Bingley had been apprised of Miss Bennet's visit to Town, allegedly by a letter from Miss Bennet herself. Your sisters did exchange a call."

"They called upon each other?" A frown passed across Bingley's countenance, and he slowly raised his glass to his lips as if unaware of his actions. A deep silence prevailed, and Darcy felt his insides twist with discomfort. Discussing such matters sat ill with him, and though he knew it to be his duty to reveal the truth to his friend, now that the depth of his transgression was revealed he waited anxiously for Bingley's reaction, be it anger or disgust.

# Chapter Eighteen

"I TRUST IT DOES not bring ill-tidings?"

Charlotte's voice startled Elizabeth, and she glanced up quickly, realising that her friend had returned bearing a tray of the promised refreshments, and she cast her an apologetic look.

"Forgive me. How ill-mannered I am, letting this intrude upon our last day together."

"Dear Lizzy! Do not make yourself uneasy on my behalf. I am merely concerned, for your expression did not signify pleasing news. There is no ill health in the matter I trust?"

Elizabeth got up and crossed the room to join her friend. "In part, for Serena travelled north to be with her father who has been unwell, which accounts for her being in Derbyshire rather than Somerset."

Charlotte poured lemon barley into two glasses and Elizabeth smiled her acceptance as she took it from her, settling herself in her usual chair by the hearth.

"Derbyshire?" Charlotte gave Elizabeth an amused smile as she joined her friend. "So Lambton is in Derbyshire – might one enquire if it is located in the same vicinity as Mr Darcy's home?"

Elizabeth shrugged. "I do not know."

Little did she welcome the return of that gentleman to the fore when the contents of her letter had finally succeeded, for however short a duration, in supplanting him.

She took a welcome sip of her cool drink. "It would seem that Mr Seavington is now recovered, and Serena is eager to be in my company. She says she begged the direction from Jane once she arrived home from the West Country."

Charlotte offered her friend a plate of biscuits, then settled herself back on her chair.

"Ah yes, her Easter visit with the Haringtons. Are she and Mr Nicholas yet on friendlier terms than they were?"

Elizabeth flicked a quick glance at Charlotte, then took another sip of her drink before replying. "Better, yes," she paused, then let out a short laugh. "You recall, then, her disapproval of him?"

Charlotte laughed. "But of course! Yet she has not visited Longbourn in recent years, so I have only ever known her when she found him the most annoying – what was it she called him – dung-fly of her acquaintance!"

Elizabeth laughed with her. "And I can still picture Nicholas' face. To be certain, he resembled less a dung-fly and more a codfish, his mouth opening and closing with no sound coming out! He did not think she had it in her to be so outspoken."

Charlotte's brow furrowed. "You and she have been such friends, yet she no longer visits with you in Hertfordshire?"

Elizabeth dropped the letter onto a side table. "I am ashamed to own that on her last visit, Mama…" she paused. "Mama was less than subtle about Serena's agility. You know full well my mother, Charlotte. Her tongue has a will all its own that no amount of censure will calm." Elizabeth looked at her friend with troubled eyes. "It was quite dreadful. Serena had the misfortune to overhear Mama referring to her as a 'cripple'. She took the word harshly, being at a vulnerable age, and sadly I have never since secured acceptance of an invitation to Longbourn from her."

"The poor girl, to believe she could ever be perceived as such. Indeed, one might hardly know, and I recall her being a demon on horseback, from the earliest age!"

Elizabeth nodded. "Absolutely. She is as skilled as any horsewoman – quite fearless. Indeed, I think her somewhat uneven gait as a child troubled her little, for she could run and skip as much as any of us. But once her thoughts turned more upon pretty gowns and social occasions, she seemed to feel it acutely."

Charlotte busied herself refilling their glasses for a moment, and Elizabeth sighed deeply. "As for her no longer travelling to Hertfordshire, I am fortunate that I have been able to spend time with her when visiting with my aunt, the Haringtons or her parents, though since their return to Mr Seavington's former neighbourhood this past year, I have seen none of them."

Elizabeth glanced once more at the letter where it lay on the table, then met her friend's gaze.

"Forgive my meandering thoughts, dear Charlotte; my attention is all yours. Do you have any scheme for our last afternoon?"

Charlotte laughed. "Sadly yes, Lizzy! I must visit old Mrs Braithwaite with a basket, and call upon one or two of the other villagers who have been in ill health of late. I trust to your not having walked yourself weary, that I might have your company."

Elizabeth took a long draught of lemon barley from her glass, and pocketing her letter she stood up, grabbing a couple of the biscuits from the platter before holding it out towards Charlotte and nodding at it to encourage her to do the same.

"Come then, let us go, and you can regale me with all Maria's news from Hertfordshire!"

Disguise of every sort sat ill with Darcy, and though his confession should have brought some relief, the silence that followed his final revelation became more than he could bear. He made to rise and excuse himself, but just then his friend got slowly to his feet.

"Darcy, I believe I have never been so pleased to see anyone in my life as you today!"

Darcy sank back in his chair, staring at Bingley in disbelief.

"Come, man! You have informed me not only that my affections were returned – Lord, let us pray that it may ever be so – but that Miss Bennet may even yet be here in London."

"But I have deceived you!"

Bingley walked over to the window. For a moment no words were spoken, but then he turned to face Darcy.

"I do not deny that it does not sit well with me that I was so – taken in, so gullible." Bingley ran a hand through his hair, then gave a self-deprecating smile. "But deceit? Do you really believe it to be so? I do not see it. Did you lie to me openly, deny her presence in Town?"

Darcy let out a frustrated breath. "Not precisely, no, but –"

"Yes - *precisely*. That is the very point." Bingley walked back over to the table. "What would you have gained from sharing such intelligence with me? You knew the lowness of my mood – you did me a kindness, for it would have been cruel to advise me of her nearness, knowing I was not at liberty to call upon her."

"But I should never –"

"Imagine if you knew someone you had such feelings for was in Town now," Bingley interrupted him once more. "Imagine if there was such a chasm between you that nothing warranted your attentions upon them. No, Darcy, you must keep it in context. At the time, we believed her to be indifferent."

Darcy got to his feet slowly, breathing steadily through the intense pain that once more gripped his insides. Bingley could not know how his words stung his friend, yet amidst his pain, Darcy accepted that he deserved every innocent blow, and if anyone was justified in the delivery, it must surely be his friend.

"Where is your anger over my interference in your affairs?"

"Anger? How can I be cross with you, when you bring me such happy news?" Bingley paused. "Though I wonder a little at Caroline's – and indeed, Louisa's – reticence. Forgive me for speaking thus of my own sisters, but I doubt their reasons for not revealing Miss Bennet's presence in Town run to such altruistic ones as yours did."

Darcy grunted and walked over to a window on the far side of the room before turning around. Bingley watched him with apparent interest, but clearly unable to suppress the smile that would linger about his mouth and almost rocking from foot to foot in his pleasurable anticipation.

"Bingley, you must be rational, you must *think*. I have done you a disservice. I have not treated you fairly. You were ill-advised, and I can blame no one but myself."

Bingley's smile faltered, and he walked over to join his friend. For a moment, they both stared out at the busy thoroughfare of Piccadilly. Then Bingley stirred, and his tone took on a rare seriousness as he spoke.

"No. No, Darcy. Let me accept my own culpability. I was a fool to be so persuaded. I have had time aplenty to reflect whilst you have been away, my friend and had long acknowledged my own culpability in this before you came to claim yours. I have been haunted by my own indecision, not by your advice to me."

"But you credited it because of my arrogant assertion."

Bingley placed a hand briefly upon his friend's shoulder.

"Darcy, for once accept that I shall stand my ground. Your fault is no deeper than mine. And let us not forget that my sisters advised me likewise." Bingley paused. "Yes, perhaps you should not have counselled me so, but you did so with the best of intentions – a friend's well-being. But I?" Bingley ran a hand through his hair again, leaving it in further disarray. "I should not have allowed myself to be thus persuaded away without endeavouring to ascertain Miss Bennet's true feelings. I was weak. I should have countered your arguments. Well, now I am doing so, and that is your penance for your original ill advice! We are both equally to blame, albeit for different reasons, and that, my friend, you will simply have to accept."

Darcy tried to ignore the distaste he felt for himself, knowing full well that he could not yet bring himself to admit to Bingley his further incentive in removing them both from Hertfordshire. He watched as his friend moved over to the door and called for his manservant.

"Can I prevail upon you to return with me directly to Mount Street?"

Bingley closed the door on the servant and crossed the room again. "Let us discuss it over some refreshment. I find my appetite has suddenly returned and have ordered a fresh meal be sent up for us. Come," Bingley indicated that they seat themselves once more and reached for the wine bottle. "Convince me I should wait at least until dawn to seek Miss Bennet's whereabouts."

Darcy eyed Bingley thoughtfully, then reached for his glass. "Bingley," he said, raising it in a toast to his companion, "If there is one thing I will promise you, it is that I shall not attempt to convince you of anything ever again." Then, meeting Bingley's wide grin with a rueful smile, he drained his glass before offering it for a refill.

The afternoon had drawn to a close by the time Elizabeth and Charlotte were once more in sight of Hunsford parsonage. Their visits were complete, yet the sun still held some warmth, and with mutual agreement they headed for a charmingly situated wooden seat against one of the garden walls.

"I shall miss your company, Lizzy," Charlotte said as she set her now empty basket upon the floor. "You do promise to write me during your sojourn in Town? I will welcome any news you can spare!"

Elizabeth grasped her friend's hand and squeezed it. "It is the least I can do, if that is all the repayment you will demand for having hosted me so gracefully these past weeks."

"Of course, your opportunity for indulgence in society is widened by the Harington connection. Should you find yourself once more in the same company as has recently left the neighbourhood, I will not be satisfied with anything less than an *Express*!

With a jolt of unease, Elizabeth recognised the truth of this, but before she could answer they both detected the approach of Maisie.

"Beggin' yer pardon, Ma'am," she bobbed an awkward curtsey, "But Cook be seeking you. Says 'tis urgent, she does."

"Thank you, Maisie. Tell Mrs Dene I shall come directly." With a sigh, Charlotte stood, stooping to reclaim her basket. "Please excuse me, Lizzy; I will re-join you as soon as I am able."

Elizabeth nodded and sat back against the bench for a moment, eyeing the pretty cottage garden in an attempt to prevent her thoughts from straying once more in a certain gentleman's direction, and as her hand brushed her pocket she recalled Serena's letter.

With a frown, she quickly withdrew it, her eyes drifting to the closing paragraphs.

*"Dearest Lizzy, there is a matter pressing upon my mind that I would share with you, yet I find myself reluctant to put it in writing. Though I am restored to my parents' home but these ten days, now that I am assured my father's health is improving, I have sought an invitation from my dear sister in Town, that I might find the opportunity to join you there before you leave for Hertfordshire. Much as I would enjoy securing your company here in Lambton, I believe to hope for it before the summer's end would be unrealistic, and I long for your kind ear*

*Thus, I beg you, Lizzy, to not make haste for Longbourn if it is within your power to extend your stay. I will trust to my sister's kind invitation by return and hope for your counsel and comfort at the soonest opportunity.*

*Your affectionate friend, Serena"*

Tucking the letter back into her pocket, Elizabeth rose from the bench and gathered her shawl. Serena's anxiety notwithstanding, it would be enjoyable to tarry a while in London and spend some time with her friend, and as the thought of Mr Darcy residing there attempted to reassert itself, Elizabeth refused to allow it any purchase as she crossed the lawn and went up the steps into the parsonage. She would pen a quick response to Serena, assuring her that she would await her arrival, and as soon as it was done, she would put the finishing touches to her packing.

# Chapter Nineteen

HALF WAY ALONG Mount Street in Mayfair stood the London residence of the Darcy family, the only double-fronted townhouse in a row of similar striking edifices, set slightly back from its neighbours and displaying an inscrutable, unadorned façade to the outside world, its door unembellished other than by plain brass fittings, and a simple bell pull located in the stone architrave.

Inside, the hallway was richly but elegantly furnished, and at this hour of the day depicted a serenity at variance with the concealed activities of some of the house's many occupants: a servant readying the tapers; the cook and her many helpers working diligently in the kitchen, keen to prepare a meal that would assure their master of their continued devotion; Mrs Wainwright, the long-serving housekeeper, personally putting the final touches to the drawing room – plumping a cushion here, tweaking the particular fall of a drape there and casting an assessing eye towards the stock upon the drinks tray before heading to the dining room to ensure that the upholstery had been adequately brushed and the flowers suitably arranged.

Upstairs, in his customary chamber on the second floor, Colonel Fitzwilliam reclined in his shirt-sleeves in a hearthside chair, a glass on the drum table near his elbow, oblivious to his manservant as he applied himself to a last-minute polish of the buttons on his coat.

The Colonel frowned into the flames before reaching for his glass. Appreciative though he was of the reason behind Darcy's precipitous departure, he could only hope that his cousin's delay in returning did not signify a dramatic turn of events. The further complication of a rift with one of his dearest friends might have serious implications upon how soon Darcy might rally his spirits.

Fitzwilliam swirled the liquor in his glass before taking a hefty swig. Notwithstanding his empathy for his plight, he had a further and equally serious concern other than Darcy's state of mind: that of his other cousin, Georgiana. After the despair she had experienced of late, he was keen nothing should disturb the marked improvement in her spirits he had detected earlier, and if she were to discern the lowness of her brother's mood, the Colonel worried for its influence.

The young lady herself was presently in her own chamber at the opposite end of the landing. Turning her head this way and that, Georgiana Darcy inspected the dressing of her hair in the looking glass, before wrinkling her nose at her reflection and getting to her feet.

Walking over to her bedside table, she picked up the note that her brother had left, frowning at its all too brief content as she read it through one more time in the hope it might even yet shed some light upon his purpose with his friend. The chiming of the clock, however, reminded her of the hour, and she discarded the note before making her way out onto the landing and set off in search of her companion.

Inside Darcy's own chamber, in contrast to the calm silence of the hallways, there was considerable bustle. Having been let into the dressing room from the servants' staircase, several retainers were busy with their appointed tasks and, assured that all was in order, Thornton turned his attention to his own duties.

Crossing over to the corner of the dressing room, he retrieved from the back of a nearby chair the garment that he had laid there earlier. He frowned as he picked the coat up and gave it a good shake before walking over to hang it upon the stand in the far corner, and taking up a nearby brush he began to sweep it over the fabric. It had been soaked from its outer layers right through to the silk lining, which had watermarked badly.

Thornton tsked and slowly shook his head. There was nothing for it: the lining would have to be replaced, and who knew how the seams would hold up in future. With a grunt, he gave the coat one last sweep of the brush before discarding his task and making his way over to the closet to select suitable attire for his master that evening.

The afternoon had all but faded by the time Darcy finally emerged from the Pulteney Hotel and began to retrace his steps along Piccadilly. It was fortunate Bingley had agreed to progress to tea rather than order another bottle of wine – though unspoken, they both had seemed to sense that anything signifying a celebration might be premature. As a result, he now felt the benefit of the decision, his only ailment being the ever-present ache in his breast.

Darcy paused as he reached a wide junction, oblivious to the noise of hooves clattering on the cobbles and the bustle of people around him. The progression of the afternoon had left him adrift, for any attempt at diversification had fallen upon deaf ears, and eventually he had conceded defeat and allowed the conversational reins to fall into the hands of his friend.

Bingley's initial preoccupation was, understandably, with Miss Bennet: establishing her whereabouts, calling upon her, attempting to repair the damage to their acquaintance. But as there was little that could be resolved instantly, thus it was her sister who ultimately secured Bingley's interest.

The sudden blast of a horn from a passing carriage startled Darcy out of his introspection, and he looked around to take stock of his present position before turning on his heel and heading up the nearest street in the direction of Berkeley Square.

Bingley's pressing for information relative to Darcy's interaction with Elizabeth had surfaced a myriad of feelings, but despite his friend's persistence, Darcy found there was little more he could offer by way of information: yes, he believed Miss Bennet had continued to reside in Town when Miss Elizabeth arrived in Kent, but whether this remained the case, he could not answer.

The only other suggestion he could offer was that it had been common knowledge in Hertfordshire that the Bennets had relations in Cheapside, and one might assume they were Miss Bennet's hosts when she was in Town and that this would also be her sister's destination on the following day.

The only likely way to discover for certain if Miss Bennet had indeed returned home would be to call upon these relations – if they could establish who they were, and where they resided – and Bingley had determined that this must be his preliminary course of action.

Darcy's reminder of Bingley's sisters' call on Miss Bennet had eventually presented itself as the perfect solution, for they would know not only the family's name, but would be familiar with the direction. Thus, Bingley had determined to send his sister, Caroline, to visit by way of penance, that she should take some part in effecting a reconciliation between them both by establishing for certain the lady's whereabouts.

Darcy frowned as he walked: he had some reservations about this, for he doubted not only that Miss Bingley would be amenable to such an undertaking but that, should she do so, her information could hardly be relied upon.

With a sigh, Darcy forced the issue aside as he made his way along the west side of Berkeley Square, where a cluster of people milled around outside the row of elegant shops, in particular near *Gunters*, the renowned confectioners and café. He made his way around an elderly couple waiting for their carriage steps to be lowered and, knowing he delayed the inevitable, he allowed himself to be drawn to the window display of a nearby book shop. His eyes flickered with feigned interest over the new editions resting on velvet-covered stands, but even this poor attempt to distract himself failed, his gaze caught by a slim volume of translations in a green leather cover. Darcy himself had it on order at his usual bookseller, yet it was the author whose name resounded in his head.

Elizabeth had been perusing, clearly with much enjoyment, a volume of William Cowper's letters during her stay at Netherfield. He knew this because, upon her quitting the drawing room after one of their frequent debates, he had retrieved the book from where she had discarded it upon the couch. *Elizabeth*... How could he put her from his mind, when the smallest thing could draw her back?

A wave of weariness flooded him, as he struggled against the memories, and he forced himself to walk on, passing the windows of *Gunters* slowly, oblivious to the array of fine cakes on display. He must rally; he was barely minutes from home and though Georgiana would doubtless provide the necessary temporary distraction, he feared that some essence of his poor spirits might reach her.

The jangling of a bell startled Darcy out of his reverie, and he almost collided with a young gentleman eagerly stepping out of the establishment, followed by a manservant bearing several gaily wrapped packages.

"My apologies." Darcy made a perfunctory bow, touching his hat.

"No indeed, it is I who begs your pardon, Sir," the shorter man bowed more formally, giving a quick, if somewhat distracted, smile before turning in the opposite direction, the servant following in his wake, and

Darcy resumed his pace, soon turning the corner into the calm of Mount Street.

Less than four miles distant across the city, in a charming townhouse fronting onto a wide thoroughfare in Cheapside, Mary Gardiner entered her sitting room and crossed to the writing desk, smiling warmly at her niece as she passed, who had looked up from her needlepoint and wished her 'good evening'.

"I fear the light is fading, Jane, dear. I have called for the lamps to be lit, but I would advise you to desist from your labours for now. Your mother will never forgive me if I permit you to strain those beautiful eyes!"

"Dear Aunt," Jane Bennet shook her head at the teasing reprimand. "Though I am more than happy to oblige you, for it does not hold my attention at all."

Mrs Gardiner settled herself at her desk, retrieving her pens, ink and a small, ivory-handled knife from the various compartments. "You are looking forward to being reunited with Lizzy."

"Oh, Aunt! I have missed her so very much. I am sure she is the remedy to fully lift me from my present melancholy."

Having removed the stopper from the inkbottle and peered carefully at her pens before selecting the one that promised the finer nib, Mrs Gardiner turned her gaze upon her niece.

"Indeed, yet we should not overlook the fact that the hoped for remedy is guilty of being a contributor to the ailment! Had she not despatched you to our care so expeditiously, and then absconded to pastures new, you might not be feeling her loss so acutely!"

Jane laughed softly, but began to take particular care in stowing away her threads and needles.

Conscious as they both were that Elizabeth was not the only loss of society that Jane felt so deeply, Mrs Gardiner sought a distraction. "Well, then we must thank dear Nicholas, must we not?"

"How so?" Jane got to her feet, her sewing basket clutched to her middle, and she walked over to where her aunt sat.

"My dear girl – is not your sister curtailing her adventures in Kent, that my Godson might have his demands met and see her before he is obliged to return to the West Country?" She paused for a moment, smiling up at her eldest niece. "But I must own that I am happy to concede to his wishes, for I, like you, look forward to being in company with our Lizzy sooner than anticipated."

Jane's eyes drifted to the open letter upon her aunt's desk. "And now we are to be reunited with Serena also!"

"Indeed! And I must attend to my reply, for she is no doubt all suspense over how soon we can receive her!" She laughed as her eyes scanned her sister's letter once more. "Serena does seem most anxious to secure some time with your sister; I trust she appreciates she may have to share her attentions!"

Jane smiled. "Dear Lizzy. She will find herself so in demand she will not know which way to turn, for wishing to satisfy us all at once."

"Aye, and I foresee Nicholas will have to curb his impatience somewhat. Serena may be a quiet little thing, but she is possessed of an iron will when the notion takes her!" Mrs Gardiner shook her head in amused affection, conscious of a real sense of happiness at the thought of being reunited all at once with a group of young people who had been as like her own offspring as any could be.

Jane walked over to the dresser and returned her sewing basket to the shelf, then paused on her way back across the room by a long side table. "Perhaps you should seize this opportunity to update your collection." She nodded towards the array of miniatures nestled on the dark red velvet runner, all done by her aunt's hand over the years.

Mrs Gardiner got to her feet and joined her. As well as images of her half-sister at various stages of her development, there were small portraits of all the Bennet daughters, albeit the majority were of the two eldest, and all the Harington offspring, including dear little Maria, who had succumbed to the fever – sadly, her baby brother had passed before any such likeness could be taken.

Letting out a short laugh, Mrs Gardiner pointed to some of her first attempts, those of Jane and Nicholas before they had reached the age of two. "Oh dear – upon reflection, I fear my talent when you were all younger lacked direction. The most recent ones are certainly more accurate renditions!"

"Dear Aunt, how can you say so? Do you not recall with what pleasure we viewed each new offering over the years?" Jane leaned across the table and picked up a particular favourite of hers of Elizabeth at around six years of age.

"Hmmm, I do. I also recall how much one can appreciate an attempt at a likeness without understanding its relation to art!" She peered at the miniature that Jane still held in her hand. "I am sure you recollect how the original differed from *that* particular portrait?"

Jane smiled before replacing it on the cloth. "You are too severe upon yourself."

Mrs Gardiner laughed. "And you, Jane, are too generous, as we all know full well. The finished version fails to depict the truth of the model, who had, as you may recall, disarrayed hair and sported a smudge upon her nose from her exploits in the garden!" She turned to cast her eyes over the table once more. "At least I may suppose that, should the time present itself, I will do better justice to Nicholas and Elizabeth. Their inability to be still for any length of time combined with my lack of expertise really does render their early portraits as unlike each other as anything, and…"

She broke off as her gaze swept the table once more, and she frowned, but just then there came a knock upon the door, and both ladies turned as the servant entered, bearing a taper and a supply of fresh candles.

Beckoning him in, Mrs Gardiner glanced at the clock and, realising the lateness of the hour, hurried over to resume her seat at the desk. Jane picked up the last of her belongings, and came over to plant a kiss upon her aunt's cheek.

"I shall leave you to your letter-writing."

Mrs Gardiner watched her niece leave and then turned once more to face her desk. Reaching for a fresh sheet of parchment, she glanced at her sister's letter before dipping her pen into the ink and beginning to write.

# Chapter Twenty

BY THE TIME DARCY crossed the threshold of his home, it wanted barely an hour until dinner and, divesting himself of his hat and coat into the hands of the waiting footman, he headed straight for the stairs, but before he had reached the first step, he was forestalled by his housekeeper who had just then emerged from the dining room.

"Good evening, Sir," Mrs Wainwright bobbed a small curtsey in greeting. "The Colonel has retired to his room to prepare for dinner, and Mrs Annesley advises that Miss Darcy is awaiting your return in the small sitting room."

"Thank you, Mrs Wainwright."

Darcy climbed the stairs, pausing at the top to send a fleeting, regretful glance towards the staircase to the second floor, longing for the refuge above. Then, he turned his steps along the landing towards the sitting room frequented by his sister. Much as he desired to see her dear face, it was of paramount importance to him that no hint escape of his troubled spirits, for she had suffered enough of late.

Darcy paused for a moment as he reached the closed door, staring unseeingly at the panelled wood in front of him. Before he had left for Rosings, he had welcomed all the signs of the return of the young sister he knew: increasing bouts of enjoyment of a well-loved piece of music, an appreciation for the arrival of spring and the resurrection of her affectionate nature – yet he could still picture quite vividly the times he had caught Georgiana's sombre gaze upon him, and how she had quickly looked away upon catching his eye. Her large eyes had seemed graver somehow, and occasionally they reflected a wariness, as if there was something that yet preyed upon her mind.

"Fitzwilliam!" With a start, Darcy stepped backwards as the door swung open, and before he could respond, his sister had let out a cry of delight and thrown herself into his arms. He hugged her tightly, the laugh that had risen within him stalling in his throat as he held her.

Closing his eyes against a sudden rush of emotion, Darcy prayed that Georgiana would detect nothing amiss. To be held once more in the comforting arms of a loved one had suddenly opened up within him a well of despair, and for a moment he was lost, unable to do more than cradle her head against his shoulder and rock her gently to and fro as he struggled to salvage his composure.

"It is so good to have you home, dear Brother," Georgiana murmured, her grip around his waist tightening. Unable to respond for a second, Darcy dropped a kiss upon her hair. Then, he cleared his throat and released her gently, quickly brushing a hand across his eyes.

"My humblest apologies, Georgie. I had not anticipated my visit with Bingley taking up so much time. Are you well?"

His sister studied his face for a moment; then she smiled and stood aside so that he could enter the room. "I am well now that you are here. I will own that I had become impatient to see you, but now you have returned I find I can forgive you anything."

Darcy smiled grimly as he followed Georgiana into her sitting room. First Bingley, now Georgiana – what bad fortune that Elizabeth was too far distant to bestow such similar mercy… Darcy blinked, and shook his head. To allow Elizabeth any purchase now would be counter-productive, and he forced all thought of her aside, focusing his attention upon his sister.

In unspoken mutual agreement they took up their usual seats by the hearth. Darcy rested his head against the leather chair and stretched his legs out in front of the fire. Unhappy he may be, but it was a comfort to be home.

"Was the journey tiring, Fitz?"

Darcy straightened up. "No – no, I am merely content with being here, with you."

Georgiana smiled, and he found himself returning it as the tightness that bound his chest loosened its grip slightly.

"There is nothing amiss, Fitz?"

"Err, no – no, there is not. Should there be?"

Georgiana shrugged lightly. "Your precipitous departure to see Mr Bingley. I was concerned that some matter of urgency had arisen. I trust all is well in that quarter?"

Darcy shook his head. "I merely had some pressing business with Bingley that could not be delayed; but I assure you, all is well."

His sister smiled and sat back in her chair. "And did you have a pleasant visit with Aunt Catherine this year – I must own to no little surprise that you extended your stay, Brother; it was most unanticipated - you must tell me all!"

Darcy shifted uncomfortably in his seat. "Err, indeed. You... did Richard not enlighten you?"

Georgiana let out a huff of breath and rolled her eyes. "You well know Cousin Richard, Fitz. He will talk until the cows come home, yet reveal nothing of import," she paused, frowning. "I believe his response implied that some unforeseen circumstance had arisen; that until you had..." Georgiana paused again, then added, "... that until you had brought the matter to a confrontation you had been unable to leave."

Conscious that his sister looked at him expectantly, Darcy leaned back in his seat again, trying to push away the memories that would intrude.

"Brother? It was nothing too serious, I trust? Was she being particularly difficult this year?"

He attempted a smile. "Do not trouble yourself, Georgie. Aunt Catherine is much as she ever was; there is nothing more to it than Richard says."

Reluctant to promote further discourse of his time in Kent, Darcy sought a change of subject. "Bingley sends his regards. He intends to call upon us on the morrow."

"Mr Bingley is not joining us for dinner?"

"No – no, he had a previous engagement to dine in Grosvenor Street, but when he calls in the morning he hopes to be in a position to advise whether or not he will be able to make any stay with us."

"But he always resides with us when you are in Town! You are not planning to remove to Pemberley? I thought we were not to travel north until closer to harvest time?"

"No..." Darcy paused. The temptation of Pemberley was strong, being a long way from any southern county, be it Kent or Hertfordshire. Perhaps journeying north would aid his recovery...

"Fitz?" Georgiana seemed to be studying him with the familiar troubled expression.

"Bingley's plans are unfixed at present, as to whether he will remain in Town a while or return to his estate."

"But Miss Bingley seemed quite certain that he was fixed in Town for the duration. She even hinted…" Georgiana blushed. "Forgive me, Fitz. It is not my place to speculate or comment, but she has implied that her brother will be giving up his estate in the country."

Darcy shook his head. "The lady is quite mistaken, my dear." He smiled gently to reassure her that her words had not been out of place. "I had best leave you so that I might refresh myself. Shall I call for you and escort you downstairs?"

"Please!"

"In a half hour? It will perchance give us a moment's respite before Richard joins us?" They both got to their feet, and Georgiana nodded as she stepped instinctively into his embrace once more. He ruffled the top of her hair, and she batted his hand away with a laugh.

"Fitz! Must I begin anew to order my curls?"

Darcy smiled down at her as she stepped away from him and turned to peer in the mirror over the mantelpiece.

"You will do very well as you are. I will be with you directly," and with that, he turned and left the room.

Bingley was late, and he knew he had only himself to blame. Ever since Darcy had left him, he had been wandering about his rooms in a state of distraction, and Overton, his valet, had clearly been running out of patience as he finally managed to cajole and coerce his master through the necessary preparations for an evening out. Recalling his valet's resigned expression as he tried valiantly to fasten the neck cloth of his fidgeting and restless charge, Bingley could suppress his merriment no longer, and let out a loud chuckle.

By the time he headed down the main staircase into the hotel lobby, Bingley was almost at a run, and he beamed happily at a rather sour looking elderly gentleman whom he passed on the stairs, before hurrying across the entrance hall.

"Have a pleasant evening, Sir."

Bingley nodded briskly in acceptance of the manager's greeting and then nodded once more towards the doorman, who leapt forward to swing open the doors.

His eyes were bright with anticipation. Indeed, he could hardly comprehend the sense of purpose he now experienced, the exhilaration of feeling that his life had suddenly turned about. In fact, he was so elated, and thus distracted, that he walked straight into the gentleman who at that moment entered the lobby from outside.

"I do beg your pardon."

"Not at all, Sir. My mistake, I assure you."

Bingley hesitated. There was something familiar about the voice, and he turned to look at the gentleman in question as he removed his hat, realising in an instant the connection.

"Harington?"

The other man turned to fully observe Bingley, whose features broke into a wide smile of recognition.

"It *is* you! Well met. I do not believe I have seen you since Cambridge days. How fares it with you? And how does that elder brother of yours?"

The man frowned momentarily as he studied the open countenance before him; then, recognition seemed to dawn. "Bingley! How are you, man? Good to see you!"

Conscious that they were blocking the main entrance as the door once again swung open, both men moved aside, shadowed by Harington's servant.

"You have been to *Gunters*!" Bingley nodded in the direction of the patient retainer with his pile of packages wrapped in the well-known shop's signature style, and Nicholas grinned.

"Yes, indeed! A dear friend arrives from the country on the morrow, and I have been purchasing gifts for her and her family."

"Aha! A young lady, Harington? What is this?"

His companion laughed and shook his head. "My lips are sealed! Have you time for a drink?" Harington gestured towards the gentleman's bar adjacent to the lobby. "I should welcome the opportunity to regale you with my brother's antics and hear all your news, that I might pass it on!"

"Sadly not." Bingley pulled out his pocket watch, which merely confirmed what he knew full well: he was late, and he had no desire to delay his opportunity to secure potential news of Miss Bennet. "I am afraid I must dash; a dinner engagement with family, you understand. But you are in residence here?"

"Indeed. You may recall that my parents have always eschewed the tradition to maintain a house in Town."

"Then shall we break our fast together in the morning?"

"An excellent notion. Ten o'clock?"

Harington held out his hand, and Bingley shook it warmly.

"I shall look forward to it. Until then," and raising his hat, he took his leave, hurrying out of the door and down the steps to his waiting carriage.

Thornton, having been alerted to his master's return by a footman, hurried the servants to bring hot water for bathing and made haste to set out the necessaries for shaving. He had just requested the placing of a warming pan between the sheets on his master's bed when the chamber door opened and Mr Darcy entered the room.

"Good evening, Sir."

"I am running late, Thornton. I have no time for a shave, a bath must suffice." Thornton struggled to mask his disapproval, but before he could respond his master continued, "I comprehend your thoughts entirely; yet as it is only my sister and my cousin who must tolerate such unkemptness, I am certain they will bear up under the strain."

"As you wish, Sir." Thornton walked over to the chair where Mr Darcy had discarded his coat and retrieved it, draping it reverently over one arm before turning to observe that two boots had been summarily tossed onto the floor near the bed. Walking across the room, intent upon reclaiming them, Thornton barely had time to take two paces before a flash of white caught his eye and, just in time, his arm shot out, niftily catching his master's discarded shirt and neck cloth as they sailed through the air towards him.

"Well caught."

Thornton bowed his head in acknowledgement of this praise, and turned to collect the discarded footwear as Mr Darcy disappeared through the door to the dressing room. Depositing the clothing upon a chair and the boots nearby, Thornton selected a dressing robe from the hook behind the door and followed in his master's wake, but as he reached the threshold he stopped, hovering just inside the bedroom, unsure whether to proceed.

His master stood in front of the stand holding the still slightly damp coat, at which he stared fixedly. Thornton was about to speak to justify its present condition when the words froze upon his lips.

Mr Darcy had reached a hand out, hesitantly; for a moment it rested, suspended in mid-air as if he was unsure of his purpose but then, to his surprise, he raised the other arm and rested both hands upon the shoulders of his coat, gripping it tightly.

Concerned that his master was displeased, Thornton moved forward, placing the dressing robe he carried onto a nearby chair as he approached the offending item on its stand.

"My apologies, Sir. I have attempted…" Thornton stopped; his master had started at the sound of his voice, and it suddenly occurred to him that he was unaware of his approach. "Forgive me, Sir."

Mr Darcy cleared his throat and stepped back from the stand, his gaze still fixed upon the somewhat worse for wear coat. "Do not concern yourself, Thornton."

"I shall be sending the coat for cleaning, Sir. I fear the lining… "

Shaking his head decisively, his master turned away and began to unfasten his breeches. "There is no need. I do not intend to wear it again. Have it cleaned as best you can – if it remains fit for wear, permit it to be distributed to a good cause; if not, dispose of it."

# Chapter Twenty One

THOUGH THE SUN HAD long set over the grounds of Hunsford parsonage, Elizabeth remained at the open window of her chamber. The sunny day had passed into a cloudless night, and a near full moon cast a shimmering glow over the garden walls.

Shivering a little as the cooler temperature permeated the room, Elizabeth drew her shawl about her shoulders and inhaled deeply, enjoying the sensation of the evening air upon her face. Much as she had enjoyed seeing Charlotte again, she could not regret her imminent departure. She longed to be with Jane, to reassure herself of her sister's present well-being, and casting one last lingering look over the grounds below, she pulled the casement window closed and dropped the latch into place.

She turned around, her eyes drifting over the familiarity of her chamber: her trunk stood against the wall, its lid propped open awaiting any last-minute belongings, her travelling clothes were laid out upon a chair, and on the table sat her writing case, surrounded by its many contents.

Walking over to the hearth, Elizabeth bent to drop a small log onto the fire which had begun to smoulder, causing it to stir and flare up. Satisfied that she had secured herself some further heat, she crossed over to the desk and began to put her pens, wax and seal into the relevant compartments of the case, before turning her attention to the pile of correspondence she had pulled out earlier with the intention of restoring it to some sort of order.

Thoughtfully, she trailed a finger over the various pieces of folded parchment, most of which bore Jane's elegant script, but then her finger slowed as it came to rest upon the last letter she had received at Hunsford – that of Serena. Elizabeth studied the neatly written direction before smiling to herself, familiar as she was with her friend's desire for guidance of some sort. With so few close acquaintances, borne of her disinclination for society in general, Serena had chosen to look to her for support and recommendation whenever troubled, a role Elizabeth undertook willingly for love of her friend more than a particular talent in that quarter.

Rousing herself, Elizabeth picked up a small bundle of letters in one hand, rummaging in one of the drawers of her case until she found what she sought: several thin pieces of ribbon. With the skill of long practice she soon had the packet neatly tied. She placed them in the case and turned her attention to the next pile and, conscious that they were all from Jane, she bit her lip thoughtfully as she fastened a bow to secure them.

She would face a dilemma once she reached her aunt's home: what should or could she reveal to Jane? It had never been in either of their natures to keep things from each other – and yet this touched upon such secrets. What of Wickham's past? Further, it would surely do her sister no good to discover that Mr Bingley had been persuaded away from his interest in her, for Jane, with such tenderness of heart, would begin anew and suffer for all that he had endured also.

She frowned. Jane's correspondence had continued to hint at a lowness of spirit, even though she had attempted to imply she did not dwell on the past. The only indication of a return of her sister's natural enjoyment of life had come with her last missive, and that seemed to be solely down to Nicholas' visit.

Elizabeth let out a rueful laugh. What with Jane's unhappiness and Serena in need of counsel, Nicholas' uncomplicated company would doubtless be the least complex of her upcoming visit.

Bestirring herself, she dropped the bundle into her case and was about to select another piece of ribbon when the hand upon one of the remaining letters caught her eye, and she suddenly recalled that she had earlier thrust Mr Darcy's letter in with all the others. Snatching it up, she turned around with it in her hand. What should she do? It was not likely that anyone would come across it, locked in the case, yet should she take the risk – or destroy it?

Elizabeth glanced over towards the fire. There was ample flame to devour one letter, yet her feet remained firmly in place as she studied the lettering on the front once more.

Was it possible that their paths might cross again in Town? She could not fail to recall Charlotte's words from earlier. How would she feel to be in his company again, should such a situation occur? How would *he* feel?

Engrossed as she was in her thoughts, she failed to hear footsteps approaching until a sudden knock came upon her door.

"One moment." Moving over to the bed, Elizabeth tucked the letter under her pillow, then crossed to open the door.

"Charlotte! I thought you had retired for the night." Elizabeth stood aside and beckoned her into the room, then frowned as she noted the bundle in her friend's arms.

"I thought I would return these to you. Maisie was about to bring them up, but I was happy to have another reason to speak with you before taking to my bed. I shall miss your company most sorely!"

Elizabeth hugged her friend impulsively, and then released her to relieve her of the now dry garments, walking over to lay them upon the bed where she hastily turned her back on them.

"That is kind of you."

"I am afraid they are both unfit for wear – come see, Lizzy."

Resignedly, Elizabeth turned back to face Charlotte, who had perched herself upon the edge of the bed to inspect the hem of the gown Elizabeth had worn on Sunday.

"It has dried perfectly well, but I am afraid my staff has limited means, and we have been unable to remove all of the discolouring from dirt."

To be fair, in the dimness of the few candles that lit the room, it was not easy to tell what was staining and what was shadow but Elizabeth made a pretence of glancing at it.

"It is of little import, Charlotte. I am sorry to have put the servants to so much trouble through my own fool-hardly behaviour of walking in such inclement weather. I am certain that my aunt will know of a place where the fabric can be cleaned satisfactorily, and if all else fails, the gown can be dyed to a darker hue."

"That is true, but I am not sure your coat will recover. Though it has dried adequately, the hem is yet much blemished and, being of such fine fabric, I fear it will not improve."

"Then I have no one but myself to blame. It is not as if my parents will find it unusual for me to have sullied an item of clothing beyond repair when rambling about the countryside. I am afraid it has been a lifetime's tendency I find hard to alter!"

Charlotte laughed, but her smile faded as she studied her friend.

"I have been worried about you, Lizzy. Though you seem somewhat recovered today, your low spirits on Sunday were out of character, as was your desire for solitude in the subsequent four and twenty hours. I would not wish to return you to your family the worse for your sojourn in Kent."

"Dear Charlotte," Elizabeth reached over and patted her friend's arm. "Pray do not concern yourself on my behalf. I am quite well and perfectly robust! If my spirits were at all dampened temporarily, it was down to nothing more than the soaking I experienced the other day."

To Elizabeth's relief, Charlotte smiled and got to her feet. "Well then, I shall leave you now and look forward to sharing an early meal with you in the morning."

Wishing each other a good night's rest, Elizabeth shut the door upon her friend before walking back over to the bed. She refolded the dress and quickly crossed to the trunk, placing it on top of the other clothes within before retrieving her coat and holding it up to the light to inspect the damage. Its condition did indeed appear somewhat poor and was likely not salvageable. It crossed Elizabeth's mind briefly that this might present some difficulty in Town, but then she shrugged her shoulders, and folding it rather haphazardly she placed it in the trunk with the gown and dropped the lid on the sight of them.

Fortunately, the weather for the morrow bade fair, and she would be journeying in a covered carriage. She would trouble herself about the need for a coat when the necessity arose, and with that thought, she applied herself to her preparations for bed.

It had grown late by the time Georgiana finally consented to retire for the night, and Darcy watched his sister reach the top of the first flight of stairs and turn to give him a small wave before she disappeared out of sight.

Turning to follow his cousin as he headed along the hallway towards Darcy's study at the back of the house, he reflected upon her obvious reluctance to leave their company. It bespoke how much she had missed them and reinforced what he had long known: she lacked company, most especially of those near her in age, and in particular female companions – friends – with whom she could interact. A small voice reminded him how he had long been imagining Elizabeth in that role, but he ruthlessly silenced it. He would not think of her.

Entering his study a few moments later, he found Fitzwilliam settled in one of the wing chairs near the fireplace, nursing a glass of Darcy's finest brandy.

"I refrained from pouring you one, Cousin," the Colonel raised his glass in a toast. "Whilst the effect upon your empty stomach is entertaining, I believe it is not always to your satisfaction."

Darcy threw him a look more eloquent than words as he walked over to the tray of drinks that had been placed upon the side table earlier; the Colonel merely snorted and took a long sip from his glass.

"We have just dined, Fitzwilliam. I think I can tolerate at least one glass before retiring." Darcy poured himself a small brandy and walked over to the hearth, staring into the fire for a moment. Then, placing his glass on a circular leather-topped table near his own chair, he rested one arm against the mantelpiece and reached for the poker, giving the logs a hefty shove that caused them to spit and fire up.

"Did you call that dining, Darce? One bread roll torn into pieces, and a meal that probably half a dozen people had a hand in preparing, moved about the plate like pieces on a chess board?"

Darcy stared into the crackling flames, before muttering, "I did eat something!"

"Oh yes, something indeed. A very little something – was it a pea? Do not think it will go unnoticed."

Darcy grunted and gave the logs one more prod before replacing the poker, satisfied that there was sufficient heat remaining to accompany their nightcap, before dropping into his chair.

Conscious that Fitzwilliam scrutinised him over the rim of his glass, Darcy reached for his own drink and cradled it in both hands, studying the amber liquid as he swirled it around restlessly.

"You performed well enough this evening, I will grant you – certainly an improvement upon the prior two. At worst your concentration drifted but rarely, and I think with the aid of my incessant chatter, and her general delight in our return, your occasional bouts of ill attention will have escaped Georgiana for now." Fitzwilliam paused.

"You do appear somewhat more at ease. I trust things went well with Bingley?"

Darcy adjusted his position, before raising his gaze to meet his cousin's. "Almost too well; I do not deserve Bingley's easy acceptance of the situation, his forgiveness. How can he not resent me?"

The Colonel laughed. "This is Bingley. He would not know how to bear a grudge if one came along and poked him in the eye."

Darcy shook his head, still somewhat flummoxed over the way his friend had managed to absolve him of all culpability, and was about to speak again when there came an unexpected knock on the door.

"Forgive the intrusion, Sir," Pagett, the butler, intoned in his solemn voice. "Mr Bingley requests an audience with you, and begs you will forgive the lateness of the call."

A flicker of concern passed through Darcy, and he cast a glance at the clock before looking questioningly in his cousin's direction. The Colonel lifted both hands and shrugged and settled back into his seat as Darcy instructed Pagett to show the gentleman in.

Walking swiftly over to the drinks tray, Darcy measured out another glass of brandy, turning around as the door opened once more and Bingley came rapidly into the room. Barely pausing to take a breath, he fetched up in front of Darcy pink-faced and positively quivering.

"She will not do it, Darcy; she will not atone, and I... I... well, can you but believe it?" Bingley huffed, opened his mouth to continue, but when no sound came out, shut it with a snap.

Darcy handed his friend the glass and raised a brow as he knocked the drink back in one before handing it back and begging a refill. By the time he had turned back with the refreshed glass, Bingley had taken to pacing to and fro near the door.

"I am in high dudgeon, Darcy."

Bingley accepted the new offering from his friend, who bit back upon stating the obvious, waiting for him to continue.

"Caroline refused, most emphatically, to assist my endeavours to trace Miss Bennet!"

Bingley tossed the contents of the glass down his throat without a second glance and Darcy retrieved it as his friend resumed his pacing.

"There will be no note despatched to Miss Bennet's aunt, nor any call to establish if she remains in Town! I have discovered no direction for them, nor have I ascertained the name of these relatives, so I am unable to find them through other means." He ran a hand through his extremely dishevelled hair. "This is a disaster!"

# Chapter Twenty Two

DARCY WALKED OVER to the fireplace as his cousin nestled back against the leather of his chair, clearly relishing the scene playing out before him. Throwing him a warning look, Darcy turned back to face Bingley, deciding it was time to point out that they were not alone, when Bingley happened to draw the same conclusion.

"Colonel Fitzwilliam! Forgive the intrusion."

"Pray, do not concern yourself, Bingley. I shall permit you some privacy," the Colonel rose to his feet, drained his glass and walked over to deposit it on the silver salver.

"I beg you would not depart on my account. I trust I have caused no offence with my lack of discretion."

Darcy felt obliged to interrupt. "My cousin is well-versed in my mistakes regarding Miss Bennet."

Bingley blew out a long breath. "Good. Then he is aware of mine also. Colonel, please do not excuse yourself. It may be that you can offer a fresh perspective."

Darcy rolled his eyes at the smug expression crossing his cousin's face, and interjected, "Oh have no doubt of that. Be prepared for all the wisdom Fitzwilliam can offer – I am sure he will not disappoint."

The Colonel bowed and, retrieving his glass along with the decanter, paused to top up Bingley's before returning to his chair, and Darcy indicated to Bingley to seat himself before resuming his own.

"So come, Bingley. What has transpired? I am certain you will find your way to overcome any obstacle that has been presented."

"You have more faith in my ability to deduce than I." Bingley sat down heavily. "Let us not deny it. I need your counsel, whether you would wish it or not."

"Did she give a particular reason for her refusal?"

"It sounded like some form of brain malfunction," Bingley said morosely, taking a large mouthful of brandy and pulling a face as he swallowed it.

The Colonel tried and failed to repress a snort but Darcy ignored him, throwing his friend a questioning look.

Bingley shrugged. "She appears to be suffering from memory loss in relation to her call upon Miss Bennet. She claims she has no recollection of the exact address, merely that it is in a – well, I shall not tell you the exact words she used, but clearly she intended me to think it a dreadfully poor area."

Darcy frowned. "Were we not almost convinced that Miss Bennet has been staying somewhere in Cheapside?"

"Cheapside?" The Colonel leaned forward in his chair to place the decanter upon a side table, his gaze moving from Darcy to Bingley. "That is no poor area of Town. It is hardly fashionable, admittedly, but it is a thriving district of up and coming businesses – a breeding ground for trade and commerce. The merchants in that part of Town are anything but poor!"

Bingley let out a derisive laugh. "Precisely. And thus I must wonder if Caroline's ailment is genuine, for this is not the first occasion upon which my sister's memory deficiency has been exposed in relation to the source of our *own* family fortune."

Darcy eyed his friend sympathetically as he observed his frustrated demeanour. Whilst he was not surprised at Caroline Bingley's resistance to aiding her brother in his quest, he was concerned at how limited their options were for discerning Miss Bennet's whereabouts. It may well be that a ride out to Hertfordshire was required after all.

Bingley, meanwhile, had put his glass down and risen to his feet as his indignation began to surface again. Standing on the rug in front of the fire, he turned first to the Colonel and then Darcy.

"Further – can you but believe it – she claims she does not even recollect the name of the aunt and uncle, that she had," here Bingley paused, and drawing himself up in height he assumed a haughty expression, and in a manner markedly like that of his sister said, *"no intention of retaining such pointless detail, for what likelihood was there of a need to prolong the acquaintance"*?"

Before either of his companions could react, Bingley had begun to pace to and fro across the rug.

"I even tried to question Louisa. She is the more malleable of the two." Bingley paused to address the Colonel with these latter words, then resumed his pacing. "And to be fair to Hurst, he did instruct her to reveal whatever she knew. Yet, when pushed, all she could come up with was that she thought their name might be 'Green', or similar; possibly something akin to horticulture. What use is that to either man or beast? *Horticulture*...Bah!"

Bingley threw himself back into his chair and folded his arms across his chest, his air and countenance indicative of the frustration he had experienced in Grosvenor Street.

Darcy studied his friend thoughtfully. He did not wish to be seen to be guiding him, yet he also felt an obligation to ensure that Bingley had every opportunity to be reunited with Miss Bennet, and he cast his mind back over all that Bingley had disclosed.

"Is there no letter from Miss Bennet? They must have exchanged some correspondence for the calls to have been paid at all."

"Destroyed. All gone."

"Destroyed?"

"So my sister attests. Her response was strikingly similar to my earlier request – why would she want to retain a letter from someone with whom she is so little familiar and with whom she had no intention of continuing an acquaintance?"

"There is one other who would know the direction," both Darcy and Bingley turned to observe the Colonel, who was clearly most satisfied with having drawn a conclusion no one else had yet reached.

Bingley pursed his lips in concentration, but it was Darcy who spoke. "Of course! The Hursts' coachman!"

Bingley sat up quickly, his hair flopping onto his forehead, and he brushed it aside impatiently as Darcy turned to face him. "There lies your answer. Your sisters would not have made the journey to Cheapside on foot."

The Colonel grunted and drained his glass. "For what it is worth, Bingley, I would make your enquiries discreetly, or you will find the poor man has been despatched to the Far East. Miss Bingley does, if you allow me, seem one very determined woman."

"That would be a fair interpretation," Bingley said, his spirits clearly rising upon discerning his purpose again. "Now we must decide..."

A loud rap upon the study door had them all turn in their seats, and once more Darcy got to his feet and called, 'Enter.'

Pagett stepped forward into the room bearing a resigned demeanour as well as a small silver tray, upon which rested a note. Walking with stately progress across the floor, he came to a halt in front of the Colonel, bowing as he offered the tray to him.

The Colonel snatched the note up and quickly scanned its contents before hauling himself to his feet.

"Excuse me for a moment, gentlemen. It is from my commanding officer and the *Express* rider is awaiting my response." With a bow he excused himself, and as Pagett slowly closed the door, Bingley turned back to face his friend once more.

"Well, I do believe we have made progress. I am all anticipation for the morrow and the opportunity to visit Hurst's household again. I only hope his coachman is not out with the carriage when I call, for I cannot leave for Grosvenor Street until late morning." He settled himself more deeply into the chair and reached for his glass.

Darcy studied his feet, troubled by a thought that had just occurred to him. He did not wish to seem as if he were opposing Bingley's decision to seek Miss Bennet out as quickly as he could; nor did he wish to offer further poor counsel. Yet, knowing from Elizabeth that her sister had suffered a cruel disappointment at what appeared to be Bingley's hand, he did wonder how she might feel upon suddenly receiving an unexpected call from him. Indeed, he was not at all sure the surprise would be a welcome one in the circumstances – yet how to tender such a suggestion, when his friend was understandably so eager to find her?

"You are-," he hesitated, raising his eyes to meet those of his friend. "You are not at all concerned about your reception, Bingley? I am not blind to the fact that my mistake over Miss Bennet's true feelings will have caused her some pain, and ..." Darcy broke off as Bingley's contented smile slowly faded, and he sat up in his seat.

"What a damn fool I am!" Bingley jumped up out of his chair and dropped his glass onto the nearby table before turning round to face Darcy. "If she was not indifferent... Lord, Darcy, it will appear I abandoned her! What will she think of me? What will her family think? I had given it little enough thought, keen as I am to see her. How should I approach her after what I have done?"

"What you have done? It is I who caused the damage, Bingley. If it were not for my actions…"

"Darcy, please." Bingley stopped him. "Let us not go over it again; you are not solely culpable here, and the sooner you accept the sharing of the blame with me, the better for us both."

"But you must tell her – if for any reason she doubts your sincerity – tell her of my interference, Bingley, and not of your sister's. If you are successful in your attempt to repair the relationship, and Miss Bingley is to one day become sister to Miss Bennet, it would not sit well with either of them to begin that connection with such an impediment between them."

"If need be, I shall tell her of my own foolish behaviour. I will not pass the blame by implying you were the sole cause of this situation."

Darcy stared at Bingley for a moment, as a tumult of feelings assailed him: a touch of frustration at not gaining his point, combined with pride in his friend's new firmness and chagrin at still being so easily forgiven.

"You really are too good, Bingley."

Bingley let out a somewhat bitter laugh and walked over to reclaim his seat. "I am not sure that Miss Bennet would agree."

Darcy ruminated upon how Bingley's sudden departure from Hertfordshire and subsequent failure to return must have been received by the Bennets. "Or, indeed, Mrs Bennet – though I am certain her forgiveness will be rapid if you put things to rights."

Bingley's face paled as he threw an appalled look at Darcy. "Oh good grief – can you but imagine the lament of Mrs Bennet?"

"I must own that imagining Mrs Bennet, lamenting or otherwise, is something I avoid at all costs."

Bingley released a huff of laughter, then studied his friend for a moment. "Are you quite reconciled to my making such a match?"

"I have no need to be reconciled. If you are convinced of your future happiness with Miss Bennet, then I wish you every success."

There was no time for further comment, as the Colonel returned to the room and walked over to join them.

"I am committed to an early meeting with my commanding officer at Whitehall, gentlemen, so I shall bid you both goodnight."

"Yes, I must away also. My apologies for the late-night intrusion." Bingley got to his feet and turned to shake Fitzwilliam's hand. "Thank you for your assistance, Colonel. It is much appreciated."

"Delighted to have been of service, Bingley. At least you have the discernment to value my input."

Darcy stood up, pointedly ignoring the smug look that his cousin threw him, and the three gentlemen turned towards the still open door.

Glancing at Bingley as he followed him out of the room, the Colonel added, "You are off on your quest at first light, I trust?"

Bingley shook his head as they walked the length of the hall towards the front door. "No, indeed. I have a prior commitment in the morning, though I doubt Harington will get much sense out of me in the circumstances." Bingley turned towards Darcy and shook his hand. "I will call to report on progress, if you are at home?"

Darcy motioned to the footman to open the door as Pagett handed Bingley his hat and gloves. "I have no plans other than to catch up on some business and spend time with my sister."

Bingley nodded, took his leave of them both and made his way out to his waiting carriage.

Darcy exchanged a few words with his butler before turning to join his cousin as they walked towards the staircase, but the Colonel turned a frowning visage upon his companion.

"Does the name Harington mean anything to you?"

"Should it?"

Fitzwilliam shrugged his shoulders as they reached the first stair.

"I have a notion it was mentioned recently, but I cannot for the life of me think in what connection or by whom."

Unable to contribute anything enlightening, Darcy shook his head and began to climb the stairs, his cousin following silently in his wake. With another long night approaching, he was less concerned with troubling his mind over unfamiliar names than attempting to close it forcibly against one other that would persist in haunting him.

Most of the windows of the Pulteney Hotel were covered against the night, and slowly the lamps within were being extinguished. Yet at one window, the drapes remained fastened, and backlit by the candlelight a figure could be discerned staring out across Piccadilly.

From his suite on one of the upper floors, Nicholas Harington would have been able to see the full moon, the rooftops of Kensington Palace and a glimpse of the tallest trees in St James Park, had his gaze been fixed upon anything at all. As it was, he leaned against the sill, a half empty glass of wine in one hand, his eyes focused upon nothing as his mind dwelled on the morrow.

An uncharacteristic melancholy lingered about him, an aura that he had struggled to conceal. Yet the pretence of assuming his normal happy-go-lucky demeanour in front of his Godmother took its toll upon him, even a mere seven days after his arrival in Town. Restlessly, he shifted his weight from one foot to the other and raised the glass to his lips, taking a hefty swig of the contents.

Closing his eyes briefly, Nicholas let the liquid slide down his throat before rousing himself, turning his back upon the darkness. Crossing over to the dresser, he drained his glass and deposited it next to the wine bottle; he wished for no more alcohol, and picking up a book from a nearby console table, he walked over to one of the leather armchairs near the hearth and threw himself into it, dropping the book onto his lap.

Nicholas stretched his legs out and leaned his head back against the chair, closing his eyes and letting memories wash over him. Instinctively, he raised his hand to his breast pocket and rested it upon the weight there; then, unable to resist, he sat up and withdrew a miniature which he held up to the light. To be certain, it was not the most recent, having been taken some two years earlier, but Nicholas had happened to observe the original as the likeness was taken. He shook his head, smiling at the memory. She had meant something entirely different to him then, and how mercilessly had he teased her – until he had been banished from the room by his Godmother.

His expression sobered, and he stroked his thumb gently over the face before him. He had known her for so many years; she was his friend, yet now he wished for so much more from her. Nicholas chewed his lip as he studied the likeness in his hand intently. This interminable wait since he had last laid eyes upon her; if he could only comprehend what was in her mind, her heart – what she really felt for him.

Then, with a sigh and a final sweep of his thumb over the surface, Nicholas slipped the miniature back into the pocket of his waistcoat and got slowly to his feet. There was little point in dwelling upon that for which he had no answer. There was only one who could help put an end to his suffering and, despite his apprehension, he could sense his spirits rise in anticipation, knowing as he did of her imminent arrival in Town.

# Chapter Twenty Three

THE CLOCK ON THE MANTEL had chimed the midday hour, yet the man seated at the leather-topped desk appeared to heed it not.

Having attended his cousin to breakfast before his early departure, Darcy had repaired to his study determined to clear the backlog of paperwork that always awaited his attention after a sojourn in the country. Yet his interest had soon waned, and he had been staring at the papers on his desk for some time, unable to find an incentive to lift the letter opener from the blotter.

With a sigh, he leaned back in his chair. Was it only days since his world had turned upside down? Was it in truth only Wednesday?

*Wednesday...* the day that heralded Elizabeth's arrival in Town. An instinctive urge to indulge in thoughts of her fought with his resolve to reject any such visitation, but his heart remained the victor, and his mind flooded with all the questions he had struggled to suppress throughout the morning.

Had she yet departed Kent? Was she even now on the road? Who accompanied her that she might travel in safety – surely her uncle had sent more than one servant to attend her? Admittedly, it was an oft-travelled route, being the main thoroughfare between London and the southeast ports, but he did not like the thought of her journeying alone and unprotected.

Feeling his agitation rise, Darcy stirred in his seat. At what time of day might she be in London? Their paths were unlikely to cross, but what if... what if he should find out where she stayed? Darcy sighed: who did he attempt to fool? If Bingley's endeavours this morning with the coachman were unsuccessful, he knew his friend's sense of purpose would have him in Hertfordshire soon after.

Once the location of Elizabeth's relations was known, he could – as an acquaintance – presume to make a call. He could, and yet he would not. He was, after all, the last man she would wish to see, and if there was something in all of this that he must learn, it was that he could not think only of himself and what he alone desired.

With a groan he dropped his head into his hands. Finally, he understood his friend's reaction on the previous day: he had been right at first not to advise Bingley of Miss Bennet's presence in Town, for the agony of being so near yet unable to justify a call combined with the longing to give in to the temptation was nigh on unbearable.

A firm rap upon the door roused him, and he sat up, running a hand through his hair as he called, "Enter."

The door opened to admit Mrs Wainwright, who dropped a brief curtsey before responding to Darcy's beckoning hand. In her wake came a young servant, who cast a nervous glance at the housekeeper before advancing towards the desk and depositing the tray she carried before bobbing a curtsey and fleeing.

Darcy studied the offering silently for a moment – a pot of hot tea and, when he uncovered the accompanying dishes, a plate of coddled eggs and some finely sliced ham – before raising his eyes to his devoted housekeeper.

"Is this an invitation or an order, Mrs Wainwright?"

The woman opposite him placed her hands upon her hips and assumed a fierce expression, belied by the sparkle in her eyes.

"Now, Master Fitzwilliam, you must partake of some nourishment." She spoke with the familiarity of having been long in service to the family, reverting to a more informal address in the absence of other company.

"But I attended breakfast with my cousin!"

"Aye, Master, that you did. Attended, but did not partake. It cannot escape me when only one used plate is returned to the kitchen, and it was hardly likely to be the good Colonel who abstained. I thought you had a mind to eat later with Miss Georgiana, but I found she had breakfasted with only Mrs Annesley in attendance."

Darcy failed to suppress a wave of resigned amusement. He had never been able to get anything by Mrs Wainwright, even when he had been a young lad. He reached for the teapot and poured himself a cup, adding a dash of milk.

"Now you just keep that plate covered and warm for a few more minutes, Master, for the gentleman outside would have a word with you, if you please."

Darcy frowned at his housekeeper's retreating back, but before he could conjecture further, Bingley presented himself in the doorway.

Getting to his feet, Darcy greeted his friend and gestured for him to take a seat before dropping back into his own chair.

"Shall I order you some tea?"

Bingley shook his head; then, as if unable to help himself, a wide smile spread across his features. "You will never believe what has happened!"

Taking a drink from his cup, Darcy assumed his friend would expound upon this, but he merely perched himself on the edge of a chair, clearly struggling not to fidget, his eyes shining brightly.

Darcy felt his lips twitch. "Nor shall I, if you never share it."

"Oh! Yes, yes of course!" Bingley laughed, "Forgive me. I am a little stunned by my own good fortune!" Then, clearly unable to handle the challenge of sitting still, he leapt to his feet and leaned on the desk, fixing Darcy with a bright glance.

"I have seen her! I have seen Miss Bennet!"

Darcy sat up instinctively as the words fell from Bingley's mouth and placed his cup carefully on its saucer, but before he could voice the obvious question, Bingley continued.

"Grateful though I am for your cousin's inspiration, I had no need to venture to Grosvenor Street mews, for I learned of Miss Bennet's whereabouts at breakfast. Who would have thought it?"

"Who indeed," muttered Darcy, struggling with a momentary vision of either a repentant Caroline Bingley arriving at the Pulteney to reveal all she knew, or Hurst's coachman himself venturing to partake of a morsel as he delivered the welcome news. "How…"

Bingley straightened up, his grin widening, and announced as though certain it would provide enlightenment, "Harington is intimate with the Gardiners! Is it not fortuitous?"

"It could well be, but I must own to being unsure as to how."

"Forgive me." Bingley chuckled. "I cannot seem to think straight. Harington happened to be explaining," he paused. "I did say that he and I were to breakfast, did I not? Anyway, he was due to make a call upon his Godmother and her family this morning, and happened to mention that said family hailed from Hertfordshire." He paused again and started to pace to and fro, his eyes darting here and there about the room as he related the events of the morning, "Of course, I went on to say that I currently had an estate in that fair county, and lo and behold, Netherfield proved the link, for we soon discovered that he was entirely familiar with Longbourn, being so intimately connected with the Gardiner family!"

Darcy leaned back in his chair as his confusion deepened, but as Bingley had clearly unfinished his tale, he held his tongue; the questions could wait.

"Of course, once I explained that I had a more than passing acquaintance with the Bennets, being a close neighbour, he announced that *Miss* Bennet presently resided with her aunt and uncle and that Miss Elizabeth was due to arrive this very day. He invited me – nay, insisted – that I accompany him upon his call – I could hardly tell him of what had occurred in the past and decline the invitation – and to be honest, nor did I wish to!"

Assailed by a wave of longing, Darcy stared at his friend. Was Elizabeth even now just a few miles across Town? He cleared his throat and ventured, "And – and how went your visit?"

For a moment, Bingley's smile faltered. He passed a hand through his hair and stopped his pacing.

"I – well, to be honest, Darcy, I do not know. A part of me is so full of joy at having discovered her, at having seen her face again – she is even more beautiful than I remember." Bingley threw himself back into his chair, all signs of agitation now fully suppressed. "But – well, she seemed somewhat ill at ease; she was rather quiet – it is to be expected, I suppose, yet for every word she exchanged with me, she must have given tenfold to Harington."

Conscious that, even against his better judgement, his every sense screamed for news of Elizabeth, Darcy fixed his gaze upon Bingley attempting to decipher everything his friend had revealed.

"So these Gardiners are the elusive aunt and uncle?" Bingley nodded, and satisfied that he finally made some sense of his friend's outburst, Darcy added, "We should assume that Miss Bennet was surprised to see you. I trust there was no way to alert her to your presence other than you simply being announced with Harington?"

Bingley shook his head. "If anything, it was worse. Harington is intimate with the family, and thus there was no announcement. Once through the door, he took me straight to the drawing room. Yet Mrs Gardiner – the aunt – welcomed me warmly."

Darcy suppressed the urge to roll his eyes at this. If Mrs Philips was any indication of Elizabeth's aunts, he had no doubt that this London version would be of similar ilk. Bingley had always been far more tolerant than he over such fawning civilities... then, realising that his friend was still talking, Darcy strove to concentrate on what he was saying.

"... a most gracious lady, and most understanding – or so it seemed – when I made the point to both her and Miss Bennet – not that Miss Bennet would meet my eye, but it had to be said, do you not think?"

"I am sorry, Bingley. What was the point that you made?"

"That I had only learned this very morning of her being at her aunt and uncle's home in Town, of course!"

"Ah." Darcy reflected upon this for a second. "And do you feel it was accepted?"

For a moment, Bingley studied the toes of his boots. "Well, Mrs Gardiner did express some polite surprise, I must own. Miss Bennet seemed more interested in listening to Harington, but I hope that she heard me. Mrs Gardiner mentioned my sisters' visit." Bingley raised his eyes and met Darcy's gaze. "I can only imagine how *that* went, but I apologised for being unaware, that somehow it had slipped their mind to advise me of it. Whether I am believed or not," Bingley raised both hands and shrugged, "the words have been spoken."

"And," Darcy hesitated, "and Miss Elizabeth Bennet. Is she – has she joined her family yet?"

"She had yet to arrive by the time of my departure, though expected imminently." Bingley smiled mistily. "Miss Bennet is clearly greatly anticipating her sister's arrival from the country, for whenever her name arose – which occurred frequently – her eyes brightened and she smiled so much more. Harington was all for waiting it out – Miss Elizabeth's arrival. But Mrs Gardiner persuaded him to return to dine instead, and Darcy, I have been invited to attend after-dinner drinks, that I might make the acquaintance of Miss Bennet's uncle. Do you think it is a good sign?"

Darcy's thoughts immediately turned again to Elizabeth, but then he frowned as the realisation dawned that he had become somewhat irritated with the repetition of the name of Harington, especially in connection with the Bennets.

"This Harington – I take it you had not seen him since your establishment in Hertfordshire, else this coincidence might have come to light earlier?"

"Harington? Not seen… no, no. He is not really a close acquaintance. We happened across each other last night at the Pulteney. His brother – the elder, not the younger – there are three of them, you see." Darcy raised a brow. "Well, quite. Anyway, his brother and I were at Cambridge together, and I met Harington – Nicholas Harington, that is – through him."

Darcy leaned back in his chair as his friend talked, recalling his cousin's notion of the previous evening that he recalled the name of Harington for some reason. It seemed to trigger a vague memory with Darcy, yet he could not place it, certainly in recent recollection.

"Darcy – what do you think about my returning so soon? I do not wish to impose upon Miss Bennet, but I had little incentive to refuse such a kind invitation, and to be certain, though she did not meet my eye, she did exchange a smile with her aunt on my acceptance." Bingley stopped, frowning. "At least, I think perhaps she did. It may have been coincidence, or just anticipation of her sister's arrival."

Conscious of a niggling dissatisfaction, Darcy got to his feet and walked over to the window. He had to acknowledge that he envied Bingley his easy manner and his swift acceptance into the fold of the Bennets' family, well aware that there would have been a time not so long ago when he would have scorned the thought of spending an evening in Cheapside.

With a start, he became aware that Bingley had come to join him at the window, and for a moment, they both stared out into the garden, which had become so green during his stay in the country.

"Come to Gracechurch Street with me, Darcy."

"I cannot."

"Nonsense – you can do as you choose."

"Then I choose not."

Darcy turned away and walked back towards his desk, Bingley following in his wake. He felt weary, defeated and empty inside.

"Miss Bennet will welcome you, I am certain. She is all that is good and kind, and you said you had renewed your acquaintance with Miss Elizabeth in Kent. Thus, they are hardly strangers to you." Bingley smiled. "I know the Bennets are not your favourite people, but you can hardly escape the acquaintance now!"

*Elizabeth…* the temptation to see her almost overwhelmed him, but he would not go. He knew full well that the best thing he could do was keep out of her way, that firstly, she might not have to endure the awkwardness of his company and secondly, that she might not fear he would intervene during these tentative first steps of a renewal of acquaintance between her sister and his friend.

"Forgive me, Bingley, but I must insist. The Gardiners and I are not acquainted. It is one thing to arrive unannounced when accompanying someone who is intimate with the family, but with your own association with them but hours old, it would be in extremely poor taste on my part."

Bingley held up a hand.

"As you wish. But if I succeed in securing Miss Bennet's hand one day, you will be unable to escape an introduction to her relatives."

The misunderstanding suited Darcy's purpose, and he chose not to enlighten his friend. "Now that you are secure in the knowledge of Miss Bennet's whereabouts, can I prevail upon you to take up your usual rooms here? They are at your disposal, should you so wish."

"I would be delighted to accept your offer. Let me away to the Pulteney directly to give Overton the necessary instructions. As I am due to be out this evening, I shall aim to join you before the midday hour on the morrow if that is convenient?"

Darcy walked with Bingley towards the door.

"Perfectly so. I have no fixed plans."

"I shall see myself out. Pagett will no doubt be stood to attention with my hat before I am but two paces down the hallway, and besides, Mrs Wainwright will not thank me if I keep you from your meal – she insisted that I not prevent you from partaking!"

# Chapter Twenty Four

DARCY CLOSED THE DOOR behind Bingley and leaned his back against it. The ache he had been carrying in his breast since Sunday showed no sign of abating, and every mention of the name Bennet and its subsequent connotations caused his head to reel. He tried to force thoughts of Elizabeth away again, and with renewed determination he pushed himself from the door and walked back to his desk, sitting down heavily and throwing the now cold platter of eggs a look of utter distaste.

Yet before he could settle upon a distraction from his thoughts, there came another knock upon the door, and once again Darcy observed Mrs Wainwright entering the room, followed by the timid servant, who removed the untouched tray, but not before she had deposited another in front of him. Merely raising an admonishing brow at Darcy, the housekeeper shepherded the maid out of the room before standing aside to admit Mrs Annesley.

Darcy got to his feet as the lady walked briskly over to his desk and dropped a quick curtsey. "Good afternoon, Mr Darcy."

Darcy returned her greeting, indicating that she take a seat.

"I thank you, Sir, but I shall not take up your time. I am here merely at Miss Darcy's request."

Darcy concealed his surprise and bade her continue. Mrs Annesley looked a little awkward, but she met Darcy's gaze firmly. "Miss Darcy has advised – that is, Miss Darcy has suggested that we postpone our walk today – if you are in agreement, of course, Sir."

"Is she unwell?"

"Not at all, Sir. Miss Darcy is in perfect health."

"I see." Darcy, who did not see at all, frowned, mystified as to why his sister would wish to postpone her daily exercise, something he knew she took much enjoyment from. "Are you in agreement, Mrs Annesley? Does the rearrangement inconvenience you in any way?"

"Sir, I am at Miss Darcy's disposal. Whether her period of exercise falls at a particular time or not makes little difference to me. I am, after all, here for your sister's benefit, not my own."

Darcy welcomed the honesty of her response. Mrs Annesley had proven herself a valuable companion to his sister, and the improvement in Georgiana's spirits that he had noted upon his return from Rosings was surely testament to that good lady's influence.

"Sir? Miss Darcy also requested that you join her for afternoon tea in the small sitting room, at a quarter after 3 o'clock," and without awaiting a response, she performed a smart curtsey before excusing herself from the room.

Somewhat bewildered, Darcy sank back into his chair, staring at the now closed door to his study. Almost unaware of his actions, he lifted his cup and drank his tea, his brow furrowed in contemplation.

It was uncharacteristic, to say the least, to receive a summons from his sister, however politely worded the invitation – and somewhat amusing. He supposed it to be a sign of her growing up. His gaze fell upon the mound of paperwork that still littered his desk, and he studied it for a moment, then glanced over at the clock. He had ample time to clear this backlog if he applied himself before his tea with Georgiana. He poured himself a fresh drink and lifted the lid on the platter that accompanied it to reveal a selection of cold meats, cheese, fruit and a basket of neatly cut bread. He looked again at the pile of post. Then, shrugging his shoulders, he pushed the paperwork aside and pulling the tray closer he turned his attention to selecting some bread and cheese.

The bells of the church of St Clements were tolling the hour of three by the time Elizabeth was finally ensconced in the room she always shared with Jane whenever they had the good fortune to be in Gracechurch Street together.

With a sigh of contentment, she looked about the room. The maid had finished unpacking her belongings, but Elizabeth had asked her to leave the soiled dress and coat in her care for the time being for she wished to consult her aunt upon the best remedy for them.

Then, having finished arranging her personal belongings to her satisfaction, she picked up her nightgown and deposited it upon her pillow before walking over to the window and gazing down into the busy street below.

Elizabeth smiled to herself as she recalled her welcome from her aunt and sister. It felt good to be amongst them again, and to heed all the potential distractions of Town. She had, however, been completely unprepared for the news that Jane and her aunt had imparted as soon as they were settled down to a cup of tea.

At first, she had felt all the shock of Mr Bingley's visit. Her immediate thought had been that Mr Darcy had had a hand in it, but as Jane related the facts she realised she gave him credit where none was due. The sense of disappointment that this engendered was a surprise to her, but she had forcibly put it aside as she attempted to focus her attention on her aunt and her sister's description of their morning callers. She did wonder, though, how Mr Darcy might react when he discovered that, despite the machinations of Miss Bingley and himself, his friend had managed to seek Jane out.

A slight disturbance on the landing roused her from her thoughts, and at the sound of the chamber door opening, Elizabeth glanced over her shoulder, greeting her sister with a smile as she came in.

"There you are! Aunt is preparing some fresh tea and bade me fetch you. Are you ready to come down?"

Elizabeth cast a final fleeting glance out of the window before walking over to join her sister. "Oh it is so good to be back here and to be restored to your company." She reached out and took Jane's hands, giving them a squeeze. "I have missed you dreadfully, and to arrive and find you in much improved spirits... Come, tell me more – you clearly felt unable to talk freely in front of our aunt."

"Oh, Lizzy, you will think me so very bad," Jane blushed and sank down to sit upon the bed, her gaze cast towards the floor.

"Impossible!" Elizabeth laughed, but then she studied her sister more closely and detecting the change in her demeanour hurried to sit at her side. "Jane, what is it?"

"I am so thankful for Nicholas's presence. All I could think of was how much I wanted to look at Mr Bingley. I could hardly believe that he was there. I wanted to stare at him, so many months has it been since I saw his face." Jane stopped, and it did not take more than a fleeting glance for Elizabeth to detect that her eyes were quite moist.

"Dear Jane. Your feelings are perfectly natural, and there is nothing wrong with them."

"But I wish to not raise my hopes. He called merely out of courtesy; yet when our eyes first met, when he first entered the room..." Jane raised her anxious gaze to meet her sister's. "I am certain I did not mistake the look upon his face. At least, whatever I saw today is entirely what I saw in Hertfordshire and... oh Lizzy, I so do not want to be led wrong again. How can I guard my heart against him, when it is even now in his possession?"

Elizabeth patted her sister's arm and stood up. "It might be wise to give Mr Bingley the benefit of the doubt over his awareness of your presence in Town – after all, we have no reason to suspect him of duplicity."

She walked over to the mirror on the dresser, feeling a little uncomfortable, being certain of Mr Bingley's innocence, and she made a pretence of poking at her hair, before espying a stray pin and using it to fasten a loose curl into place before turning back to face her sister. "And indeed, he has agreed to return this evening to meet Uncle Gardiner, has he not?"

Jane nodded, smiling wistfully. "Nicholas has given me much cheer these past seven days. It is impossible to indulge in melancholy when he is near. And oh, dear Lizzy," Jane broke off and laughed, "he was so comical this morning, quite put out to discern that you were not expected until the afternoon. He knew not, of course, that uncle's carriage had been delayed from setting out for Kent until later than planned. He insisted that he would not remove himself until you had arrived! Indeed, Mr Bingley seemed most amused, though I am sure he misunderstood. All the signs might well lead him to think Nicholas enamoured of you!"

"And why, pray, should that amuse you so? Am I so unpalatable a choice?" Elizabeth pretended indignation, but could not keep her face straight and laughed.

"Dear Lizzy, you are more than palatable. Indeed, I can still recall Mama's disappointment when he last visited Longbourn, so certain was she that she could find a wife for him between either you or I!"

Elizabeth laughed again. "Poor Nicholas! He has never braved the wilds of Hertfordshire since. And poor Mama – how I have thwarted her matrimonial hopes." She faltered, fully cognisant of the one disappointment she would ever have to conceal from her mother. "But Nicholas is just too… agreeable. And I am not, and you know I could never marry a man who is!"

"Lizzy!"

"But continue, you were telling of Nicholas' tantrum!"

"Aunt Gardiner refused to let him sit and wait and eventually shooed him out the door like a disgruntled bantam. He had determined to return this afternoon, but Aunt has banished him from the house until this evening, claiming that you would be in need of rest after your journey, not torment, and that it is only fair I should have first claim upon your time today."

"Well, I cannot fault her for that." Elizabeth pulled open the drawer beneath the mirror, seeking another hairpin. "Jane, would you please pass me my comb – it is on the bedside table."

Jane walked over to Elizabeth's side of the bed and picked up the comb. "What is this?"

Elizabeth turned to glance at Jane who held the book she had been attempting to read during her journey from Kent.

"Oh, nothing. It is but a marker for my page."

Walking over to the dresser, Jane handed her sister the comb before opening the book to where the marker protruded.

"Dear Lizzy! How typical of you!"

"It is a morsel I retrieved from the ground when I stretched my legs at Bromley. Why should it amuse you so?"

Jane threw her sister a fond look and replaced the neatly woven stick into the pages before closing the book once more and placing it on a nearby table.

"It is not its purpose that amuses me. It is what is says about you. No fine tooled leather or elegant embroidery will suffice as a marker when nature can provide her own alternative."

Elizabeth gave her hair one final pat and turned around.

"Aye, well – show me a man that can fashion a marker from wild grass, and I shall prefer him every day to one who can handle a needle with finesse!"

"*Lizzy!*"

The girls met each other's eye and the sheer contentment of being together again caused them to slide into a bout of giggles. Then, composing themselves as best they could, they linked arms and left the room to join their aunt downstairs.

At the appointed time, Darcy found himself outside the door to his sister's sitting room, and at her bidding he let himself in. Georgiana stood near her writing table perusing a letter which she put aside before coming to greet him.

"Good afternoon, Georgiana,"

"Good afternoon, Brother. I apologise if my request for your company disrupts your business."

Darcy placed a kiss upon her forehead before steering her over to the chairs by the hearth, noting the strategically placed tray of tea, cakes and neatly sliced bread and butter on a small circular table.

"It is no disturbance, I can assure you. There is little to interest me upon my desk." Darcy took the chair across from his sister as she seated herself and studied her thoughtfully for a moment. The girl opposite him differed vastly from the one who had greeted him so enthusiastically on his return from the Pulteney the day before. Though she met his gaze quite firmly, she was pale and her manner quite strained.

He had hoped for a full return of her customary spirits, yet today she seemed reminiscent of the saddened, changed Georgiana of recent months.

"Are you well, Georgie? You seem somewhat subdued."

"I am perfectly well, Brother." Georgiana paused and swallowed visibly. Then she shook her hair back over her shoulder and sat up straight in her chair before fixing Darcy with her eye. For a moment, he felt a shiver of apprehension, yet before he could speak she said, "I – I wish to ask you what took place in Kent."

Darcy blinked once, and then shook his head as if to deny her words, but before he could react further she added, "I want you – I would very much like for you to tell me – about Miss Elizabeth Bennet."

# Chapter Twenty Five

THE SILENCE THAT FOLLOWED Georgiana's request lengthened as Darcy stared back at her. His foremost thought, to utter a denial, he quickly negated. The anxiety he could detect upon his sister's countenance at her own boldness was belied by the set of her shoulders and the gleam in her eye. He felt instinctively that she was confident he could not deny knowledge of Elizabeth. But what else might she be privy to?

Darcy moved restlessly in his chair before clearing his throat. "How – who – how came you…"

"How came I to be familiar with that name?" Georgiana smiled slightly and shook her head at him. "How many women not yet of my acquaintance do you think you have ever written of to me?"

Darcy blinked, his mind devoid of an answer, and as his gaze met his sister's once more, she nodded.

"Precisely. It is rare enough that you refer at all to your social interactions in our correspondence, and never do you allude to the new female acquaintances you make. All I have ever had from you is a vague *'the female company'* or *'the ladies present'*, and even, if I recall correctly on one occasion, *'there were few who were not men'*." Georgiana let out a small huff of indignation. "So you see, Fitz, that having mentioned this particular lady's name, as you did once in a letter from Hertfordshire, coupled with this intelligence of her in Kent…"

The reinforcement of her earlier words sent a tremor of foreboding through Darcy, and he stood up abruptly, running a hand through his hair and then clasping his hands together to still his fingers. He stared at Georgiana, who had fallen silent the moment he had risen to his feet. She stared back at him, a combination of determination and nervousness on her countenance. Then, he expelled a frustrated breath.

"I shall throttle your cousin."

"Anne?"

"Richard."

"What has Richard to do with this?"

"Then it was not he who…?"

"Who what?"

Darcy's gaze dropped to the floor. "Nothing. There is nothing."

"Truly, Brother?"

"Absolutely."

"Then what Anne alludes to in her letter is…"

Darcy's head lifted at these words. "Anne has written to you?"

Georgiana gestured towards the writing table in the corner. "Yes, I received word from her this morning – and she most pointedly asked me to advise you that her talent with the pen is a little more superior than she is given credit for." She frowned. "I could not comprehend her meaning – to what does she refer?"

Darcy shook his head before sinking back onto his chair again.

"Fitz?"

He eyed Georgiana carefully for a moment, then sighed. "A comment her mother made about Anne's health being an impediment – that it hampered her ability to write. Clearly, Aunt Catherine underestimated her." Darcy leaned back into his chair, muttering under his breath, "As did I."

What had Anne observed, in her quiet watchfulness? What had she heard or surmised? And more to the point, what had thus been imparted to his sister? Desperate to comprehend what might yet be salvaged of the matter, Darcy said tentatively, "I did not know you were in communication with Cousin Anne?"

Georgiana shrugged her shoulders. "I am not – not regularly – and have never received a letter from her of such length or intrigue."

His sense of unease increased upon hearing these words, and Darcy moved restlessly in his seat.

"You do not ask what she has written."

He tugged at his neck cloth, which seemed to be tightening its grip upon his throat, attempting to feign a nonchalance that was belied by the racing of his heart.

"I do not see that she has much to relate. It is quite true that Miss Elizabeth Bennet, whose acquaintance – as you point out – I first made in Hertfordshire, stayed in Hunsford at the same time that Richard and I made our visit with Aunt Catherine. Yet I fail to recall ever seeing Anne in direct conversation with the lady."

Georgiana all but rolled her eyes at him. "She may say little, but she has both eyes and ears, Brother, which she clearly uses to much effect. From her letter, you are all but players on the stage to Anne."

Darcy was silent. This unexpected source – how could he have given no thought to what Anne might have supposed? Reluctantly, he met his sister's determined gaze. "Then please enlighten me. What is it that Anne has seen or heard regarding Miss Bennet that persuades you to ask such a question?"

Georgiana studied him for a moment. "She wrote that I should observe your disposition carefully. What she does not understand is that I had been doing thus these many months."

"These many months?" Darcy stared at his sister in confusion.

Georgiana pushed herself out of her chair and walked over to the writing table to retrieve the letter before turning to face him.

"Yes, Brother. Since your return from Hertfordshire. And I have had much time to think on it – so much so that my concern for you has overridden my reproach of myself. And, sad though the distraction is that has pulled me from my self-absorption, I have welcomed the release it has brought – even though at your cost."

Darcy paled as his sister walked back towards him, the letter in her hand. "*My* cost? What is your meaning?"

"Oh, Fitz!" Georgiana stopped beside his chair. "Can you not tell? I have become distracted by my worry for *you*. We have been brother and sister these 16 years – yet rarely have I seen you thus."

Grappling with the sudden realisation that his attempts to conceal his struggles over his attraction to Elizabeth had been all too apparent, even if the cause was not, Darcy clasped his hands together. "There is naught amiss with me. I am quite well."

Georgiana let out a huff of breath, turning on her heel to reclaim her seat, where she perched herself on its edge before fixing her brother with a stern look.

"Do you think me a simpleton? I have watched you, Fitz. If I had concerns before, it is nothing to this. You are pale and distracted; you ate nothing at dinner last night and your eyes… there is pain in your countenance and despondency in your air. I am no longer a child – do not treat me as such. Tell me what ails you, for if you do not, I shall have to resort to desperate measures."

Feeling his insides lurch in trepidation, Darcy sat up rapidly in his seat. "And what might those be?"

"I shall consult Richard. I know he is privy to more than you own for I did not miss your reaction, Brother. Why should you wish to throttle him? What might he have told me that is to do with Miss Bennet and Kent that you will not share?"

A rising sense of panic gripped Darcy. "Nothing. I had no recollection of mentioning the lady by name to you, so could only assume Richard had advised you of our encountering her."

Georgiana narrowed her eyes, as if contemplating the validity of his response. Glad of the brief respite from her verbal onslaught, Darcy studied her carefully for a moment, then shook his head. "There is something different about you – you are altered."

"Yes, Brother, I am. I have been a fool, but the experience at Ramsgate has done me much good; yet I would have wallowed longer in self-absorption had I not taken on board some of your regret."

Darcy frowned. "How so?"

"Do you recall what you said to me after Ramsgate? How you regretted that you had not been more observant of my demeanour, more attentive to me, paid me more notice? That had you been more discerning, perhaps..." Georgiana paused. "Well, I have been doing for you, Brother, what you wished for me."

Darcy stared back at his sister, unable to respond. It was as if she bloomed before his very eyes, and he was quite transfixed.

"When you returned to Town from Hertfordshire I immediately detected a change in you. You were withdrawn most of the time, uncommunicative. At first, I blamed myself – I pondered that perhaps you were dissatisfied with me, that you had reflected upon your easy forgiveness of my stupidity; yet your manner towards me was as loving as ever. I watched you carefully over the following weeks – I thought you might well have determined my purpose, for occasionally I would be caught out in my study of you – and I continued to observe your distraction and low spirits, despite your attempts at concealment."

Darcy slowly shook his head from side to side as if he would deny her claim but remained powerless to do anything but listen.

"… and now you return from your travels, and I am devastated by the alteration, for you are clearly worse than before."

As his sister's revelations unfolded, Darcy tried to marshal his thoughts. Prevarication might well have worked thus far, but clearly it only brought a temporary respite. Notwithstanding the fact that disguise sat uneasily upon him, he had had sufficient time to reflect over the past four and twenty hours and realised that his sister may make the acquaintance of at least one Miss Bennet in the none too distant future. Would it not avert the potential for awkwardness in the future if he revealed a part of what had come to pass? If a day should come when Georgiana might encounter Elizabeth…

As this thought crossed his mind afresh – a notion that he had once entertained such hopes for – he could contain his agitation no longer and, getting to his feet, he walked over to the window and stared out over the walled rear garden. Then, turning on his heel, he faced his sister, who watched him intently from across the room.

Swallowing hard on the rising emotion that gripped his throat, he found himself unable to speak at all, and turning his back once more, he leaned his head against the windowpane. Conscious that Georgiana had moved, Darcy became aware of her presence at his side, and he put his arm about her shoulders, hugging her to him, comforted by her own arm slipping around his waist and giving a reciprocal squeeze.

"You have been a father-figure to me these many years, but you are not Papa. You are my brother – and I can be here for you just as you were for me." Releasing her hold upon him, Georgiana stepped out of his embrace and peered up into his face. "And this you will have to accept."

Darcy turned to face her, noting the concerned eyes in a determined face. "I begin to see our cousin in you, Georgiana."

"Anne?"

He smiled ruefully, and shook his head. "Richard."

Reaching out, Georgiana took his hands in hers, squeezing them tightly. "Tell me about it, Fitz – tell me what has affected this change in you. Let me share in what ails you, I beg of you – if not for yourself, then do it for me, that I might be put out of my misery."

Darcy let out a low, disbelieving laugh. "So it would be more selfish of me to abstain from sharing my feelings – I should consider your anguish over mine?" He observed her pleading expression, then sighed wearily. "I cannot deny you, Georgiana. So – enlighten me, my dear.

What does Anne claim to have discerned? Until I comprehend this, I am uncertain what it is you would have me account for."

"Anne writes that this visit would stay in your memory – that you would not soon forget it." She hesitated and bit her lip. "She advised me that a lady who had been making some stay in the neighbourhood had frequently been in company with both yourself and Richard and that at the first opportunity, I should ask you about her. She gave the lady's name as Miss Elizabeth Bennet, and she implied..." Georgiana paused and swallowed, her manner visibly weakening as she dropped her gaze. "She believes, it would seem, from what she has observed, that you – that you are…"

Conscious of the tightening in his chest, Darcy leaned back against the wall. "That I admire the lady?"

Georgiana's head shot up and her eyes widened as they met her brother's uneasy gaze.

"Yes! Precisely! Oh, Fitz – it is *true*?"

Darcy ran a hand through his hair and studied his sister's expectant face thoughtfully. He could see no escape. It was far preferable that he gave an abbreviated version of events to his sister than allowed his cousin full rein. Uncomfortable enough with the need to dissemble, how could he not learn from the past? It was true that he had regretted not being more observant of his sister that he might have saved her some anguish, and he could not deceive Georgiana in this for disguise would benefit neither of them.

Darcy turned to stare out of the window again, conscious of his sister's silent vigil at his side.

"I made the acquaintance of the lady when residing with Bingley, as you know. By chance our paths crossed once more in Kent." Darcy paused as the memory of that first encounter at Rosings rushed through his mind. Nothing could have prepared him for how overwhelmed he had felt to lay eyes upon Elizabeth again.

Georgiana laid a hand upon his arm, and Darcy turned to face her.

"Aunt Catherine had advised me by letter before our visit took place that her parson had found himself a wife in Hertfordshire. She followed the announcement with the knowledge that the new Mrs Collins was attended by a Miss Elizabeth Bennet…." He paused. "I had to see her, and once I did I knew my mind had played no tricks upon me. I did – I do – like her… very much."

Tentatively, Georgiana took his hand. "But I do not understand. Why would you be so disturbed over finally finding someone whom you can so admire?"

"I am afraid it is perfectly simple." Darcy looked down at their clasped hands. "Whilst I think very highly of the lady, she does not return the sentiment; in fact, quite the contrary."

# Chapter Twenty Six

GEORGIANA STARED AT HIM in disbelief.

"But why would Miss Bennet not admire you? And how is it that you are so certain of her feelings? I cannot comprehend how *anyone* could not like you."

"No – no, I know you cannot, dearest." Darcy patted her hand gently. "But trust me that her reasons are perfectly sound. Some of her impressions of me were misguided, but I cannot deny that all were so. There can be no doubt of Miss Bennet's opinion of me, for she told me of it herself. Thus if I seem a little low in spirits..."

Georgiana shook her head. "I cannot comprehend... how could she hope to find a better man than you?"

Darcy gave a short, bitter laugh. "How indeed! With great ease, I suspect – certainly in Miss Bennet's eyes."

"But then she cannot see you as I do – as you really are."

Conscious of his own recent failings where the portrayal of his character was concerned, Darcy refrained from sharing with his sister precisely how he felt about the man he really was.

"Do not be distressed, Georgiana. Did you not say that I would aid you better by revealing my troubles than concealing them?"

Though she attempted a smile, he could see that tears were rising, and Georgiana threw her arms about her brother and hugged him tightly. Keeping a firm grip on a sudden wave of emotion that threatened to overwhelm him, Darcy stroked his sister's hair gently whilst she sniffled into his chest.

"You must not upset yourself, Georgie. I will be well; *we* will be well."

They remained thus for some minutes; then, conscious that she spoke, Darcy lowered his head to catch her words.

"What does Richard know of this?"

He grunted. "Sufficient. His interrogation methods are not dissimilar to your own."

Georgiana gave a watery giggle, and Darcy released her, the tightness in his throat easing as she fished in her pocket for a handkerchief to wipe her cheeks dry. A sudden knock caused them both to turn about, and Darcy was unsurprised to see Fitzwilliam's head appear around the door.

"There is no need to look so morose, the pair of you. I have been away but a few hours."

Darcy patted Georgiana reassuringly on the shoulder as she stowed her handkerchief away, and as the Colonel strolled into the room, he walked over to join him before the fireplace.

"I trust your meeting went well?"

There was no immediate response to this enquiry, as the Colonel's gaze had fallen upon the tea tray containing the platter of food, and Darcy smiled faintly at Georgiana as she retook her seat.

Conscious that he had lost his own chair to his cousin, who now paid court to a slice of cake, Darcy seated himself on the arm of his sister's chair.

"You were a long time, Richard," Georgiana remarked. "You are not about to leave us for an extended period?"

The Colonel shook his head. "Temporarily, it would seem, but not for any lengthy duration, as I understand it." He shoved the last morsel of cake into his mouth, munching with apparent contentment as his gaze moved from one cousin to the other. "So – have I missed anything of interest?"

Darcy exchanged a quick glance with Georgiana. "No – no, you have not," but upon observing his cousin's raised brow added, "We were discussing our visit with Aunt Catherine."

The Colonel's eyes narrowed at this, and once again he looked from Darcy to Georgiana, pausing to study her face more thoroughly before returning his gaze to her brother. "Ah. I see." He paused. "At least, I think I do."

Conscious that both his cousin and his sister were now observing him, one thoughtfully, the other with compassion, Darcy pushed himself off the arm of the chair and walked back over to the window again, yet barely had he taken up his position before his sister spoke.

"I have received a letter from Anne, Cousin."

Darcy turned towards Georgiana in alarm, but the slight shake of her head in his direction assured him that she had no intention of revisiting their earlier conversation. Conscious as he was that Fitzwilliam possessed the knowledge Darcy most wished to conceal, he looked quickly in his cousin's direction, but typically that gentleman had detected a different line of enquiry.

"Good Lord! Wonders never cease! Did her companion pen it for her?"

"Certainly not! She had much to say, Richard – indeed, she commented on your robust appetite with great relish!"

The Colonel looked somewhat discomfited at this observation, and Darcy could not help but smile at his cousin's countenance. "I trust Darcy did not go unscathed in this letter?" Fitzwilliam let out a snort of derision, "Though Anne would hardly comment upon your brother's eating habits, for there would be nothing to report."

Georgiana shook her head. "I can assure you, Richard, that Anne had much to say about you. She particularly drew my notice to your love of adding liberal amounts of liquor to your after-dinner coffee!"

Darcy laughed. "It is a fair point, Fitzwilliam. You will have to exercise more restraint in future!"

The Colonel's mouth opened and closed once, then twice, before he managed a blustering, "Well. What is Anne about, making sport of her mother's guests?"

Darcy smiled, but Georgiana remained serious. "Anne is alone for much of the time. In company, a whole new world is revealed to her."

"But she has her companion," interjected Darcy.

"Ah, but Brother, Mrs Jenkinson is not Mrs Annesley, who is a woman of infinite kindness, good sense and intelligence."

"Anne does not find these qualities in her own companion?"

"She says Mrs Jenkinson believes there is no difference between a sonata and an aria, that Berlin is in Ireland and green tea is, without question, the restorative of all ailments. What is your opinion of her sense and education?"

Darcy exchanged shocked glances with his cousin. "But how could our aunt engage such a woman?"

Georgiana shrugged. "For her meekness? For her inability to either speak her mind, or argue a point?"

The Colonel smiled at his cousin. "Since when did you become so wise, old thing?"

"I am not. I merely have a good memory and am thus repeating what Anne herself noted in her letter."

Darcy sighed heavily. "Anne has not lived a full life. We should have done more for her, invited her to stay with us. I feared raising Aunt Catherine's expectations by paying attention in that quarter, but I believe we have failed our cousin somewhat."

"Come, Darce. Do not take it upon your own shoulders so. We are all equally culpable. Perhaps Georgiana will now be able to enter into a regular correspondence with her – that will be a beginning."

Georgiana nodded enthusiastically at this suggestion, and Darcy suppressed an urge to groan. The last thing he desired was for his sister and his apparently observant cousin to begin discussing his *behaviour*. Yet, before he could mull too heavily upon this possibility, he realised that the Colonel addressed him.

"What news of Bingley?"

Observing Georgiana's quick frown, Darcy was unable to respond before she said quickly, "Mr Bingley? What of him?"

Throwing his cousin a warning look, Darcy turned to his sister. "Bingley paid a visit after you retired last night. Your cousin and I were trying to help him resolve a small matter."

"But did he not call here this morning as well? Mrs Annesley said that she saw him in the hallway."

The Colonel let out a snort of laughter. "Good Lord, the man clearly enjoys your company, Darcy. If he is here so often, why does he not move in permanently, pray?"

Darcy walked slowly back across the room; it would not do for his cousin to let slip any mention of Miss Jane Bennet at this juncture, and he hoped Fitzwilliam understood that.

"Bingley will join us on the morrow."

"So soon?" The Colonel fixed his eye on Darcy. "And the matter that caused your friend some concern – did he manage to resolve it to his satisfaction?"

"Indeed."

"Ah. I see. Well, Darce – can you spare me a half hour or so in your study? I have some business I would discuss with you prior to my departure for the south coast."

Conscious that every subject they were presently touching upon seemed fraught with possibilities, none of which he wished to favour, and thus feeling the distraction would be most welcome, Darcy turned to look at his sister.

"Will that be amenable to you, Georgie? We have not yet spent much time together since my return."

"Do not concern yourself, Fitz." She smiled up at him, then got to her feet and walked towards the door. "Besides, I promised Mrs Annesley that I would practice my music once our tea was over…" her voice faltered for a moment, and she cast a guilty glance towards the neglected tray. "Will you call for me before dinner?"

Darcy walked over to join her and held the door open, conscious that his cousin had hauled himself out of his chair to select a slice of buttered bread from the platter.

"With pleasure, my dear. Come, Fitzwilliam. Let us repair downstairs where you can set out this business of yours more readily, without the distraction of food."

Maisie Cooper enjoyed her work as a serving girl at Hunsford Parsonage. To be certain, Cook could sometimes be a little sharp, if Maisie did not complete her tasks with due haste, and she found the Master somewhat intimidating – something to do with his wordiness (Maisie was not very good with words) – but the Mistress was fair, and the work varied for, with so few servants in the house, it was understood Maisie would turn her hand to whatever was asked of her.

Thus it was that today, following the departure of the parsonage's recent guest, Maisie had been instructed to strip the bed and bring the linen to the wash house, then clean out the chamber fireplace and, finally, sweep the floor, and she knew that her bowl of broth would not be forthcoming until she had completed her duties.

Yet she was at present unaware of the passage of time, or the cooling dish awaiting her in the kitchen, for she faced a dilemma. Perhaps a person of keener intelligence might not have seen the matter as such a predicament, but Maisie, though a sweet girl, was quite devoid of anything approaching common sense. Thus it was that the occurrence of anything untoward would cause her no end of worry – and something unexpected had indeed arisen.

Setting to with a purpose, she had stripped the sheets from the bed, humming softly to herself and anticipating her meal with relish, when something had caught her eye, and she had watched in fascination as a folded piece of parchment fell from beneath the pillow she had just picked up, twirling gracefully to the ground near her feet.

Picking it up warily, she had been staring at the parchment in her hands for several minutes. Clearly, she held a letter, and most assuredly it belonged to that nice Miss Bennet – not that she could decipher the direction, for Maisie had never learned to read – but who else could have placed it between these pillows? And did that not signify that it held some importance? But the lady had long departed for Town – what should she do with her find?

The faint slam of a door down below roused her from her thoughts, and she glanced about the room hurriedly before biting her lip. She had not even completed one of the tasks she had been assigned, yet she was certain that she should not delay handing the letter over. After all, no one knew better than Maisie – or indeed the cook – just how forgetful she could be. Cook! Of course! She would ask her for guidance, and perhaps her having acted so promptly would lessen the scolding over her being so far from completing her duties.

With a decision made, Maisie opened the chamber door and stepped outside. Yet she had gone but two paces when she espied someone at the opposite end of the landing, and she smiled with relief. Surely this was the perfect solution, for if she were to hand the letter over to another, it would no longer be her concern, and she, Maisie, could return to her duties, completing them before Cook was any the wiser.

Unaccustomed as she was to drawing attention to herself, Maisie took a deep breath before stepping forward and executing a somewhat awkward curtsey. Then, her eyes still lowered respectfully to the floor, she thrust the piece of parchment unceremoniously under the nose of her saviour – the Reverend William Collins.

# Chapter Twenty Seven

AS SOME POORLY FOLDED pieces of paper were thrust unceremoniously under his nose, William Collins lowered the prayer book that held his attention. Instinctively, he raised his free hand to take the offering, but barely had the tips of his fingers brushed against it when another hand reached over his shoulder.

"Pray allow me, my dear," said Charlotte, moving past her husband to take the letter, adding "Thank you, Maisie," before giving the girl a nod of dismissal.

As Maisie turned and fled back whence she had come, Charlotte glanced quickly at what she held, unsurprised to see her friend's name, but struck immediately that something was amiss. Turning to face her husband, who still held aloft his book, she met his bemused expression with a calm that belied her curiosity.

"I shall forward this on to Lizzy, my dear." She indicated the sheets she held in her hand. "She must have overlooked it during her packing."

"Of course, of course," mumbled Mr Collins and, with a formal bow, he continued along the landing towards his chamber, his nose buried once more in his prayer book.

Charlotte's thoughtful gaze followed her husband's progress until the door closed behind him, the purpose of her own presence on the landing long forgotten, before turning to retrace her steps. She glanced quickly at the letter once more, and her astonishment at what she perceived brought her to a halt at the top of the stairs, for it bore neither direction nor postmark and thus could only have been delivered in person. Further, the hand, though unrecognisable, was most decidedly masculine in form, yet Elizabeth's only acquaintance in the neighbourhood consisted of the occupants of this very parsonage and the residents of Rosings Park.

Hurriedly, Charlotte made her way down the stairs and along the narrow hallway to her private parlour. Dropping the letter onto her desk under the window, she methodically pulled together the implements required for writing and, having ensured that the door to the room was secured, she hastened to light a small candle before returning with it to the desk.

Despite her curiosity over its sender – though in truth there could surely only be two possible suspects – and thus its purpose, Charlotte determined to secure the letter as soon as possible. She reached for the ill-folded and rather crumpled pages, intent upon straightening them well enough to affix the seal, but a shaft of sunlight suddenly fell across the desk, and before she could close her mind to it, she saw the final words just visible along the bottom edge of the page: *God bless you, Fitzwilliam Darcy.*

Having escorted Georgiana to the music room at the back of the house, the gentlemen crossed the hall to the study, where Darcy sank into his chair behind the large, leather-topped desk, waving his cousin into the seat opposite.

"So what is this peculiar business, Fitzwilliam? It necessitated a summons by *Express* only last evening, yet now you are not to depart until the morrow."

The Colonel stretched his legs out in front of him. "Another *Express* arrived whilst I was at Whitehall, and thus my role has become investigative rather than preventative."

Darcy frowned. "That sounds rather ominous."

The Colonel shook his head. "Not so much. There was some trouble brewing within a regiment under the command of a colleague. Today's message confirmed the rabble-rouser has absconded; yet my commanding officer insists that I pay a visit to the encampment. I am not sure what I can do in the circumstances, but far be it from me to disregard an order."

"And when do you hope to return?"

"I anticipate being absent from Town no more than four and twenty hours." The Colonel sat forward in his chair. "This was not the business that requires a moment of your time."

Darcy eyed his cousin warily. "Would you care to enlighten me?"

"There are two matters, to be precise, the first of which relates to your conversation with Georgiana."

Darcy sighed. For how much longer would he feel obligated to talk about such things? Tapping his fingers on the desk, he held his cousin's gaze for a moment. "What is it you would know?"

"All I ask is what you have revealed, lest I step amiss with her. Less than you have shared with me, I suspect, though I must own that the atmosphere was a trifle thick upstairs."

"I told her as much as I felt I could."

"I did not expect you to tell her aught." The Colonel studied his cousin for a moment. "Though your spirits remain somewhat depressed, I am at a loss to discern how she could identify the cause."

Pushing himself out of his chair, Darcy walked over to the full-length windows that led out into the walled garden. The view was reminiscent of that from Georgiana's small sitting room on the first floor, and the emotions rising in his chest were strikingly similar also, evoking a strong desire to escape into the garden's seclusion.

"Darce?"

He turned back to face his cousin. "Georgiana has harboured some concerns for me since my sojourn in Hertfordshire, fearing I was – not myself. Having remarked a change in my demeanour upon my return from Kent, followed by..." Darcy clasped his hands together to still the agitation of his fingers. "Followed by the letter from Anne this morning-" Darcy threw Fitzwilliam a helpless look.

"Hmph. So I was not the only one she chose to abuse in her letter. Yet I suspect she had more telling observations about you than your digestive habits?"

Darcy dropped his hands to his sides and turned back to stare out into the garden.

"Yes – yes, she had, and thus I have admitted to admiring Miss Elizabeth Bennet, and that my sentiments are far from returned, but nothing more. I could not – I would not tell Georgiana of my rejection. She would break her heart over the – over my-" He sighed heavily. "I cannot allow that."

The Colonel walked over to stand beside him. "I am of a mind to agree. Yet-"

"Does there have to be a *yet*?"

The Colonel smirked. "I fear so. But come now, *think* man. You have put things to rights with Bingley – at least as far as you are able without unduly interfering once more. It is down to him to act, if he is to secure Miss Bennet. You have cleared your name regarding Wickham's infamy. You know that the lady is due in Town today, is she not?"

Involuntarily, Darcy's eyes flew to the clock on the mantel. At this late hour of the afternoon, Elizabeth would most certainly be in Town – then he forced the thought aside and returned his gaze to his cousin once more.

"Of all these things I am aware, Fitzwilliam, but I will not indulge in false hope. Even if her ill feeling towards me has eased somewhat, there remains too wide a chasm between her original abhorrence and any likelihood that she could... that she would ever consider accepting my attentions."

A surge of emptiness swept through him as he spoke these words aloud, and Darcy turned back to the windows and released the catch, pushing them wide and stepping outside into the cooling afternoon. He drew in a deep lungful of air, relishing in its freshness before breathing out slowly.

"But, Darcy, surely you can-"

"No, Fitzwilliam, I can*not*." He turned to face his cousin where he stood framed in the open doorway. "Please do not attempt to persuade me otherwise. Besides, as I have previously told you, there is the further impediment of the lady harbouring feelings for another."

The Colonel shook his head. "I disagree. Taken in she may have been, but I believe the lady to have too much good sense, once apprised of Wickham's true character, to remain enamoured of the man. Even Georgiana, who believed herself fully in love with the scoundrel, has admitted to me that she is cured of her affection."

Darcy stared at the Colonel.

"You may well be surprised, Cousin, but it is true. Once his real intent came out, it did not take Georgiana long to admit an infatuation for what it was. Her spirits have been badly affected, I grant you, but she has lately owned to me that it was down to self-reproach for her own gullibility, coupled with despair over having caused you such concern."

For a moment, Darcy was silent as he absorbed these words, acknowledging both the relief they brought him on his sister's behalf, and their veracity. Her demeanour and indeed her own words that very afternoon had proved her to be more than adequately recovered.

"Thus, what is there to lose in seeking out a certain lady?"

With a frustrated gesture, Darcy threw his cousin a warning look, to which the Colonel responded merely with a shrug of his shoulders. "I am at a loss to understand why you will not attempt a continuation of the acquaintance."

"Yet I am not. You do not fully comprehend the depth of Miss Bennet's antipathy for me. Even should she recover from her disappointment over Wickham, there is no reason for her to think sufficiently well of me to – she – I –" Darcy expelled a deep breath as he flexed both hands restlessly. "Her poor opinion of me was well-ingrained long before Wickham became part of the local populace."

The Colonel studied him, eyes narrowed, for a moment. "And so we come to it. There is more to this than just Wickham and Bingley."

Turning on his heel, Darcy strode down the steps and set off along the path that ran the length of the garden, unheeding of the effects of the spring planting that had reached its full potential, or the pleasing signs that summer fast approached.

"So Miss Elizabeth Bennet's ill opinion precedes Wickham's attempts to blacken your character." His cousin's voice followed him down the path, as did his footsteps, his boots crunching loudly on the gravel.

Refusing to heed him, Darcy's eyes scoured the edges of the path as he walked. Then he shook his head at his own stupidity; his garden was far too well tended to offer up what he sought.

"Would you care to enlighten me, or do I make my own assumptions? Be warned. In case you have forgotten, I am not infallible in my deductions." Garnering no response, the Colonel continued. "She had a poor opinion of you formed in relation to *what*, Darcy? What did you do?"

Darcy pointedly ignored his cousin's question, continuing his rapid walk towards the rear of the garden, yet his action did not deter his pursuer, who kept pace with him, continuing his ruminations aloud.

"I say, Darce, would it perchance have anything to do with what Miss Bennet spoke of at Rosings – you recall, I am sure, that evening at the pianoforte?"

Coming to a halt as he reached the terrace near the far wall, Darcy looked about in vain, he knew not what for, but his cousin was relentless in his pursuit, and stepped onto a neighbouring flagstone.

"She referred to the occasion of your first meeting, did she not?"

Swinging on his heel to face his cousin, Darcy bit out: "Be done, Fitzwilliam."

"Oh no, this is far from done. I am close to the source of the matter, it would seem. Now, let me think... yes, did not the lady tell me so herself? She first encountered you at an assembly, where you would not trouble yourself to dance with any of the local populace."

"I was in no mood to become acquainted with... with anyone."

The Colonel shook his head resignedly. "Please tell me that you did not do that stupid thing whereby you stand there all stiff and bored-looking – being tall renders you impossible to look down upon but permits you that liberty by default."

Feeling a wave of discomfort sweep through him, Darcy walked over to the wooden summerhouse that had been built for Georgiana that she might be able to sit in the garden regardless of the weather.

"I have observed you these many years, Darce; you exude disapproval, did you know that?"

About to lift the latch and open the gate, Darcy's hand dropped to his side, and he turned to face his cousin. "I beg your pardon?"

Colonel Fitzwilliam gestured with his arm. "In society – even be it the highest the *ton* can offer. And I deem it most likely that you presented the same countenance and air to a small country neighbourhood – yet there you would not be forgiven, would you?" The Colonel grunted. "Country town society, for all its inadequacies, possesses more honesty, less sycophancy. I do not say the latter does not exist," he continued, acknowledging Darcy's sceptical look, "but that, unlike amongst the *ton*, it is not prevalent."

Shaking his head, Darcy turned back and swung the trellis gate open, ducking his head as he stepped into the summerhouse before walking over to throw himself down onto one of the benches that lined the sides.

# Chapter Twenty Eight

COLONEL FITZWILLIAM FOLLOWED Darcy into the summerhouse and took up the seat opposite.

"Come, Darcy, you must own that no amount of ill humour, nor indeed dismissive demeanour, can forestall the society ladies nor their families from fawning over you. Yet I suspect that in Hertfordshire, for all your wealth and standing, such behaviour was not tolerated."

Darcy stared at his booted feet, blatantly aware of the accuracy of his cousin's words. Indeed, had he not acknowledged something similar himself, only yesterday during that interminable carriage ride?

"What perplexes me is why you will not make the attempt now to improve Miss Elizabeth Bennet's opinion of you. You have much to offer: you are from an old and wealthy family, a good master with a sound reputation and in possession of a good character." Fitzwilliam paused, then sighed affectedly. "It pains me further to acknowledge that you are not unhandsome either, though I am of course biased, and perhaps you are not half as well-looking in other's eyes."

Drawing a shallow breath, Darcy lifted his gaze and stared unseeingly out of the summerhouse into the garden. "Just tolerable, perhaps?"

The Colonel laughed. "Well, perhaps, but I am not so harsh!"

Darcy shifted his position before looking back at Fitzwilliam. "Yet there you have it, Cousin."

"I do not follow you, Darce. You speak in riddles."

"I refer to the occasion of my first making the lady's acquaintance at that assembly in Hertfordshire."

Colonel Fitzwilliam's eyes widened. "You cannot mean that someone had the gall to refer to you as such? You must have presented yourself in a rare old strop. Did the rustic ale not rest amiably in your refined stomach?"

Darcy released a frustrated breath before meeting his cousin's smirking countenance. "It is worse than you can ever suppose. It is how I described Miss Elizabeth Bennet to... so that... to avoid having to stand up with her." The final words came out in a rush, and there was silence as his cousin's amusement turned to astonishment.

"*Avoid?*" Fitzwilliam spluttered as he cast an incredulous look upon his cousin. "Darcy, I will never understand you. A woman of Miss Bennet's charms and you would not stand up with her? You deemed her only tolerable and, dear Lord, are you saying that somehow this came to her attention?"

"It was an attempt to forestall Bingley's enthusiasm for making me dance; a defence, a reaction, and most certainly not said with the intention of being overheard by the subject, nor did I perceive that it had been... " Darcy swallowed with difficulty, attempting to douse the memories of that night as they flooded his mind. "Though I suspect it to be so."

The Colonel shook his head. "So, you were both offensive *and* indiscreet. That is an expensive education well bought! One can only assume you missed the lecture upon how to recommend yourself to young ladies!"

"I am glad that I am providing you with some entertainment, Cousin," Darcy snapped; then, he sighed. "What is done is done. I cannot undo creating a poor first impression, nor reinforcing it with my subsequent behaviour thereafter."

The Colonel pursed his lips. "So, you troubled yourself little with concealing your distaste for the local populace during your stay, adding to the poor impression you had begun with. But Darcy, you can ensure it is not perpetuated. Miss Bennet has yet to recognise the other aspects of your character. If you encounter her henceforth, then is it not also likely that you will gain an introduction to her connections in Town? What better opportunity could there be?"

Darcy got to his feet in agitation. "We move in diverse social circles, and reside in completely different parts of London. I will not seek her out, and thus I am unlikely to encounter her. Besides, there is more than distance that separates us, as we have discussed interminably."

The Colonel got to his feet as well, studying Darcy in silence for a moment.

"There is some truth in what you say; but not in all – and thus you lead me neatly into the second matter of business I wished to raise with you."

Darcy eyed his cousin warily; a change of topic would be welcome, yet somehow he felt little confidence that his cousin bore any intention of letting go his purpose.

"And that business is?"

"Bingley. Am I correct in my assumption that his coming to stay here means he had success in ascertaining Miss Jane Bennet's whereabouts?"

"You are."

"Then he determined the direction from the coachman?"

Darcy shook his head and walked back over towards the gate of the summerhouse, staring out over the garden. "No – no, he did not. Fate intervened before there was any occasion to do so. Not only did he find out what he sought, but he also paid a call this very morning."

"Good Lord! How did that come about?"

Darcy turned round and leaned against the gate, folding his arms across his chest as he met his cousin's enquiring gaze. "There was an unexpected connection, a mutual acquaintance with whom Bingley breakfasted this morning. He is intimate with the elusive relations."

"Really? This... Harington, is it?"

"Indeed."

"How fortuitous." The Colonel eyed his cousin thoughtfully and then frowned. "Why is the name Harington familiar to me? I still cannot for the life of me recall why."

Darcy shrugged, conscious as he had been that morning that he too had felt some peculiarity over the name, as if he should have been cognisant of it. Yet keen though he was to further his cousin's latter train of thought as opposed to the former, he simply said: "And what of Bingley?"

"Ah yes. Bingley. This re-acquaintance of his with the eldest Miss Bennet – you must comprehend that you stand in imminent danger of encountering her, and thus by association, Miss Bennet's sister?"

"Not if I can help it."

"But you *cannot* help it."

Darcy shook his head and turned to unlatch the gate, his fingers struggling with the catch in his agitation. "I am secure here – Miss Bennet can hardly pay a call upon Bingley. Even should she wish it, convention forbids it. Bingley may elect to call upon her as much as he chooses, but I need not fear the reverse."

"But if he is courting the lady's society, you may, as his close friend, encounter her elsewhere, as may Georgiana, by accident."

Darcy paled. It was not that he had not hoped and wished for the acquaintance these many months, but now... *now* what might his sister, in her newfound determination to be of aid to him, draw the courage to say if such a situation presented itself? Darcy felt his skin grow cold as a rush of possibilities flooded his mind, and finally releasing the latch, he pulled the gate open and strode rapidly out of the summerhouse, across the terrace and down onto the gravel pathway.

"Come, Darcy. This may be something even you cannot control."

Fitzwilliam's voice proved him to be hard on Darcy's heels, and with a pointed tap upon the shoulder, he managed to stall his cousin's rapid pace. "Just promise me one thing."

Turning to face the Colonel, Darcy met his look with scepticism.

"Do not, during my brief absence, exclude me from any forthcoming plans you may make."

Darcy's eyes narrowed at this but he said nothing, turning and resuming his walk along the path towards the house, but at a steadier pace, aware that his cousin had fallen into step beside him. He threw Fitzwilliam a glance, then sighed.

"I have no fixed plans at present, though there is as always a plethora of invitations to sift through. I am as little disposed as ever to partake of the London social scene."

"Which is precisely why I caution you not to exclude me when you do, Cousin. It is blatantly obvious you will need my support if you are entering into the fray."

Darcy grunted. "I am entering no fray, Cousin. Miss Elizabeth Bennet's aversion to my company followed her from Hertfordshire to Kent – I am under no illusion that she would find my presence any more palatable in London."

Having reached the steps that led up to the rear entrance to the house, Darcy stopped again, and faced his cousin once more. "Thankfully, our mutual desire to avoid each other's society will doubtless secure us no little measure of success, should the unlikely event of a potential encounter arise."

The Colonel gave an ill-suppressed snort. "You cannot become a hermit! Do you propose to never leave the house? How will you explain yourself to your guest, Bingley? How can you deny Georgiana some form of escape?"

Darcy shook his head. "I shall not be secluding myself, for there is little need. Our paths will not cross. The Bennets are as likely to frequent Mayfair as I am to have business in Cheapside."

"Truly?"

"For pity's sake, what would you have me do? Selfishness and arrogance have been the beginning and end of my present situation. I cannot continue to live in the same way. I have to begin considering the wishes of other people, not just my own. What do you honestly think the lady desires most? To have me purposefully seek her out, or to never lay eyes upon me again?"

Darcy and the Colonel glared at each other for a moment, before a movement at the window to the left of the doorway caught their eye. Georgiana stood at the music room window, watching them, and she raised her hand in a hesitant wave.

Forcing a smile, Darcy lifted a hand in response, nodded to his cousin and turned on his heel, striding purposefully up the steps and back through the open study windows.

The Colonel shook his head at his cousin's departing back and turned to grin reassuringly at Georgiana, whose wary gaze had moved from where her brother had been stood to her cousin's face. Fitzwilliam rolled his eyes, tilted his head in the direction of Darcy's study and shook his head at her, relieved to see the concern upon her features ease and the quick smile that graced her face.

Bowing deeply, the Colonel raised a hand as she waved in response and turned to follow his cousin.

Having enjoyed their afternoon tea and the opportunity to catch up on each other's news, a lull in the conversation in the drawing room at Gracechurch Street left Elizabeth more than conscious of her concealment of much regarding her sojourn in Kent, to the point that she had failed entirely to mention the gentlemen who had been in residence at Rosings. Keen to deflect any possible attempt by her companions to question her further about her stay with Charlotte, she reverted to the theme of their extended party by way of diversion.

"I am looking forward to seeing Nicholas this evening, Aunt. Is he much altered since we last met?"

"Dear Nicholas," Mrs Gardiner smiled at her nieces. "He has been such a joy in my life – as have you both, my dears. But altered? I think you will find him as teasing and exacting as before. He seems as ill-disposed as ever towards bearing his own company, and he is certainly most keen to see *you*, Lizzy, and makes no secret of it!"

"Indeed, we have spent every day in his company since his arrival from the country, have we not, Aunt?"

Mrs Gardiner laughed. "Jane is quite correct. I begin to wonder if it would not have been easier on your uncle's horses had we all taken up residence at *Grillons*!"

"Then he does not come to Gracechurch Street often?"

"Oh but he does – with persistent regularity!" Mrs Gardiner smiled. "And we are, without fail, delighted to see him. Yet he will continue organising outings and expeditions, and all are across Town. I believe he has something planned for every day going forward, and I do not know how my housekeeper is managing the demands we have made of her over the upkeep of our attire!"

Elizabeth's smile faded as she recalled her minimal wardrobe.

"Pray, child, is something the matter?"

"No indeed – at least, nothing too dire, yet I do have a confession to make, Aunt. The clothing I have with me is likely to prove inadequate for any length of stay in Town, and it has been further depleted by the soiling of one of my better gowns and the only coat I chose to bring away. I fear they may both be beyond remedy."

Jane's countenance assumed a concerned air but her aunt merely shook her head.

"Dear girl, what misadventure has found you this time?"

"But Lizzy!" Jane leaned over and laid a hand upon her sister's arm, her expression earnest. "What has happened? Were you in any danger; have you suffered any injury?"

"Dearest Jane," Elizabeth shook her head, pushing aside the memory of her fall and its outcome. "I am quite well, I assure you."

Meeting two pairs of enquiring eyes, Elizabeth shrugged her shoulders. "I was merely caught in some extremely inclement weather, and my clothing took the brunt of the rain and the subsequent dirt underfoot. I must own that I hoped you would be able to recommend someone, Aunt, who might restore them to wearable condition. There were such limited means at the parsonage, and I would so dearly like to retain the use of them. Indeed, without my coat I shall be unable to venture out of the door at all unless the sun graces us with its presence!"

Mrs Gardiner nodded and got to her feet. "Then come, let us repair to your chamber, consider the damage and see if we cannot find a solution."

# Chapter Twenty Nine

ONCE UPSTAIRS, ELIZABETH laid the dress and coat upon the bed, that her aunt and sister might examine them and draw their own conclusion. For a moment, Mrs Gardiner studied the staining along the hemlines and ran a hand over the texture of the fabric, paying particular attention to her niece's coat.

"Though dyeing the fabric to a richer hue is certainly an option, I believe it might be best if we were to take the opportunity whilst you are in Town to order a new one?"

Elizabeth ran a hand over the material. "I am sure your advice is sound, Aunt, but I am particularly fond of this; I do not wish to dispose of it. Could we not at least attempt the darker shade before committing to a replacement?"

"Of course, my dear." Mrs Gardiner patted Elizabeth's hand, before glancing sideways at her. "We shall take it with us in the morning when we attend our appointment with the dressmaker."

Elizabeth looked up at this and then, catching her sister's eye, she laughed. "And is this something that you were going to advise me of once we were in the carriage, Aunt? I can assure you that I have almost outgrown my reluctance to attend the dressmaker!"

"Indeed, Lizzy?"

Her niece had the grace to look a little guilty. "Well, suffice it to say that whilst it will never be my favourite pastime, I believe I can tolerate the experience with more grace than I did when younger!"

"More grace, my dear? I believe it was a question of less elusiveness! If it had not been for your efforts I am certain your uncle and I would never have realised our home contained quite so many opportunities for concealment!"

Elizabeth laughed. "You attempt to distract me, Aunt! For what reason are we to make such a visit?"

"A couple of weeks ago, Jane and I ordered some new gowns to be made up. Your uncle had once again received a delivery of some particularly fine fabrics, including the most delightful silks. He bade me order a dress for you as well. Jane helped to select the design and colour, for she understands your preference best. There are always belongings of Serena in the house, and we used one of her gowns for measurements as you share a similar frame."

"Oh Lizzy, the fabric is truly most beautiful." Jane's eyes shone. "Our appointment on the morrow is for final fittings and for the length also to be determined with your gown, for we shall need them this coming Monday."

Elizabeth's smile widened. "I am most grateful! How kind of Uncle Gardiner to allow us such a treat – but what is the necessity for dressing so well on Monday? Has Nicholas managed to secure an audience with the King himself?"

"And well might you mock such an occasion, Lizzy, but I am confident you will be pleased with Nicholas' invitation all the same. There is to be a May ball hosted by his aunt, Lady Bellingham, at her home. You may recall that you were introduced to her?"

"But of course! She is a most formidable lady by appearance, and indeed reputation, yet I found her perfectly cordial."

Jane looked a little uncertain. "To be sure, Lady Bellingham is a little intimidating."

Mrs Gardiner patted her on the arm. "I suspect that her manner varies dependent upon how close a vicinity she is in to the other presiding custodians of *Almacks*. When in company with only her immediate family, she displays a much less strident demeanour, and I believe Nicholas' father holds much sway over her Ladyship, and in the company of her brother – and by default, his children and their close acquaintance – she is perfectly amiable. And connections Nicholas may have, but the ability to obtain sufficient invitations to *Almacks* is beyond even his charming manners, relative or not!"

Elizabeth smiled at her aunt. "Then Uncle's timing is fortuitous, is it not? Do you think we shall pass muster in our new finery?"

Jane responded in all seriousness: "Dear Lizzy, you will be delighted with Madame Eliza's work. We examined some finished models when we took the fabric along to her premises. Her needlework is quite exquisite."

Elizabeth directed her curiosity towards Mrs Gardiner. "How is it that we do not visit your usual dressmaker?"

"Sadly, she is not so able now, Lizzy. She finds close work rather trying on her sight, and though she has two promising apprentice needlewomen, they are not yet of sufficient standard."

"Well, I am certain to enjoy ample wear of this wondrous new gown, for I am poorly equipped for all the society that would appear to be awaiting. Will it suffice for a walk in the park, do you think?"

Mrs Gardiner laughed and got to her feet. "It most certainly will not, my dear, and to your good fortune, I will add one other."

Walking over to the cupboard doors that lined the opposite wall of the chamber, Mrs Gardiner pulled them aside before saying over her shoulder. "I must assume you have not examined your closet since the maid unpacked for you, Lizzy?"

"Indeed not, for I received an urgent summons to take tea!"

Mrs Gardiner pulled forward from the back of the closet three of her niece's better gowns, including the evening dress she had had made up for the Netherfield Ball.

"There! These will at least render your appearance acceptable, shall they not?"

Elizabeth's eyes widened and then she laughed. "Last I saw, they hung in the closet at Longbourn!"

"As soon as the invitation was extended to make some stay with us, your uncle sent an *Express* to Longbourn, seeking permission from your father for the change in plan and asking your mother to return a box containing some of your better gowns and accessories to Town."

Somewhat relieved, though she did not stop to examine the reason why her appearance should concern her so much on this occasion, Elizabeth examined the hem of the soiled dress on the bed.

"My bonnet took a rather severe beating too," she confessed. "Not that I can bear to wear one unless there is inclement weather."

"In Town, my dear, you ought to wear some form of head covering when we are out."

Elizabeth sighed as she met her aunt's eye, and nodded reluctantly.

"Do not concern yourself. We have several items here of Serena's, including a couple of Spencers. With the warmer weather approaching, either will suffice, I am certain, and you may borrow whichever you prefer. You share a similar lightness of figure, though you are much the taller."

Jane smiled at her sister. "There, Lizzy. You have all the clothing you could possibly need to enjoy a sojourn in Town." Then she laughed and patted the dress on the bed between them. "I was going to ask if you were pleased, but I forget to whom I am speaking! You would be perfectly content with only these dear items restored."

Elizabeth laughed and shook her head. "Certainly not. I must own to being quite excited! Is it a phase, do you think, or am I regressing? I fear I may have spent too much time with Kitty and Lydia of late, and without your soothing company, Jane!"

"Lizzy!"

Elizabeth merely smiled and turned to her aunt. "Does Madame Eliza have a workshop nearby?"

Mrs Gardiner shook her head. "Alicia Harington recommended her to me some time ago, and she wrote a note of introduction which Nicholas brought with him after I had written to her and described the bolts of fabric. In truth, I have promised one to her also."

"Then we are to cross town?"

"Yes, we are, though this is one outing for your uncle's carriage that has not been precipitated by Nicholas' design!"

Elizabeth's smile faltered as the realisation dawned that Mayfair was likely their morning destination. Then she shook her concerns aside; it would prove too large a coincidence if she were to come across Mr Darcy when venturing into that neighbourhood for a few hours. Surely she could visit the district without detection?

Pushing the notion aside, she smiled at her aunt and let out a contented sigh. "Then I shall look forward to our adventure!"

Having resealed Mr Darcy's letter as hurriedly as possible, for fear that accident or temptation might reveal any of its content, Charlotte carefully folded it inside the one she had then penned to her friend, and ensuring that the direction was clearly legible, she again applied the seal to some wax before getting up and leaving the room.

She paused as she passed the tray in the hallway where correspondence was normally left for a servant to take to the post, the letter in her hand. She had neither the desire nor the reason to think so ill of her household as to consider them underhand enough to seek to determine the contents of any letter, but some instinct warned her not to leave this particular package there. No – this she must personally place into the postman's bag herself, and without delay.

Indeed, had it not been that sending for an *Express* rider would have roused suspicions in her husband and might well cause all sorts of awkward questions upon the letter's delivery in Town, she would have sent it by that method – for she had little doubt that whatever its content, Elizabeth would have had no intention of leaving this letter where it might be accessible to anyone but herself. Whether her friend had even missed it, Charlotte could not answer, but the sooner it was restored to its rightful owner, the better for all parties.

Once the seal had dried, Charlotte tucked the letter into her pocket and made her way out into the garden. She had considered any and every possible reason for Mr Darcy to take such a step as addressing Elizabeth by letter, but nothing made any sense. With a sigh, Charlotte pressed her fingers to her forehead. She would resolve to think on it no more in the hope that Elizabeth's response would alleviate any concern.

Conscious suddenly of the changing light indicating the rapid progression of the afternoon, she secured her shawl about her shoulders and hurried down the path and out onto the lane that led to Hunsford village.

Mayfair was fully cloaked in darkness and, undisturbed by any passing carriage, the peace of Mount Street was complete. Candlelight flickered through windows as yet uncovered, causing ghostly shadows to shimmer across the railings, the silence broken only by the sporadic neigh of a horse stabled in the mews that ran behind the houses.

Behind its dignified façade, the drawing room of the largest house in the street was filled with a beautiful melody, a fire burning brightly in the grate that, along with the glow from the many candelabra, contributed to the warmth that pervaded the room.

Leaning back against the worn leather of his armchair, Darcy's gaze was drawn neither by his sister at the pianoforte, or the Colonel in the chair opposite, but by the sky outside. As it had darkened from blue to indigo and finally to black his eye had been caught by the sight of a pale moon that stared moodily back at him from its lofty perch above the rooftops. Yet his thoughts, despite the severe reprimand he bestowed upon himself, were firmly fixed in another part of town.

The dinner hour had been over for some time in Gracechurch Street and from her position at the drawing room window Elizabeth bestirred herself. At her aunt's request, she had come to close the drapes, yet she had found herself transfixed by the beauty of the night sky, and in particular an early summer moon just visible through the new leaves that were opening up on the trees that lined the street.

With one last lingering look at the heavens, she released the ropes that restrained the curtains so that they fell swiftly and heavily into place and ran a hand down the fabric to ensure its evenness before returning to seat herself next to her aunt. Accepting a cup of tea from her, Elizabeth then turned to continue her observation of her sister.

Jane Bennet's attention had been lost to both her companions for some time; lost in fact since the bell was pulled and her uncle and Nicholas had excused themselves to partake of a post-dinner glass of port with the newly arrived guest.

"I suspect we shall have to occupy ourselves until the gentlemen join us, Lizzy."

The quietly spoken words brought Elizabeth's attention back to the lady by her side, and she turned towards her aunt with a smile.

"Indeed. Let us hope that Jane rouses herself sufficiently upon their return. From what I have heard, poor Mr Bingley struggled to draw any response from her this morning."

A sense of unease passed through Elizabeth as she uttered these words, and she turned to regard her sister again. Jane faced slightly away from them, staring into the fire, the abandoned book upon her lap testament to her distraction. Conscious as she was of her sister's concern over protecting her heart, Elizabeth feared that her efforts might effectively seal her fate once and for all – if Mr Bingley had been convinced of her lack of interest in Hertfordshire, what might the gentleman make of her efforts to disguise her true feelings?

"Lizzy? My dear," Mrs Gardiner rested a hand upon her niece's. "You are quite as distracted as your sister!"

"Forgive me, Aunt." Elizabeth hesitated, then added in a low voice, "I am concerned over the effect of Mr Bingley's reappearance."

Mrs Gardiner followed Elizabeth's gaze to where her other niece sat. "You worry for Jane's spirits, her having rallied so recently?"

"Yes, though I have concern also for Mr Bingley." She turned in her seat. "Dear Aunt, all I wish is that, whatever the outcome of their re-acquaintance, it is one that leaves neither suffering."

"My love, it is a good wish, but the interference of others before now would appear to have led to much mischief. We must allow them to find their own way."

Appreciating that her aunt's advice was sound, Elizabeth nodded just as the sound of laughter out in the hallway heralded the gentlemen's approach and, getting to her feet, she could not help but glance anxiously in Jane's direction as the door opened.

# Chapter Thirty

"MY DEAR," MR GARDINER crossed the room to take his wife's hand before turning back to face his companions. "As you see, we have been joined by Mr Bingley. I have just had the pleasure of making his acquaintance, but we refrained from tarrying too long in my study, for he wished to pay his respects to the ladies before departing."

Mrs Gardiner smiled. "Mr Bingley, it is a pleasure to see you again. But please, if it is no inconvenience, at least stay long enough to partake of some tea."

Elizabeth noted Bingley's fleeting glance towards Jane before stepping forward to bow in her aunt's direction. "I would be delighted, if you feel it is no intrusion."

"Not at all, Sir. You are most welcome. And you were not able to reacquaint yourself with my other niece this morning."

With a warm smile, Bingley stepped towards Elizabeth, sketching a small bow.

"How delightful to see you again, Miss Elizabeth. Darcy informed me only yesterday that you were London-bound, and I am pleased to have been presented so precipitously with the opportunity to renew my association with yourself and, of course, Miss Bennet."

Surprised that her name had been mentioned by his friend, Elizabeth hastily dropped a curtsey as Bingley continued, "I trust your journey passed without mishap?"

Elizabeth smiled at him. "I thank you, it did. And have you been in Town all this time, since we last saw you in Hertfordshire?"

"Indeed, I have." Bingley paused and glanced over towards Jane, who had joined her aunt in preparing some fresh tea. "Had I been able, I would have called upon Miss Bennet before today. Had I known she resided in Town these several weeks, the visit would have long been paid ten-fold, but it was only this morning that I learned of her place of residence."

Elizabeth could not help but smile at this blatant admission, and the colour flooded Bingley's cheeks.

"That is… I mean to say, that I would have wished to call upon *any* of the family – even your mother… no, that is not quite my meaning – I – er - had I known – that is, if I had been conscious…"

"Mr Bingley," Elizabeth interrupted him gently, "I assure you, your meaning is perfectly clear, and I thank you for the sentiment on behalf of *all* my family."

Bingley gave a self-conscious smile before excusing himself, and Elizabeth watched him as he made his way over to her aunt and Jane, accepting a cup of tea from the former before standing back to allow the latter to precede him over to a seat near the fireplace.

Her aunt beckoned her over, and Elizabeth crossed the room, resting her hand briefly upon her uncle's arm as she passed him, deep in conversation with Nicholas, and he threw her a quick smile as he patted her hand in response. Taking the proffered cup from her aunt, she then followed her over to a small couch opposite her sister and Mr Bingley. Seeing that the ladies were all settled, Mr Gardiner and Nicholas took the two remaining chairs before the former turned to his wife.

"Young Mr Bingley here recalls this district well, my dear. His grandfather had premises in both Cornhill and Moorgate, and he can distinctly remember visits with his father."

"Indeed?" Mrs Gardiner smiled at Bingley, who, upon hearing his name spoken, turned his attention from the lady at his side to his hostess. "How do you find being master of your own manor, Sir?"

Bingley looked a little sheepish for a moment.

"I must own, Mrs Gardiner, that I have not proved myself yet. But Netherfield is a fine estate, and when I have… that is to say, if – *if* I am able to resolve some outstanding matters whilst I am in Town, then I can safely say that I shall soon be in residence again, and nothing will persuade me to give it up."

"I am very pleased to hear it," replied Mrs Gardiner. "My Godson would do well to emulate you, would you not, Nicholas?"

The note of mild admonishment in her voice did not go unnoticed by its intended recipient, and Nicholas laughed.

"Come now, Aunt. We must not descend into yet another debate about my idle lifestyle in front of a guest." Bingley looked confused, and Nicholas added, "Having not seen you for some time, you are probably not aware that I am now one of a rare and curious breed."

Elizabeth laughed. "Indeed, Nicholas, most rare and curious!"

"Lizzy!"

"Dear Aunt, surely you will not censure me for agreeing with him? It would be more disrespectful to contradict him, I am certain."

"My wife's Godson refers to his situation in life, Mr Bingley," interjected Mr Gardiner. "He is in the fortunate position of being a second son without need of a profession."

"Ah, Uncle, but not so fortunate as my younger brother – for surely to be a third son without need of a profession is rarer yet!"

Mr Gardiner smiled and inclined his head. "Indeed, indeed."

Nicholas turned a satisfied countenance towards Elizabeth, who rolled her eyes. "It is perhaps providential that you have no need of a profession."

Mrs Gardiner turned to look at her niece. "Hmm, and what wisdom would have you say that, Lizzy?"

"Oh she means to be severe upon me, of that you can be sure!" Nicholas laughed, his expression challenging, but Elizabeth refused to be deflected.

"Why, Aunt, that he is eminently unsuitable for the most common professions of second sons: the church, the law or the armed services."

"And pray, child, why is that?"

Elizabeth tilted her head to one side and studied the subject of their conversation for a moment, who bore her scrutiny silently, though clearly suppressing amusement.

"Nicholas could never be sufficiently serious to deliver a sermon, has not the patience to absorb a legal document, and he is neither tall nor fierce enough to fight his fellow man."

"*Lizzy!*" Jane's voice was drowned out by Nicholas's shout of laughter.

"You know me all too well, dear girl." Then, he turned towards their guest. "I blame my parents, Bingley, for making an idle man of me. They have deemed it unfair that my brother and I should have no right to a share in the family coffers, merely through the misfortune of being born after James. As such, instead of securing their entire estate solely upon the heir, both Patrick and I have been willed our own manor in neighbouring counties to Somerset, along with some independence of income. As such, I am presently much as yourself – learning to be master of my own estate by instructing my steward in things that he knows better than I, and to devote my time and attention to living the life of a gentleman."

"Then perhaps we could compare notes?"

"I would be delighted. I have only recently taken up the mantle, and I am demonstrating all the reluctance to shoulder its burden that my aunt's criticism implies, yet if I can persuade you, perhaps you would care to visit once I am fully in residence?"

Bingley nodded. "Be assured that I would! In which county is your manor?"

A fleeting and almost indiscernible shadow crossed Nicholas's face, and Elizabeth frowned as he cast a quick glance in her direction. "Wiltshire. I chose Wiltshire."

"Chose?"

Nicholas shrugged his shoulders, then his face broke into a smile once more. "My one advantage over my younger brother. As the elder of the two, I am permitted the choice of two smaller properties that have, through our maternal grandmother, passed into the possession of our family."

Mrs Gardiner interjected at this point. "With your love of the sea, I would have expected you to opt for Rowlands." As she spoke these words, Nicholas pushed himself up from his seat to walk over to the side table to refill his cup, and his aunt turned to address their guest.

"My Godson has always professed a desire to live near the coast, and the manor house at Rowlands is dramatically situated on the rugged cliff tops of north Devon. I must own, Nicholas, that I am curious to hear the reasoning behind your choice." She turned to study her Godson's back as he busied himself with the tea urn, but when no response came she prompted him.

"Nicholas?"

Dropping a spoon onto the marble-topped table with a clatter, Nicholas turned about. "Forgive me, Aunt. My concentration was all with the tea urn! It seems to be in need of replenishment."

Mrs Gardiner laughed. "Then let me make amends for it." She got to her feet to ring the bell for more water, before making her way over to take the vacated chair next to her husband.

"Sutton Coker is a beautiful estate," Bingley said, as Nicholas crossed the room and seated himself in his aunt's former place beside Elizabeth. "I had the good fortune to pass a summer there during my Cambridge years."

"It is indeed, Sir," Mrs Gardiner smiled warmly at him. "My dear friend, Alicia has turned the house into a wonderful home."

"Hence our reluctance to leave it for pastures new, Aunt, albeit they are our very own!"

Mrs Gardiner fixed her Godson with a serious eye.

"Now, Nicholas. Tell me – why *did* you forsake Rowlands? Admittedly, Crossways Court has the finer park – indeed, one might say it is the finer property. But you have always had an affinity for the water, and have you not, since your earliest days, claimed a desire to open your windows to the sounds of the sea?"

Detecting a restless movement from the man at her side, Elizabeth turned to look at him, but his attention was with his aunt.

"What can I say? Such youthful fancies have left me – surely it is acceptable to mellow one's concept of such things?"

"It is indeed, my dear. I am merely curious given your earlier sentiments."

"I – well..." Nicholas hesitated, and sensing his reluctance to expand upon the matter, Elizabeth glanced quickly about the room.

"But Wiltshire is such a beautiful county, is it not? I have not seen Crossways, but we have travelled that way before and the Downs are quite breath-taking."

Following her niece's lead, Mrs Gardiner nodded.

"I do not think Salisbury Plain can be rivalled for its undulating beauty."

"Good fishing territory too, Boy." Mr Gardiner nodded his head.

"Indeed, Uncle. There is a fair-sized lake near the main house, and I have no doubt that you will be able to indulge your passion whenever you make any stay with me."

"Well, Nicholas," Mrs Gardiner smiled affectionately at him. "Though I am surprised by your choice, I am pleased with it, for you will not be so far away from us, and Crossways is more accessible for Bath and London, and you always did have a stronger inclination for Town than Patrick."

"And it is conveniently situated from Hertfordshire!" added Bingley.

"Are they not renowned also – the Plains I mean – for walking?" Jane's soft-voiced contribution was her first to the general conversation, and Elizabeth smiled at her sister.

"They most certainly are. Something that I shall take keen advantage of, if Nicholas chooses to invite his Hertfordshire connections to visit!" She turned towards him now, yet when she faced him there was a strange consciousness about his expression as he caught her eye and held it. "It is commonly acknowledged that I love to walk – but I will own that, like most ladies, I prefer a gentle incline to a steep one any day!"

"That is precisely what I thought!" exclaimed Nicholas eagerly. "I thought… I hoped –" he hesitated, and glanced quickly about the room, as though suddenly recalling the company. With a slight laugh, he shrugged his shoulders. "I had hoped it was the right decision, and I begin to feel it is."

Elizabeth returned his smile, confident that whatever his choice, Nicholas would be happy with it. It was not in his nature to be dissatisfied with whatever life might send his way, and he could be relied upon to see the positive in any given set of circumstances.

"But Harington…" Bingley's voice interrupted Elizabeth's train of thought, and she looked over at him. "Excuse my curiosity, but if all your family lands are in the West Country, and the Bennets have long been in Hertfordshire, how is it that you spent so much of your youth in company with each other?"

Mr Gardiner exchanged a smile with his wife before saying, "I believe you are familiar with my sister, Mr Bingley."

"Indeed. I had the pleasure of making Mrs Bennet's acquaintance in Hertfordshire."

"No doubt, no doubt. Well then," Mr Gardiner winked at Elizabeth across the room. "With five such lively young ladies all arriving into this world within a period of close to six years, you can perhaps imagine the strain upon my sister Bennet's – disposition."

Ignoring the slight snort that emanated from the man at her side, Elizabeth threw another quick look towards Bingley, but his countenance merely expressed polite interest.

"My wife and I," Mr Gardiner reached over and took his wife's hand, "were blessed with the care of the two eldest so that my sister could devote her attentions to the three youngest – and Jane and Elizabeth have been like our own children. For a large part of each year, they would both reside here in Gracechurch Street, and for much of the remainder, my wife would accompany them to Hertfordshire."

A look of comprehension filtered across Bingley's face, and detecting Elizabeth's eye upon him, he smiled at her. She knew exactly what passed through his mind, for it was not the first time such a realisation had occurred – there were many who failed to understand quite how the two eldest Miss Bennets came to be so different to their younger sisters. Once it was understood that their raising had largely been in the hands of their relations in London, the difference in their intellect, good sense and decorum became more comprehendible.

"We could not, of course, keep them too long from home as they grew older. Lizzy has always been close to her father, and he played a large part in their education, and she has also long preferred the countryside to Town; as for Jane," here Mr Gardiner threw his other niece a fond look, "She has a nurturing instinct that meant she longed for the opportunity to help care for her younger siblings."

Mrs Gardiner smiled. "But despite that, both Jane and Lizzy have continued to reside with us for long periods of time over the years, and with the close connection between myself and Alicia Harington, and Nicholas being my Godson, the young people were frequently in each other's company – either here in Town or in Somerset – along with Serena, of course."

Just then, a maid entered with the hot water, and Mrs Gardiner got to her feet, holding out her hand to her husband for his cup. She turned to offer the same service to her guest but then registered the blank expression upon Bingley's face. "Forgive me, Ma'am." He handed her his empty cup. "Serena?"

"Of course – you would not know. Serena is my half-sister." She threw a general look about the room as she turned towards the table hosting the tea-making accoutrements. "We anticipate her arrival here next week."

Nicholas grunted. "Are you certain she will come? She may decide against it."

Mrs Gardiner, tea canister in hand, turned to frown at her Godson. "That is a rather singular comment. What would lead you to suppose such a thing?"

He gave a dismissive shrug. "She can be a little changeable."

"Nicholas, that is ungenerous of you." Mrs Gardiner shook her head at him.

"Forgive me." He smiled apologetically. "I meant no disrespect; I simply would not wish for you to be disappointed, should she decide not to make the journey. To be certain, it is a fair distance from Derbyshire to Town."

Mrs Gardiner picked up the now replenished cups of tea. "She will not disappoint me – and indeed, it is far less an expedition than Sutton Coker to Lambton, which she undertook only a matter of weeks back!" She walked over and handed Bingley his freshened cup. "I would be honoured if you would allow me to introduce her to your acquaintance."

"I would be delighted." Bingley beamed about the room, his gaze finally coming to rest upon the lady at his side. "How singular that we have all been guests at Sutton Coker in the past, though our paths did not cross there, yet that very connection is what has reunited us in Town."

# Chapter Thirty One

ELIZABETH OBSERVED HER sister as she met Bingley's eye, the colour rising once more in her cheeks, before Jane rose to her feet, excused herself with a small curtsey and moved to the side table to replenish her own cup. As her uncle engaged their guest once more in conversation, Elizabeth's gaze followed her sister anxiously. How did she feel to be in company with Mr Bingley for the second time that day? His attentions towards her seemed as marked as ever, but even Elizabeth herself could detect Jane's reticence.

Unbidden, Charlotte's voice came to her: *"a woman had better show more affection than she feels"*.

Deep in such uncomfortable thoughts, it was a moment before she recalled the man at her side; until, that is, he touched her arm to gain her attention and said in a low voice: "I cannot tell you how relieved I am that you are come, Lizzy."

Having turned her head at his touch, Elizabeth laughed. "Except that you previously have. Do you not recall saying as much to me as we went into dinner?"

"The repetition must surely be proof of my sincerity!"

"And why, pray, are you so pleased to see me? I am not used to such an effusive welcome."

Conscious that Nicholas had cast a quick glance over towards Mr and Mrs Gardiner, the latter of whom had now retaken her seat, Elizabeth followed his gaze, noting that they were engrossed in a discussion with Mr Bingley, and they both turned their eyes back to each other at the same moment.

"I must own that there is something that I would ask… that I would speak to you about."

Elizabeth turned properly in her seat to face him, almost forgetful of where they were, her glance distracted for a moment by Nicholas raising his hand, as if involuntarily, towards his breast pocket before dropping it suddenly to his lap. Catching his eye, she was startled to see that his face had paled, but before she could respond they were interrupted.

"Nicholas! Lizzy! What are you whispering about now?" Mrs Gardiner's voice carried across the room from her place beside her husband. "Come now, I appreciate that you have not seen each other for some time, but you cannot continue as though we were all family here tonight." She turned towards their guest, who had risen to his feet out of courtesy as Jane retook her seat at his side.

"My apologies, Sir. The friendship between these young people extends to their earliest days. It is no excuse for such lapses, but I do beg your forgiveness that you are being accorded no more attention than if you were one of the family."

Bingley resumed his seat. "Oh please do not concern yourself, Madam. I would only wish that I were... that you might treat me so... that is, I – forgive me." Bingley looked somewhat mortified at what he had just said, and swallowed visibly.

Mr Gardiner shook his head. "Do not disturb yourself, my dear Sir. We fully comprehend your meaning."

Bingley smiled weakly before adding under his breath, "That is what I feared." He was rewarded however by a quickly smothered laugh from the lady at his side.

"I can only apologise, Bingley. My excuse is that we have long been the best of friends-" Nicholas turned towards Elizabeth and took her hand, squeezing it lightly before releasing it. "Have we not, Lizzy?"

Meeting his gaze, Elizabeth could not help but let out a small laugh. "Indeed we have!"

"And yet not always to your advantage," added Mr Gardiner.

Nicholas gave an exaggerated sigh. "I do feel it most unjust that friends who, through no fault of their own, are of the opposite sex, cannot partake of indulging in a private exchange once in a while."

"We are full aware of your thoughts upon the matter, my boy, and stop acting like the convention ever prevented you from achieving your aim."

Elizabeth noted the surprise on Bingley's features and said quickly, "It is not quite as serious as my uncle implies, Sir." She turned to the man at her side. "Perchance, Nicholas, you should explain the legend of Ben and Harriet?"

Nicholas laughed. "Ah yes – and our downfall. I remember it well."

"As do I," interjected Mr Gardiner.

"As do we all," added Jane in an undertone, and Bingley turned to look at her.

"Would you care to tell the story, Miss Bennet?"

"I can share but a part of it, only learning of the situation later. As a secret held between Nicholas and Lizzy, though I believe they meant no harm by it, I feel one of them should do the honours."

All eyes turned upon the couch where the two perpetrators sat and with a laugh, Nicholas turned towards Elizabeth. "Shall I?"

"Oh, I think you must, else Mr Bingley will fear the worst!"

He faced the room and grinned. "What can I tell you, Bingley? There we were, two such good friends, yet we lived no little distance apart. Whenever we had occasion to make any stay in the same part of the country, we would spend much time together, yet as we grew from children into our youth, we found greater restrictions being placed upon us." Nicholas paused and pretended a heavy sigh. "Simply by nature of our sex, we were unable to spend time alone together. It was most unkind."

"It was nothing of the sort, as well you know!" laughed Mr Gardiner. "It is not unkindness to teach young people about convention and propriety."

"But a lesson sorely learned at the time, Uncle, nonetheless. We had enjoyed such freedom as children – to suddenly find ourselves having to conform to society's demands severely curbed the enjoyment of our friendship!"

"So what did you do?" Bingley's eager interjection caused everyone to smile.

Mrs Gardiner turned towards him. "What did they do, Sir? They found a way around such restriction, by devising a way of staying in touch that had all the appearance of legitimacy!"

"We decided to strike up a correspondence," Elizabeth said, catching Jane's eye momentarily and smiling. "Unable to share things privately when in each other's company, we derived much satisfaction and pleasure from sharing them by word when apart."

"But did you not take the risk of being discovered? What if one of the letters had fallen under someone's eye?"

Jane shook her head. "They had thought of that. They both made efforts to disguise their own hand." She paused and looked quickly at the man beside her. "And to secure the matter, Lizzy signed her letters with a boy's name, and Nicholas with a girl's. Thus, should anyone happen across their correspondence by chance, they would detect nothing amiss."

Bingley grinned and looked over at Elizabeth. "Ben?" and then turned towards Nicholas, "and Harriet?"

"Indeed, indeed," said Mr Gardiner. "Inspired by their family names, they each took ownership of a name of the opposite sex."

"Yet you stated the downfall of your scheme?"

Nicholas attempted a resigned sigh, but could not refrain from breaking into a wide grin. "Indeed, Bingley. I was so proud, having attained the age of fifteen years, of being allowed my first glass of wine, that I made the mistake of taking another. Suffice it to say, before long I began to address Lizzy as Ben to her face."

With a short laugh, Bingley turned to face Jane. "And were you all present? Was it a family occasion?"

Delighted to see her sister more herself, Elizabeth smiled as Jane turned her attention to the gentleman by her side. "Indeed, Sir, it was. My aunt and uncle and all our family were present."

Elizabeth patted Nicholas's arm. "He was, of course, severely chastised – both for the over-indulgence and the liberty-taking. And thereafter, both he and I were banned from continuing our innocent correspondence."

"Which, of course, we adhere to... most of the time."

Mrs Gardiner eyed her Godson narrowly for a moment. "Yes – well, perhaps the less said about that, the better?"

Jane threw her sister a somewhat shocked look. "You would not... you did not – *continue?*"

"Dear, Jane. He is teasing..."

"... or is he?" Nicholas interjected, waggling his brows in a comical fashion, and Elizabeth laughed.

"And let that be the end of the matter," announced Mr Gardiner, who then turned to address Bingley once more. "So, Sir, have you been travelling this spring, and are only just returned to Town?"

"No, indeed. I have been in residence since quitting Hertfordshire. You must forgive the tardiness of my call upon Miss Bennet, Sir. I was unaware of her presence in Town until only yesterday. My friend had been making some stay in the country, and upon his return Darcy shared the good tidings with me."

Elizabeth's eyes widened in surprise and, unable to restrain herself, she blurted out, "But I thought you found your way here through Nicholas!"

"Oh but I did, Miss Elizabeth! I learned of the direction from him, receiving confirmation that Miss Bennet continued to reside in Town. But it was Darcy who informed me only yesterday that she had been in London for some time."

Mrs Gardiner exchanged a puzzled glance with her husband. "Mr Darcy? How would Mr Darcy be privy to such knowledge?"

Struggling with this unexpected intelligence, yet conscious that it brought her pleasure, so much so that she could not help but smile, Elizabeth realised that Bingley floundered for a response and said quickly, "I happened across Mr Darcy whilst staying in Kent, Aunt. Jane's being in Town came up in conversation."

Jane frowned. "How could you just happen across Mr Darcy?"

Elizabeth hesitated as she saw her aunt exchange a puzzled glance with Jane, and was unsurprised when she turned to look at her and prompted, "Lizzy?"

"Mr Collins' patroness and Mr Darcy's aunt are one and the same. By coincidence, Mr Darcy and his cousin were staying with Lady Catherine de Bourgh during my visit with Charlotte."

Conscious that both her aunt and sister would be ruminating upon how she had managed to avoid mentioning this during their afternoon together, Elizabeth was mightily relieved when Bingley took up the conversational reins.

"Are you acquainted with my friend, Mrs Gardiner?"

"No, not at all. But the Darcy name is not unfamiliar to me – I grew up in a village not five miles from Pemberley, and I learned from Lizzy's correspondence last year that the family had made the gentleman's acquaintance in Hertfordshire."

"Darcy is the best of men."

Elizabeth's mouth opened slightly as words of concurrence almost fell involuntarily from her lips. Swallowing the sentiment that had almost escaped her, she leaned back in her seat and released a slow breath as the conversation continued around her. This unexpected news caused her some confusion of mind. Mr Darcy had indeed informed his friend of the situation, and this gave rise to feelings of gratitude towards him that were both unprecedented and unsettling.

Closing her eyes, she leaned her head back against the upholstery, conscious of a sensation of weariness stealing over her. Something inside had eased, falling away from her, and as it slipped from her grasp she began to feel a release of tension and a great desire to sleep.

The chiming of the clock caused Elizabeth to start, and opening her eyes she became conscious that the company had been reminded all at once of the lateness of the hour. Sitting up, she tried to shake off the heaviness and recall her attention to the room.

With a grimace, Nicholas caught his Godmother's eye. "I fear we have outstayed our welcome, Aunt."

"Nonsense, dear boy. It has been a pleasure, as always, to share your company." She paused, catching sight of Elizabeth as she discreetly tried to conceal a yawn behind her hand. "Yet some of us have had more wearying days than others, and perchance we should postpone further conversation until our next meeting."

Everyone rose to their feet and made a general movement towards the drawing room door. Having prearranged between themselves that Bingley would take a hired cab to Gracechurch Street, permitting the two gentlemen to travel back to the Pulteney in Harington's carriage, a servant was despatched to ensure that the conveyance be made ready at the door, and the guests took their leave of the company.

Having exchanged the requisite pleasantries with his hosts, Mr Bingley approached Elizabeth, and she shook aside her drowsiness and broke immediately into speech.

"Forgive my curiosity, Sir, but did I understand you correctly? Did you say that Mr Darcy informed you of my sister's presence in Town?"

Bingley nodded. "He advised me of many things, not least of which was a result of a conversation with yourself. I am grateful for your openness with my friend, and wish to reassure you that your sister's well-being is my utmost concern."

Elizabeth could not help but wonder what might have been said by Mr Darcy to his friend, but certain as she was that he would not have divulged *all* that had occurred in Kent, felt the legitimacy of making an enquiry after a common acquaintance.

"And how fares Mr Darcy?" she feigned nonchalance, ignoring the fact that her insides seemed to be turning themselves into knots the moment his name passed her lips.

"Quite well, Miss Elizabeth. He did me the honour of calling upon me within an hour of arriving in Town, and I spent a very pleasant afternoon in his company. I did suggest that he accompany me this evening, but he felt it would have been an imposition."

Elizabeth felt the warmth flood her cheeks upon hearing these words. The notion that Mr Darcy might have walked through the door this evening had not crossed her mind, for she knew full well he would not wish to associate with the connections that he had so denigrated during his proposal, nor could she picture him wishing to pay a call in an area of London so far removed from the lofty drawing rooms of Mayfair.

Conscious that Bingley awaited a response, she pulled herself together and smiled widely at him. "Forgive me, Sir. I am distracted. I am sure that my aunt and uncle would have been more than happy to welcome Mr Darcy into their home, but I believe I understand his reservations."

"I will let Darcy know that you enquired after him, if I may?"

Elizabeth hesitated, unsure what she could say; to request that he not do so would seem most odd, yet she would not have Mr Darcy believe she patronised him. Unable to think of a suitable response, she merely inclined her head before excusing herself, walking over to join Nicholas and her aunt and uncle as they waited by the door for Bingley as he took his leave of her sister.

Under cover of the confusion as hats and canes were distributed and the door opened to the night air, Nicholas turned to Elizabeth. "I will call as soon as the hour is acceptable in the morning."

Before she could respond, her aunt had intervened. "Indeed you will not! We ladies have better things to do with our time than sit around awaiting calls from young men!"

Mr Gardiner chuckled at the expression on Nicholas' face. "Come now, we must leave the ladies to their purchases. If you have time upon your hands you could always attend me at my business – I am certain I should find you something by way of occupation!"

"But-"

"Have patience, Boy! Our paths will cross later in the day, for shall we not all meet in the evening, when we attend the recital?"

His face brightening immediately, Nicholas turned to Bingley.

"You must join us! It is in Hanover Square."

Bingley looked a little awkward, and he threw a glance towards Jane, who made a deal of brushing imaginary creases from her skirts. "You are very generous. Perhaps I could leave word at the Pulteney? I am removing to my friend's home and would need to consult his plans before excusing myself from his company so precipitously."

On that note, the gentlemen took their leave, and having been urged to get some rest, Elizabeth made her way up the stairs, her tired mind struggling to absorb all that she had discerned.

The clouds that had slowly gathered finally succeeded in obliterating the moon. On a dirt track running across open fields some twenty miles from London, a horse and cart drew slowly to a halt near a wayside marker.

Jumping down from the seat next to the driver, the passenger walked up to the stone and ran slender fingers over the engraved wording: *Meryton 3 miles*

Straightening up, the figure stepped back up to the cart and handed over a few coins before receiving a pack and a cane from the silent driver in return.

"I am much obliged to you."

The driver grunted, and with a flick of the reins and click of his tongue, the horse slowly moved on, the cart rattling in its wake.

Having watched the retreating conveyance until it was swallowed by the night, the figure hoisted the pack up and set off towards the town, the stick striking the ground by way of a guide in the darkness.

# Chapter Thirty Two

DAWN HAD BROKEN IN Gracechurch Street and, having lain awake for some time, Elizabeth had been privy to the light filtering into the room as it turned from darkness to pale grey. Turning her head on the pillow, she observed her sister, whose eyes remained closed. Elizabeth had not been aware of Jane retiring for the night, so deep had her repose been, and she could barely recall getting herself ready for bed at all, other than a sensation of the utmost relief that her mind was too weary to dwell upon the evening's revelations.

Yet comforted though she was to be once more amongst family and familiar surroundings, she could not quite settle herself to enjoy it, and it seemed to be her inability to dismiss Mr Darcy that remained the main cause of her disquiet. Not only had he been her last thought before sleeping, but soon after waking he came once more to the forefront of her mind.

His call upon his friend so soon after arriving in Town, and his purpose in doing so, had left her eager for more. Further, on hearing that Mr Bingley intended to reside with Mr Darcy, it seemed clear no rancour existed between the two. There was a time not so long ago when her instinct would have been to believe that either Mr Bingley was simply too forgiving, or Mr Darcy had not made known the full extent of his interference.

Now… *now*, though, she felt nothing but deep gratitude towards Mr Darcy for not only making such a precipitous confession to his friend, but also for what else he might have disclosed, for Mr Bingley's own words to her on his leave-taking the night before convinced her that he was conscious of a deal more than just her sister's being in Town.

Realising that she was once again indulging in the very pursuit that so frustrated her, Elizabeth turned her head restlessly on the pillow. This gradual reversal of her opinion of Mr Darcy could not cease to astound her. Here she was, not five days from having spurned the offer of his hand and declaring to his face that he was no gentleman, forced to accept that the two considerable blights upon his character, that she had felt defined him as the worst of men, had been in one case destroyed as myth and in the other, considerably atoned for.

Sighing, she rested her arm across her forehead and closed her eyes. Having little left to reproach him for, she was left with her continued growing awareness of him as a man, and once again she was unable to prevent her thoughts from rushing back towards that moment outside the parsonage when he had caught her as she fell. Even now, eyes closed to her surroundings, she could smell the spring rain, feel its wetness upon her skin, sense the fine fabric of his coat beneath her hands, the solidity of the frame beneath it of the man who held her…

Feeling the heat steal into her cheeks, Elizabeth stirred restlessly. *Can there be so much awareness in a man's touch?*

"Lizzy?"

Elizabeth gave a start and moved her arm to the pillow as she opened her eyes, letting out a huff of laughter at herself.

"Are you well? You are flushed."

Kicking the covers from her legs, Elizabeth rolled onto her side so that she faced her sister. "I am a little warm, that is all." She studied Jane for a moment, then smiled. "And you? I trust you slept well and your dreams were pleasant!"

"Lizzy!" Jane rolled onto her back and lay much as her sister had been a moment earlier, staring at the canopy above the bed.

Propping herself up on one elbow, Elizabeth threw her sister a speculative glance, but before she could express what was on her mind, Jane spoke.

"So it would seem Mr Bingley intends to return to Netherfield, once his business in Town is resolved."

"If the timing is fortuitous, perchance he will return to Hertfordshire when we do."

Jane turned her head on the pillow. "Yet he may take Nicholas up on his invitation and head to Wiltshire instead."

With a laugh, Elizabeth shook her head. "I think the likelihood of Nicholas confining himself to his estate in the foreseeable future is negligible."

"I do hope that Mr Bingley was not too shocked by the banter between you and Nicholas, Lizzy. For someone unfamiliar with the relationship between our families, it must seem quite… quite…"

"Forward? Lacking in propriety?"

"No! Not entirely. It is just…" Jane sat up and wriggled up the bed until she could lean back against the headboard. "I fear I may have been reckless in contributing to the tale of your youthful indiscretion."

Elizabeth laughed. "Dear Jane! You truly are too good. How could you imagine that *you* were reckless? Besides, I doubt the rather dubious behaviour of any of your siblings will cause Mr Bingley any undue concern."

She sat up, plumping up her pillows before reclining against them next to Jane. "And Nicholas has been as a brother to us both, for all that we were not raised in the same household. I am quite certain the level of comfort that exists between us caused minimal distress. Indeed, Mr Bingley seemed as though he would wish to be part of it."

A sigh emanated from her sister, and Elizabeth turned her head to observe her. "I would not wish to give Mr Bingley the wrong impression."

Elizabeth could not help but laugh. "Dear Jane – what impression would you wish to give, precisely?"

"Why, that we meet as mere common acquaintances!" She threw her sister an anxious look. "I find it so difficult to meet his eye without betraying my feelings, and you know how much I wish to guard myself from that. Oh Lizzy," Jane grasped her sister's hand tightly and turned to face her. "I am struggling to maintain an air of indifference."

Suppressing the urge to snort, Elizabeth settled for rolling her eyes. "You are exuding disinterest to any but those closest to you. I wonder if perhaps you should cease the attempt." Jane shook her head, but Elizabeth continued, "Perhaps it is time to have some faith in your sister."

Seeing the puzzled look upon Jane's face, Elizabeth smiled. "As I said when Caroline Bingley sent you that letter, Mr Bingley is in love with you."

"Yet if it was so back in Hertfordshire, then why have we not heard from him in all this time?" Jane's gaze became clouded as if caught in some memory. "And now he is moving in with his friend… do you not also recall that part of Caroline's letter? Both families desire a connection between them, in the form of an alliance between Mr Bingley and Miss Darcy."

Elizabeth shook her head. "Miss Darcy is but a child, Jane. She is almost of an age with Lydia. All we are privy to is Caroline Bingley's desire for such a connection. Besides, Mr Darcy would never permit a potential suitor for his sister to reside under his roof. As for Mr Bingley's not seeking you out, you heard from his own lips, not once but twice yesterday, that he was unaware of your presence in Town. He is as honest as the day is long. He told no lie; and his pleasure in being re-acquainted with you is writ plain for all to see – and indeed, Jane, you would have seen it for yourself, had you but looked with a little more frequency!"

"But-"

"Be sensible, Jane!"

"I fear I have forgot how."

"Impossible!"

Jane laughed reluctantly. Giving her a hug, Elizabeth then sat back, her hands on her sister's shoulders.

"Now listen to your Aunt Lizzy. The next time we encounter Mr Bingley – and you cannot fail to understand that he intends to continue the acquaintance – you pay him some attention. The poor man is positively begging for it!"

Jane could not help but smile as her sister gave her a gentle shake before releasing her; then her expression sobered once more. "But Lizzy – what of Mr Bingley's taking up residence with his friend."

Elizabeth felt a flicker of apprehension pass through her. "What of it?"

Jane shrugged her shoulders. "Perchance there may be occasion for us to meet with him. If Mr Bingley, as you say, intends to court our society, then it stands to reason that we may encounter his closest friend – do you not think?"

Elizabeth sighed. Denial was hardly more likely to make it impossible.

"Lizzy?" Jane spoke hesitantly. "I trust – I do hope that you will not mind? I am full aware that you and Mr Darcy are far from the best of friends."

Letting out a huff of laughter that held little humour, Elizabeth dropped her gaze to her toes. Friends? She and Mr Darcy as friends was something she could never imagine – too much had gone between them for something so tame as friendship.

"No, you are quite right. We are not the best of friends. But," she raised her head and forced a smile, "I will own that by the time of my departure from Kent, we had progressed to being able to hold a conversation in complete civility! Do not concern yourself, dearest. I promise to behave and be perfectly cordial should our paths cross."

"Oh yes! Dear Lizzy – how could you forget to mention your being in company with Mr Darcy when telling us all about your sojourn yesterday!"

Swinging her legs around, Elizabeth got up and walked over towards the window, saying as casually as possible, "I did not think that it would be of much relevance. Besides, we had far more interesting things to talk of."

Jane had also risen and even now headed towards the dresser holding the pitcher of water, and Elizabeth turned to pull the curtains aside to look out upon a morning of thick cloud overhead. She studied the greyness of the sky, assessing the likelihood of a downpour and the chance of taking some air, but her attempt to distract herself failed miserably. The ominous threat of rain merely reminded her of Sunday and a certain gentlemen.

Was an encounter with Mr Darcy imminent? Would he be cognisant of the danger himself? And how would such an occurrence affect him? When she had last seen him, his mood had been influenced by the proximity to Sunday's unpleasantness and also by the shock of her unexpected presence at Rosings. But now? He would have had ample time to reflect upon her cavalier dismissal of his offer and her unfounded slurs against his character.

Elizabeth chewed her lip. Not so long ago, the notion of invoking Mr Darcy's displeasure had concerned her little; she had cared nothing for his approbation and had even welcomed his perceived disapproval of her. Yet now... *now*, what did she feel? It was galling to realise that she had no answer.

Having risen early to see his cousin off on his mission, Darcy had chosen to retire to his study until a more civilised hour, attempting to concentrate on the paperwork that had failed to grasp his attention on the previous day.

With grim determination, he worked through the remaining piles of correspondence until the only items in need of his attention, some two hours later, were the stacks of invitations that had accumulated in his absence. As these held as little interest as ever for him, it was with considerable relief that he responded to Mrs Wainwright's summons for him to attend his sister in the breakfast room, and now, as the meal drew to a close, he pushed his chair back and walked over to one of the windows to finish his cup of tea in silent contemplation of an almost deserted Mount Street.

Georgiana's unspoken affection and support for him had been almost more of a trial than his cousin's persistence in making him speak out. They had made gentle small talk throughout the meal, yet all the while he could detect the compassion upon her face, and the blatant intention of distracting him with any possible subject she could call to mind. In his turn, determined that she not be concerned for him, he had made every effort to converse with her, whatever the topic she raised, and had found the entire exercise exhausting. Yet he was relieved that she had specifically requested that he accompany her on her daily walk once her music practice was over, and it was this intended foray outside that had drawn him to the window.

"There is a deal of cloud about, Georgie."

Darcy studied the grey skies for a moment, before turning to regard his sister in her place at the table where she finished her meal. "You are certain that you wish to risk a walk? We could always take the carriage out if you prefer." Georgiana wiped her fingers on her napkin and got to her feet, coming to join him at the window, and as she too peered up at the rather heavy looking sky, he rested a hand on her shoulder. "Shall we wait to see how things fare once your practice is over?"

She nodded, still staring out of the window, and he felt her twist under his hand as she leaned forward and suddenly exclaimed, "Why, it is Mr Bingley! He is come!"

Darcy followed the direction of her gaze to see a familiar carriage drawing up outside the house. He walked over to replace his cup on the dresser, prepared to go and welcome his friend, when a thought struck him that stopped him in mid stride. Bingley was, in all likelihood, going to be full of his evening in Cheapside. In truth, Darcy was torn between wanting to hear everything and wishing to know nothing, that he might not regret his own absence, but it was not this thought that gripped him as he stood motionless near the dresser.

How could it have escaped his attention that some of the first words out of Bingley's mouth were likely to contain the name Bennet? And how could he circumvent it?

# Chapter Thirty Three

DARCY GLANCED QUICKLY in his sister's direction, disconcerted to see the look of grave concern upon her features.

"Brother? What is it? What troubles you?"

He frowned, conscious of the disturbance out in the hallway that indicated Bingley's arrival in the house. He had no notion how to avoid the imminent situation arising, frustrated with himself for not considering the impact of his friend's residence and aware that a brief, carefully worded explanation of Bingley's acquaintance with the family would probably have sufficed for Georgiana, but that now there was no time to deliver it.

He shook his head. "All is well, Georgie." There was no time for further discourse, as the door was pushed aside and Bingley entered.

"Good morning, Bingley. You are very prompt."

"Darcy, how do you do? And Miss Darcy," Bingley bowed in the latter's direction, before turning a smile upon them both. "Forgive my early arrival. Overton was so expeditious in his packing that I found myself at a loose end, so I summoned my carriage and was on my way forthwith. I trust that it is no intrusion?"

Darcy shook his head, attempting to forestall his own anxiety. "You could never intrude, Bingley, and as always I would ask that you treat our home as your own." He indicated the nearby table. "Do you wish for sustenance?"

"Indeed no – I thank you. I am well fed, but would not say no to a cup of tea."

Georgiana touched her brother's arm lightly. "If you will excuse me, Fitz, I will repair to the music room for an hour or so."

Relief at the temporary respite from what could have been a difficult moment swept through Darcy. "Of course. I shall be in my study when you are finished."

Georgiana made her way towards the door, and Bingley turned an eager countenance upon his friend, who had walked over to pull the bell beside the fireplace.

"I will not take up too much of your time, Darcy. I have an appointment with my attorney in a half hour. I am most anxious, though, to speak with you regarding Miss Bennet."

Unsurprisingly, Georgiana's hand stilled on the door handle, and she threw a startled look towards her brother, who gave a slight shake of his head, but before he could stall her, she said, "Miss Elizabeth Bennet?"

Bingley turned a surprised countenance towards her. "No, Miss Jane Bennet."

Georgiana's eyes grew wider. "And does Miss Jane Bennet have a sister?"

Glancing over at Darcy, Bingley laughed. "Your brother would say she has all too many!"

"I will see you after your practice, Georgiana," the note of authority in Darcy's voice was somewhat belied by the uneasy expression upon his face, and he could well observe from his sister's face that she was ill-disposed to curb her curiosity until a more appropriate time. They stared at each for a moment in silence as Bingley moved to take up a seat at the table, and then the door opened to reveal a servant. He was soon dispatched with the master's request for more hot water, but the distraction had been sufficient for Darcy to gather his wits and the firmness in his countenance must have been adequately conveyed for, with a resigned sigh, Georgiana muttered *"I am all anticipation, Brother,"* and left the room.

Blowing out a breath of relief, Darcy turned to join Bingley, whose countenance had sobered somewhat as he idly twirled a teaspoon in his fingers.

"You were quite right, Darcy, in your caution to me yesterday. Miss Bennet clearly harbours some – not resentment so much as misgivings. I suspect she doubts my motive in renewing the acquaintance."

Taking a seat, Darcy frowned.

"I am sorry to hear it."

Bingley toyed with the teaspoon for a moment longer before casting it aside, and Darcy could feel guilt welling up inside him; his friend did not deserve to be suffering such uncertainty, and he felt his own part in it deeply.

"It grieves me that it did not go well, Bingley, but I must reiterate that which I related to you on Tuesday: Miss Elizabeth Bennet is adamant that her sister's hopes have been disappointed and that Miss Bennet returned your affections most sincerely."

Bingley lifted his shoulders and then let them fall again.

"I do not doubt your word; and I appreciate your attempt to rally me; I fear I little deserve it." He ran a hand through his hair and then picked up the spoon again. "Perchance it is not so dire. I am merely impatient. Miss Bennet was perfectly civil – even friendly on occasion, but I did not feel anywhere near as secure in her returning my regard as I once did. The evening progressed better than the morning visit, but I believe the hurt I unwittingly caused has come back upon me tenfold. I shall have to work hard to overcome her wariness."

"I am so sorry."

"Let it be, Darcy. I allowed it to happen. If she cannot forgive me, it is my fault alone – but I will not give up without effort. She is worth every ounce of it." Bingley laughed but without much humour. "Perchance I should take a leaf out of Harington's book."

"Your friend? In what way?"

"He has such easy manners," Bingley paused, clearly wrapped in a memory from the previous evening, and Darcy almost let out a snort of disbelief. That Bingley of all people should envy another's easy manners struck him as nothing but ridiculous.

"Now I reflect on it, he had an ability to draw Miss Bennet into the conversation where no one else could." Bingley fidgeted in his seat for a moment. "Indeed, the only occasions when she became animated were when he talked of his new residence or of some childhood misdemeanour! He is most entertaining company, Darcy, and has no artifice. I believe you would like him."

The door opened to admit a servant with the hot water and a maid carrying a tray of clean cups and saucers, and Darcy frowned as an uncomfortable notion crossed his mind. The frequent repetition of Harington's name in association with Miss Bennet, coupled with Bingley's report of his first meeting with her on the previous day, when her attention had been more fastened upon this other gentleman than Bingley, gave him cause for disquiet. Even knowing from Elizabeth's passionate avowal that her sister had held Bingley in the greatest of esteem and that she had suffered deeply from the loss of his regard could not reassure him that her attentions had not been diverted in the aftermath of what appeared to be Bingley's neglect.

"Bingley?"

Having secured his friend's attention from the sugar bowl, Darcy cleared his throat.

"Do you – how do you find this Harington?" Bingley sat up straighter in his chair as he dropped a sugar lump into his cup. "Forgive me, but are you not... uneasy?"

Bingley frowned and rested his spoon carefully in his saucer. "Uneasy? Why the devil should I be – and about Harington, of all people? He is from an excellent family."

Darcy gestured with his hand. "No – no, I do not question the man's credibility or character. It is just..." he hesitated. "It is just that Miss Bennet seems somewhat taken, do you not think, with him?"

To Darcy's utmost surprise, instead of causing his friend a disturbance of mind, or even worse, further heart-searching, a familiar wide smile immediately appeared.

"Indeed, she is not!" Bingley sobered for a moment. "I must confess that I envy him his ease within the family. He is but a Godson to Mrs Gardiner, but his place seems more that of their own child. And with the Bennets it is apparent that the acquaintance is both of long-standing and almost equal intimacy."

"And you are not concerned over his level of... intimacy with Miss Bennet?"

Bingley pursed his lips as if attempting to give the matter the seriousness of thought that Darcy seemed to think it warranted. "I perceived no particular notice from him towards her other than the friendliness of manner one would expect at their level of acquaintance – though I might have been jealous of the attention she paid him, had I observed aught to indicate anything other than a familial bond."

Feeling somewhat relieved, though not totally convinced, Darcy poured himself a cup of tea and tried to keep a rein upon his desire to question his companion in detail about his evening in Gracechurch

Street, but before his resolve to ask no questions could be properly tested, Bingley spoke once more.

"But I remain confident that if he has any intentions beyond that of a friend, they lie in quite another direction." Bingley sipped his tea, then met Darcy's eye with a smile. "I know you and Miss Elizabeth Bennet never got along, but I can assure you that it is quite the contrary with that young lady and Harington."

Darcy blinked as these words were uttered, and his insides lurched uncontrollably amidst the hope that he had misunderstood his friend's meaning. Gripped by a desperate urge to know more, he swallowed a mouthful of hot tea and allowed the liquid to burn a trail down his throat. Was this the way of it? Was Harington interested in Elizabeth? Feeling a fool for not considering the possibility, he tried to focus on his friend.

"He is a single man of good fortune, and indeed good family. It is a fair prospect for Miss Elizabeth. In some ways, they are as brother and sister – if you could only hear their banter and tales from their childhood – but I am not so certain that is all it is. I was privy to his anxiety to wait upon the lady before her arrival, and his attention was most decidedly fixed upon her last evening."

Darcy got quickly to his feet and walked over to his earlier place at the window, where he glared at a passing phaeton. Here was his first real mention of Elizabeth, something he had both feared and longed for, and yet it was coupled with this faceless man whose name had begun to haunt him – a man about whom he suddenly possessed a driving need to know more.

With an air of disinterest contrary to his aspirations, he said, "Remind me; how is it you are acquainted with him?"

"I attended Cambridge with his brother. You are well familiar with the wiles of the *ton*, Darcy. Fortune alone holds little sway with them. Fortunately, the aroma of new money did not affect James Harington's nostrils as it did others'. Once he had befriended me, being of an old and wealthy family, others followed."

Darcy's eyes narrowed as he stared out of the window. There was most definitely something familiar about the name James Harington – and he briefly cursed the absence of his cousin, for Fitzwilliam had also indicated some recall of the family name. He turned around and leaned against the sill.

"I feel I should know them – the family. Where do they hail from?"

"Somerset; Sutton Coker – their estate – is but thirty miles from Bath. Indeed, they own a good deal of land in the West Country."

"And the connection between them and the Bennets?"

Darcy could ill account for his questioning his friend in such a way. It was fortunate that Bingley remained distracted by his own affairs, for he could offer no defence for such singular curiosity.

"Harington – Nicholas Harington, that is – is Mrs Gardiner's Godson. Mrs Gardiner, as I am given to understand, has been a very close friend of Mrs Harington from their earliest years, and she is also aunt to both Miss Jane and Miss Elizabeth Bennet.

Darcy mulled for a moment upon this close connection. Much as he did not wish to admit it, it *was* a fair prospect for Elizabeth – but would she see it as such? Did Harington merely pay court to her, or did she return his interest? Had his cousin been correct, that Elizabeth's affection for Wickham would not survive the revelation of his true character, and if so, did that leave her ripe for an approach from another, especially one with whom she was not only intimately acquainted but whom the family welcomed? Had she not vowed to his cousin that only deep affection would tempt her into matrimony, and did he not have proof himself that merely securing a situation was insufficient to tempt her? He knew Elizabeth had now turned down at least two offers of marriage, either of which, despite their disparity, would have secured her family's future. Would she...

"Darcy?"

With a start, Darcy realised that Bingley had finished his tea and had risen to his feet.

"You are to depart?"

"I must be in Piccadilly directly, so I will leave now and seek you out on my return."

Accompanying his friend along the hallway, Darcy struggled to put aside his interminable thoughts, but if he hoped for no further mention of Elizabeth, he was to be disappointed. Bingley received his hat and gloves from the footman, who then opened the door for him, but before he stepped outside he turned to Darcy once more.

"I almost forgot! Miss Elizabeth asked after you last night. I did explain that I had asked you to accompany me, but she said that she understood your reservations in not calling in Gracechurch Street."

Darcy winced, well aware of the underlying meaning such a turn of phrase could carry.

"Darcy?"

Conscious that Bingley eyed him with a somewhat puzzled countenance, he forced a smile. "Forgive me, my friend. I appreciate your passing on the message."

Bingley gave a nod and turned to leave, but then he paused on the threshold and said over his shoulder, "I must say, Miss Elizabeth is looking remarkably well, and she is most certainly in good spirits." Bingley shook his head. "She and Harington," he laughed, "they are a most entertaining couple. Well – good day, Darcy. I will see you anon."

And with that, he walked briskly down the steps and along the path to his waiting carriage, leaving Darcy prey to all manner of black thoughts as he proceeded down the hallway to his study alone.

# Chapter Thirty Four

WITH THE BREAKFAST HOUR over, Elizabeth climbed the stairs to ready herself for the appointment with the dressmaker, much relieved to have a reason to escape from her aunt's gentle interrogation as to why she had failed to mention Mr Darcy's presence in Kent, when not so long ago her niece's correspondence had been full of him.

*But that was when I despised him,* she mused as she reached the landing, and immediately came to a halt as the implication of such a thought struck her. Had it become so very natural in so short a time to instinctively put her dislike of the man into the past? And had she truly mentioned him so very much in her correspondence to her aunt, even when she professed to detest the man?

Refusing to dwell upon this unsettling reminder of her poor judgement, she pushed open the chamber door to find Jane seated at the dressing table attending to her hair, and she met her sister's reflection in the mirror with a smile.

"Aunt Gardiner has gone to select a coat and bonnet for me from Serena's room, and I heard her order the carriage be brought round as I came upstairs."

Getting to her feet, Jane walked over to the closet from where she retrieved her Pelisse. "I had not anticipated being in company with Serena again so soon. It will be most pleasant for us all to be together, will it not?"

"It will indeed." Elizabeth walked over to the chest of drawers and picked up her reticule, before turning to watch her sister as she gathered two pairs of gloves from the closet and pulled out their outdoor footwear. Accepting the latter, Elizabeth sank onto a chair and kicked off her slippers, but instead of making any attempt to step into her shoes, she frowned as she recalled Serena's letter and looked up at Jane.

"How did she fare? Was she well?"

"Well enough in the circumstances. Why do you ask?"

"I received a letter from her when I was in Kent."

"Yes, I knew that she wished to write to you, for she wrote for the direction."

"Her words were somewhat mysterious. She wishes to consult with me about something that troubles her." Sitting back in the chair, Elizabeth met Jane's gaze. "I know that is nothing new, but there seemed to be some pressing urgency in the matter. And yet, she gave you no indication of any such thing?"

"No, there was no hint of any particular concern when in Town; though I think she feels her disability more now that she is of a certain age – but then, you are more her confidante than I, Lizzy."

Jane sat on the bed to attend to her own footwear. "She appeared to have a most enjoyable stay here, and though we heard nothing from her over Easter, we then learned of her being in Derbyshire once our aunt received news of her father's bout of ill health."

Elizabeth nodded, conscious that there was little she could do until Serena arrived, and she bent to slip into her shoes. "No doubt all will become clear when she joins us."

"If I think on it," Jane said thoughtfully, "She did seem somewhat in two minds about paying the visit to Somerset, but Mrs Harington was most insistent and Serena is so attached to her that she could not deny her."

"That may have had more to do with Nicholas being in residence."

"What do you mean?"

Elizabeth bit her lip, then got quickly to her feet, waving a hand dismissively. "Oh, nothing in particular. You know how she and Nicholas can be."

Jane stood up also and picked up her bonnet. "I shall go down, Lizzy, as I am forwarder than you."

"Yes do. I shall join you directly."

As Jane closed the door behind her, Elizabeth walked over to the mirror where she studied her reflection for a moment, her thoughts with her friend. Serena and Nicholas had sparred continuously as they grew up; thus, discovering that her antagonism had turned into a stout affection had distressed Serena greatly. Turning her back on the mirror, Elizabeth sighed. She disliked keeping anything from Jane, but this was something she had been sworn to secrecy on. As for Nicholas, Serena took such prodigious good care to disguise her true feelings from the object of them that it was likely he would never know.

Further, Elizabeth did not know that anyone would ever supplant him; how anyone could. Serena lived a quiet and confined life, meeting few new people and thus having little to distract her. She would not partake fully of society, even when opportunities presented, for even the adapted Patten that Uncle Gardiner had acquired for her could not suffice in the drawing room or on the dance floor in the way it did on the street...

Elizabeth's train of thought was interrupted by a light knock upon the door heralding the arrival of Mrs Gardiner, and with relief she pushed aside her concern for her friend and turned to see what her aunt had managed to find.

"Here we are. I feel this one will complement the colour of your gown best." Mrs Gardiner walked over and handed a familiar Spencer to her niece, who took it and held it up, smiling.

"Dear Serena – how she loved this when it was first made up! I recall her reluctance to remove it even when indoors, so much did she admire the cut and the fabric!"

Mrs Gardiner helped her niece into the coat, smiling. "Well, I suppose the novelty must have worn off for it to be relegated to her London closet!"

"To be fair, Aunt, I think it more likely that it is rather too fine for country use. The red and cream narrow striping is very unusual, and the needlework very detailed. Did not Mrs Harington have it made up for her?"

"She did indeed. Alicia cannot do enough for the girl," an expression of sadness filled Mrs Gardiner's eyes for a moment. "I think she helps soothe the loss of her own little one, even now." She fastened the final button. "There. You look very well, Lizzy."

Elizabeth smiled at her aunt as that lady passed her a deep red satin bonnet, and fixing it quickly into place she tied the ribbons beneath her chin before holding out both her arms and laughing.

"Serena and I may share a similar frame, but I think we see the discrepancy of our height here! My arms would appear to be a little longer than hers!"

"Oh dear." Mrs Gardiner stared at the gap between the end of the Spencer's sleeves and Elizabeth's gloves and then glanced about the room. "Where are those ribbons we acquired the other day?"

Hurrying over to one of the bedside tables, she picked up a tissue-wrapped package, from which she took several strands of ribbon.

"Which shade do you think? The red is not a good match, I fear…" she inspected them carefully before selecting two pieces of cream fabric. "Here, try this."

Indicating to Elizabeth to hold out her arms, she neatly tied a piece of wide ribbon to each of her niece's wrists, concealing the small expanse of flesh that had been left exposed.

"There!" Mrs Gardiner smiled as she patted her on the arm and turned towards the door. "Come, or we shall be late. Much as I know you dislike frippery and layers, you are at least sufficiently attired to face the eyes of Mayfair – indeed, you may even inspire a new fashion!"

With a laugh, Elizabeth held her arms out to inspect the effect of the ribbons, which was surprisingly complimentary if a little more dressy than was her custom.

"Be warned, Aunt. I may begin to giggle incessantly and talk of nothing but balls and red coats, and if I do, I charge you to please come to my aid and remove them!"

Darcy's attempt to give Georgiana as brief an explanation as possible of Bingley's acquaintance with Miss Bennet had been thwarted somewhat by his sister's interest in the matter. When she did not attend him in his study, he had repaired to the music room thinking that perhaps she had become lost to time whilst enjoying her instrument, only to find that the pianoforte had long been discarded in favour of investigation. He found Georgiana in her sitting room, engrossed in a letter – a letter, it turned out, from himself, penned during his stay at Netherfield, as were the others that she had then produced from her pockets.

As he shepherded her up to her chamber to prepare for their outing, he endured her quietly voiced but persistent curiosity as best he could, agreeing that the '*daughter of a local gentleman*' that he had initially made mention of was indeed the Miss Elizabeth Bennet that he had later described, and yes, she was the sister of the Miss Bennet of Bingley's acquaintance. Further than this he refused to be drawn, merely agreeing with her that he had failed to inform her that Miss Elizabeth had several sisters, that Bingley seemed very interested in the eldest and that yes, Miss Bennet presently resided in Town, but no, he did not anticipate renewing his acquaintance with her, despite the fact that his friend had.

His sister seemed a little puzzled by this statement, but Darcy firmly ushered her, still bristling with curiosity, into her room and closed the door upon her with the warning that he would collect her in a half hour.

Thus it was that, some thirty minutes later and dressed for the outdoors, he accompanied Georgiana down the stairs towards a recently returned Bingley.

"Are you quite certain that you wish to accompany us, Bingley?"

"Absolutely. Miss Bennet is to attend to some shopping this morning, so there is little point in my making a call in Gracechurch Street. Overton is making it blatantly obvious that I hamper his unpacking, and as I have just passed an hour in the smokiest office imaginable whilst having some documents drawn up, a stroll in the fresh air is all I desire!"

Allowing Georgiana to precede them out of the door, Bingley turned to Darcy as they made their way down the short path and out into Mount Street. "Did you have a particular direction in mind?"

"Georgiana?" Darcy offered his arm to his sister. "Do you have a preference? Would you prefer St James Park to wandering the neighbourhood?"

"I would rather head for the Square, Brother. Should the rain start, then at least we can shelter in comfort."

Bingley beamed at her. "You would not, by any chance, be an admirer of *Gunters*?"

"I am! I do not think I have tasted the equal of their iced pastries."

"Indeed, no. Harington – an acquaintance of mine – brought some of the very same with him when we called upon Miss Bennet only yesterday morning, and very well received they were too."

Struggling with an irrational wave of jealousy at the mention of Harington's name, and conscious that Georgiana had cast a quick, enquiring glance up at him, Darcy sought frantically for a change of subject, but before his mind could oblige him, he felt her disengage her arm from his and step ahead to walk alongside his friend.

"Do you think that we might encounter Miss Bennet during her stay in Town, Mr Bingley?"

Suppressing a groan, Darcy quickened his pace in order to keep up with the two people in front of him, though he derived little comfort from overhearing their discourse.

"I should think it very likely! I am certain she would be most honoured to make your acquaintance." Bingley exclaimed, and he threw a laughing glance over his shoulder towards Darcy. "Your brother has met her, and I am certain there could be no objection."

"Yes, so I have just learned."

Taking the arm offered to her by Bingley, Georgiana threw her brother a look of smugness, before returning her attention to her companion. "Now, Mr Bingley, tell me all about Miss Bennet and how you came to meet her."

With their visit to the dressmaker concluded to everyone's satisfaction, and the necessary accessories purchased to complete their attire for Monday's ball, Mrs Gardiner had despatched the servant to load the carriage with their packages, along with the instruction to await them in Berkeley Square.

A pleasant ten-minute stroll later and the ladies were entering *Gunters* fine establishment, well disposed to partake of the refreshments on offer. As soon as they arrived, they were assisted into seats near the bay window and immediately turned their attention to the tasselled menu card. Heads together over the table as they poured over the list of cakes, pastries and ices on offer, they were oblivious to the passers-by in Berkeley Square.

Having made her choice of dessert, Elizabeth sat back in her chair, leaving Jane and her aunt to continue debating the benefit of marzipan over icing. Removing her gloves quickly, she then released the ribbon beneath her chin, relieved to be freed of the oppression of such garments, but as she lifted the bonnet from her head her eye was caught by the gentleman who had just entered the café.

"Nicholas is here!"

Elizabeth's announcement caused her two companions to withdraw their noses from the menu card and look towards the new arrival, who made his way towards them between the tables and chairs.

"Good morning, Aunt. Jane." Nicholas bowed, then turned his attention to where Elizabeth sat, and meeting her eye with a keen look, bowed once more. "Lizzy."

Elizabeth studied Nicholas thoughtfully as he acquired a chair from a nearby table and settled himself by her side. He looked extremely pale, and she reached out a hand and touched his arm to draw his attention. "Are you well, Nicholas?"

"Quite well, I thank you." She saw him flick a quick glance towards her aunt and sister, who had turned their attentions to the waiter, now patiently awaiting their order, before returning his gaze to her.

"I am a little surprised to see you?"

Elizabeth smiled at his apparent confusion. "We had need of refreshment; shopping is a wearisome venture!"

He smiled faintly, his eye drawn to one of her hands where it now rested upon the table. He touched the edge of her sleeve briefly, where it met the wide piece of ribbon that had been tied around her wrist earlier, before lifting his eyes to hers, a brow raised in question.

"I had need of borrowing a coat. This is Serena's."

"Yes, I remember it well."

"It is a becoming shade, do you not think?" Elizabeth laughed, before turning her attention to the waiter and placing her order. A moment passed whereby Nicholas requested a cup of coffee; yet the waiter had but turned from their table before Mrs Gardiner called him back, wishing to change her choice.

Turning quickly to Elizabeth, Nicholas muttered under cover of the distraction, "Lizzy, I would – I *must* talk to you."

Surprised at the urgency of his tone, and indeed the seriousness of his expression, Elizabeth hesitated a moment too long, and before she could respond her aunt addressed her companion instead.

"So - to what do we owe the honour of your presence, Nicholas? I hate to disappoint you, but we have completed our purchases, and they are safely ensconced in the carriage."

"I shall bear the deprivation as best I can, Ma'am." Nicholas inclined his head in his Godmother's direction with a smile. "But it is, indeed, most fortuitous that you are now at liberty, for I would very much enjoy some company. Would you be so good as to join me in a stroll around the gardens?"

Mrs Gardiner eyed her Godson fondly. "We shall be delighted to join you, I dare say, but not until we have partaken of our ices! A morning's shopping is always certain to stir a lady's appetite!"

# Chapter Thirty Five

ON REACHING THE CORNER of Berkeley Square, the party from Mount Street paused for a moment, and Darcy once more studied the sky. Though the cloud was as thick as ever, it had not darkened and the threat of rain seemed less likely than it had earlier.

"Do you wish for refreshment, Georgiana, or shall we walk in the gardens and call back later?"

"Oh, a walk first, I think – do you not agree, Mr Bingley? We were having such a pleasant conversation."

Darcy shook his head at his sister as she threw him a guileless look, and she bit her lip before mouthing 'forgive me' at him. Despite his discomfort, he found himself unable to be anything but slightly amused at her persistence, and as Bingley had clearly welcomed the opportunity to expound upon his favourite subject there was little he could do about it. He was quite certain that Georgiana, for all her curiosity, would not say anything inappropriate.

They crossed the street and entered the garden, and Darcy reflected for a moment that his friend had been as good for his sister as he had been for him.

"Shall we stroll towards the arbour?" Bingley turned to look at Darcy, who shrugged his shoulders.

"As you wish. Lead the way."

Offering his arm once more to Georgiana, who took it with alacrity, they set off, with Darcy following, his pace slower and his mind elsewhere; thus it was that he failed to overhear Georgiana's words to his friend as they rounded the corner of the path ahead.

"So tell me about Miss Bennet's family – and her sisters! Please tell me all about her sisters!"

Having enjoyed their refreshments and in good spirits, the party from *Gunters* made their way safely across the cobbles into the gardens in the centre of Berkeley Square.

Observing Nicholas as he fussed over Mrs Gardiner and Jane, offering to hold shawls and who knew what else as they readied themselves for their walk, Elizabeth smiled to herself. He was so kind, such a good man. Indeed, were he not like a brother to her, she would have considered a match with Nicholas to be highly desirable.

She sighed. Perhaps holding out for love was a mistake, for what had she seen of late that hinted of that condition bringing joy and pleasure? The indications were that it brought quite the opposite. What was the worst pain of loving – bearing an unrequited love in silence or the reality of rejection?

Rousing herself as Nicholas approached, her sister and aunt walking slowly along behind him, Elizabeth smiled, attempting to shake off her dismal thoughts.

Taking his offered arm, they turned towards the centre of the garden, and welcoming the opportunity to talk to him without interruption she said thoughtfully, "Do you recall when we were younger, Nicholas, and we talked of the future?"

"I believe the subject came up on more than one occasion. To which particular instance do you refer?"

"Most particularly – of marriage."

He looked at her searchingly. "You had some youthful, optimistic view of the state."

"Then you recall my assertion that I would marry for naught but love!"

Nicholas grunted. "Indeed, though then you were but a child and could be forgiven such foolish impetuosity!"

Elizabeth laughed as they came to a junction in the path, and Nicholas looked to her for a decision. Nodding to her left, they turned their feet in that direction before she responded.

"I was twelve! At such an age a girl's mind has long turned to matrimony!" Elizabeth glanced over her shoulder towards where Jane and her aunt were following. "Well, suffice it to say, I am beginning to doubt my own opinion."

"Upon what, precisely?"

"That only love should induce one into matrimony – from what I have seen of late, love brings the person bold enough to feel it nothing but pain."

Sensing the sudden tightening of his arm under her hand, Elizabeth glanced quickly at Nicholas to surprise a strange look of consciousness upon his countenance. "If one discovers it is not returned, perhaps."

Thinking of her sister, Elizabeth smiled ruefully. "And even before that – the not knowing, the uncertainty before a declaration is made – whether the hopes and dreams will be answered…"

She stopped; how was it that those words immediately brought to mind Mr Darcy and how he must have suffered? If he really had loved her as ardently as he declared – and she must assume he spoke no lie, for she certainly was no catch compared to the ladies of the *ton* – then was he not likely to be harbouring strong feelings of rejection?

Conscious that her insides seemed to be tying themselves in knots, Elizabeth drew in a deep breath. Though she doubted her earnestness, she could almost believe it might be best if resentment truly had set in, that his anger might guarantee him some form of protection.

Aware that Nicholas had turned to look at her, studying her face intently, she gave him a rueful smile.

"Forgive me; my mind is all distracted this morning."

Nicholas shook his head and patted her hand where it rested on his arm. "In that you are not alone, dear girl." He looked around. Mrs Gardiner and Jane were some distance behind and ahead there was only a stranger.

"Lizzy, I feel you have read my mind. We must find an opportunity where I can speak – away from company or interruption. It is my sole purpose in coming to Town…" He stopped as the grip on his arm tightened, but glancing at his companion's face he saw he had lost her attention. Following her gaze, he looked again at the stranger ahead of them on the path, but as his back was to them, he could not discern his identity.

"Lizzy? What is it?"

Feeling all the perversity of fate, Elizabeth let out a low, disbelieving laugh. She shook her head at Nicholas to assure him she was well, then turned back to look at the figure ahead of them. She recognised instinctively the broad set of those shoulders.

Perfectly aware that she might be the last person he would wish to encounter, and with no clear idea of what she could possibly have to say to him, she did not stop to examine her purpose. Releasing her hold on Nicholas' arm, she walked quickly after him, and as soon as she was sufficiently close to be heard, spoke his name with quiet authority.

"Mr Darcy."

On hearing his name spoken, Darcy's step faltered. Knowing full well whose voice had accosted him, he threw a desperate look towards the curve in the path ahead whence Georgiana and Bingley had only just disappeared from sight before drawing in a much-needed breath.

"Mr Darcy? Sir?"

Turning swiftly on his heel, he faced Elizabeth, startled to realise that she was much closer than her voice had implied. Instinctively, he bowed formally, barely able to mutter a soft "Miss Bennet" in greeting as he struggled to come to terms with the fact that the very situation he had felt certain to avoid was upon them both.

She curtseyed, and as she raised her head and met his eye, he felt a warmth invade his cheeks, unsurprised to discern the colour upon her own.

For a moment, silence reigned; then he said quickly, "Forgive me. You are – your presence is – I did not expect to see you – here."

Her smile was genuine and unexpected, and he swallowed hard on the uprush of emotion evoked by such a simple gesture, so rarely had it been bestowed upon him.

"In truth, Mr Darcy? Your memory does you a disservice. Had you so soon forgotten my destination on leaving Kent?"

"No – no, I had not. I meant..." He paused and studied her face for a moment. "You do, of course, completely comprehend my meaning." He was rewarded with another smile, and he quickly cleared his throat. "Err – and did you – how was your journey?"

"Much as one would expect; and yourself and the Colonel, Sir? I can see that you arrived safely, though I do not see your cousin accompanying you?"

"He had some business to attend out of Town, but will return directly."

"And thus you are obliged to walk alone?"

"No – no, I am not. I am escorting my sister…" Darcy stopped as Elizabeth raised a questioning brow, her glance moving to his left and then his right before her eyes met his once more.

"Are you quite certain, Sir?"

In spite of the unexpectedness of her presence and the agitation within his breast, the edges of a smile touched his lips.

"I am. I do assure you that Miss Darcy is hereabouts – only she has walked on ahead of me with Bingley-" he broke off suddenly, conscious of the last time they had discussed that particular gentleman. "I – err… I must have been keeping a slower pace; they will wonder what has become of me."

"Then I trust you will excuse me for having detained you further."

There was a slight pause, during which they eyed each other warily; then, she spoke again with a light laugh, "Indeed, I am hampering my own party's progress likewise!"

He cast a quick glance beyond where she stood and observed a small group of people some way down the path, one of whom he determined to be Miss Bennet.

Following his gaze, Elizabeth looked over her shoulder briefly before turning back to face him. "As you see, I too am accompanying family. We could not resist the temptation of taking the air as the rain seemed to be holding off."

This mention of relatives roused Darcy somewhat and conscious that, despite his recent defamation of them, such common civility should have been some of the first words out of his mouth, spoke now to atone.

"Forgive me for not asking sooner. Your family – I trust they are in good health?"

She looked somewhat startled at this courtesy, and a twinge of guilt stole through him.

"Oh! Yes, I thank you. From their letters I must assume that they are, and of course, for my eldest sister, I have the proof of my own eyes." She paused. "Indeed, she is in much improved spirits of late, for which I offer my deepest gratitude."

A silence fell between them once more as he absorbed what she had said, their eyes fastened upon each other. That he could adequately surmise whence her gratitude stemmed, he could not deny; why was it, then, that the notion gave him little pleasure?

A sudden movement then caught Darcy's eye, and his gaze was drawn once more to Elizabeth's walking companions. As he glanced in their direction, Miss Bennet happened to look up and, detaching herself from their company, she walked up to where they stood.

"Miss Bennet."

"Mr Darcy."

He greeted Jane Bennet with as much composure as possible, unable to keep at bay the remembrance of Elizabeth's heated avowal of her sister's feelings. Despite his attempt to put matters to rights, he felt all the guilt of causing her distress and, as a consequence, struggled to find words other than the commonplace, and once he had enquired after her health and stay in Town, fell silent.

Fortunately, his companions were more adept at pleasantries, and as Elizabeth acquainted Miss Bennet with the knowledge that Darcy walked with his sister and Bingley, he found his attention wandering to their companions who remained in quiet discourse further down the path.

That the lady might be the aunt, he could not deny, but she was quite contrary to his expectations. Not only was the frippery of dress observed in Mrs Bennet lacking, but he would have expected her to be putting herself forward, making an introduction inevitable. His gaze rested briefly on the young man engaging her in conversation, and he frowned. This must be the elusive Harington, the man whose name had begun to haunt him, the man who was considered a good match for Elizabeth. He was unsure whether or not he wished to put a face to the man; picturing Elizabeth on the arm of another, of *him*, would be all too easy if he did.

Conscious of a surge of longing towards her, combined with a twist of pain that he could accredit to nothing but envy, he drew in a sharp breath, and in so doing, earned the attention of both of the ladies before him.

Elizabeth's expression was unreadable, but before he could raise any conjecture as to its meaning, she spoke. "Forgive us, Mr Darcy. We must importune no longer upon your time. You must be anxious to re-join your sister and your friend."

He blinked, realising that she had perhaps interpreted his behaviour as impatience and, despite his desire to find Georgiana and remove with her rapidly, away from such temptation as Elizabeth's company, he faltered. To part from her now leaving behind the impression that he had been anxious to quit her company, regardless of how much she might well be desiring such a release, was beyond him. Determined to show her that he had listened to her and had begun to acknowledge the mistakes he had made throughout their acquaintance, he broke hurriedly into speech.

"It is no inconvenience, I assure you. My sister is in good hands. Bingley has been as good as a brother to her these many years."

Elizabeth threw a lightning glance towards her sister, before meeting his eye once more.

"It is very generous of you to say so, Sir. But we must also take our leave; unlike the other members of your party, ours have been obliged to stand still these few minutes which is somewhat contradictory to their professed desire for exercise!"

Darcy wished to cause no further offence towards Elizabeth, nor to her family and connections. It would take but a moment to affect an introduction, and the courtesy of requesting it would, he trusted, bear longer approval from Elizabeth, which was all that he desired.

"I would not wish to intrude upon your outing, but I would request a few moments further of your time. Miss Bennet, Miss Elizabeth – would you do me the honour of introducing me to your companions?"

# Chapter Thirty Six

WANDERING SLOWLY ALONG THE path towards the arbour, Georgiana smiled to herself. She had encouraged Mr Bingley to talk of his time in Hertfordshire, her ears anxiously awaiting any mention of a certain Miss Elizabeth Bennet, yet she presently endured a further monologue on the virtues and beauty of her elder sister.

Hiding the smile as best she could, Georgiana began to wonder why Mr Bingley had left his manor for Town in the first place, but then suddenly she sensed they were no longer being followed by her brother. A quick glance over her shoulder confirmed her suspicion, and she came to an abrupt halt, causing her companion to stop also and throw her an enquiring look.

"Fitzwilliam – he is no longer with us!"

Releasing the arm of her escort, Georgiana walked a few steps back down the path. "It is most odd. What could have become of him?"

Bingley shrugged. "He was not five paces behind us when we last spoke." He threw a glance at the sky, laden with grey cloud. "We had best continue – perchance he took another way to the arbour."

Georgiana held her ground, shaking her head. "But he would not desert us – something must have delayed him."

She threw Bingley a beseeching look, and he laughed. "Come then. We shall retrace our steps and track him down," and offering her his arm again, they walked back down the path they had followed not moments earlier and turned the corner where they had last seen Darcy following them.

They had barely taken two paces further before they spotted their quarry, and on this occasion it was Bingley who came to a halt.

"Why, it is Miss Bennet!"

Georgiana's eyes widened as she stared at her brother's back ahead of them; he did indeed appear to have encountered some acquaintances. That one of the party was Miss Bennet drew interest enough, but the incidence of other ladies in the group caused Georgiana to drop her grip on the gentleman's arm and, heedless of his attempt to stall her, hurry forward as fast as she could without defying all decorum and breaking into a run.

Avidly, her eyes scanned the small party as she hurried along. A young lady dressed in a dark blue pelisse stood next to her brother, and as she came closer she saw a gentleman facing them, another young lady at his side, and an older lady, who just then noticed Georgiana's presence and gave her a warm smile.

Suddenly recalling the inappropriateness of putting herself forward, Georgiana's step faltered, and with embarrassment she stopped and lowered her gaze, wondering how she would justify her actions to her brother.

Having heard the rapidly approaching footsteps, Darcy glanced over his shoulder.

His sister stood a mere two paces away, a deep colour on her cheeks and her eyes cast down, as Bingley fetched up beside her, a wide smile overspreading his face.

Darcy's immediate concern at now having to force the acquaintance upon Elizabeth was overridden by Georgiana's clear embarrassment at having thrust herself into a situation involving so many strangers. Conscious that Bingley, who was previously known to those present, would cause sufficient distraction for now, he bowed briefly and stepped away as his friend took his place and, putting an arm around his sister, they walked a few paces back along the footpath.

"Do you feel up to making some new acquaintances, Georgiana?"

She nodded as the colour in her cheeks receded somewhat.

"Forgive me, Fitz. I did not think – when Mr Bingley mentioned his Miss Bennet, I was so eager to join you. I do not wish you to be obliged to introduce me, yet nor do I wish to cause offence now that I have foolishly put myself in their way."

Content from the sound of voices behind him that they were being afforded a moment of privacy, Darcy studied his sister thoughtfully. Then, he sighed.

"It is true that I had not intended for you to make the acquaintance of Miss Elizabeth Bennet. It is difficult for me to say more, but please be assured that my reasons for saying such are not through any objection to the lady herself." He stopped, conscious that his sister's eyes had widened and a tentative smile appeared.

"Miss Elizabeth Bennet is here? She is one of the party? I did wonder - I hoped…"

Darcy shook his head. "There is nothing to hope for, Georgie; on that we must be clear. But yes," he paused and glanced quickly over his shoulder, reassured that their behaviour seemed to be causing no particular concern, though he had the distinct impression that Elizabeth had at that very moment withdrawn her gaze from them. "She is walking with family, to whom I have just been introduced. In the circumstances, I feel it would be fitting to include you, provided you are comfortable with the notion."

Straightening her shoulders, Georgiana looked up at him and smiled fully. "Well, Brother, I begin to feel I know the eldest Miss Bennet, so that is one less stranger, is it not?"

With a small laugh, Darcy took her hand and placed it on his arm and then turned around to lead her back to the others.

A small silence fell upon the company as Darcy and Georgiana rejoined them, and he was conscious of his sister's grip tightening upon his arm. Absent-mindedly, he patted her hand, struck in an instant that every face before them was open, welcoming and friendly – such a stark contrast to many of the *ton* when an introduction was about to be made, whose expressions would mirror a chilling superiority or a sickening familiarity, dependent on their understanding or otherwise of the wealth and status of the newcomer.

"Ladies, Mr Harington – please allow me to introduce my sister, Miss Georgiana Darcy, to your acquaintance. Georgiana," Darcy looked down at her, "This is Mrs Gardiner."

The lady came forward, and as his sister stepped aside to exchange a curtsey, Darcy fought the inclination to look over at Elizabeth. How she must wish him at the other side of the world.

The remainder of the introductions were soon performed, and conscious of the deepening colour in Georgiana's cheeks, Darcy sought a means of easing her immediate discomfort, but before he had determined upon a topic of conversation, Bingley spoke.

"What a happy circumstance, that we should all meet this morning when we thought our occupations led to the contrary!"

"Indeed, Sir. Quite the coincidence!" Mrs Gardiner turned her smile upon Georgiana. "It is a pleasure to make your acquaintance, Miss Darcy. This is a pleasant garden for taking a stroll, is it not?"

As she gently encouraged his sister into conversation, Darcy eased himself away from Georgiana's side. Conscious that Elizabeth likely regretted the introduction, and probably planned as soon as practicable to remove from Town to Hertfordshire, that the acquaintance might remain nothing more than passing, he sought to distance himself from where she stood, feeling it was the least he could do in the circumstances.

Bingley picked up the threads of his conversation with Harington, and Darcy turned to join them, attempting to focus on their dialogue. He hoped that Georgiana would not feel he had abandoned her, and with half his attention on the interaction before him, to which he contributed the occasional comment, he slowly adjusted his position so that his sister could catch his eye should she require his assistance.

Yet from his place at Harington's side, Darcy realised that he was well able to observe Elizabeth, who now conversed easily with his sister. Georgiana, though clearly striving to maintain her newly growing confidence, seemed to be listening far more than she spoke, but he could see from her stance and the alert expression upon her face that her interest in Elizabeth far outweighed her nervousness.

Permitting his gaze to rest upon the lady in question for a moment, Darcy realised for the first time that she was not dressed as he was accustomed to seeing her, charming though her appearance was, but then a movement caught his eye and, conscious that Elizabeth had caught him staring at her, he quickly looked away. The colour that washed her cheekbones anew he could easily explain, for he understood the awkwardness of this meeting for them both, and he was certain that she felt far less at ease than her manner towards his sister implied.

He risked another glance in her direction and then sighed. Elizabeth remained as lost to him today as ever, and seeing her again only reinforced that loss. The sooner he made his excuses and they departed with their respective parties, the better for them both. To that end, he turned to his friend.

"I believe we should continue on our way, Bingley. The cloud becomes ever darker, and I fear our opportunity for walking will soon be over."

Casting a quick glance to the skies, the other gentlemen concurred, and turning as one they approached the ladies. The success of the meeting on Georgiana was apparent even now upon her features, though she seemed somewhat disappointed over their imminent parting.

Even though he was conscious of his desire to free Elizabeth of his company, Darcy could not help but indulge his wishes for one last moment, though he suspected he would chide himself thereafter for the indulgence. He bade farewell to Harington, whom he begrudgingly allowed to be as likeable as Bingley had implied, Mrs Gardiner and Miss Bennet before turning to face her fully for the first time since their initial words at this unexpected meeting.

"Miss Elizabeth."

"It was an honour to make your sister's acquaintance, Sir."

"I am certain that the pleasure is all hers." He cast a glance towards Georgiana, who waited with Bingley for him to join them, unsurprised to see her attention quite fixed upon them. "She is but little in company as yet."

"But she is full young, Mr Darcy, and I believe she coped admirably with so many new faces."

Warmed by her approbation, he smiled, feeling the tightness about his chest ease a fraction as she returned the gesture. Unable to look away, a silence settled upon them as those around them made their farewells. Then, he cleared his throat.

"It has been a pleasure to see you, Miss Elizabeth."

"Goodbye, Mr Darcy." She dropped a quick curtsey; the moment was over, and returning the farewell gesture with a bow, he straightened slowly.

"I wish you an enjoyable stay in Town. Good day."

With that, they turned to re-join their respective parties. Offering Georgiana his arm, a position she accepted this time with alacrity, leaving Bingley to wander on ahead of them, Darcy fought with the desire to look back at Elizabeth, but had no wish to see her at Harington's side.

As they reached the corner in the path that once more led to the arbour, his sister did precisely that, glancing over her shoulder towards where the other party were now moving away in the opposite direction, only to observe that Elizabeth Bennet mirrored her action.

Turning back quickly, she bit her lip, keeping to herself the thought she dare not utter: *"You may suspect that the lady does not like you, Brother… but whatever her feelings, I believe she is not indifferent."*

As the Gardiner carriage trundled slowly around Berkeley Square and out onto the main thoroughfare of Piccadilly, Elizabeth stared unseeingly out of the window, conscious of the murmur of voices but hearing nothing of her companions' discourse.

She felt strangely unsettled and, on reflection, could find nothing of comfort. That Mr Darcy wished to escape her company was certain for, their initial exchange excepted, he had addressed no words to her until they took their leave, and the distance he sought to put between himself and her was most evident, something she could hardly blame him for in the circumstances.

Yet it all seemed so contradictory. Though good manners had obliged him to introduce his sister, there was no denying that he had chosen of his own free will to meet with Aunt Gardiner, yet he must have known that this might be one of the dubious connections that he had denigrated during his proposal.

The remembrance of that incident caused Elizabeth to stir restlessly in her seat, and conscious of the warmth invading her cheeks, she rested her face against the coolness of the window, chastising herself for her impetuosity. What on earth had inspired her to approach the man in the first place? What must he think of her?

"Lizzy, dear? Are you quite well?"

Turning to face her aunt, Elizabeth summoned a smile. "Perfectly well, Aunt. I was merely reflecting on Mr Darcy's request for an introduction to yourself and Nicholas; I am quite astounded by it."

Mrs Gardiner looked amused. "Indeed? Are we such poor company?"

"Of course not, dear Aunt! My words were a reflection of my opinion of Mr Darcy, not of yourselves!"

"I suspected as much. Yet Mr Darcy does not appear the proud and arrogant man you would have had me believe. There was an element of reserve in his manner, I will own, but he was more than civil."

Elizabeth exchanged a swift glance with Jane. "I have never seen him so willing to converse, or so open to meeting strangers."

Mrs Gardiner frowned. "I am not ignorant of the family as you know, but it was Mr Darcy's father who ran the estate when I was a child.

Thus my only intelligence of this particular generation comes from one source. *You*, Lizzy."

Elizabeth blushed. Her feelings of discomfort were growing, and she knew not what to say.

"The gentleman whom I just met," her aunt persisted, "he bore little if any resemblance to the man you described in your letters."

"It is true that Mr Darcy's character is not as black as I believed it to be." Elizabeth sighed. "He can be both proud and disparaging, but he does not possess the blackness of nature that I believed. I am ashamed of myself, most especially for being so liberal in sharing my negative opinion of him with others." Lowering her gaze to her, she blew out a frustrated breath. "It is only in recent days that I have discovered just how in error my judgement was, but I assure you I feel it deeply."

Raising her head, Elizabeth caught the end of a look of surprise exchanged between her sister and her aunt, and Mrs Gardiner patted her gently on her knee.

"Do not distress yourself, my dear. It is not as if the acquaintance has any particular significance." She paused. "Yet I would be interested to know how you found yourself so misled and how the truth of the matter revealed itself."

"It is not possible for me to reveal all that I have learned. What I can tell you is that we are much deceived in Mr Wickham."

Jane looked troubled, but Mrs Gardiner had little to say other than express her surprise. Elizabeth was fully cognisant of her aunt's concerns over her previous regard for Wickham.

"I am afraid it is so, Jane. His word cannot be trusted. I have been unsure whether to advise our family of his duplicity, for they were much in company with him."

"Has he not left the neighbourhood?"

"The regiment was for Brighton before I set off for Kent." Elizabeth paused. "I shall talk to Papa on my return, and he may then decide what should or should not be revealed."

Mrs Gardiner, taking her cue from Elizabeth and seeming to understand that the matter was not up for further discussion, returned the conversation to their new acquaintance.

"Miss Darcy is charming. Shy, undoubtedly, but utterly charming."

Elizabeth smiled. "I have learned that she has been raised by her brother, along with a cousin – a Colonel Fitzwilliam – whom I had the pleasure of meeting in Kent. They have shared guardianship of her since her father died five years ago."

"Then they have done an outstanding job. It cannot have been easy for them – for Mr Darcy in particular – inheriting an estate the size of

Pemberley and then raising a young girl, for he cannot have been much into his own majority at the time."

Her aunt's words were giving Elizabeth cause for reflection; she had never before considered the responsibilities that Mr Darcy shouldered, dismissing him as she had done as the idle rich. With a smile, she glanced over at her sister. "Jane never believed Mr Darcy's character to be so deficient."

"Dear Jane!" Mrs Gardiner smiled at her eldest niece. "You would never believe ill of anyone." She then turned her gaze upon Elizabeth. "He was very solicitous of his sister when she joined us so abruptly, and the level of affection between them was apparent. There is much to admire. He is, of course, an extremely well featured man and has a fine figure!"

"Aunt!" Elizabeth exchanged an astonished look with Jane.

"Pray, am I not allowed to acknowledge the fact? I may be old enough to be your mother, Lizzy, but I can appreciate a fine looking young man as much as anybody!" Elizabeth laughed, then her aunt added, "He was not liberal with his smiles, so far as I could see, but there is a pleasantness about his mouth when he speaks."

"Dear Aunt," Jane said, smiling, and as the conversation moved on from the morning's encounters to discuss their anticipated evening, Elizabeth turned away to resume her window gazing, conscious of her cheeks warming once more and wishing to disguise any tell-tale colour that might be evident.

Mr Darcy's mouth, however pleasant, was not something she wanted to dwell upon, and of her dream she adamantly refused to think, though it had come immediately to mind. Deeply unsettled, she stared unseeingly out of the window, willing the carriage onwards to the calming sanctuary of Gracechurch Street and away from the gentleman's disturbing presence.

To be continued in

# Volume II – Darcy's Dilemma

# About the Author

Cassandra Grafton has always loved words, so it comes as no surprise that writing is her passion. Having spent many years wishing to be a writer and many more dreaming of it, she finally took the plunge, offering short stories to online communities. After that, it was a natural next step to attempting a full length novel, and thus *A Fair Prospect* was born.

She currently splits her time between North Yorkshire in the UK, where she lives with her husband and two cats, and Regency England, where she lives with her characters.

http://www.cassandragrafton.com

https://www.facebook.com/cassie.grafton

https://twitter.com/CassGrafton

Printed in Great Britain
by Amazon.co.uk, Ltd.,
Marston Gate.